Dying to Ski

Books by Maureen Meehan Aplin

Dying to Ski, a Mary MacIntosh novel

Snake River Secret, a Mary MacIntosh novel

Powder River Poison, a Mary MacIntosh novel

Pandemic Predator, a Mary MacIntosh novel

DYING TO SKI

a Mary MacIntosh novel

Maureen Meehan Aplin

iUniverse, Inc.
New York Lincoln Shanghai

Dying to Ski
a Mary MacIntosh novel

Copyright © 2007 by Maureen Meehan Aplin

All rights reserved. No part of this book may be used or reproduced by any means, graphic, electronic, or mechanical, including photocopying, recording, taping or by any information storage retrieval system without the written permission of the publisher except in the case of brief quotations embodied in critical articles and reviews.

iUniverse books may be ordered through booksellers or by contacting:

iUniverse
2021 Pine Lake Road, Suite 100
Lincoln, NE 68512
www.iuniverse.com
1-800-Authors (1-800-288-4677)

This is a work of fiction. All of the characters, names, incidents, organizations, and dialogue in this novel are either the products of the author's imagination or are used fictitiously.

ISBN: 978-0-595-43490-9 (pbk)
ISBN: 978-0-595-87817-8 (ebk)

Printed in the United States of America

For My Children

Acknowledgements

Dying to Ski was originally named *Geyser* and was the first novel I crafted. In order to gain the skills and experience necessary to craft fiction, I needed and used the valued professional coaching of University of California—Irvine's Creative Writing Director, Dr. Lori Miller. I remain grateful to Dr. Miller, as she was so deftly able to persuade me to throw away my first manuscript and start anew. Remarkably, she encouraged me to do this a few more times before we had what she considered a working manuscript. From there, the editing commenced.

In addition to Dr. Miller, I wish to acknowledge three editors. Jerry Gross, Kay Garrett, and Bill Scarff, all of whom improved this novel greatly. Also, I would like to thank the staff at iUniverse for assisting with line editing this novel.

I pitched this book many times, and for valuable feedback, I'd like to acknowledge Kimberly Cameron, who suggested that I rename the novel. Other editors and agents who offered valuable insights include: Beth deGuzman, Barbara Bova, Elizabeth Larsen, Barbara Harris, Kimberly Whalen, Jane Chelius, Susan Crawford, Amy Rennert, and Clare Ferraro.

I must acknowledge the *National Parks and Conservation Association* for information regarding geothermal riches and "bioprospecting" rights in return for information and royalties.

Finally, heartfelt thanks and love to my family and friends who have supported me. I am grateful for your praise and encouragement. Most importantly, I acknowledge my children, Chase and Allison. You make me smile a dozen times a day. I love you.

Chapter 1

"What was the last thing you said to Preston before he died?" I asked Michael O'Connor, our firm's newest client. Michael looked away and started rocking back and forth in his mother's rocking chair; his sandy blond hair was getting wavier each time he swept his right hand through it. "Your arraignment hearing is the day after tomorrow," I reminded him, trying to push the words out of his mouth.

"Answer her," Michael's mother ordered, as if he were still her little boy, despite the fact that he was thirty-nine years old. Michael looked at his mother sheepishly with his sky blue eyes, and then lowered his gaze back to the shag carpet that covered the hardwood floors of his childhood home in Jackson, Wyoming.

"I don't remember my exact words," Michael said, almost defiantly. Harry, the senior partner of our law firm, stood and reached for his coat. Michael obviously got the message. "We were arguing about business, all right? But it was no big deal. We argued about business all the time."

"Let me explain this to you," Harry said, setting his gray pinstriped Massimo Bizzocchi suit jacket back down. "The grand jury must have had enough evidence to indict you for Preston's murder, so now's the time for you to come clean. The grand jury's final report of its finding and recommendations to the presiding judge detail plenty of evidence of motive and opportunity. There's even an affidavit from a confidential source that you hired a hit man to kill Preston. Let's start by where you were, what was said and how, and who said it." After forty years practicing law, Harry always dispensed with the small talk. He'd moved to Jackson Hole about twenty years ago. Formerly a partner in a large law firm with offices all over the world, Harry had practiced out of both the New York and San Francisco offices, jet-setting the coast regularly. On a skiing vacation one winter, he fell in love with Jackson Hole. Not longer after, he cashed in on his partnership, convinced his wife, Jane, of the benefits of living in fresh air, and hung his shingle in Jackson. A former full academic-scholarship Stanford football star, his outgoing nature helped him establish his practice in Jackson. His taste for expensive British apparel made him stand out. He was famous in court as a relentless questioner.

"Like I told the police," Michael stammered, "We all went up the tram together and I told Preston that I wanted to take an advanced ski run back down the hill and-"

"Who's 'we all'?" Harry interrupted.

"My mom, Kelly, Preston, and I went skiing together that day." Michael's mom nodded in agreement.

"Preston was your business partner and Kelly was his wife, right?"

"Yes. Actually, Kelly was *my* friend before she was Preston's wife."

"I see. Go on."

"When I told everyone that I wanted to ski Granite Canyon, Preston insisted on tagging along. I tried to talk him out of it, but no one could talk Preston out of anything he'd decided to do. He followed me to Granite Canyon, which is out of bounds. When we got to the first chute, I again tried to tell him not to try it, but he kept on following me. As we made our way to the second chute, he was trying to convince me that he was doing the right thing in Asia for our business. I adamantly disagreed-"

"So you wanted to take an expert ski run and Preston wanted to follow you to talk business?"

"He wanted to convince me that he was right. But he wasn't. Preston was selling Geyser drugs in Asia for the wrong reasons, and we both knew it." Michael suddenly stopped rocking, but his right eye began to twitch and he put his index finger over his eyelid to stop the reflex. "He told me he was going to do the deal in Asia with or without my consent. I guess my exact words were something like, 'Over my dead body.'"

"Is that what happened? A dead body? Only it wasn't yours—it was his."

*   *   *   *

My name is Mary MacIntosh, but Harry calls me "Mac." He's the only person in the world I would allow to give me a nickname that makes me feel like a cheap meal. I've been working for Harry for six years. He hired me straight out of law school, even before I passed the bar exam, and put me to work doing the most routine clerical tasks, so that I would "learn the ropes" of practicing law—and so he could mold me to practice law like he does.

"What do you make of him?" I asked Harry on the ride back to the office after our meeting with Michael O'Connor.

"My son went to school with him—says that he's smart. He certainly hasn't wasted any time building a huge pharmaceutical company. He's not much of a talker," Harry said.

"Maybe he's turned it all inward," I suggested. "It's like pulling teeth to get information from him," I said as Harry pulled up to our office to drop me off. I'd left my Honda there.

"Notice how he brought up the fact that Kelly was *his* friend before she married Preston? She's the one that testified against Michael at the grand jury hearing. She must have given them enough to make the case."

"Did you notice the pictures in Michael's mother's house? When you were talking with Michael, I took a look around. I asked his mom about the girl who was in many of the pictures with Michael when he was a little boy. She said that the little girl was Kelly Flanigan, now Kelly Parker. Mrs. O'Connor said that they were best friends growing up. I can't believe that Kelly testified against him in front of the grand jury."

"She didn't have much of a choice. But I hear that they gave her immunity in exchange for her testimony. Kelly's a lawyer. I'm sure that she struck a good deal for herself," Harry said. I nodded in agreement. I opened the door to Harry's black Yukon and stepped onto the curb, bumping my head on the frame of the car door. Being tall has its drawbacks. The sub-zero evening air slapped my face. I turned toward Harry.

"I'll see you in the morning."

"Not first thing. I promised Hal Bennet that I'd meet with his kid tomorrow morning before his parole hearing, so I'll be at the jail. Let Lela know, will you?"

I hustled to my car and turned the starter, praying that my old Honda would turn over and that the heater would gain strength before I reached home. Harry waited, following me out of the parking lot to the last street possible before he had to turn toward his house, without making it too obvious that he was making sure that I made it home all right. The streets were slippery on this cold January night.

I dashed into my basement apartment, dropped my clothes at the foot of the bed and snuggled in under the comforter with Ted, my calico cat, who firmly believed that he was a dog. I grabbed my laptop from my nightstand and logged onto the Internet. I pulled up Jackson's local paper and did an archive search on Michael. He'd made the local papers a number of times growing up for his scholastic and skiing achievements. But he made the front cover of the newspaper on the day that he buried his father. I looked at the picture of a young boy seated at the edge of a casket, holding a folded United States flag. The article told of how Patrick O'Connor, a prominent local doctor, had died from a heart attack on the ski slopes. I wondered whether Michael was with his father on the slopes that day? Did he see his father die? How ironic, I thought to myself, that his father and his business partner both died on Jackson Hole ski slopes.

My mind strayed, taking me back to one of the only childhood memories I have of my father. He'd tied the toboggan to the back of our old blue snowmobile and taken my brother and me on a moonlit ride. At some point, the toboggan tipped over, spilling us on the side of the trail, and we could only watch as his lone headlight disappeared into the blackness of the night. By the time he discovered that we were no longer his passengers, our faces were near the burning stage of frostbite. This is the clearest memory I have of him. He died later that winter in an accident during the worst snowstorm that Colorado had seen in decades. After learning that Michael lost his dad at a young age too, I felt kind of connected to him.

Exhaustion overwhelmed me. I logged out of my computer and fell asleep to the sound of Ted's purring.

The next morning, I got up in time for my ritual morning jog and arrived at the office around my usual time, seven o'clock. Normally, Harry beats me to the office, but when I entered the pitch-black foyer, I remembered that he had an early meeting at the jail. I flipped on the lights in the reception area and headed straight towards my computer. After logging on, I turned around to hang my jacket on the hook behind my door. There he stood, tucked into the corner of my office, his dark, beady eyes burning through me like lasers. He was a heavy-set man with a navy blue ski cap pulled down over his face. Panic overwhelmed me, to the point where I couldn't scream for help. I backed slowly toward my desk, hoping to get close enough to grab the phone. When I saw the gun in his hand, I realized that the phone wouldn't save me, so I reached back and felt around for my silver letter opener or a sharp pencil. As I fumbled with my hand over my desk, he came at me with the pistol in his right hand. He grabbed me by my ponytail with his black-gloved hands and jolted me to the ground. With the gun now pressed against my right temple, he used his teeth to pull off a piece of silver duct tape off a roll he pulled from his jacket. He slapped it around my mouth.

In a low, gruff tone he said, "Take all of your clothes off." His breath smelled like a stale cigarette. He was breathing hard on my neck and all I could think about was rape. This man was going to rape and kill me.

"If you want money-" I tried to say, but the tape over my mouth kept the words from making sense.

"Shut up and strip."

"I know of someone who can help-" I mumbled again.

"Shut the fuck up," he said, and he pressed the gun hard against my forehead.

I fumbled with the buttons on my blouse, trying to get what seemed like oversized buttons through the tiny holes. "Faster," he sneered as my blouse fell to the floor. He unleashed his grip on my hair and reached out with his left hand to touch the strap on my bra. "Your skirt next."

I unsnapped the clasp on my gray skirt and unzipped the zipper as he grabbed the reigns of my hair again and tightened the cinch. As he jerked my head back, my skirt fell to the floor. "Take off the nylons. Now!" I tucked my thumbs under the waistband of my panty hose and peeled them over my hips. He yanked on my hair to balance me, while I stepped out of each stocking leg. He forced me to stand erect. "The bra," he whispered, as if he was gaining control. I unfastened the clasp from between my breasts and peeled away my dignity. He watched as my bra hit the ground. He took the barrel of the gun and made figure eights around my breasts, and then he stopped and put the barrel over my nipple. He rotated the barrel back and forth. "Are they real?" he asked, in a faint tone. I didn't respond. He pressed the cold metal of the gun against my chest as he used his hand to feel me up. "Yes, they're real," he repeated. "I like the real ones." He fondled the other nipple with the gun and then took a step back. The graveyard of clothes lay at my feet, and I stood nearly naked before him. I leaned back towards my desk, trying to find a weapon, but I could only feel papers under my fingers.

"Turn around and face the window," he said. I turned around slowly. He shoved me up against the desk so hard that he rammed my thighs into the credenza. I reached forward to brace myself. "Put your hands behind your back." I kept my hands forward, frantically looking for something sharp to grab. "Get your fucking hands back here now." I reached back. "Take off your underwear." I paused. He snapped my head back and jabbed the gun to my right temple. I slid my panties over my hips and they dropped to the floor. He let go of my hair long enough to slap handcuffs around my wrists.

As the handcuffs clicked, I thought back on my self-defense classes from college. If I did try to kick him, I would have to heel him in the groin so hard that it would drop him to his knees suddenly. Then I would have to stomp on his hand to get the gun away and then I'd have to run for my life. The odds of making this work without getting shot and killed weren't good. I braced myself. I should have made my move before the handcuffs were snapped. I'd missed my opportunity. I was mad at myself for not thinking quicker. Now that I was naked and cuffed, his assault was a foregone conclusion. I decided to pretend that I was auditioning for a play. I audition for parts regularly at Jackson's local repertory theater. I'd just auditioned for Tennessee Williams' *The Case of the Crushed Petunias*. I'd tried out for the role of Dorothy Simple. Of course, I was offered the role of Mrs. Dull.

I decided in my own mind that the only way I was going to survive this attack was to be compliant and cooperative. Maybe this creep would get off in whatever way was necessary and he'd leave me alive, if I cooperated. I took a deep breath as I felt his gloved hand clutch my narrow hips.

"Skin and bones," he said. "I like a little meat on my bitch." I closed my eyes, thinking of Mrs. Dull. Her opening line in the play was, "I want a pair of wine-colored socks for my husband." I decided to rehearse the play in my mind and avoid feeling what was happening to me. But I couldn't. The rage was growing inside. All I could think about was getting away from this man. I said a silent prayer to my father to help me.

Just as I heard him unzip his pants, I heard Harry's voice. "I forgot the Bennett file," Harry yelled from the foyer. When the thug heard Harry, he turned. This was it. I kicked him with my heel as hard as I could in the groin. He lunged forward. "Fucking bitch," he howled. He pistol-whipped me on the side of my face and then ran out of my office, knocking Harry to the ground on the way.

"What in the hell?" Harry ran into my office and gasped. "Oh my God. What in the hell happened? Are you okay? Did he hurt you?"

I couldn't answer. I just stood there, naked. Harry tore the tape off my mouth and then took off his trench coat and wrapped it over the front of my shoulders. He held me tight for a second, and then grabbed my phone. He called the cops, all friends of his.

"A man just attacked Mary MacIntosh," Harry started. He shouted the details to the dispatcher and then slammed the phone down.

He sat me down in the chair, glancing at the wound on my cheek. "What happened?"

I couldn't find words, sitting naked in my boss' coat, still handcuffed, cold and horrified. I could feel my lower lip trembling. The tears poured down my cheeks. "It's going to be all right. You're going to be okay." Harry put his arm around me and reached over for the phone again. "I'll call Jane."

Jane, Harry's wife, rushed through the reception area. Her rail-thin body was clad in a white terrycloth sweat suit. She hadn't showered yet, and her brown hair was matted to her head on the right side. A smudge of mascara encircled her eyes. "Oh, baby, are you okay? I'm so sorry. So sorry," she said, holding me close. Jane had sort of adopted me as her own daughter after Harry hired me. Educated at an Ivy League school, Jane showed me a different world than the one in which I'd grown up. She was delighted to help me buy the right clothes, suggest good books, take me to nice restaurants and introduce me to the art of food and wine. I'd often wondered why she and Harry didn't have more children, but Harry cautioned me early on not to bring it up.

"Can you think of anyone who'd want to hurt you?" Harry asked, wiping the mascara-laden tears away from my cheeks with his Hermes silk handkerchief.

I took a deep breath, finding my voice. "Aside from a few of our less reputable clients, I c ... can ... can't think of anyone."

"What about that boyfriend of yours?" Harry said in a less than approving tone.

"He broke up with me last month, but that man was *not* my ex-boyfriend. He would never do something like this. God, Harry. To even suggest ..."

"Now, come on, you two. You're shaking, dear," Jane said. "Can I get you anything?" Before I could answer, Harry picked up Jane's coat from the floor and draped it over me. Harry was the closest thing I had to a father. My mother remarried not long after my dad died, but my stepfather was more interested in getting a new mom for his two kids than serving as a father to me.

Harry was pacing the floor of my office. "Has anyone been following you? Stalking you? Have you received any strange phone calls?"

I shook my head.

"Maybe the guy was here to steal something and you just happened to interrupt him," Harry said. "Is anything missing?" Harry walked out into the reception area and looked around.

"Jesus Christ! Lela's desk has been ransacked!"

Jane and I followed him. Files were scattered about Lela's cubicle, with drawers open and papers yanked out from their files. Lela's computer was on, but it was flashing on the password screen.

"He must have tried to get into her computer," I said, pointing to her computer screen. "He was obviously looking for something."

"Excuse me," a voice interrupted from behind us, "we're responding to your call. I'm detective Trammel and this is my partner, Detective Abrams." They flashed their ID's. Detective Trammel stood about five-feet-five, with wide hips and short, dark hair. She took one look at the mess and reached for her gun. "Stay put. Abrams and I will check the place to make sure that the assailant is gone. He could've had an accomplice." Trammel motioned to Abrams to follow her as they cased the office. "All clear," she said when they returned. She put her gun back into the holster and reached for her notebook. She turned to Harry. "What happened?" Harry told her his version. Then she turned to me.

"He was about my height, say five-feet-nine, and he had heavy-set shoulders," I told the police. "He had on a dark-colored ski mask and gloves, so I couldn't see his face. Harry said that he had big boots with red shoelaces. That's about all I can remember. I think his eyes were brown, but I can't be sure."

"Are you sure he was your height?"

"Pretty sure. He might have been a little shorter than me. He certainly wasn't taller than five-feet-nine." Detective Abrams, a short, overweight man with thick brown hair and bifocal glasses, took notes as Trammel fiddled with the handcuffs until they finally snapped free.

"Describe his voice?" Abrams asked.

"It was low. Gruff."

"And you say that he was wearing dark clothes and a ski mask?"

"Yes."

"Anything that you can remember about his clothes? Was he wearing a sweat suit, or a jacket?"

"I don't remember. I think it was a jacket with a zipper, but I'm not sure. He had a zipper in his pants, I think."

"He asked you to take off your clothes?" Trammel asked.

"Yes."

"Did he touch or assault you?"

"Yes." I looked down.

"Would it be better for you if I asked you these questions in private?" Trammel asked. I nodded. She walked me back into my office and closed the door. She saw my clothes in a pile on the floor.

"Why don't you get dressed, and then we'll talk, woman to woman-like." She stepped out of my office for a few minutes, like the nurse does at the OB-GYN. She knocked a few minutes later and entered.

"First of all, you have nothing to be ashamed of, dear. This isn't your fault." I nodded. "Tell me what happened." I told her how I'd gone to hang up my coat and there he'd been, hiding in the corner. I explained that he'd duct-taped my mouth and held me by the back of my hair and made me take off my clothes.

"Did he touch you?" she asked, reaching out for my hand. I instinctively pulled away.

"He drove his gun around my breasts like they were a racetrack. He stuck the barrel of the gun over my nipples," I said, tears spilling out of my eyes, watering my mouth. "I thought ... I thought he was going to rape me. He made me turn around and-"

"It's all right. Did he rape you?"

"No," I managed.

"Then let's focus on that. We'll find out who did this to you, but we'll need your help. I'll need you to come down to the station and give a composite description."

"A composite?"

"Yes. We need to have a picture for the press to get-"

"For the press? I don't want this on the evening news! I don't want everyone in town to know that I was ... assaulted."

"Miss MacIntosh, it's important that you cooperate with us. Don't you want us to catch this guy?"

"Of course I do, but I don't want the world to know about it. We have this big trial coming up and I'm sure that it's going to be in the news. I don't want to be the sub-story after the headline about the Michael O'Connor case."

"I see. Well, I can do my best to keep it confidential, but in order to get the word out that there is a possible rapist running around, we're going to have to publish at least a physical description of the guy. And that description will be given to the media. That's standard procedure. You understand."

I understood it perfectly. In this small town, every household would know about it by dinnertime. But I didn't really have a choice. I agreed to cooperate. I watched as they dusted for fingerprints and collected samples. They even took a sample of my auburn hair.

"You're representing Michael O'Connor, aren't you?" Abrams asked on his way out. Harry nodded. "Knew him in high school. Smart guy. Great skier. Kept to himself, though. I was on the ski team with him. Always had his nose in a book. Do you think he did it?"

Before Harry could answer, Detective Trammel reprimanded him for asking such a question.

By the day's end, the trauma of the office burglary had set in. Lela, our secretary, was out ill—otherwise, I would have asked her if I could stay at her place. Sleeplessness plagued me even on good days. I couldn't imagine sleeping alone tonight. Luckily, Harry and Jane insisted that I stay at their house, so I gathered

Ted, my cat, from my apartment and settled into one of their spare bedrooms. Ted was no stranger to the Harrison home—he'd been housed there many times when I'd gone on trips. Ted liked moving in on Harry's Labrador.

Before bedtime, I approached Harry working in his den. "Do you need help getting ready for tomorrow's arraignment?"

"As a matter of fact, I was going to ask you to do the O'Connor arraignment. It would be great experience for you to handle something high-profile. But, after what happened today, maybe now is not the time."

"N-n-no, not true. I can do it. I'm okay. Let me do this." I couldn't believe Harry's timing. I've been begging for a murder arraignment for two years now, and he chooses the day that I've been assaulted at gunpoint to hand one over to me.

"Of course, I'll first-chair the case, but it's time you get a murder arraignment under your belt."

I plopped down into the leather chair opposite Harry and let out a sigh. My head was spinning and my hands were shaking.

"You need a glass of wine. Follow me." I followed Harry into the basement of his remodeled Victorian home. He flipped on the lights to his pride and joy: a wine cellar that is the envy of every jetsetter in Jackson Hole. He walked around, studying a few labels before he chose the right vintage. "Nineteen ninety-one Caymus Vineyards Special Selection Cabernet Sauvignon. This is a wonderful bottle."

His wine cellar is organized by region, type and age. Every bottle has a hand-made label. He walked the bottle over to his mounted antique opener, popping the cork instantly. "This needs to breathe," he said, while pouring the Cabernet into a decanter. I watched the burgundy wine spin in an orbit while Harry gave me one of his famous wine lectures. "When you taste this full-bodied wine, concentrate on the black cherry and coffee aromas, along with a veritable potpourri of vanilla, mint and berry on the medium to full-bodied palate."

Harry grabbed two large wine glasses and the decanter and motioned for me to follow him back to his den, where we sipped wine and talked strategy late into the night.

Chapter 2

The morning headlines were direct: *New York Times*: "O'Connor Arraigned for Geyser Partner's Murder" and *Boston Herald*: "Geyser Stock Plummets Over Murder Charges." The local paper included the headline I feared most: "O'Connor's Attorney Sexually Assaulted." As Harry and I flanked our now famous client, Michael O'Connor, the reporters flogged us on our way in the courthouse. "Is the assault related to the case?" "Have they caught the guy yet?" Question after question. I felt sick to my stomach. The closer I got to the defense table, the higher my panic rose. The courtroom was as crowded as I have ever seen it. The bailiff looked nervous, like a country boy in the presence of royalty. The prosecutor looked over at me as I arranged my files.

Christopher Bain, prosecuting attorney, is tall and thin with thick, dark hair that sweeps down in front like a horse's forelock. He is forever whisking it back with a sudden whip of his neck, causing a reflexive blink which, in turn, makes his glasses slip down his ski jump of a nose. To get them back in place, he repeatedly twitches his nose like a rabbit. It was comical to watch.

Bain's expensive-looking suits belie his public servant's salary. I often see him shopping at the outlets. His ties never quite match his suit. Conversely, his leather belt and well-shined shoes always match. Bain's take-no-prisoners style is adored by juries, but not always by judges. Bain looked over in my direction and shook his head. Today, his white shirt was molded to his athletic body. Normally, he would not approach the defense table before a hearing, but over he came.

"I'm so sorry to hear what happened to you. Are you doing okay? I'm here for you if you need to talk." He reached over to pat my shoulder and I about jumped out of my skin. I could feel the tears welling.

All I could manage was, "I'm okay." Then I turned to Harry and whispered, "Switch me places. I can't do it. Not today."

"What?"

"You know that I want to do this more than anything else. But I'm shaken up today. It took half an hour to cover the bruise on my cheek with make-up. Please do this arraignment. Let me do the next one." I hated hearing the words coming out of my mouth. I was angry with myself for being such a weakling, for letting the reporters shake my confidence. I was angry at Harry for offering me the opportunity at the most vulnerable moment in my life. I hated myself for not having enough courage to take on the job. The look of disappointment on Harry's face screamed volumes.

"This kind of opportunity doesn't present itself often," is all that he said. He escorted me to his left and took the place of the first-chair attorney—the one that was cued to speak. I noticed that Bain was watching the musical chairs. He shook his head slowly and mouthed, "I'm sorry." I averted his stare as Judge Furmer took the bench. Bain followed my gaze and looked directly at the judge. She didn't bother to look back. This was clearly disappointing to Bain, who likes everyone to take notice of him, especially women.

Bain has a reputation in Jackson as a ladies' man. He loves the transient state of many of the women in the town—they are either tourists or ski bums willing to be wined and dined by one of the few men in town dressed in a suit. Bain's law office is perched above an art gallery near the town square, giving him a full view of the town's patrons du jour. Jackson's most distinguishing and eye-catching feature is in fact its town square, a picture-perfect city block, flanked on all four corners with St. Louis-style gateway arches, each one made from hundreds of elk antlers.

Bain once told me (at a county bar association meeting after a few beers) that he particularly liked the town arches in the winter because they are draped with little white lights, which remind him of the eyes that once guided the elk through the expanse of forests in Yellowstone and Grand Teton National Park. He said the lights also remind him of his sacred belief that the courageous animals live on—a reincarnation of sorts—which is what Bain believes life is all about. He loves to talk about reincarnation, rebirth, and reinvention. If I didn't know better, I would think he was from Berkeley instead of Wyoming. Bain loves to tell his newly made lady friends that the Tetons got their name from French-Canadian trappers who called them "Les Trois Tetons," meaning "The Three Tits." He tells me that there's something titillating about being able to say "tits" in front of a woman on a first date. I never know what to believe from him after he's had a few drinks.

"All rise, the bailiff announced to the courtroom on the first day of Michael O'Connor's murder trial. "The Honorable Sheryl Furmer presiding." With standing room only, the reporters were crammed in the back row, their notepads and pencils poised for prose.

The courthouse in Jackson is unremarkable from the outside. It looks like any other government building—gray, rectangular, with many small windows that suggest entombment. But the interior of the courtroom is sufficiently decorated, with slate-blue carpeting on the floors, which gives a calming effect and probably hides dirt well, and with comfortable black canvas bucket-seat chairs, a dark wood partition separating the gallery from the public, and an impressive, dark, oak-stained bench, behind which the judge reigns. Above the judge's bench hangs the Wyoming state seal with this inscription: "Equal Rights: Livestock: Mines: Grain: Oil."

"Please be seated," Judge Furmer said. "The People of the State of Wyoming versus Michael Brian O'Connor, case number WC000599. Counsel, please identify yourselves for the record."

Bain whipped his hair back, adjusted his glasses and said, "Good morning, your Honor. Christopher Bain on behalf of the People of the State of Wyoming."

"Good morning, your Honor. Andrew J. Harrison on behalf of the defendant, Michael O'Connor." It was peculiar to me to hear Harry call himself Andrew J. Harrison. Everyone in town knows his as "Harry."

"Good morning, counsel. Mr. Bain, please present probable cause," Judge Furmer said.

"The defendant, Michael O'Connor was Preston Parker's business partner in a pharmaceutical business named Geyser, Inc. Michael O'Connor was the last person seen with Preston Parker on the ski slopes. A witness can testify that the last thing he heard the defendant say to the deceased was: 'Over my dead body.' The witness claims that the two men were having a fight over business practices. Within an hour of this argument, Preston Parker's unconscious body lay bleeding in the trees of Granite Canyon, an out-of-bounds ski run on the slopes of Jackson Hole Ski Resort. In addition, Your Honor, the State has an affidavit from a sworn witness who claims that Michael O'Connor hired him as a hit man to kill Preston Parker.

"The autopsy notes that Preston Parker suffered blunt force trauma to the head. Toxicology reports indicate that the deceased was also poisoned. Michael O'Connor was present at the scene of the ski accident and was present both at the hospital and at the after-care facility where the poisoning likely took place. Motive and opportunity, Your Honor. Significantly, Michael O'Connor stood to gain control of Geyser, Inc. if Preston Parker was dead."

"Thank you, Mr. Bain," Judge Furmer said. "Mr. Harrison, you may address probable cause."

Harry cleared his throat. "Mr. O'Connor is present before the Court this morning and we acknowledge receipt of the State's indictment. We waive Mr. O'Connor's right to have the indictment placed on the record and hereby move the court enter Mr. O'Connor's plea of not guilty to the charges identified on the grand jury indictment." Harry told me that he would not address probable cause because he knew there was enough evidence to indict Michael and he didn't want the State to put any more evidence on the record. The press would have a field day with the information that they already had.

When Harry first hired me, I was a glorified secretary, really. When I passed the bar, my job didn't change much at first, but little by little, Harry gave me more lawyerly responsibilities. I now sit "second chair" at all of his trials, which means that I do all of the grunt work preparing for trial. I organize all of the documents, evidence and testimony. I subpoena and help depose the witnesses, draft the pre-trial motions, and otherwise do whatever Harry needs done before he steps foot in the courtroom.

Normally, when Harry is doing an arraignment hearing, I'm in the "War Room," which is what we call our conference room, working. Not today. "An attractive lawyer might help Michael's case. This case is going to be tried by the media," Harry had said to me with a wink and a nod. "You know, being defended by a good-looking woman may serve him well, since he is single, young, and filthy rich. Not to mention that it might also rattle Bain's cage if you're here." Harry used any opportunity to push Bain. He and Jane have tried to set me up with him more times than I can count. Bain is the perfect match for me, they say. He's well dressed, has some culture, is a lawyer and he finds me attractive. I've tried to explain that Bain is attracted to every decent-looking woman in town, but they don't believe me.

I felt Michael shifting back and forth in an effort to stand still next to me. He was dressed in a navy blue suit and a white button-down shirt. His sky-blue tie matched the color of his eyes. His light-colored, wavy hair was combed back off his high forehead, accentuating his rosy cheeks. In yesterday's local paper, which is really little more than a gossip column, his fifth grade teacher had described him as a "handsome boy as a pupil." I noticed him looking nervously around the courtroom at what once were familiar faces: schoolteachers, classmates, parents, and grandparents—townsfolk who are all very interested in his predicament. Funny how that is, I think. None of these people called or wrote to Michael when he was on top of the world, running one of the fastest-growing companies in America. Maybe they supposed he was too busy to respond. But they are happy to have him back, to show their support, like they would have if he had been part of the championship football team so many years ago. They have surfaced from the tourist shops and ski slopes, wanting to be a part of something larger and more exciting. Looks like they'll get what they came for.

"The defendant's plea of not guilty is noted on the record. Have the prosecution and defense reached an agreement with respect to bond?" Judge Furmer asked as she looked up from her podium for the first time. Recently appointed to the superior court, she'd served as a municipal court judge for more than thirteen years. I've appeared before Judge Furmer many times, watching while she handled municipal cases, and I have spoken to her a few times at Rotary Club meetings. Judge Furmer has never had a high profile case like this one. She knows that the press will be all over this case and she welcomes the publicity—so much so that I heard through the grapevine that she took yesterday off to have her hair and nails done, just for the camera. If she handles this case well, an appointment to the Wyoming Supreme Court is a real possibility. I'm told that she wants the appointment in the worst way.

"The State asks for bail in the amount of two million dollars," Bain said.

"Your Honor, that's absurd," Harry said. "Mr. O'Connor is not a flight risk. He has family in town and is a founder of one of the country's leading pharmaceutical companies. He's a reputable citizen without a prior criminal record. We ask that bail be set at one hundred thousand dollars."

"Bail is set at one million dollars," Furmer said.

"Bond arrangements are in place," Harry said. The bond had been wired to the bank, and I had arranged for our legal service to pick it up after the hearing and lodge it with the court.

I could see out of the corner of my eye that Michael was not paying attention to the judge. I followed Michael's gaze—he was staring at Kelly. I admit, her natural beauty is like a sunrise—making it hard to stop staring. She was seated directly behind the prosecutor in the courtroom. She wore a navy Chanel suit with a cream silk blouse, a long strand of pearls circling her neck, and diamond solitaire and pearl earrings in her ears. Her long black hair fell freely over her shoulders, perfectly framing her oval-shaped face. Kelly's emerald eyes met Michael's and she gave him a nod. He darted his eyes back toward the judge.

I wondered how Kelly felt about Michael's bail arrangements. It's not every day that the wife of the victim consented to bail. Bain had merely said that Kelly consented. But I think that Kelly was obliged to Michael for many reasons. Kelly's hands kept clenching and unclenching, as if she were trying to decide whether to hold on or let go. She looked back at Michael, who was standing before her. Her childhood friend and her college buddy—these were reasons to help. But—if someone were accused of murdering my husband, I don't think I could help spring him from jail—even if he had been my best friend.

"A pre-trial conference is set in ten days. If no plea bargain has been reached by then, the case will be set for trial," Judge Furmer stated for the record. She struck her gavel and adjourned the hearing. She stood and stared out in the gallery a few extra seconds for effect, then collected her files quite deliberately, cradling them to her breast. After the click-click of the cameras, Judge Furmer vanished like a phantom in a black cape through the door to her inner chambers. According to lawyer gossip, the cameras in the courtroom were Judge Furmer's idea. In Harry's forty-some years of practice, he'd only tried one other case where the media were allowed to photograph the trial.

As we left the courtroom, I heard Michael let out a big sigh, probably relieved to have made it through the first part of his criminal proceeding. I watched his every move, trying to get to know him one gesture at a time. Michael didn't look directly at Kelly, but he looked down at her shoes—navy, square-toed, with sensible yet fashionable heels. As he stared at her shoes, I allowed my eyes to venture up a few inches, distracted by her perfectly defined calf muscles.

Kelly and Michael both grew up in small Wyoming towns, not that there are many large cities in the state. Wyoming is America's ninth-largest state, enveloping nearly ninety-eight thousand square miles, yet it has the smallest population of any state. Most towns are small, leaving most of the land wild and predominately undeveloped. Speaking of small towns, from what I gathered from yesterday's meeting, Kelly probably wasn't wishing to revert to her small-town days. Michael mentioned that Kelly hated small towns—hated the small-mindedness of the people. But Jackson is the exception to her small-town rule, because Hollywood had taken over and there were now movie stars, wine bars, latte shops, and lingerie boutiques where there once was only the corner drugstore and the five and dime.

Jackson is not a typical Wyoming town. For a small town, Jackson is as good as it gets. Crowned on three sides by Snow King Mountain, East Gros Ventre

Butte and the Gros Ventre Range, the town itself is a tiara of beauty. Venture in any direction outside of the crown and visitors will be graced by the Grand Tetons, national forests extraordinaire, and amazing wildlife—bears, buffalo, elk, deer, moose, all wandering freely and openly, unconcerned about the human population (until hunting season, that is). The Snake River winds its way through valleys of splendid wildflowers and willows, while geysers spout the earth's thermal liquid free from captivity. And trees thicken the landscape—splendid, old, tall vegetation offering an umbrella of protection to all the creatures scampering above their roots. Yes, I imagine that, for Michael, it would be all right to be a small-towner at this stage in the game—tending his garden, hiking, fishing, camping, skiing, and rafting,—all for the asking, outside his back screen door.

Buffalo, Wyoming, where Kelly grew up, is the quintessential small town, where everyone knows everyone else's business. I watched as Kelly momentarily forgot to play the role of the mourning widow, glancing at the cameras with a slight flirt of a smile, almost smug, a look of assurance that only accompanies a woman who truly understands the power of her beauty, and is willing to use it.

We inched toward the mob, the noise volume increasing. I watched Michael's shoulders rise, as if he were trying to muffle the noise and hide at the same time. He must have felt the strength in Harry's left hand, as Harry grabbed him by the elbow. Still carrying his twenty-pound briefcase in his right hand, Harry cut a swath through the sea of reporters—a move that probably served him well in his football days.

"Look confident and don't answer any questions," Harry said to Michael.

Chapter 3

"Mr. O'Connor, how does it feel to be charged with murder?" "Why did you do it?" "Did you do it?" "Are you going to take the stand in your defense?" "Are you confident that you have good lawyers? Didn't one of them get raped yesterday?" I stopped dead in my tracks to find out which reporter had the nerve to utter such a question. I could feel Harry nudging me forward, saying over and over, "No comment … no comment … no comment." I dug my heels into the carpeted steps and grabbed the railing tightly. I heard the rude reporter's voice ask another ridiculous question. I honed in on him, letting him know in my silent way that he should take heed. Instead, he shoved a microphone into my face and asked, "Do you think there's a connection between your assault and the O'Connor case?" Harry unwrapped my knuckles from the railing and escorted me out.

When we reached the door to the outside world, the cool, brisk air shocked my lungs. Low clouds blocked the sun, reminding me of a solar eclipse I'd seen long ago. As we crowded into Harry's black Yukon, a cameraman ran up to me. Before I could tell him to leave us alone, he said, "Hey, I'm sorry about what just happened. That reporter should be canned. He's a jerk."

I wanted to thank the cameraman, but Harry forced me in the car and closed the door. I watched him as we sped away to the safety of our now police-guarded office. My heart fluttered. The sincerity in the cameraman's eyes stole my breath.

* * * *

"Let's get cracking," Harry shouted, the minute we reached the War Room. "We've got a ton of work to do to get ready for trial."

We normally handle local cases, meaning that the witnesses live nearby. This case was different. The alleged crime happened here, but the other possible suspects and witnesses live in different towns, states and even countries. "You'll finally have a chance to see some of the world, Mac." Harry's a world traveler. He's been on me for years to take a trip overseas to learn about other cultures. I've been more concerned with paying down my college loans. Ironically, I finally have an excuse to get on an airplane and see something besides wide-open spaces, but since yesterday's attack, I'm afraid to go.

I grew up in Boulder, Colorado. Nestled against the face of the Rocky Mountains, Boulder is framed by three gigantic rock faces shaped like the hot side of an iron; hence the name, the "flatirons." It was originally home to the Arapaho and Southern Ute Indian tribes. I attended the University of Colorado at Boulder, which is the central nervous system of the city. I found Harry through the career placement office on campus. He wanted someone fresh out of law school so that he could pay the poor soul next to nothing to learn how to be a "real lawyer." He has been faithful to both promises: I still haven't managed to make more than my minimum payment on any school loan, but today I feel like a real lawyer.

Our office is located on the upper floor of the Bank of Jackson Hole. The Bank has a façade that makes it look like a cabin built with knotty pine and river rock. The roof is cantilevered in the front in two tiers—the second tier housing a clock tower lookout, yet the roof over our part of the building has a flat line that gives the office a low industrial ceiling.

Harry's office is decorated in Stanford red and white and has a beautiful cherry-stained U-shaped desk, which is kept relatively clear of paperwork. He only allows active files and pleadings on his desk, meaning paperwork from cases that he's currently working on. If he's not working on the case, the files go in a labeled box. Papers and books get stacked on top of these boxes. It gets out of control at times and that's when he calls Lela in over a weekend to do a clean up.

Other than these stacks of boxes on the floor, Harry is a very neat and tidy man. Everything has a place in his world, even in his garage, which is lined with white shelving on the upper half of the walls. The bottom half of the wall has corkboard with all of his tools and yard equipment outlined by shape and hung in order of size. Jane tells me that he organizes his closet by color. I'm sure that his Louis Vuitton cap-toed black shoes are not next to his John Lobb brown shoes. Harry would keel over if he looked in my closet. I'm lucky if I'm not wearing one black shoe and one navy shoe (they look the same in the early morning hours).

Harry is an outdoorsman in every way, as evidenced by the prints that line the walls in his office. He has beautiful shots of the Tetons, and of wildlife photographed by local artists, hanging on the walls. The one thing missing from his office is a computer, as it would simply collect dust. He does all of his research the old fashioned way—via books or via his associate. He keeps telling me that "one of these days" he's going to take a computer class. He often stands behind me in awe as I access the Internet and get information with the touch of a few keystrokes. I do most of my research on CD-ROMs, websites and legal search vehicles. I love the fact that I can learn anything about anyone with the touch of a few buttons.

"Let's go over the facts of the case," Harry grumbles, as he slams the thick file on the wooden conference table. "Michael and Preston are Harvard roommates who started Geyser, Inc. together in Boston," Harry says. "They're here in Jackson, Michael's hometown, for a convention and take a day off to enjoy some skiing. Michael's an expert skier and he takes Preston on an expert run. Somehow, Preston winds up unconscious in the trees. Preston is taken by the ski patrol to the emergency room. Despite everything that is done to save him in the hospital, he dies the next day."

"Here's an odd thing. From the minute Preston was transferred to the hospital, the police were there to question Michael," I added. "Why would the police have been called? I doubt they run to the emergency room every time someone gets hurt on the slopes."

I watched as Harry digested the facts of this case. He contorted his forehead in thought, causing me to focus on the broken capillaries around his nose, which stood out like tree roots in the dead of winter. "We need to interview the ski patrol, the treating doctor, the pathologist, Deputy Tim Marshall, Kelly, Michael, Michael's mom, Michael's research assistant, Preston's secretary, and the members of the Geyser board of directors, for starters," Harry said. He was on a roll. I wrote all of these names down on the easel, as fast as I could.

"We need corporate records like profit and loss statements, and the relevant financial filings for a public company like Geyser. I will need all hospital records subpoenaed and a copy of any police interrogations and statements given by witnesses to the police. Find out what Bain's strategy is for this case. Scratch that. I will call Bain myself. He already saw you in court today. That might be as much as he can take of you for one day." Harry gave me one of his wry smiles, a half-smirk flanked by dimples. He teased me at every turn about Bain.

Bain's a ladies' man, for sure, but Harry is convinced that he is in love with me. For the record, Bain is not in love with me. I think he flirts with me because

I'm a challenge to him. According to my last boyfriend, I'm fiercely independent, not given to commitment, extremely private, and economically challenged. I guess I agree with his psychological evaluation for the most part, except for the commitment thing. I could commit. Just not to Bain, or to my ex-boyfriend. Bain needs something new to stoke his fire constantly, anyway. He wouldn't want to commit. He just likes to flirt with me, and everyone else in a skirt. I think he enjoys me because I'm nearly as tall as he is and he loves my long red hair. He calls my hair a wildfire in a season of drought.

"I'll get the subpoenas going right away, but how do you want to divide the task of interviewing all of these people?" Harry hates to travel on business any more. He did so much of it in his early years of practice that he got burned out on airports and hotels. He likes to be either at the office, home, or outdoors surrounded by nature and his sporting equipment. Accordingly, he assigned me all the witnesses in Boston.

I had Lela make the travel arrangements. Harry had hired Lela straight out of high school. Actually, she'd dropped out of high school at age sixteen, and marched into his office one day, begging for a job. He liked her spirit and her short skirts. Lela is a Shoshone Indian and the daughter of a Shoshone Chief. She wasn't the type who valued a formal education, but she had street smarts and ambition. Harry prefers common sense to raw intelligence. He says that it's worth more. Harry trained her and promoted her up through the ranks. Now thirty-four, after eighteen years at Harry's side, Lela is a part of Harry. I like the fact that Lela is a year older than me. I often tease her about it.

Lela arranged for me to fly to Boston with Michael on his early morning flight back to his home, where his pharmaceutical company had its headquarters. That meant that I had only a few hours to prepare dozens of subpoenas and pack my bags. Darkness surrounded the office long before I left. I wasn't really anxious to go home.

I met Michael at the airport the following morning. After checking in and going through the security checkpoint, I sat in the waiting area and enjoyed black coffee and a freshly baked bagel. I will never lose respect for the everyday pleasures of life. From what I'd witnessed, Michael didn't appreciate ordinary pleasures—his pleasures were achieved through experimentation. For instance, he bought two coffees—one black and the other with cream and sugar. He was drinking the one with cream and sugar leaving the black one idle, like an abandoned car. I wondered whether he thought I would drink one of them, or if he liked his first cup souped-up in preparation for the full dose of caffeine on his second. I got my answer within the hour. The second cup of black coffee was used to keep his souped up version hot over the long haul. He would drink a gulp of his creamed-up coffee and then add just a little of the black reserve. He repeated this routine for nearly a half hour during our conversation. Finally, the loudspeaker announced our flight.

"I hate commercial travel," Michael said. "How long can the police impound the corporate jet?"

"As long as they want … at least through the trial. We'll file a motion to have it released from custody after we get word that they've finished with forensics," I said.

"How long does forensics take?"

"It depends. It can take days, weeks, months."

"What are they looking for in the jet? I didn't even fly in the jet here. Preston did," Michael said. "He always had the jet."

"They're looking for any evidence that can be connected to his death, like threatening letters. They'll do fingerprint, hair and fiber analysis to see who else has been in the jet. Who knows what they're looking for?"

"They can do that sort of a fishing expedition? They don't have to say what they're looking for?"

"It depends on what the search warrant says. In this instance, the police got a broad warrant, so they can look for anything that could be connected to the alleged crime, unless we file a motion for a protective order. Is there a reason we should file for a protective order?" I asked. Michael's eyes darted quickly back to the newspaper.

"No. Of course not. I was just wondering."

"Harry tried to narrow the scope of the warrant, but the magistrate didn't grant his motion. Around here, the police seem to have a pretty long rope when it comes to investigating a crime." Michael nodded, then looked away.

For my traveling comfort, I wore my standard black wool slacks and a taupe turtleneck, boots with heels, a black leather coat and a black silk scarf. After the jet discussion, we sat in an uncomfortable silence as we drank our coffee. I would have loved to break the ice, but I wasn't quite sure where to begin. I knew that Michael and Kelly were childhood friends who had gone to Harvard University together. I also knew that they somehow met Preston Parker at Harvard and that eventually, Michael and Preston became business partners. I knew that Kelly and Preston married sometime after that. I knew that Michael, Preston and Kelly were in Jackson together for a company conference and that Preston was gravely injured on the ski slopes and died shortly thereafter. I needed to know more.

As we prepared to board the small commuter plane, the airline ground crew summoned stand-by passenger Miller to the podium. A man approached the podium, picked up a boarding pass and cut ahead of us in line to board the plane. Something about him looked hauntingly familiar. As I found my seat on the plane, I noticed the man staring at me. A chill shot up my spine.

"What's wrong?" Michael asked.

"Oh, it's probably nothing. That man in the back of the plane is staring at me."

"He's probably just admiring your beauty."

"Right," I said, half-embarrassed. I wasn't trying to call attention to myself. Something about that man's eyes gave me the creeps. I shook it off and cinched the seatbelt. I could feel the man's eyes burning a hole in the back of my head. I loosened my seatbelt and popped my head over the headrest. He was still glaring at me. I narrowed my eyes on him in a stare down, which was interrupted by the airline attendant announcing preparations for take-off.

We alighted with a bumpy start. The views of the Tetons were spectacular on this clear, brisk morning. I could see mountain ranges for miles and miles. The plane's engine, sounding like a revved-up electric mixer, blared in my ear, detracting a bit from the natural beauty beneath me, but nothing could spoil my appreciation for the wonders of mountains. I thought about Lewis and Clark and how they must have been in awe of the West: the rugged peaks, the floral valleys, the wide-mouthed rivers and the statuesque trees. Even from this altitude, the snow glistened on the crest like diamonds embedded in a mine.

Michael read the local coverage of his arraignment hearing. He must have sensed my gaze because at that same moment, he briefly raised his head from the newspaper and glanced my way. The front page had a picture of him leaving the courthouse yesterday with Harry at his side. The caption read: "Local Man Arraigned on Murder Charges." The story told about how Michael was born and raised in Jackson. Now at age thirty-eight, he's a research doctor for one of the largest pharmaceutical companies in America, and one of its founders. The article suggested that Michael and Preston had had an argument on the ski slope and stated that Preston wound up dead a short time later.

Michael thumbed through the paper to continue reading the article. He looked at the buried headline: "O'Connor's Lawyer Sexually Assaulted." Michael read on fervently. A few minutes later, he lowered the paper. "This happened to you two days ago?"

I rolled my eyes. "Yes. I'm not sure what's more horrific—the act itself or having it smeared all over the papers."

"I'm really sorry. I hope you're doing all right. Have they found the guy yet?"

"No. As far as I can tell, they have no leads. He didn't leave much evidence behind. He didn't … hurt me."

"How can you be back at work so quickly? Most people would be curled up in their beds being taken care of by their mother."

"I haven't told my mom about it." As the words escaped my lips, I realized how remote they sounded. I hadn't realized how much I'd isolated myself from my family, even my own mother. I hung onto Michael's words for a moment. If I had confided in her about the assault, or any other problem in my life, she would have started her monologue with a scolding of how I should not have been in the office alone. Nor should I live alone. Nor should I be alone. Somehow, my being single in my mid-thirties threatened her. It was as if she'd failed me. Over the past few years, every time I call home, the first five minutes of our conversation is filled with updates about my high school and college classmates who've recently married. Michael must have sensed my guilt.

"Sometimes we need to think things over before confronting someone that we love," Michael said.

I was about to respond but the plane dropped a few hundred feet without warning. The pilot came on the loud speaker to let us know that we'd encountered some turbulent air and to make sure that our seatbelts were fastened tightly.

* * * *

When we changed planes in Salt Lake City, the man in the back of the plane followed us to our next gate. While Michael stopped at the newsstand to look at every major headline, I pretended to read the back jacket of a best-selling paperback. The man passed closely behind me, wafting his cigarette-laden breath as he passed. The smell was distinct. I panicked.

I stashed the book back on the shelf and dashed to Michael's side. He looked over at me with a half-glance, as if I'd invaded his personal space.

"Are they calling our flight?" he asked.

"Uh, yes … I think so." I tagged beside him, looking nervously around until we were settled on the next flight. I decided it was time to ask Michael a few questions, and it would help the time pass. Maybe I'd learn something, and I didn't have to be too obvious about it. First, I asked Michael about Kelly's job.

"She's an associate lawyer with Jenkins & Brode. She clerked for them while in law school and they hired her after she passed the bar. As far as I know, she mostly does medical malpractice defense work. She also sits on the board of directors of Geyser. She's the corporate secretary. That's why I had her take care of the bail arrangements. Her firm handles some of our corporate work."

"Must be a big firm."

"It is. And you?" I told him about how I wound up working for Harry. He seemed genuinely interested and asked a lot of questions about criminal defense law. My turn.

"How did you and Kelly meet?"

"Our fathers met at Harvard Medical School. After finishing medical school, Kelly's dad set up his medical practice in Buffalo, Wyoming and my dad established his in Jackson Hole. We got together for holidays and learned to ski together and that sort of thing."

"Are you a good skier?"

"I was on the high school ski team and I was on ski patrol, so I guess you could say that I'm a decent skier," he said.

"What about Kelly? Is she a good skier too?"

"She's all right. She's been skiing since she was a kid and she used to be pretty good, but she was too busy being cheerleader and homecoming queen to be serious on the slopes."

"What about Preston? Was he a good skier?"

"Not really. He thought he was better than he was. He learned to ski on the East Coast, at places like Sugarloaf. I skied with Preston a few times. He usually skied beyond his limits."

I could sense Michael's competitiveness, and gave this a bit of thought. Preston was injured while skiing with Michael on some pretty advanced terrain. If Michael didn't think that Preston was a decent skier, why would he have allowed Preston to ski with him in expert territory? I really wasn't intending to interrogate, at this point—I was simply trying to make conversation. Apparently, my moment of silence plagued Michael, because he shifted in his seat and turned in my direction.

"Anyway, Kelly and I both got accepted to Harvard and our dads made us go."

"How did you meet Preston?"

"Preston was my dorm mate our first year at Harvard."

"You two must have hit it off for you to have gone into business together. I couldn't stand my dorm mate my first year of college."

Michael looked at me intensely. He furrowed his brow slightly and focused on me. "Preston was the best thing that ever happened to me up to that point in my life. I was awkward in high school—too skinny to play rough and tumble sports like football and too shy to join any social-type clubs. Preston took me under his wing right away and made me part of his group of friends. He called us the 'Parker Posse.' His friends were my friends. He invited me to share holidays with his family. He made sure that I was never the fifth wheel. He changed my life." Michael's eyes welled with tears. He obviously cared about Preston. I wasn't sure what to say.

Luckily, the steward was serving lunch and interrupted the uncomfortable silence with rubbery chicken, a scant salad, a dry roll and a brownie with nuts. I passed on the in-flight meal service. I did join Michael in his request for red wine—sangre de toro, as my college roommate used to say. Blood of the bull.

After Michael gulped down his glass of red, he opened a mysterious looking medicine container and popped two little white round pills. I tried to read the label, to no avail. Within a few minutes, he was fast asleep, slumped over in my direction. I reached over and slipped the paper out of his hands and started reading the coverage on the trial. Ten minutes into page three, he started talking in his sleep. I couldn't make out what he was saying, but it was something like, "Either you're in or you're out." He suddenly jerked awake and shook his head, then slumped in the opposite direction, passing out against the window of the plane. He slept the remainder of the flight.

We landed smoothly at Logan International Airport in Boston, although I was sure we were landing in the Atlantic Ocean until the plane made a sharp turn back toward land at the last minute. Michael escorted me into a taxi and checked me into the Four Seasons Hotel in downtown Boston. If one wants elegance and luxury, this was certainly the place to go. My mom had taken me to New York when I was in college. She's an interior designer and she goes there every year for a convention. She introduced me to fabrics and furniture through her designer eyes. While Michael spoke to the lady at the reservations desk, I wandered around the lobby.

The marble floor in the foyer was polished to a luster equal to the crystal chandeliers dangling overhead, reflecting a prism of light with every move I made. The mahogany banister up the circular staircase looked like it belonged in a palace. The lounge chairs were covered in gold chenille, all coordinated by the concentric circles of marble in the core of the room. The grand piano was mahogany. The firelight flickered from the open hearth.

"Geyser holds most of its conferences here. The majority of our key vendors and customers stay here when they're in town," Michael said, catching up with me. Lucky customers. Michael had requested a suite for my stay in Boston.

The bellman opened the door and said, "Madam, the television is in the armoire, along with your minibar. The room key will open the minibar and automatically charge anything you select from it to the room. Over here, we have modem and fax capabilities. The luxury spa tub is here, and this switch will automatically lower your bathroom blinds for privacy. The dual-head shower has a massage unit and the bidet is adjacent to the toilet. Shall I arrange for a turndown service for you this evening?" the bellman asked.

"Uh, sure," I said. I didn't know what would be included in a turndown service, but I hoped that it was better than it sounded. Michael handed the bellman a bill and then looked back my way.

"I figured that you may be here a week or so, and that you will need a place to work. No offense, but I would feel uncomfortable having you set up shop at Geyser's headquarters. I hoped that you could work here and have any of my employees you need to talk to meet you here or in the lounge. Just charge what you want to the room and I'll take care of it," Michael said. "Now, I'll let you get settled. I need to get home and take care of a few things. If you need anything, please call me." He walked over to the desk, wrote his home and cell number on the back of his business card and handed it to me. "Thanks for your help, Mac. I appreciate everything that you and Harry are doing." I gave him a light embrace and a strong pat on the back.

"We'll do everything we can for you. We'll need your help, though. Take a day or two to think of everything leading up to the ski accident. No detail is too small, at this point. You can make a list if you need to. Write down every person that you can think of who could possibly help your case. Make a second list of anyone or anything that might hurt your case. Then we'll meet to discuss it. In the meantime, I will need to meet with Preston's secretary," I said. I watched as he pulled a three by five note card out of his shirt pocket and made notes on it. He scribbled out a few items, scratched his head, and added a few more. He put his note card and pen back in his shirt pocket.

"Why do you want to meet with Carol?" Michael asked suspiciously.

"If Carol is anything like Lela, Harry's secretary, she knows more about Preston than anyone. That's why I would like to meet with her."

"I doubt she'll be of much help. She's more of a busybody than a secretary. I'd rather that you left her out of this."

"Sorry, Michael. It's important for me to meet her. The prosecution might notice her deposition. I want to get her story up front."

"I'll think about it."

"I would like to see Preston's office tomorrow, too."

"I don't see why you need to see his office."

"Because the prosecution will want to see it. I'm sure that they're already getting a search warrant for it."

"Can they do that?" Michael asked, running his right hand thought his wavy blond hair.

"Yes."

"Can we block it?"

"The warrant? We can file a motion opposing the issuance of a warrant, but it's up to the judge or magistrate to make the call."

"I want you to oppose any warrant to search Geyser headquarters. I don't want anyone nosing around," he said on his way out the door. "We have huge issues with trade secrets. All pharmaceutical companies do. No one gets into Geyser headquarters unless I say they do. I don't trust anyone, especially nosy cops. Do I make myself clear?"

I nodded as I watched the door close behind him. I stood there a minute or two. I walked over to the window and looked out onto the Public Garden. Michael had told me about it during the taxi ride. The Public Garden is one of the oldest botanical gardens in America and the pond in the middle is famous for its foot-pedal swan boats. I changed into my jogging suit and took a jog through the garden before darkness set in. When I was a little kid, my mom read me the book, *Make Way for Ducklings,* the one about Jack, Kack, Lack, Mack, Nack, Ouack, Pack and Quack—ducklings who took up residence in this very pond, following the swan boats around collecting peanuts from the tourists who rode on them.

I visited the statues of the ducks and watched as families rode on the swan boats, feeding the ducks along the way. At least that many ducklings paddled near the pond's edge, so I bought some peanuts and took pleasure in feeding them. I saw a young couple picnicking on the grass, sharing in the ambiance of their love. I felt a pang of homesickness, and, yes, loneliness too.

It was getting dark and my mind started to plague me with thoughts of my attacker, so I hurried back to my suite. On the way, I noticed a bulky man following not too far behind me. I took a side path, and he followed. I picked up my pace to a half-jog, half-walk, as did he. My heart started palpitating and a wave of anxiety overwhelmed me. A very busy street separated me from the hotel. I held up one hand and dashed into the street. A taxi nearly hit me. It screeched on its brakes, missing my legs by only a few inches. I kept running, darting behind a van and around a limo. The man darted across the street right behind me. I ran into the hotel lobby, hysterical.

I was afraid to get on an elevator, in fear that he would get on too and we would be alone together, trapped. I looked desperately for the staircase. I saw the exit sign indicating stairs, but realized that I needed to use my electronic room key to access the stairs. My hands trembled as I tried to line the card into the slot. The red light turned green and the door clicked open. I thought for a half-second about being trapped in a vacant stairwell with this hulk of a man. No one would be able to hear me scream. I let go of the stairwell door and ran back to the elevator.

I reached around a group of people waiting for the next elevator to appear. I pushed the "up" button and then took a fleeting look at the others in the lobby. I couldn't see the man. The elevator door opened and I got in. Several other people stepped inside. The door was just about to close when a hand jabbed through the crack, springing the door back open. The man got in and looked around. Panic filled my veins as I tried to hide behind the gentleman standing in front of me, who was obviously annoyed with the proximity in which I was standing. He inched forward, separating us, allowing a gap of space for my enemy to glare at me. When we got to my floor, I zipped out as quickly as I could and then sprinted to my room. I was gasping for air.

I entered my room and double bolted the door behind me, collapsing on the bed. I didn't know whether my imagination had got the best of me or whether the man had been after me. He looked familiar, something in the eyes.

After I calmed down, I unpacked my laptop from its black carrying case. I plugged it into the telephone jack and e-mailed Lela to let her know that I had arrived safely, but mentioned the incident with the guy in the park. I wanted someone to know, in case something terrible happened to me.

Chapter 4

After I calmed down, I got to work. Since Geyser was a publicly traded company, I used the Internet for a business search. I didn't want to waste time asking Michael or anyone else about Geyser when I could probably find out as much as I needed to know for now on my own. I learned from the Geyser website that Michael and Preston had formed the company together ten years ago with the help of start-up capital from Preston's dad, who was the president and chief executive officer of PKR Tobacco Company. I remembered reading a case in law school about PKR Tobacco. PKR was sued for failure to warn about the dangers of smoking. It was one of the seminal cases requiring tobacco companies to put warning labels on their products.

The website showed a picture of a geyser in Yellowstone National Park erupting high into the air, with Preston and Michael in front of it each holding a test tube filled with a cloudy liquid. The article profiled Michael first, explaining how he had learned about the organic life that exists in the geysers through his research with Professor Kincade of Montana State University. Michael had been hired on as a research assistant during summer breaks from Harvard and conducted some elementary experiments with the geyser water and discovered all sorts of organisms never known to exist. The article discussed Michael's own "personal experiments" in the woods. Michael drank a vial of water from a particular geyser and got an immediate erection with no external stimulus. Michael had never tried Viagra at that time, but thought that the reaction must be similar. So he got a prescription and tried Viagra, then compared it to the reaction from the geyser water. He found that the geyser water worked more quickly.

While in medical school, Michael contacted the National Park Service Director and the Yellowstone Superintendent through his contacts in the Jackson area and arranged for a meeting under the umbrella of the Cooperative Research and Development Agreement (CRADA). He convinced them of the benefits of conducting "bioprospecting" in the geysers in an effort to discover cures for impotency and cancer. Michael was granted an opportunity to develop a business plan for the Yellowstone Superintendent, detailing the type of research he wished to conduct. The National Park Service agreed to allow the research so long as Michael agreed to give the NPS information about endemic organisms that the NPS could not afford to inventory itself. Michael formed Geyser Inc. with Preston and they hired biologists, environmentalists, chemists, and other experts to help in this "thermophile" research. Under CRADA, Geyser would share a portion of its product royalties with the NPS.

The website then profiled Preston—the son of a business tycoon in Boston. Preston had a Bachelor's degree in business administration from Harvard and an MBA from Harvard Business School. The article told how Preston had secured the financing for the thermophile research and launched a worldwide marketing campaign for sexual dysfunction products for both men and women.

The rest of the website was dedicated to testimonials, success stories, self-screening questionnaires, patient summary information and comparisons with competing drugs such as Viagra. Geyser's claim to its ever-increasing market share was that competing pharmaceutical drugs had serious potential side effects like cardiac arrest, blood pressure problems, chest pains, dizziness, and nausea. Geyser is an herbal medicine, created from organic life from a particular geyser and enhanced with botanicals such as pellitory and ginseng. The remedy is wholly natural, faster, and completely safe without the risk of side effects, the web page explained.

I decided to dig deeper. Following the reference links to the ".edu" sites, I learned more. Michael's research team manufactured a pill from the geyser water that could be taken by men before intercourse, which enhanced the smooth muscle relaxant effects of nitric oxide, a chemical that is normally released in response to sexual stimulation. This smooth muscle relaxation allows increased blood flow into certain areas of the penis, leading to an erection.

The team created a patch for women that simulated the introduction of androgen into the female adrenal glands causing an increase in the natural production of testosterone, androstenedione, DHEA and DHT—all necessary elements to female sexual arousal. The combination of the geyser microbes and the natural libido enhancers were a near-perfect simulation of the body's natural hormonal state at approximately age twenty-five, for both sexes. Free from the side effects of chemically produced drugs like Viagra or the estrogen/testosterone patch, Geyser's products were the natural sexual dysfunction solution. No wonder their market share had climbed astronomically.

Michael's personal statement on the Geyser website was: "Erectile dysfunction affects millions of men. Now there is a safe way to help with this problem without the serious potential side effects that accompany many of the pharmaceutical ED drugs on the market. Even men with high blood pressure or men using nitrate drugs can safely use Geyser for Men." There was a picture of the container next to the statement with a few pills lying nearby. The pills were bright yellow, and the label on the pill container pictured the phallic geyser shooting high into the air.

Michael's personal statement continued: "There are few treatments available for women suffering from sexual disorders. Geyser for Women has been created with the specific mechanisms that help stimulate a sexual response in women. Natural enhancers including a potent combination of ginger, soy and nutmeg boost a woman's drive. The natural microbes from the geyser help women produce the right balance of hormones to enhance their sexual drive." The container for the women's patches showed a beautiful turquoise-blue geyser pool glistening in the sunlight. Another cheer for the marketing team. Even I wanted to dive in—and I know how scalding hot geyser pools are.

The website had several links to more detailed clinical studies and comparisons in the pharmacology world. I didn't read them all, but it all looked very scientific, with charts and graphs and tables.

I then did a search on Michael Brian O'Connor. He was born in Jackson Hole, Wyoming, and made the local paper first for winning chess tournaments and ski races. He had published several papers and articles for the *Journal of American Medical Association* and had received marks of distinction for his thermophile research. He had given a number of speeches to various organizations and had been featured in many magazine articles. One article described him as a "scientific mastermind and devoted husband."

A devoted husband? He never mentioned a wife.

I needed to get to bed. The time had slipped away and I knew that the East Coast time change was going to kill me in the morning if I didn't wrap it up soon. I shut down my computer and melted into a pillow as soft as a cloud and the firmest mattress I had ever known. Still, I couldn't sleep. A devoted husband? I wasn't aware that he was married. I turned on the overhead light and made a list of questions to ask him, including the whereabouts of his wife.

Chapter 5

I got up earlier than expected and went for a jog around Boston. It just didn't seem right to be in the cradle of America's independence and not explore the Freedom Trail on foot. I scurried back to the Four Seasons and felt immensely underdressed in the elevator, but happy to be among hotel guests that didn't look like they were about to attack me on my way back to my room. I hit the shower—make that a massage shower—then I called Michael at his office, expecting to get a voicemail message, but his secretary picked up the phone and plugged me directly in to him.

"Good morning, Michael," I said in my ready-to-work voice. "If it is okay with you, I would like to meet with you at some point, whenever it is convenient." I heard him take a sip of coffee. "I also need to meet with Preston's secretary, and with the Chief Financial Officer of Geyser. If you can think of anyone else who may be helpful to your case, please feel free to volunteer names. The more information I have early on, the better off we are. I'd like to visit the plant today too, if possible. I want to see Preston's office."

"I'm really busy this morning playing catch-up, but I will arrange for Carol to meet with you as soon as she's settled in this morning," was Michael's hurried answer. "I still don't see why you need to see Preston's office. I'll have to think that one over. I'm not sure that Carol would let you in there anyway."

"What do you mean, 'let me in there'?"

"Be warned. Carol defends Preston like he's her own son. She worked for his father for years before joining our team."

"I see. Nevertheless, I need to be able to look around his office and elsewhere."

"Like I said, I'll give it some thought. In the meantime, let me check to see if Dan Silverberg, our CFO, is available today. I don't know his schedule, but if he is around, I'll send him your way. Can I communicate with you by e-mail?" he said, in a friendlier tone.

"E-mail is fine," I said and gave my address: "MaryMac@hotmail.com."

It was only six o'clock a.m. Mountain Daylight Time when I called my office. Harry is an early riser. I figured that I could brainstorm with him before his day exploded.

"Harry here," he answered.

I told him about my research the night before and about my conversation in flight. "He talked in his sleep on the flight, something about setting someone up. What do you make of that?" I asked.

"Who knows? People have bad dreams when they're under a lot of stress. I wouldn't get too bogged down on an utterance in his sleep. Concentrate on the witnesses that Bain will be subpoenaing for trial."

"I am."

"To be honest, I'm more worried about you being alone in that big city than I am about the case. Lela told me about the guy who followed you yesterday. You should've called the police."

"I told Lela not to tell you. I knew that you'd just worry. It was probably my imagination getting the better of me."

"Jogging alone in a city isn't smart. You should know better than that. Jane is worried sick about you. She wants you to call her today. Do you have your witnesses lined up for interviews yet?"

"I'm working on it."

"This isn't a vacation. You should have a line-up ready. You'll make the most of your time there, and then be back here, ready to-"

"I will be back as soon as I can, ready to work."

I opened the room-service menu and ordered breakfast. After I placed my order for eggs benedict, toast, crispy bacon, freshly squeezed orange juice and coffee, I leafed through the rest of the hotel guide. I could order toys for my children, room service for my pet, a terry cloth robe for my relaxation.

* * * *

Carol Leahy knocked on my suite door. I was expecting her to look like the consummate professional secretary: short, sensible haircut, horn-rimmed glasses, white blouse, brown cardigan, and tweed wool skirt. But Carol Leahy did not fit the mold. She was a glamorous woman in her mid-fifties with frosted hair swept back off her high forehead. Her defined cheekbones glistened with peach blush. Her lips were outlined and highly glossed. Her shimmering eye shadow illuminated her hazel eyes. She possessed the kind of style of a well-polished breed, wearing a light yellow suit and a beautiful scarf around the neckline. Carol escorted herself in like she owned the place and I imagined that she had set up more than one meeting here. I wasn't sure how she felt about being ordered over for an interview, but she seemed cooperative and pleasant enough.

"Our interview will be recorded, if that is all right with you," I said.

"Fine," she said. "I've known Preston since he was born," she said.

I knew at this point that I wouldn't need to ask many questions.

"I started working for him when he started Geyser. I worked for his father for nearly twenty-five years prior to that. The Parker men are good people. They don't deserve for this to happen." She started to cry and reached into her Gucci handbag for tissues. I offered my condolences. I wondered how she felt about Michael. He was now probably her boss.

"Tell me about the relationship between Preston and Michael."

She looked at me for a moment. "When the boys started the business, it was because Michael had discovered this impotency drug that was all natural. Michael is a very capable scientist, but he doesn't know a thing about running a business. At least he was smart enough to ask for help. So, Preston took charge. His dad pitched in, and the two of them got the company up and running. They hired me to answer the phones, and we were set to go. It was slow at first, to be honest. Preston was worried that Geyser wouldn't be able to compete with Viagra and other drugs like it because most people in the age-range who take Viagra are not into herbal medicine. They're more likely to go to an old-fashioned doctor and get prescription medications. So, we struggled at first," Carol said.

"How did the struggle affect Preston and Michael?"

"Michael was very frustrated by it. He couldn't understand why any man would opt to take a prescription drug with potential side effects when he could take a natural remedy. He blamed Preston for not pushing harder in the U.S. market."

"How do you know all of this?"

"My desk has always been at the center of things. I sit right outside Preston's office. Preston does most of his business on the speakerphone and I can overhear almost all of it, as annoying as that can be. There's always been some tension between Michael and Preston. And sometimes, Michael would come down to Preston's office from his lab and they would fight."

"What would they fight about?" This was making me nervous. She was making a good witness for the prosecution. This didn't match with how Michael had described their relationship.

"At first, they argued about the U.S. market problems. Then, as the company started growing by leaps and bounds, Michael seemed upset by that too. We had a big growth spurt due to Preston's marketing presence in the foreign market. And Michael wasn't happy about that for some reason."

"Anything else?"

"Well, don't get me wrong. Michael is a really nice man and everyone in the lab loves working for him. Things went well between Michael and Pres once the product was out on the market. But when his wife died, Michael apparently went over the deep end a little."

"Wait a minute," I said. Last night, I was surprised to learn that he had a wife. Now, Carol says that she's dead. Dead like his business partner? "What do you mean? Michael's wife is dead?"

"Again, I don't know all the nitty-gritty. Some of the girls in the lab could probably tell you more, but he became a workaholic, more than he already was, after Brianna died," Carol said. She leaned in a little closer. "She had breast cancer. Terrible tragedy," she said. She then inched her way back. "When she was alive, he and Brianna and Preston and Kelly would go out together all of the time. After Brianna died, I heard that Michael became a hermit and wouldn't talk to anyone for days at a time. He hissed like a cat at the people in the lab if they didn't get research done right, and he and Preston got into it, too, sometimes."

I watched her deflate again. "Pres was always so upbeat, and he worked so hard, especially in the foreign market. I just can't imagine why anyone would want to hurt him." She started to cry. I went into the bathroom and got more tissues for her.

"Can I get you some water?"

"Please." Room service had left the pitcher of water from my breakfast order. I poured her a glass. She drank. I thought about what Carol was telling me. The reference to the foreign market sounded a bit rehearsed. Had she met with Preston's father before coming to meet with me? I wasn't sure. She was very well informed about company business.

"Let's talk about the week of the Jackson Hole conference. What was going on around the office?"

"The week before Preston died, I found Michael snooping in Preston's office. I told Preston about the snooping incident and he said that he would handle it, and handle it he did. They had quite an argument. Preston told Michael to keep his nose out of marketing and to worry about the laboratory. Michael was becoming a menace to the company. He'd decided to learn more about running the business and he was ruffling a lot of feathers. He's not the most suave man, if you know what I mean."

"How well do you know Kelly?"

"I don't know her that well. She keeps her distance. She didn't call Preston too often at work, but when she did, she was curt on the phone. Rumor has it that she works a lot and shops a lot."

"What kind of-"

"I did attend their wedding. It was beautiful. They had it on Martha's Vineyard at a very romantic inn. Over five hundred guests," Carol said, turning her head slightly sideways while raising her eyebrows.

"Sounds expensive."

"Oh, it cost Hugh a pretty penny. I'm sure he doesn't know the half of it. Phyllis doesn't settle for anything but the very best."

"Wouldn't Kelly's parents have paid for it?"

"They helped a little, but I'm told that they don't have much savings. The Parkers would never have allowed a low budget wedding. I'm told that Hugh paid for almost all of it. It was very extravagant."

"Tell me what Preston was like to work for."

"Preston was excellent at leadership and vision, but I have to admit, he's a chip off the old block. He's a control freak. He was the youngest of four boys, and all of his brothers work for his dad at the tobacco company. Preston liked being the boss. Truth be told, I think that he got his training from Hugh, who is extremely organized and progressive. He could make any deal happen in any language in any country at any time. Bangkok. Bali. Singapore. Hong Kong. Like I said, Preston was a chip off the block."

Sounded too good to be true to me. I couldn't get Carol to admit to anything negative about Preston, so I decided to change the subject.

"Did Preston and Kelly ever argue?"

Carol looked away for a moment. "They argued about having children."

"Did they want children?"

"Kelly did. Preston didn't."

"Why not?"

"It's not that Preston didn't want to have children. The truth is that they weren't having any luck getting pregnant. Kelly wanted to try fertility drugs and he wouldn't agree. She blamed him for traveling so much. He blamed her for working out too much and not eating right."

"You said earlier that Michael's wife died. How long ago did she die?"
"A few years ago."
"Has he started dating?"
"I wouldn't know. I don't see much of him. He stays in the lab most of the time." Carol leaned in toward me and in a near whisper, continued. "Although office rumor has it that Kelly visits Michael in the lab from time to time. One girl that works in the lab told me that she thinks Michael's been giving her fertility shots behind closed doors. She saw empty vials in his garbage can. But, like I said, that's just office gossip."
"Did Preston have any enemies?"
"Of course not! Everyone loved him. He was a very charismatic young man. He'd walk into a room and everyone would look his way. He was so handsome. He dressed very well. His clients clamored over him."
"Any threatening letters or phone calls ever come his way?"
Carol furrowed her brow the best that she could. He forehead was frozen in place. "I don't think so. Oh, well, there was this man in Singapore that was really mad at him over some business deal, but I think it got worked out. He used to send a fax every hour on the hour for days until Preston finally called him back. And there have been occasional business deals that have fallen through, but nothing out of the ordinary. It's a competitive world out there."
"Do you remember the man's name that sent the faxes?" Carol looked at the ceiling and pursed her lips.
"Frank Hwong, or something like that. I could look it up. I kept the faxes in a file."
"Please. If you could get me that file, I'd appreciate it."

* * * *

After Carol left, I took a walk down Newbury Street, Boston's street for high fashion. I didn't have much time for window-shopping, though. Michael was sending over two members of his research staff for interviews.
As I walked past the Ann Taylor boutique, I noticed a refection in the window from the other side of Newbury Street. In the reflection, I saw the same man that was following me in the Public Garden yesterday. He was wearing a chestnut brown jacket over blue jeans, which was different from his forest green jacket yesterday. But it was the same face, same stocky build, same hair. He was leaning against a brick wall, pretending to read the paper. I didn't want him to know that I spotted him, so I quickly picked up my pace and watched him through the

reflection of the next store. Sure enough, he was on the move. At the intersection, I turned right and headed down Arlington Street, knowing that he'd have to cross the street to catch up. I looked back, and he was hot on my tail. I started jogging, turning left on Boylston, in the direction of the hotel. He was still on my tail. Again, I ran into the lobby and to the stairwell. This time, I waited after the door closed behind me to see if he followed me to the stairs. As his face pressed against the diamond-shaped glass, my heart pounded like a drum. He grabbed the handle of the door and tried to open it, but access was denied. I stood pressed against the wall until I saw him leave, and then I bounded up the first flight of steps. I dared to look back and there he was, watching me. I ran.

Chapter 6

▼

The piano lounge was illuminated by a fireplace so inviting that I couldn't avert my eyes from it when Michael walked through the door. It was his idea to meet at the lounge at the hotel. I found him standing over me wearing khaki Dockers, a white shirt and a turquoise tie that matched his eyes. His tie was loosened and his blond, wavy hair was a tad tousled. He looked taller to me, perhaps because I was sitting down.

"Nice fire," Michael said. I agreed. I wore my standard black crepe dress with seamed hose and black pumps. I'd let my hair down and had applied a little extra gloss to my lips. I didn't get the opportunity to go out much and enjoyed the opportunity to dress up.

Soon into our conversation I asked, "Have you ever been married?" Michael looked at me in pained surprise. I couldn't retract, so I decided to elaborate. "I was reading your website last night and it says that you are a 'good' husband."

"I *was* a husband," he said. He sunk into his chair as if it were a grave. He removed his thick glasses. "I had the most perfect wife," he continued. "She was my research assistant, my friend, and my soul mate. She passed away a few years ago." I felt a lump form in my throat. I wasn't sure where to go with this. I felt awful for prying, but it was my job. And I had learned from the best: "In this line of work, there are no good surprises," according to Harry.

Michael motioned for the waiter. "Why don't we have dinner here instead of ordering room service," Michael suggested. "We can adjourn to your suite after dinner if it's necessary to wrap it up there. The food is better here."

"Tell me about your relationship with Preston." I said, hoping to change the subject. The waiter brought us a bottle of chardonnay that Michael had ordered.

He opened the bottle and handed Michael the cork, poured a sample and Michael took a sip. Michael nodded to the waiter. The waiter filled my glass. I swirled it and then smelled the aroma before I took a sip. The wine was crisp and cold and had a bit of a sweet aftertaste. "Good choice of wine. The finish is long and clean, with rich flavors of fig and oak." I could feel my nerve endings lying back in place, like the veins of a butterfly's wings freed from the confines of a cocoon.

"I didn't realize that you knew so much about wine."

"I don't, really. Harry is obsessive about wine, so I've picked up a few clues about tasting over the years. So, tell me about Preston."

"I didn't have many friends growing up," Michael started. "I was what you might call a nerd. I didn't play football or do any of the things that make guys popular. When I went to Harvard, I was looking for a fresh start. I wanted to be somebody. I wanted to matter. I knew that I could contribute to the world. Preston and I were assigned to the same dorm room. At first, I thought I was in big trouble; he was a tall, good-looking guy from a wealthy family. But Preston took me under his wing and made me part of his social circle, both old and new. When it came time for me to go to medical school and for him to get his MBA, I thought that we would part ways. Even then, though, Preston went out of his way to maintain our friendship. Sure, he was cocky and arrogant and spoiled, but he was also protective and loyal. So, when I started dabbling in my microbe research and thought that I was onto something big, I asked Preston to be my partner. I knew that he would know how to get a company started and I knew I could count on him to keep my secret safe until I had done enough research and testing to prove myself right.

"So, when you did get the company up and running? How was it to work with Preston?"

"It was a big transition at first. Preston and I have different styles. I guess you could say that I'm a workaholic. Not that Preston didn't work hard, he did—but he always made deals fast and loose, in my opinion. He had this way of cramming something down your throat, smiling all the while. I swear, he could talk anybody into anything. I called him the 'smiling assassin.' I guess that's why I had such a hard time when we started Geyser. I thought he would be able to capitalize on the American market in no time. It only made sense to me that men would scramble for a drug that didn't have serious side effects. But it didn't work out that way. Geyser was very slow to infiltrate here. But it did great overseas."

"Carol mentioned that you and Preston had some run-ins."

"We did. I'm not going to sugarcoat it for you. We had our moments, like any business partners do. Preston had a hot temper. He was used to getting everything his way. I'm an only child and I'm used to getting things my way too. Sometimes we clashed."

"Carol also mentioned that she caught you snooping in Preston's office just before the … accident," I said.

"Sounds like all you and Carol did was gossip."

"Not true. I'm not here to dig up gossip on you or anyone else for that matter. That's not what this is all about. I'm trying to formulate a defense for you, and in order to do so, I need to understand the relationships and the business. Believe me, the prosecution will be doing the same; they will try to paint a picture of you as the jealous business partner, or something like that. I need to know as much as possible in order to examine the evidence from all sides."

"Well, I was looking around in Preston's office because there were some strange things going on and I couldn't put my finger on it."

"For example?"

"It appeared that Preston was doing business with a pharmaceutical company in the Rocky Mountain region, but there were no files for the sales rep in that area and there wasn't a master file for the customer base." Michael paused as if I should be surprised by this notion or that it should ring a bell. It didn't.

"So?"

"So, I did some investigating. It turned out that Kelly's dad was distributing some of our products for Preston on the side."

Just as I was about to follow up on this, the waiter came to take our order.

"We'll have the pan-seared Ahi tuna appetizer. I'll have your Pla Duug and my guest says that she's willing to try your Chilean Sea Bass, cooked Miso-Yaki style."

"All good choices. I'll have your tuna out promptly," the tuxedo-clad waiter said.

"The Pla Duug is incredible. You'll have to have a taste," Michael said.

"What is it?"

"A whole catfish prepared crispy outside, then laced with Thai chili garlic sauce."

In a few minutes, the waiter brought the appetizer. Michael snagged a chunk of green stuff with his chopsticks and plunked it into a small bowl. Then he poured some soy sauce, and mixed the concoction together. He picked up a piece of the tuna, dunked it in the sauce, and put it in his mouth. He moaned lightly.

"Umm. Excellent."

"It looks rare. It's not cooked?" I asked.

"It's seared, meaning that the chef puts it over high heat on each side for just a few seconds, to seal in the juices. The inside is rare. It's delicious."

"What's the green stuff?"

"Wasabi. Japanese horseradish. It's hot. Take a little and mix it with soy. It's very good." I followed Michael's directions. I then tasted the mixture from my chopsticks. The sauce was so spicy that it cleared my sinuses. I took a deep breath. "You can add more soy sauce to temper it down a little," Michael said. I did. Then I took a piece of the tuna, dipped it and ate it. I was surprised at how tasty and tender it was.

"It's good," I said.

Not long after, the waiter brought us dinner. He took great pains to set everything up just so. He set down Michael's fish. It was a whole fish, including a head with eyeballs. It had slices of lemon around it and sprigs of some green herb. Michael ate a piece of the fish's cheek first.

"The cheek is the most tender. It's a delicacy." He sliced off a bite and handed it to me. I tried it.

"That's amazing."

"See. Looks are deceiving."

At this point, I'd lost my train of thought. The wine had obviously gone to my head. "How did Kelly's dad play a part in this?"

"He was distributing Geyser products in Indonesia for Preston on the side, meaning that the profits weren't on the books. I was getting screwed," Michael said in a raised voice.

"Are you sure?"

"Pretty sure."

"Is Kelly involved?"

"I don't know yet."

"What is your relationship like with Kelly?"

"We're good friends, always have been, always will be. I thought she would sever ties with me when I was charged with Preston's murder, but she really hasn't. She has been very supportive. I know she believes that I'm innocent."

"Is that why she testified against you before the grand jury?" I asked. Michael shot a wry look at me.

"It's not her fault. What choice did she have? It was either her or me. They were going to try to pin this on one of us, so we decided that she should testify," Michael said.

"So you *knew* that she was going to testify against you?"

"Yes."

"And you're okay with it? It sounds like she ratted you out."

"What can I say? Like I told you, the cops were trying to pin this on one of us. I don't think she ratted me out. She just told them the truth. But in doing so, she cut a deal for herself. She's a good lawyer."

"But it seems like she served you up to the grand jury."

"That wasn't her intention."

"How do you know?"

"I know. I know Kelly better than anyone."

Better than anyone? I thought to myself. "Be careful about what you say to Kelly. I know that she's your friend, but she may have other motives here. Don't admit or deny anything to her. If she asks you anything about the case, tell her that your lawyer warned you not to talk about it. From a lawyer's standpoint, she should understand. For all you know, Michael, she could be testifying on behalf of the prosecution." He changed positions in his chair, tore at a piece of bread, dipping it over and over into the balsamic vinegar and oil. He took a bite and chewed long, methodical bites.

"She won't testify for the prosecution. I'm not worried about it. They can't use her grand jury testimony against her in court."

"How do you know so much about the law?" I asked.

"Kelly. Plus I discussed it with Harry."

"Tell me about Kelly's relationship with Preston," I said.

"I introduced them during our first year at Harvard. They went on a few dates and hit it off pretty well, but it didn't work out. They were on again, off again during undergrad. Then she went to law school and he got his MBA. I think they got together during that period on occasion, but nothing serious. They reunited, I guess, around the time that my wife died, and married shortly after that."

"Do you think that they had a good marriage?"

"I don't know."

"What do you mean?"

"Well, Preston traveled a lot on business, so that was hard on Kelly. She needs a lot of attention."

"I see. Doesn't she work long hours herself? Carol mentioned that she works a lot."

"Kelly's a hard worker. The firm that she works for puts a lot of pressure on her to make billable hour requirements. It's ridiculous, really. Those guys expect her to bill ninety hours a week. Not everything she does is billable. That means that she has to be there probably one hundred hours a week. That doesn't leave much time for sleeping, or anything else."

"Carol said that Preston and Kelly were fighting over whether to have children."

"She told you that?" Michael reached for his wine and took a long pull. "That information wasn't for public consumption."

"So it's true?"

"Yes. Kelly wanted children. Preston didn't. I'm sure that they fought about it."

"Carol also mentioned that Kelly likes to shop."

"She does. What woman doesn't? She likes to shop, workout and work. I think that's about all she does."

"What kind of workout does she do?" Her workouts weren't pertinent to Michael's defense. I simply wanted to know how this woman kept her legs looking so perfect.

"Kelly's always into the latest thing. When we went to college, she couldn't leave home without her Jane Fonda tapes. Then she got into running. Then power walking. Then spinning. Then kickboxing. Then tae-bo or tai chi or something like that. Then yoga and more yoga and more yoga. You name it, and if it is the thing to do, she's doing it. At the moment, I believe the workout du jour is Pilates—but don't ask me exactly what it is. Kelly says that it's used by prima ballerinas. That's all I know."

"Why does she work so hard? It can't possibly be for the money."

"I don't know exactly, but Kelly's always been a workaholic. She's very competitive and she thrives on proving herself. She just bought a new Porsche, so she probably wants to pay it off."

A new Porsche. According to the annual reports filed with the Securities Exchange Commission, Preston had been making several million dollars a year. As was Michael. Why would Kelly feel the need to "pay off" a new Porsche? Their combined income could pay for twenty luxury cars—and then some.

"Do you know whether Kelly ever confronted Preston about his travel schedule?"

"I don't know about that. Bri would have known, if she were alive. Kelly and Bri were very close." He picked up the dessert menu and looked it over. He handed it to me. "Does the chocolate soufflé sound good to you?" he asked.

"Sounds great." We ordered dessert and cognac. (I was just going with the flow—I had never had cognac before, but I liked it.) The waiter brought the soufflé. It was out of this world.

"Carol mentioned that you and your wife and Kelly and Preston went out a lot together."

"We did. Kelly and Bri became very good friends and the four of us had a lot of fun together. I miss that," Michael said. His eyes glazed over and he looked exhausted. "Kelly and Preston didn't marry until after Bri died, but when they were together, times were good."

"And when they weren't together?"

"Kelly would sink into depression. They usually broke up because she caught him cheating on her. After a while, I guess she would forgive him and they'd get back together. It was a roller coaster."

"Did Preston cheat on her after they were married?" Michael looked away and then bit his lower lip.

"I don't know."

"You don't know, or you don't want to say?"

"It's possible."

"Possible or probable?"

"Both."

"You know more than you're telling. This is important."

"Let me think about how I want to answer that one. By the way, I was able to track down Dan Silverberg. He can meet you tomorrow," Michael said as he rose. He motioned for the waiter to bring his check, which he didn't even look at while signing. "Why don't we continue this conversation later in the week. I'm exhausted." With that, he got up and left. I watched him walk out of the piano lounge.

When I got back to my room, I drew a hot bath and luxuriated in the bubbles and jets. I intended to take full advantage of this place. I might never have this opportunity again. There was a phone next to the tub. I just couldn't resist. From my bath, I called Kelly at her office. At this late hour, I expected to get her voice mail. Instead, she answered on the first ring.

"Kelly Flanigan Parker," she said.

"Hi Kelly. This is Mary MacIntosh. Could I trouble you for an hour or so sometime this week? I need to ask you a few questions."

"The problem is that I'm in deposition all day tomorrow and the next day. I'm preparing as we speak. How long are you going to be in town?"

"Only a few more days. Is it possible to meet you in the morning before your depo?"

"Well, I take an exercise class at six o'clock in the morning. It's the only time I have in the day. You could meet me at my gym and we could talk there." She gave me directions to the gym and said goodnight. Thank God Harry wasn't here. He would rather die than be caught doing yoga.

Harry was a workout buff, but his idea of a gym was the local YMCA. He loved to run the track there or pick up a game of basketball. He lifted weights religiously and often rode the exercise bike. Since his college football days, he'd always stayed in great shape. However, yoga was not part of his regime.

*   *   *   *

The phone rang ten minutes before the wake-up call. "You okay?" Harry asked. "Jane's worried about you. She thinks that you may have a stalker."

"I'm fine, Harry," I managed, looking at the clock and realizing that it was already five thirty in the morning. "What are you doing up? It's only three-thirty there."

"Had to let the dog out. I figured you'd be up, seeing as how you never seem to sleep."

"Actually, my wake-up call is due any minute. I'm meeting Kelly Parker at the gym for our interview." I could hear Harry laughing as he hung up.

I brushed my teeth, washed my face and pull my hair back. My sweatsuit smelled a little from my run the day before, so I sprayed a little perfume on it and hoped it was as good as new. I took a cab to the gym and waited in the lobby for Kelly. In Wyoming, gyms don't have lobbies. This gym was almost as nice as the hotel I was staying in. The floors were marble, the countertops granite. The people working behind the desk were tan—in the middle of winter. And there were mirrors everywhere. Many people were piling in at this ungodly hour for a workout. Kelly rushed through the door, wearing a black tankini with black tights. Her long black hair was pulled back into a ponytail. She wore no make-up. Still, she looked more beautiful than ever. Her olive-colored skin glistened and her teeth were as white as milk. She passed the front desk without hesitating and motioned to the attendant that I was to follow her. I did. She grabbed my arm and stuffed my extras in her locker and rushed me to the front of her Pilates class. "This is the only workout I do," she said. "Seems easy, but you will feel it tomorrow." We spent the next hour stretching things I didn't know I had. This was going to require Ibuprofen later, I was sure. After I got the hang of it, we started to talk.

"How are you doing?" I asked.

"Fine, under the circumstances. As you can imagine, this has been one hell of a month."

"You seem to be handling everything so well. Have you had a lot of support from friends and family?" This was always a good question. People either simply say "Yes," or they go on for days in the "No" category. I was hoping for the latter because I could get so much more information that way.

"Everyone's been very supportive."

"How are Preston's parents dealing with their grief?"

"Differently. Hugh is very angry and wants Michael to pay. Preston was his boy, his favorite son. He won't admit that to you, but he was. Preston is the youngest of four boys and he is the only one who chose not to work for Hugh's company. Hugh always loved Preston's confidence. He's sure Michael is guilty. Phyllis hasn't said much. He was her baby. I think that she's still in shock."

"I'm sure she is. And you?"

"My heart aches all the time. I miss him so much. He was my soul mate," she said, using her workout towel to wipe a tear from her eye.

"How would you describe your relationship with Preston?"

"Pres and I had a long-term relationship. We certainly had our ups and downs. We dated for a bit in undergrad, but we broke it off. We saw each other on and off for years, but didn't really get serious until Bri was in the hospital. He came to visit her when I was there, and we reconnected. I think he felt the depth of my despair over losing Bri and tried to rescue me from a fall. We knew she wasn't going to make it, yet I somehow felt like I could save her from her pain. I think Preston came to rescue me from my pain. I was vulnerable, and his timing was right." Kelly wasn't a vulnerable person, by any means. In fact, she seemed to be the type to pour herself into her work to avoid feeling pain. And it seemed odd to me that she would describe their union as a perfect blend of vulnerability and opportunity. Not love. Not passion. Not compatibility. Vulnerability combined with opportunity.

"I heard that Preston traveled a lot."

"Who did you hear that from?"

"Carol mentioned it."

"He traveled too much, I thought. He was in Asia most of the time. It's how he made the company a success, but it was hard on our marriage, to say the least," she said. She put her body in a pose that I knew I shouldn't even try to mirror. It was like she was exorcising a demon. She had a look of sheer determination on her face.

"Was Preston faithful to you?" I asked. I know it sounds awful, but let's face it, when a spouse is missing or dead under questionable circumstances, the other spouse is generally a suspect. It was my job to rule her out or to try to find other directions to point the finger. A good criminal defense lawyer will convince the jury that there are other possible scenarios that have been overlooked by the police or the prosecution. Personally, I love this part of my job. It's the juicy part. It helps fill in the gaps of my rather boring existence. But sometimes, I walk away from an interview without making any new friends. This might be one of those times.

"Why do you ask?"

"I'm sorry for the intrusion into your personal life, but it is standard fare to ask in a criminal case. As a lawyer, I'm sure you can understand. It's like what you do in a medical malpractice case: try to find a way for the jury to think that another doctor could have been responsible for the mess-up. I'm not suggesting anything here. I'm simply covering all of my bases." I think my analogy satisfied her for the moment. Her furrowed brow relaxed a bit, but maybe it was because she unwound her legs from behind her back.

"Of course he was faithful," she said as she put her legs on a giant red ball and started doing sit-ups. She twisted to the left and then to the right and then straightened up again, over and over. She let out a deep breath after each crunch. "Once we married, Preston would never have cheated on me," she said. "Did Carol put these ideas in your head?"

"She-"

"Carol is the nosiest woman in the world. I swear, she wants to know everything from A to Z, whether it's her business or not."

"No, Carol didn't say anything about it. Why? Would Carol know about these things?"

Kelly looked at me as if I were a simpleton. "She is Hugh's mistress. She knows everything about everything when it concerns the Parkers."

"Hugh is Preston's father, right?" trying to keep the names straight.

"Yes. Carol worked for him for years and then, when the sexual harassment laws changed a few years back, his advisors suggested that she be 'transferred' to another position. So, she was delegated to Preston. She babied him like he was her own son. I think she's a tragic romantic, believing that one day, Hugh will leave Phyllis for her. But that will never, ever happen. Believe me."

This was getting better by the minute. The murder victim's dad was having an affair with the victim's secretary. The victim might have been having an affair in a faraway land and his lawyer wife suspected him. The victim's business partner was mad at him about some crooked business practices. A trainload of suspects was emerging. Cases were never this glamorous in Wyoming. Sure, we had the jealous wife/husband/lover thing. But one would just get drunk in a bar, brandish a gun at the other and shoot. There were usually plenty of witnesses and the cases were usually cut and dried. Most were settled through plea bargains. This case was becoming much more interesting. Wait until I tell Harry. He loves it when it gets crazy. I decided to move on. Kelly was done with her crunches and was lifting weights. I grabbed a few barbells and we started pumping in unison. No wonder this woman looked incredible. She did more in one workout than I would consider doing in an average month at a gym—if I belonged to one, that is.

"Do you run?"

"No," Kelly said. "I used to run years ago, but I never run now. I just work out in the gym. You?"

"Almost every day. It is the one thing that relaxes me the most. My feet hit the pavement in the morning and I feel free and alive. I try to run five days a week." Kelly nodded, as if I'd made the grade.

"Michael mentioned that your dad was in business with Preston." Kelly shot a look.

"I don't know what you are talking about." She picked up a heavier set of weights and started doing curls. "My dad has an orthopedic supply business in Wyoming. He didn't work with Preston."

"Maybe I misunderstood Michael. It was late when I talked with him."

She looked at her watch and compared it to the clock on the wall. "Class is over. I've gotta run to make it to the deposition on time."

"Thank you for letting me meet with you this morning. May I call you if I have more questions?"

"Sure." She gave me a smile and a homecoming queen parade wave and she was off to the locker room. I followed her in to get my things and then hailed a cab back to the hotel. As the cab rounded the curve of Charles Street near the hotel, I realized that I'd left my wallet in the locker at the gym. I asked the cabbie to go back. He looked at me through his rearview mirror with suspicious eyes.

"I'm not trying to pull a fast one on you. I can't pay you unless I go back and get my wallet." As we pulled up in front, I saw Kelly standing on the street corner talking to a man. As we inched closer, I recognized him as the guy who'd been following me in the Public Garden and on Newbury Street. I witnessed Kelly handing him an envelope and him turning and walking away. She then proceeded to the parking garage. As I exited the gym with my wallet in hand, I saw the taillights of a new red Carrera convertible speeding past the taxi.

Chapter 7

"Your office looks like Harry's," I said to Michael as I passed by the door with his name on it. His desk was a large beveled glass table with only a few piles of paperwork on it. The floor, however, was jammed with stacks of computer printouts, magazines, boxes and files, all neatly filed and organized.

"I've been meaning to clean it for years. It's just low on my priority list," Michael said. I meant that his desk was clean. He missed the point.

"Your laboratory is state-of-the-art," I said. The high-tech lab was decorated in red, yellow and blue tiles set out in complicated geometrical designs. Churning sounds penetrated the air as did the smell of sulfur. Huge machines rotating test tubes flashed green and red lights. Data spewed from a mainframe computer. Technicians in white coats and plastic gloves bustled around.

"We can talk in private in here," Michael said as I entered his office. A picture of his parents and a picture of himself and Bri on their wedding day sat next to his computer. One tabletop was littered with small, framed photos of this and that—Michael at the foot of a geyser; Preston and Michael making a toast; a pale, blonde woman in a hospital bed, surrounded by Preston, Michael, and Kelly. "Bri died of cancer," Michael offered.

I nodded my head. "I'm sorry."

"Thank you. She was an amazing woman. I really miss her. She could light up a room with the warmth of a smile. Kelly misses her too."

What intrigued me the most about his photo gallery was the pictures of Kelly—he must have had seven or eight pictures of her scattered about—from childhood to very recent. I picked up one of the photographs. "Where was this taken?" I asked.

Michael cleared his throat. "That's of Preston, Kelly, Bri and me ringing the bell on Wall Street when we took Geyser public. That was a great day," Michael said. He looked very happy in the picture, arm in arm with Bri on one side and Kelly on the other. "I'll show you around the rest of the office," he said abruptly. We took a flight of stairs up to the second floor, and I could already feel the pain of the morning workout.

"Here's the office that you've been *dying* to see." I entered.

Preston's office was handsomely decorated in hunter green and taupe, with hints of maroon to compliment his mahogany, L-shaped desk. The rest of the building was quasi-industrial-looking, with gray-carpeted cubicles for offices with computers at each station. "Our sales reps all have office space here. We're networked worldwide," Michael said. I nodded.

"Can I have a few minutes in Preston's office? I want to look around." Michael shrugged his shoulders and walked out. I opened every drawer, but they were all empty. I walked back out. Michael was waiting around the corner.

"What happened? Did you have his office cleaned out?" Michael fixed his eyes on me. I waited for him to answer.

"It was time. We're looking for a replacement CEO."

"Where's all the stuff that was in his office?"

"In storage."

"I'd like to look at it."

Michael didn't respond. He just looked at me. I decided not to press the subject. He's Harry's client. I decided that I'd better be polite.

"I'm heading back to Wyoming tomorrow. Here's my card. Please call me if you think of anything in the next few days that we've missed." I decided to put the onus on Michael. He'd given me mixed messages about his willingness to help us defend him. Sometimes, it seemed like he wanted to be open and honest, but other times, it seemed like he wanted me out of his hair. "I have probably overwhelmed you with demands, but the more you help us cultivate your defense, the better prepared we will be. This case is going to be expensive, Michael." He grimaced when I said the word expensive. But Michael was rich. Geyser was worth millions and the annual report filed with the Securities Exchange Commission revealed that he paid himself a seven-figure salary last year. I couldn't imagine why he would worry about the expense of his defense. He could go to prison for life. With his budget, I would think that money was no object. Yet, Michael seemed frugal, at least when it came to spending money on himself. Everything at Geyser was state-of-the-art, but Michael's clothes were not designer-made, and he drove a company car, a Ford Taurus.

"Please do whatever you need to, to get me out of this mess." Michael rubbed his eyes with his thumb and index finger. The weight of reality probably had hit him like a hammer and he looked suddenly fearful. "But keep me posted on the attorney's fees."

"Remember, don't talk to the media. No one. Not even someone who claims to be interviewing you about your company. *Anything* you say can be used against you, no matter how innocuous it may seem. Be very careful. Do not speak about Preston or the accident at all to anyone except Harry or me."

"Understood."

"That includes Kelly." He shot me a narrow-eyed look. "I'm sure that Bain will offer us a plea deal by the pre-trial conference next week. We'll call you when that happens." We said our goodbyes and I headed directly to Kelly's office. She wasn't expecting me, but I was hoping that I could make contact one last time, if possible. I had a sneaking feeling that she was holding back. She was hard to get to know. I also was curious to see what big-shot lawyers' offices looked like. I had always dreamed of working in a professional firm with design interiors and a big cherry wood desk with a blotter and a lamp with a green shade.

When I announced myself to one of the three receptionists at Jenkins & Brode, she told me in her heavy Boston accent that "Miss Pawker is in a deposition. She's due back in a few oz." I gave the woman my card and told her that I was a lawyer-friend from school and asked if I could drop something off in Kelly's office. Amazingly, she agreed.

Kelly's office was the office of my dreams minus the green lamp. Her color scheme was sharp: reds, golds and creams. Silk stripes and florals covered the sofa and side chairs. I stared at her beautiful antique desk with a matching secretary and bookshelf. She had Asian art on the walls and the bookends on each shelf were Asian-style warriors that looked like monkeys with crowned temples on their heads. A ceremonial mask towered in one corner, set on a stand, probably from Thailand: a large head with bulging eyes, oversized teeth with tusks on each side, wild colors accenting each facial feature. But the most exquisite piece in her office was a mannequin head sitting on a round antique table. The mannequin was the face of a young Balinese girl with large, almond-shaped eyes and ruby-red lips. She had dark, arched eyebrows flanking a red exclamation point painted between her eyes. She wore a golden crown tightly bound and brocaded with frangipani blossoms. The entire piece was protected behind glass. The table had a long runner made of glittery gold with a red liner. The colors made the flanking chairs dance with life. I wondered whether Kelly had accompanied Preston to Asia a time or two, to have developed such a brilliant style in art and décor.

Her office overlooked Boston Harbor and she could ponder her doctors' cases while watching yachts find their slips. I closed her door quietly. I looked around for security cameras. No sign of one, so I slipped behind the desk and opened the drawers. In her pencil drawer, I found a stack of credit card receipts. The top receipt had today's date and was from Bloomingdale's department store. She had told me that she would be in deposition all day, yet she had had time this morning to spend four hundred fifty-eight dollars at Bloomingdale's before lunch. That seemed odd. I thumbed through more receipts: Barneys, Ann Taylor, Sacks Fifth Avenue.

I opened a side drawer. Form files for discovery, court filings, motions, and dismissals were labeled. Her "Misc" file had more legal stuff in it. I noticed a box next to her credenza. I found stacks of newspaper clippings about Preston. Most of the articles detailed Preston's dealings in Geyser, Inc. A few clippings were from their engagement and wedding. Under the clippings were two framed photographs: one of Kelly and Preston on their wedding day and one of Kelly, Bri, Michael and Preston on Wall Street—the same picture in Michael's office. I glanced around the office and noted that there weren't any pictures of Preston in the room.

Under the photographs was a large manila envelope from Mason & Associates Detective Agency. I opened the envelope. There was a cover letter from Bob Avery, private detective, requesting the balance for services rendered for successfully locating and photographing Preston engaged in an extra-marital affair. The next page was a map of the Pura Dalem in Bali, Indonesia. On the bottom of the map in scrawled handwriting, it said, "Pura Dalem means Temple of Death." *Temple of Death*?

Several pictures followed, showing Preston wearing a sarong wrap, walking into a temple accompanied by a gorgeous woman. Bob Avery must have had a macro telephoto lens, for he was able to snap some complicated shots of the two of them intertwined in the Monkey Forest in a most compromising manner. I flipped from one photograph to another, twisting the 8 ½ x 11s this way and that, trying to figure out exactly whose arm or leg or other body part was whose. Preston was very well built—muscular, broad chested with a narrow waist and well-defined thighs. His arms were cut and flexed as he held himself over the woman in strenuous positions set against the sharp volcanic carved temple gods. The woman was very light-skinned and slender. Her legs were no bigger around than my arms. She had short, bobbed black hair revealing a long, graceful neck that, in the shot I was looking at, was extended completely back in utter ecstasy. Her breasts were small, yet shapely. Her skin looked smooth as cream. Her make-up seemed a little harsh for her petite features, the scarlet red lipstick stood out like blood. What stayed with me the longest was the fact that she wore four-inch heels in this rugged terrain and had kept them on in the Pura Dalem. If I wore heels like that, the temple would have lived up to its name—Temple of Death. I would have killed myself just walking down the steps.

The next picture showed Preston walking with the Asian woman as she held a baby, with a toddler running in front of them. Preston's left hand was on the infant's shoulder. Both children had very light skin, and wide round eyes. Whose children were they? Preston's? Not only was he unfaithful, but did he have a family in Indonesia? That was what the pictures indicated. Maybe he had a completely separate life in Asia and that's why he spent so much time there. Had he a common law wife and two children to take care of? Perhaps Kelly lied about Preston's infidelity because she didn't want anyone to know about his children from another woman. Not only had she learned of his unfaithfulness, but she was bulldozed by offspring. Rumor had it that Kelly wanted children and Preston didn't. Maybe it was because he already had children. Perhaps Kelly figured it out, hired a private eye to confirm it and then formulated a plan to get rid of her lying, cheating husband.

Just as I was about to turn another page, I heard a noise outside Kelly's door. The handle jiggled. I shoved the lid on the box and scrambled to the floor. I pulled myself into the fetal position under her desk. But just as the door opened, I remembered that my purse lay on her desk! In one swift move, I reached up and grabbed the strap and gave it a firm tug. The purse crashed on the ground, along with a file from her desk. I slid out of hiding and tried to slide the papers back into the file, but it was too late. I heard footsteps coming my way so I crawled back under the desk and held my knees to my chest.

"Ill be down in a minute, Mr. Brode. I need to grab the file," Kelly said. I watched as her Bottega Veneta shoes rounded the corner of her desk and planted themselves squarely in front of the fallen file. She bent over and picked the file up and slammed it on the desk. "Patty is such a pig. She can't even put a file on a desk properly, let alone type a letter without getting her dirty little fingerprints on it," Kelly said, under her breath. I assumed that Patty is her secretary.

Kelly sat in her chair and scooted it closer to her desk, compressing me like a garbage compactor. I watched her open her side drawer and grab a yellow legal pad and a file. The drawer slammed and she stood, but then a pencil from her desk rolled to the floor. Just as she leaned over to pick up the pencil, the phone rang. "Yes, Mr. Brode, I'm on my way," she said, snatching the pencil up before slamming down the receiver. "Impatient asshole." She scurried out of the office, leaving the door open.

I took a huge breath and remained still for a few seconds. Still holding the private eye's report, I skimmed it quickly while camped out under her desk. Bob Avery identified the mistress as Nyomi Janger. I wrote down her name and the Balinese address listed for her. I perused the rest of the information about her as quickly as possible, and found out that Nyomi Janger was a Geyser employee in Indonesia. I closed the file and slipped it back into place, closed the box and scribbled Kelly a note:

"Kelly,

I dropped in to say goodbye and to leave you my card. If you can think of any information that might be helpful to Michael's defense, please contact me. Expect to receive a trial subpoena after the trial date is set—standard procedure, as you well know.

Best regards,

Mary MacIntosh"

While waiting at the airport for my flight, I used my wireless connection and sent Michael the following e-mail:

"To: MichaelO@Geyser.com

Re: Confidential

Michael: I have gained some information that is crucial to your defense. Please confidentially and secretly investigate your Indonesian sales representative named 'Nyomi Janger.' Do not contact her on your own, as any contact needs to be made through me to provide attorney-client privilege. We need her date of birth, citizenship, bank records, former employment status, and anything else that Geyser personnel records may have about her. Thank you. E-me back asap. Mac"

As I sidestepped down the airplane aisle in search of seat 27C, I caught the eye of a man seated in 24A that looked familiar. His face was immersed in the in-flight magazine, but he poked his head up the minute he caught sight of me, then he ducked back down. I stopped dead in my tracks, just a few inches past the back of his seat and stared at his profile. In the overhead compartment was the forest green jacket I'd seen him wearing in the Public Garden. He was tailing me.

Only two people knew I was en route today—Michael and Kelly.

Chapter 8

Despite my close connection in Salt Lake City, I waited until the man in 24A deplaned. Every other soul had retrieved their overhead luggage and had made their way to the front, but he just sat there, as if he was waiting for something … or someone. He kept looking back, but I was scrunched down as far as possible behind the seat in front of me. I could see him perfectly through the tiny space that separates the seats. The airline attendant came down the aisle and stopped at 24A. "Sir, this is a destination flight. All passengers must deplane." I heard him grumble and gather his things. He was looking back the entire time he walked forward through the aisle. When the attendant came to my seat, I motioned to her to be quiet. When I could see that he was gone, I addressed her.

"I think that guy is following me. I'm afraid."

"Should I call security?" she asked.

"No, I don't think that's necessary. I'm overly tired and my imagination could be getting the better of me. But just to be on the safe side, could I wait and deplane with the attendants?" She agreed. Her crew walked me to my next gate. I kept looking for the guy in the terminal, but I didn't see him. Maybe I was being paranoid. Being sexually assaulted at gunpoint does that to the psyche.

* * * *

For Harry, the worst part of a murder case was right after the indictment, because he was inundated with a tidal wave of evidence against his client. He was on the phone when I approached his office, and he didn't look especially happy.

I, on the other hand, loved this moment in the case. I saw it as a time to travel down circuitous paths of truth, lies and consequences. It was like putting together a two thousand-piece jigsaw puzzle without being able to see a picture of what you were making. Challenging, but not impossible. It was thrilling to me to think that Bain knew things that I didn't, and it was up to me to find the puzzle piece that slipped off the table and under the sofa before he found it. I went through the mounting pile of paper that Lela had so carefully stacked on my chair and that Harry had so carelessly rampaged through. I then logged in to my e-mail and saw that I had two messages, one from Michael and one from Kelly. I couldn't decide which to open first. Michael was paying my salary at the moment, so I double-clicked on his name.

> "From what I have found so far, Nyomi Janger worked as a rep for Geyser, but she resigned a few days before the Geyser convention in Jackson. I'll see what else I can find out.
>
> Michael"

Then I read Kelly's message:

> "Sorry I missed you on your way out. My depo went longer than expected. Keep me posted on any developments.
>
> Sincerely,
>
> KFP"

I printed the e-mails for the file and put a copy in Lela's filing stack. I logged into Lexis/Nexis, my legal search software, and clicked on "People Locator." I typed in "Nyomi Janger." In about twenty seconds, I'd learned that she has dual citizenship—Indonesian and U.S. She has a social security number and a residence in the Bay Area. I then clicked on "Property Locator" and discovered that she owned a condo in San Francisco. This was good news. Anyone who owned property in the Bay Area had to have qualified for a loan. I could find out just about anything from a loan application, once I got my hands on it.

I clicked on "Public Records" to search for a possible criminal record. She had none. Neither did Michael. Or Preston. However, Kelly Flanigan did have a record. She had been busted in law school for vandalism of a professor's car. Interesting. I printed the case file locator and put it in the file labeled "Kelly F. Parker."

I could hear the menacing grizzly bear heading my way. Harry had a most distinctive walk. It was sort of a shuffle-hop, shuffle-hop—as if he was too lazy to pick up his feet, but half way through the drag, the friction was more work than it was worth. It sounded like his knee was bothering him more than usual today. I hauled my eyes away from the flickering screen to give him full attention. It wasn't a court day for Harry. He wore tan silk slacks and a Polo sweater.

"Don't get too comfortable in the five-star hotel digs, Mac. We have some problems here. I just got off the phone with Christopher Bain."

"Weak plea bargain?"

"No plea bargain." He stopped for a couple of beats, to let it sink in. "Bain said that Deputy-Sheriff Tim Marshall, the officer on duty when Preston was brought to the hospital, has just detained and arrested a local kid named Duane Towns. Towns claims that Michael hired him to kill Preston." The words hung in the air.

"Hired him to-"

"It gets worse. I know Duane Towns. He's my son's roommate. John and Duane played football together in high school."

"Oh. That guy. I know who you're talking about."

"He's a loser. Always was. Always will be. I wish John could figure it out."

"Could this create an ethical dilemma for you? I mean, do the Professional Rules of Conduct address whether you can defend someone whose alleged hit-man is living with your son?" I couldn't imagine that the rules were that specific, but it was worth looking into. I would hate to get to the courthouse steps the day of trial to find that we had been disqualified to represent Michael on a technicality.

"That's your job. Figure out the answer to that question first, Mac. I don't know. I doubt it, but I don't know," Harry said as he planted himself in the chair across from where I stood by my desk. "So, tell me what you learned on your vacation," he said. I told him everything. He stood and leaned over my desk, taking in every word.

"I'm going to follow up on this Nyomi Janger lead and see if I can find her," I continued. "She needs to be deposed. It's possible that Preston broke it off with her recently, and that's why she quit her job or was forced to quit with an incentive package. She could be the scorned lover. She could also be the single mother of children belonging to one of the richer men in America. She could be a whole lot of things. I also need to figure out Kelly. She just doesn't make sense to me. And I need to follow up on this deal about Preston doing business with Kelly's father. Kelly was obviously stunned and maybe even annoyed by my suggestion that they were in business together."

"I'll figure out what's going on with Duane Towns," Harry said. "I'm on my way to the big house now to pay him a visit. They're detaining him. I might drop in on Bain, too, and see if we can have a meeting of the minds on this case." That was Harry—always the mediator.

"It might be prudent if you let me figure out the ethical rules before you meet with Bain. He'll rub it in your face if he thinks we can't represent Michael."

"I'll call you from the clink," he said as he shuffle-hopped out of my office. I just had to take a moment to watch him leave. He overpronates so much that his Gucci loafers look underinflated, like balding tires on an old Dodge farm truck. He turned back at me. "Whatever happened to that guy who you think was following you?"

"I'm not sure. I think he was on my plane back, but he was a few rows ahead of me. When we landed, I tried to find him at the airport, but he wasn't there."

"Are you sure it's the same guy?"

"I think so. But I'm not one hundred percent sure."

"Maybe you should stay with Jane and me for a few days, just to be safe."

"I'm okay. Thanks anyway. I've got to learn to deal with my fears."

"The offer stands," Harry said, as he left my office. I heard him bark eight or ten orders at Lela on his way out. She grumbled at him, and then started typing.

I pulled out the dusty "Professional Conduct" book that I hadn't looked at since I took the Wyoming State Bar Examination over seven years ago.

As promised, Harry called me after visiting the jail. "Good news. If your son was the alleged hit man, we might have a problem. But since your son only associates with the alleged hit man, we have the Wyoming Supreme Court green light."

"More good news. I met with Duane Towns," Harry said. I could hear the sound of an energy bar wrapper being opened on the other end of the phone line. Harry kept talking, stuffing a bite of something into his mouth. "He can't seem to make up his mind about what happened. He's told Bain that Michael hired him to kill Preston. He told me that Michael really didn't 'hire' him per se, but that Michael 'suggested' that Duane take Preston out. When I asked him what he meant by 'suggested,' Duane said that it was more of a hint. Duane and Michael went to high school together, along with Deputy Tim Marshall. Duane said that later, every time Kelly came to Jackson to visit Michael's family, that all of the local boys would find an excuse to hang out at Michael's house, because they all had a crush on her. Duane said that he and Michael have kept in touch. When Michael comes home to visit his mom, he calls Duane and they have a beer together. Well, Michael called Duane when he came to Jackson for the Geyser convention, and Duane said that they were joking that Kelly was in town and Michael said, 'Wouldn't it be nice if Preston weren't in the picture?' Duane said that he took that comment as a suggestion that he should snub Preston out."

"That seems like a stretch-"

"I'd say. I asked Duane whether Michael had offered him any money to kill Preston, and Duane got a little wishy-washy on me. He said that Michael had hinted that there would be a reward in it for him, but backed off that statement when I pressed him about it," Harry said. "After I left the slammer, I called John and asked to meet him at the apartment he shares with Duane. I'm here now. Can you come over?"

"Now?"

"You've got to see this."

"I'm on my way." I scribbled down John's address and hopped into my Honda. The driver's side door screeched every time I tried to open or close it. The standard transmission was so tight that it was impossible to tell if the car was in first or third, until the clutched popped and the car stalled. The odometer read two hundred ten thousand miles and at this point, every mile counted. I flipped a U-turn and headed toward John's apartment.

John and Duane's apartment was in the east part of town. It's in a two-story, dark-shingled building with a balcony protruding from each of eight apartments. They had an apartment on the second floor. I walked up the stairs and through the first door on the second story, straight into their living room. The burnt-orange carpet was heavily stained and smelled of skunked beer. The white walls had black scuffmarks and the kitchen smelled like rotting food. I walked past the kitchen and into Duane's room, where Harry was. Harry pointed at the walls. I walked around the room slowly, looking at every picture and newspaper article thumb tacked to the corkboards that covered his room. Duane had pictures of Kelly everywhere. Grade school. High school. Homecoming Queen. Graduation. Marriage. Every picture that had been in the newspaper about her was tacked to his wall. "This is creepy," I said.

"Very. I'm calling Bain. Maybe we have our killer, Mac. Maybe Duane Towns has been stalking Kelly and killed Preston to get him out of the picture."

Bain showed up about five minutes later, with Deputy Sheriff Tim Marshall in tow. They looked like the odd couple. Tim is short, overweight and has a cigarette hanging from the corner of his mouth. Bain is tall, well-dressed and has a nice physique. Tim took pictures of the room. Bain stood at my side.

"I think you've charged the wrong man with murder," Harry said.

* * * *

After leaving John and Duane's apartment, I grabbed a veggie sandwich at my favorite deli. As I waited for my sandwich, I looked out the window and saw Lela, our secretary, emerging from a restaurant across the street, arm in arm, with a man. Lela was known to have a variety of male companions, some "just friends" and some "none of your business." Lela was also well known in town for her provocative dress code. Today, despite February Freeze, as the locals call it, she was wearing a skin-tight short denim skirt with red pumps and a red low cut blouse. Lela rarely wore a coat, regardless of the temperature. She told me that her Shoshone blood kept her warm.

Something about the man looked familiar. As they parted ways, she pecked him on the cheek as he slid an envelope into her purse.

The man disappeared around the block and Lela j-walked across the street. I grabbed my sandwich and slapped a bill on the counter, then rushed out the door behind Lela. She ducked into the main lobby of the Bank of Jackson Hole as I watched her make a large cash deposit. As she exited the bank lobby, I greeted her at the staircase that leads to our offices on the second floor of the bank building.

"Who was that guy you were with?" I asked. Lela took a shallow breath and whirled her hair around swiftly, catching it in her left hand while swirling it up into a French twist without a thought.

"Just a guy." She fidgeted with the backings of her earrings, turning toward the stairwell.

"He looked familiar to me, Lela. Who is he?" Three steps up, she turned toward me and lowered her glare.

"I said, he's just a guy." She turned and bolted up the steps in her four-inch stilettos. I had to avert my eyes as I followed her up the steps. As they say in the White House, "The higher the monkey climbs, the more you see of his (or her) behind."

* * * *

My computer brought me back to reality with its friendliest message: "You've Got Mail." It was a response from Bob Avery of Mason & Associates Detective Agency. I had e-mailed him earlier regarding Nyomi Janger. His response read:

> "Dear Ms. MacIntosh: I received your inquiry about finding the whereabouts of one Nyomi Janger. Our agency would be happy to help you locate her. Please forward any information you have. I have attached a copy of our contract for services to the e-mail. Once I receive a signed contract and the requisite retainer, we will begin the search.
>
> Sincerely,
>
> Bob Avery"

He hadn't taken the bait. I hoped he would respond by saying something like: "Small world—we just found someone by that name for another client." No such luck. I downloaded and printed the attachment. We needed Bob Avery to testify at trial about Preston's affair, so I signed the agreement and faxed it to him.

I toggled to my research screen and did a property profile for the San Francisco address of Ms. Janger. Her condominium is owned by a REIT, or a real estate investment trust, but managed by a large property management company. I called the contact person and left a voicemail message about Ms. Janger's condo. His secretary called me back shortly thereafter and told me that the condo had been subletted to two men. I asked the secretary whether she had contact information on Ms. Janger, and she said that she wasn't allowed to give out that kind of information without a subpoena. That's California for you. I was going to have to rely on Michael to get the personnel records on her and go from there. Bob Avery might just get to double-bill for his work, after all.

* * * *

"Bain's on a roll," Harry said, as he stomped into my office. As I mentioned, it was usually a shuffle-hop, but when Harry was pissed, he stomped like a two-year-old.

"Duane Towns has an alibi for January eighteenth. He was snowmobiling with John. I called John and he confirmed it. Duane admitted to Bain that he has had a 'crush' on Kelly, but denied being a part of the alleged murder. He's now retracting even the hit man part of his story and has asked for a lawyer."

"That's good news, isn't it?"

"It gets worse. Bain has the forensics and it's not looking good. Between the hit man allegation and the forensics, we're sinking like the Titanic without a lifeboat." Harry grabbed a pencil from my penholder and snapped it in half for effect. "Bain said that he's scheduling dozens of depositions over the next two weeks. You'd better help me disprove motive and opportunity in a hurry, Mac."

"I need more time with him to develop Michael's defense," I said. "But, I'm sure that we have some other viable directions to point the finger." I told him about Kelly's hiring a private investigator to trail Preston's extra-marital affair with an exotic beauty. I also explained that the exotic beauty had been an employee who was fired only days prior to Preston's death. There were the mixed-race children that looked like Preston. Then there was Preston's mysterious connection with Kelly's father—a connection that Kelly denied any knowledge of.

"This is not going to be a finger-pointing defense. I hate it when defense lawyers pass the buck. We need to look deep into the circumstantial evidence facing us and figure out the truth. I want to know the forensics inside and out. I want to know more about Duane Towns. We're going to figure out every nuance of this trap and solve it with finesse and honesty. And then we are going to defend it with vigor, understood?"

"You bet." I had learned how to handle Harry. When he felt threatened, he got on his high horse, orated about the principles of the matter, and rallied the forces behind him. I knew how to rally and cheer, put on my armor and mount my stallion. And how to draw my weapon and ride bravely into the charging militia. It calmed Harry down to know that I had my weapon drawn. It charged me up to know that I needed to find something I could use for the offensive. In order to find a weapon, I needed the medical records to depose the treating physician. And I needed to go back to Boston. A trip to Bali wouldn't be so bad either, but that would have to be approved by Michael. First things first.

Chapter 9

▼

Harry is no stranger to forensic science. He has defended dozens of medical malpractice cases during his civil practice. In fact, he probably knows more about forensics than most doctors. The only reason that he assigns it to me is that I had specific training on the matter during undergrad, and I think he likes to think he's getting his money's worth out of me. Let's take it a step further. Harry has a wife and he needs to go home at some point during the evening. I, on the other hand, only have a pet. I can stay as long as I like. When I'm not dating anyone, which is now, I tend to stay very, very late at the office. It's my own kind of therapy—avoidance therapy. Harry keeps close tabs on my personal life in order to gauge how much work he'll be required to do.

I'd asked Lela to get me a copy of the medical chart and the post-mortem forensic toxicology report from the autopsy on Preston and I spent the rest of the evening putting the pieces together. Unfortunately, the pieces didn't fit. The forensic toxicology report detected a substance called succinylcholine in Preston's blood. I logged into the Mayo Clinic website and discovered that succinylcholine is a depolarizing neuromuscular blocking agent typically used during anesthesia. Succinylcholine poisoning is difficult to detect for the forensic toxicologist because of its rapid hydrolysis, meaning that it metabolizes very quickly in a water-soluble state. Was the toxicologist saying that Preston was poisoned? Harry wasn't going to like this one bit.

* * * *

I didn't intend on returning to Boston over the weekend or I never would've left. I took a red-eye flight back and due to my exhaustion, Kelly agreed to meet me at the hotel. The minute she walked into the foyer of my suite, I felt underdressed. I was wearing navy sweats and a red fleece sweatshirt. She was wearing a black pantsuit with a leopard-print blouse and matching leopard-print wedge shoes. She sported frameless glasses and her dark hair was pulled back in a French twist with decorative chopsticks holding it in place. She eased herself into a yoga-proper position on the couch and took a deep cleansing breath. I guessed that this was my cue to begin.

"Thank you for taking the time to meet with me," I said. "This must be a very difficult time in your life."

"It is very difficult, but I'm managing," Kelly said in a rather flat tone. There was evidence of dark circles under her eyes, which were carefully camouflaged with concealer, and a champagne sparkling dust of eye shadow.

"Tell me about your relationship with Michael," I said.

"*For the record*," Kelly said in a sarcastic tone, "I loved my husband very much and I am in deep mourning over his death. However, I don't believe that Michael O'Connor killed him. That's why I'm here today. I desperately want to see the killer of my husband brought to justice, if there is a killer. It's quite possible that Preston accidentally hit a tree while skiing and died of head trauma. The doctors in the emergency room treated his injuries as those resulting from a skiing accident, and the initial cause of death was ruled an accident. So, as far as I know, he died from a skiing accident. Like I said, I think it was an accident. But if it wasn't, there were plenty of people that Preston screwed along the way. Figuratively, of course," she said. Kelly rubbed her neck for a few seconds. "Geyser has lots of competitors. Getting rid of Preston could mean opportunity to a competitor. If this wasn't an accident, there are so many other possibilities. I can't stand thinking of Michael taking the blame. I know he didn't do it. I mean, I'm sure he didn't. This is pure speculation on my part, but that's what I think."

"Tell me about your relationship with Michael."

"Relationship? What do you mean by *that* word?"

"I mean relationship. Your history, in the-"

"Oh. Michael and I are childhood friends. Our fathers went to medical school together. We got together frequently for holidays and such. Our dads taught us how to ski together. We went on family vacations together. We met at summer camps. We were buddies growing up. When it came time to apply for colleges, we both applied to Harvard. Luckily, we were both accepted. We drove together to school and helped each other settle in. Preston was assigned as his roommate. Michael was very shy—Preston brought him out of his shell. If it weren't for Preston, Michael would be working in research at a university somewhere, making very little money and receiving little, if any, recognition. Preston made Michael who he is today in the business world and as a research scientist," Kelly said, as if she were somehow a catalyst in his success.

"Did Preston and Michael get along as business partners?"

"For the most part, yes. They had their conflicts and growing pains, like any other partnership. But, overall, they were able to work well together, I think. Preston was great at people skills; Michael was great at research and development. Together, they were able to create, promote and sell an amazing remedy that has helped millions of people all over the world. I'm very proud of both of them. As a kid, Michael was so shy and underdeveloped. I was almost hesitant to go to Harvard with him because I thought he would cling to me like a monkey and I wouldn't be able to make friends of my own. I never dreamed that he would prosper like he did. Not only did he make friends of his own, he matured and became a confident and outgoing person."

"Were you aware of any conflicts between Preston and Michael right before your trip to Jackson Hole?"

"Nothing out of the ordinary, but things were crazy right before we left."

"How so?"

"Preston had been traveling a lot, as usual. I was swamped at work. Michael seemed … distracted. Put it this way, I felt tension going to Jackson, but once we were there, it was great to be there-"

"What kind of tension were you feeling?"

"Tension from taking time off work. My firm expects a lot out of me. I bill nearly three hundred hours a month. I'm their top-producing associate. If I take a few days off, I fall behind."

"Did you feel tension with Preston?"

"No. Not really. I just hadn't seen him much. That's all." She sat upright and pulled the chopsticks out of her hair, allowing the dark mane to fall free over her shoulders. "Truth be told, we were trying to have a baby. When he traveled on business, it made it … difficult." I looked at her inquisitively, not sure what she was suggesting. "Fertility assistance," she said, closing the gap. "I was taking fertility injections, and we were supposed to try three days in a row around ovulation, but when Preston was gone, it was impossible. The drugs wreaked havoc on me, emotionally. I was due to ovulate in Jackson during the convention, so it was important that I went along to the convention. Normally, I don't go to their trade shows, but I wanted some time with my husband." She bit her lower lip as it quivered. Her eyes were wet with tears. "I'm over thirty-five. Getting pregnant isn't as easy as you think."

"I understand how you must have felt," I suggested. But as I stared into Kelly's eyes, I saw a desperate woman, but not desperate for the loss of her husband.

"What happened the day of the accident?"

Kelly took another deep breath and closed her eyes as if she were immersed in meditation. "Saturday was a great ski day for Jackson in January. We had clear skies and it wasn't too cold, for Jackson, that is. Preston and I met up with Michael and his mom and took the aerial tram up to the top of the mountain. I remember that Michael was wearing a hideous outfit—an orange down field jacket, the kind popular in the 1970's, with brown sheen pants, red gloves, and a red hat. I was half embarrassed to be seen with him. His pockets weren't deep enough to hold his cell phone, so he asked me to keep it in my fanny pack. He and Preston skied the intermediate slopes as a warm up while Ann and I followed along. After a few runs, Michael was itching to ski some harder terrain. He was going to go off by himself and meet up with us later for lunch, but Preston asked to go along. Michael just turned and skied away, and Preston followed him. Michael yelled over his shoulder that he was going to Granite Canyon. I remember Ann cautioning the guys because Granite Canyon is an out-of-bounds area and there had been a recent snowfall. She was worried about avalanches. But Michael is such a good skier, she finally let it go. We agreed to meet for lunch at the Mangy Moose at one-thirty. Ann and I skied away together while Preston and Michael headed for Granite Canyon. We arrived on time for lunch, and waited for them for over two hours. By then, we were frantic. Ann insisted on reporting them missing to the ski patrol, so we did. Just as we walked back in to the Mangy Moose, Michael walked in … alone," Kelly said. She took another deep breath and continued.

"We asked him why they were so late and he looked confused. He said 'We?' and we said, yes, we. He said that Preston had taken a few turns in Granite Canyon and had decided almost immediately that it was too tough for him, so he headed back through the trees toward groomed runs and was to meet up with us for lunch. Michael said that he hadn't seen Preston again. He said that he had run late because he had overshot the lift at the bottom of Granite Canyon and had had to make his way back to the top in order to ski down to the Mangy

Moose. He claimed the ski lift lines were forty-five minutes long each. He seemed as surprised as we were that Preston wasn't there."

"So, what did you do?"

"I tried to call Preston on his cell phone, but no one answered. I remember Michael getting a cell call around that same time, so I handed him his phone out from my fanny pack, but it wasn't Pres. Michael only said 'yes' and 'good.' I figured it was nothing important. So we went back to the ski patrol together and reported Preston as missing. The ski patrol told us to wait at the First Aid Center because if he had been injured and was found, he would be taken by toboggan there, so that's what we did."

"What happened next?"

"Around four thirty in the afternoon, a C.B. radio call came in from the ski patrol to the First Aid Center, stating that Preston had been found. Out of bounds. Unconscious."

I was relieved to realize that Kelly's version of the accident coincided with Michael's version. Kelly told me about Preston's medical care after they brought him in, and what had happened to him in the hospital. As I listened, I walked over to the bar and filled two glasses of water. Kelly followed me to the minibar and opened the fridge.

"Do you mind?" she asked as she grabbed a small bottle of chilled white wine.

"No, of course," I said. She'd already uncorked the bottle and poured two glasses. She handed me a glass and nodded that I follow her.

Kelly stretched out on the couch and kicked off her shoes, taking a long pull off the wine glass as she changed the topic, enlightening me about Michael's wife, Brianna, and how hard it had been on him when she died.

"Brianna's funeral was the worst day of both Michael's and my life." I found this statement odd, since she had just buried her husband. "After Bri's death, Michael retreated into his work. He lost his heart and soul when she died. He still wears both of their wedding bands on a chain around his neck. The rings are in the Irish tradition of two hands holding one heart with a crown over the heart. A perfect description of their love." Kelly reached into her handbag and handed me an envelope that looked like it had been toted around for years. I reached over and met her hand, as I hesitantly accepted the envelope.

CHAPTER 10

▼

I opened the envelope and pulled out the note, handwritten in near-perfect penmanship on ivory-bonded paper:

"Dear Kelly,

You are and will always be my best friend. You helped me learn how to live high and how to live low and how to live in-between. You have so much to offer the world—I hope that you will choose to spend your love and talents on someone who will mirror your inner and outer beauty and will treasure you for who you are. I have watched you emerge from your cocoon and turn into a beautiful butterfly. You need your wings to fly—be free—to be loved and to love.

I know that Michael loves you. He has loved you since he was a little boy. It would give me eternal pleasure if the two of you found each other. If it ever did happen, you would not be violating me in any way. I would rather have Michael be loved by you than anyone else in the world. He deserves to be loved by someone who treasures him, too. He is a treasure—as are you.

All my love,

Brianna"

I didn't know how to respond. I stared at the words and felt the meaning behind them. I folded the note back into its perfect V and slid it back into the envelope that had cradled it for so long. Kelly was obviously still in deep mourning over the loss of her best friend. But it occurred to me that maybe she was projecting the loss of her husband onto the old loss of her friend, resurrecting some of her feelings. I'm no psychiatrist, but common sense told me that some of this sadness was about Preston. Why couldn't she face it straight on?

I hated to change the subject, but I didn't really want to know any more than she had just told me. I understood what she wanted me to understand: that Bri was a pivotal person in Michael's life and her life and that both of their lives had changed irrevocably after Bri had died. This was all very useful and informative, sure, but it was also possibly damaging, too, especially to Michael. Bain could turn this into the psychological profile of a man who had snapped after his wife died and gone after his partner in order to be with his partner's wife.

"Thank you, Kelly, for sharing this with me. I'm sure it was very hard to do so, but it helps me understand you and Michael. I don't mean to change the subject, but I did background checks on everyone, and it popped up that you were arrested during law school. What happened?" I asked, giving her my look of deep concern. Kelly stood, pulled her hair back tightly and then unraveled it again, letting it fall loose on her shoulders for just a second. She pulled it back tightly again, twisting it into a knot at the nape of her neck and affixing the chopsticks back in place. She crossed her arms and walked over to the window, keeping her back to me.

"I wasn't really *arrested* per se. There was an incident on campus, that's all. It was ironed out," she said. She turned and looked at me, or more like through me, her green eyes narrowing. "Why were you snooping into my background, anyway?"

"I search the public records on everyone that we intend to put on the stand during trial. It's standard procedure, so that witnesses aren't discredited by prior bad acts. As a lawyer, you understand. Anyway, the search results that I got said that you were charged with vandalism to a professor's car on campus."

"The record was supposed to be expunged," she said. "Do you want to know what really happened?" After the monologue on Brianna, I knew that I should get comfortable. She had apparently missed her therapy appointment last week.

"This is how I remember it," Kelly stared. "It was the first day of law school. I took a seat in the classroom, feeling anxious and nervous. This asshole of a professor, Albert Bates, took the podium with a scowl. Without looking up, and before all of us were even assembled in our seats, Professor Bates said, 'Miss Flanigan, what is the holding of *Benedict v. Martin Industries*?' Shocked to hear my name, I started rifling through my casebook. I barely had time to look up when, again, the professor blurted: 'Miss Flanigan, did you read the first case in your assignment? It was posted on the bulletin board outside my office. I expect you to be prepared.' I was embarrassed. I understood that law professors used the Socratic method—I just didn't expect it the first minute of class. Needless to say, I didn't like Professor Bates from that moment on. He took great pride the rest of the semester in trying to make me look like a fool. To get even, after final exams, I used my car keys and scratched the paint off the driver's side of his car. Unfortunately, I didn't see the video cameras in the parking lot. I got caught and I am ashamed of doing it. Even though I wasn't dating Preston at the time, his dad came to my rescue and resolved the situation with the law school so that I didn't get kicked out. The police record was supposed to be expunged," she said. "I think Hugh knew even back then that Preston and I might eventually get back together. He liked me. He didn't want me to tarnish my reputation."

"After we left the gym the other day, I accidentally left my wallet in the locker and had to return. When the taxi pulled up, I saw you standing on the corner talking to a man. Who was he?" I asked. Kelly stiffened. She bolted upright and slipped on her shoes and grabbed her handbag in one swift motion.

"I don't know what you're talking about."

"He was a bulky-looking guy. You handed him something."

"You must be mistaken."

"No. I'm sure it was you. In fact, afterwards, I watched you walk to the parking structure and drive away in your Porsche."

"Oh, I know what you're talking about," she said, with a slight smile. She walked a step or two and then reached down and grabbed her wine glass, swallowing the remaining half in one smooth swig. "That must have been Jerry. He was the guy that watched our house while we were in Jackson."

"What line of work is Jerry in?"

"I'm not following you," Kelly said, reaching for her keys inside her handbag.

"I'll level with you. I'm quite positive that the man you were meeting with has been following me since I've been in town. I saw him in the Public Garden the day I arrived and then he followed me yesterday on Newbury Street." I watched for her reaction, but she gave no sign.

"I don't know anything about that. Boston is a big city and it's good to always be on the lookout, but maybe you're mistaking him for someone else. I don't know Jerry well. He came recommended as a house sitter from a lawyer at the office," she said on her way toward the door.

"Does Jerry have a last name? I'd like to talk with him."
"Most people do have last names, don't they?"
"Do you think you could get his last name for me?"
"Take care of yourself," were Kelly's parting words.

*   *   *   *

I bolted the door behind Kelly after she left. I cupped my wine, staring into the golden hue. As I swirled the contents of the glass, I thought of gold—money. Was Preston's death a crime of passion? If so, was it a passion for love or for money? There definitely was more research to do. I booted up my laptop and got to work. I needed to find out more about Geyser in order to have a good discussion with Michael about a number of things. I also wanted to figure out what was going on with James Flanigan, Kelly's father. It struck me as odd that Kelly didn't know or claimed that she didn't know that her father had been doing business with her husband.

I started by researching the business sections of major newspapers and magazines for articles on Geyser. Several articles reiterated that Geyser was struggling for market share in America but that its overseas sales were strong. Michael's face was splashed across the cover of *Newsweek* after the successful initial public offering had been consummated. After getting an even better understanding of the company, I decided to see if I could figure anything out about how Kelly's father played into the mix.

When I had done my public records search on Kelly, it hadn't dawned on me to search her father. I wished that I had.

Chapter 11

As it turned out, James Flanigan's medical license had been suspended in Wyoming for sending his patients to an x-ray and MRI facility that he owned with a group of doctors. Apparently, it is illegal to refer your own patients to a facility that you have a financial interest. Dr. Flanigan was issued warnings for doing so. Instead of complying, James sold his interest to a straw man, who then sold it to a limited liability company. The problem was that James Flanigan was the sole member of the limited liability company. In other words, he had sold his interest in his company to himself once removed, and had gotten caught. The medical board suspended his license and he agreed to probation. According to the file, he still had not complied with the community service part of his probationary terms, and his medical license remained suspended. Meanwhile, he had set up a pharmaceutical company that sold medical supplies in the Rocky Mountain region consisting of Montana, the Dakotas, Wyoming, Colorado, and Idaho. How defiant of him, I thought to myself. Maybe that's where Kelly gets her icy edge.

* * * *

Michael suggested that we meet at Luciana's Ristorante, a quaint Northern Italian restaurant tucked in the heart of Boston, for dinner. He gave me directions and warned me that it is hard to find, especially at night. I was to look for the red, green and white barber light outside. Thank God he mentioned it, or I would have never spotted it. Even the cabby hadn't heard of this place. It made me wonder.

I entered. The smell of garlic permeated my pores, like salt air hovering over the ocean. I could see into the kitchen, which is always a good sign at a restaurant—no hiding behind closed doors. In a restaurant, I want to see what's happening, hear the sizzling, smell the aromas, watch the flames roar to life with the excitement of gastronomical creations. The chef of Luciana's was busy and happy and full of life. He shook a skillet over a flame, flipping the contents into the air, while singing Italian opera in a baritone voice. Michael motioned me to a back table and pulled out my chair for me. As far as I'm concerned, chivalry is in—it has always been in. A simple, gentlemanly gesture is lovely.

Michael's navy blazer was draped over the back of his chair. His blue and white striped shirt was unbuttoned and he wore no tie. He had on khaki pants and loafers. I wore a cream sweater and jeans, and as I looked around at the other patrons, I realized I fit right in. This was a very casual place. Michael motioned to the chef and he hurried over to our table.

"Joey, I'd like you to meet Mac. This is Joey Lugano. This was his mother's restaurant," Michael said.

"My pleasure to meet you, Princess," Joey said. He kissed my hand. "Michael is my favorite customer," he said with a whisper, so as not to offend his other favorite customers, I suspected. "What will it be tonight?" I looked at the menu quickly.

"What do you recommend?"

"My special tonight is the Ravioli di Luciana, which is ravioli stuffed with fresh herbs and smothered in fresh tiger prawns, mussels, manica clams, and sea scallops served with a zesty marinara sauce."

"Sounds fantastic. I'll have that."

"I think I'll try something new tonight," Michael said. "That Linguine di Vitello sounds good. And let's have a carafe of house Chianti."

It's no secret that there is no such thing as good seafood in Wyoming, unless it is trout caught fresh in a lake. When I can have great seafood on the coast with delicious homemade pasta, I'm a happy woman. The warmth of the flush from the Chianti, the zesty sauce, and Michael's company made me feel whole. I didn't feel like bridging into a business conversation, but I knew that the clock was ticking and we needed to solve this crime before the fast-approaching trial.

"How's your detective work coming along regarding Kelly's father?" I asked. I thought of my first meeting with Michael before his arraignment hearing. He told me that he and Preston had some pretty big arguments about some of Preston's business dealings. Michael had questioned Preston about the huge volume of drugs being shipped overseas. Something just didn't seem right to Michael. Now he launched into an explanation.

"Before this nightmare started, I'd been snooping around the office, careful not to act suspiciously or to tip off anyone. I worked my normal routine during the day, but when the employees went home, I snooped. Before heading to Jackson for the convention, I had reviewed all the national shipping and receiving invoices for the past three years. There were regular, fairly large shipping invoices to a company called Rocky Mountain Pharmaceuticals in Billings, Montana. The company was unfamiliar to me. I didn't recall seeing Rocky Mountain Pharmaceuticals on any of the advertising or promotional logs. Most of our steady customers have been a target of one or more of our promotional campaigns. It was a mystery to me." Michael poured both of us another glass of wine and leaned back.

"I followed up by logging into Preston's computer. Rocky Mountain Pharmaceuticals was not on the preferred customer list. In fact, it was not on the customer list at all. Next, I went to the client file drawer but there was no customer file for RMP there either. It is company policy to have a customer file for every client, which includes customer financial information for billing purposes and a supply shipping log to track the lot numbers of the drugs shipped to each company for CDC purposes, in case of a negative reaction to any drug," Michael said. "Next, I called telephone information, but there was no listing anywhere in Montana for Rocky Mountain Pharmaceutical. The next day, I approached Preston's secretary, Carol, and asked her who the sales representative was for Rocky Mountain Pharmaceuticals and she said that it wasn't assigned to anyone. That was odd. Next, I called Kelly's office and asked to be transferred to her paralegal, Richard. Kelly's office often helped us out with small legal research questions like this one, so it was nothing out of the ordinary for me. I told him that I needed the incorporation information on RMP. Within ten minutes, a fax came though from Richard. Rocky Mountain Pharmaceuticals, he reported, was incorporated in Wyoming. Its president is James Flanagan. My heart dropped into my stomach. Why was James buying large quantities of Geyser products?"

"Did you figure it out?"

Michael's gaze moved from me to the well of his wine glass. "Not entirely, but I figured out enough to know that something reprehensible and improper had been going on at Geyser."

"Who's involved?"

"I'm not sure. Preston was certainly at the heart of the mess. I think that James was too. I was curious about what Kelly knew, so before our trip to Jackson, I asked her to dinner. I wanted to ask her in person so that I could see her reaction."

"Why? Did you think that she was involved?"

"No. Not really. But I wanted to make sure." He poured more wine into my glass first, and then into his. He took a slow, long swallow with his eyes closed, as if he were elevating to higher ground. "This is how I remember it."

"Kelly pulled up in her new red Porsche Carrera convertible and parked it in front of the restaurant. She knew that I ate out often after late nights at the office. I've hated eating alone at my house since Bri's death.

"I'd deliberately chosen an out-of-the-way restaurant so that we would not run into anyone that we knew. I wanted to know whether her father, James, was involved with Preston, and whether she knew anything about it. I began by telling her that Geyser had a new client called Rocky Mountain Pharmaceuticals and asked her if she had heard of them. She said that she hadn't. I asked her the name of her dad's company. She told me that it was called Powder River Pharmaceutical. In fact, she pulled out her wallet and found one of his business cards and showed me. I asked her what kind of business Powder River Pharmaceuticals was in, and she said it was a medical supply company. I asked if Geyser could possibly be doing business with her dad's company, and she said that we were in completely different markets. After that, I remember her asking me whether I was looking forward to the conference in Jackson. She said that she couldn't wait to see the mountains and ski in crisp, fresh air.

"The next morning," Michael continued, "I called Richard again and asked him to check on Powder River Pharmaceutical for me. Within a few minutes, the fax machine started churning out paper. Sure enough, James Flanigan was the president. The same address was listed for its principle place of business as Rocky Mountain Pharmaceuticals. So, it was confirmed. James was doing business with Preston. But why? Why would a medical supply company want to purchase sexual dysfunction drugs? At that point, Preston was due back in the office on the following Monday. I had the weekend to figure it out. I wanted to be more up front with Kelly about her father's possible involvement in something fishy, but I feared that she might take it the wrong way or be defensive and overreact. I was fairly certain that she knew nothing about it. But I couldn't be sure. James is her father. Preston was her husband. The next time I tried to log into Preston's computer, the password didn't work. I tried a few possible alternative passwords and they didn't work either. I worried that somebody—maybe Preston—knew I'd been snooping around. It was odd because he was still overseas.

"I went to my lab and logged in. I had always been in charge of Geyser's computer system and had programmed a separate weekly back up of the system from the mainframe. I accessed the back-up files from the previous week. I checked the history from Preston's computer. Preston had been deleting files while working on his laptop in the South Pacific. I started retrieving deleted files from the back up. I spent that Sunday trying to solve the mystery. I was devastated by what I learned."

Chapter 12

The tiramisu that Michael ordered tasted better than it sounded. And the cappuccino brought me back to earth. Good timing. "What did you figure out?" I asked.

"I found several obscure e-mails addressed to NJ@javanet.net from Preston's computer. All the messages to this address had been deleted. I was able to pull them up from archives. That's how I learned that Preston was confirming or arranging shipments for Rocky Mountain Pharmaceutical to locations in Indonesia and Thailand, and then immediately deleting the request," Michael said.

"Do we know who the e-mail address belongs to?"

"I didn't at the time. In fact, I didn't figure it out until you e-mailed me about Nyomi Janger. When researching her file for you, I found her e-mail address. It didn't register before because all Geyser employees have Geyser.com e-mail addresses, except for the employees overseas. I then searched our main database to find out where the e-mails had been received: some were in Bali, some in Bangkok, and some in Singapore. Our Asian connection."

"So, what does it mean? Even if Preston was using James to ship products to Asia and Indonesia, so what? Many companies have middlemen, right? There must be a million ways to distribute."

"I asked myself the same question. Was I being paranoid? Maybe. But it just didn't make sense. I've worked very hard in the med/science community to gain scientific recognition for my research. I know that the products that we have created are good and useful, and that's very important to me. I play by the rules in research and development. I don't cut corners or fudge the numbers so that my studies turn out a certain way, like some drug manufacturers do in order to get

FDA approval. I have earned the right in the scientific community to be considered a pioneer in thermophile product development and manufacturing. I promised my wife that I would do something good for this world. Something fishy was going on. And after looking deeper into the goings-on of my own company, I figured out that I was being taken for a fool. I don't like being deceived."

"I can understand that, but what do you mean? I'm not following you?"

"I told you earlier that the Geyser products had mediocre market share in the U.S., right?"

"Right."

"But we attained extraordinary market share overseas, particularly in parts of Asia and Indonesia. I think I had just figured out why, before I left for Jackson," Michael said. Just as he was about to elaborate, Joey came over and asked us how our dinner was. We commended Joey for his delicious fare. As we were finishing our small talk, Michael's cell phone rang. He looked down at the Caller I.D. window and took the call. "Excuse me," he said as he got up and walked toward the restrooms. I watched him rub his eyes and look at his watch as he nodded into the receiver. He came back over to the table and said, "I need to go. Kelly has locked herself out of her house and I'm the only other person with a key." He motioned for the waiter and handed him his credit card. "I'm sorry to cut this short. May we continue tomorrow?"

"Sure," I said, wondering desperately what he knew, realizing that I would not get any sleep trying to figure it out, especially after the cappuccino. "No problem."

While waiting for my cab, I walked Michael to his car. I noticed a child's car seat in the back of his Ford Taurus.

"Babysitting duties?" I asked, pointing at the car seat. Michael's eyes flashed a look of surprise and then darted sideways nervously. He lumbered back and forth on the edges of his loafers, searching for words.

"Babysitting duties. Right. I took my neighbor's kid home from preschool as a favor. I guess I forgot to take the kid's seats out," he said as he jumped into the driver's seat and started the engine, waving good-bye as an afterthought.

* * * *

When I got back to my hotel room, my intuition was confirmed. There would be no sleeping tonight. It was eating me alive, not knowing what Michael was about to tell me. I wanted to call him at home, but I didn't want to appear to be obsessive. I turned my attention to Kelly's dad, James Flanigan. What could he have wanted from Preston? I thought about it for a while. Money? Did he lose his life savings when he lost his medical license? Possibly. Jealousy? Did he want part of the action? Was his daughter living the life that he secretly wanted—so this was his way to edge his way in the back door? This led me to think about betrayal. Why wouldn't he tell his daughter that he was working with her husband? Wouldn't that be the natural thing to do? If he was hiding it from her, why? There must have been something to hide.

When I'm trying to figure out someone's motive, I look to my crime-solving nine deadly sins: greed, lust, envy, pride, deceit, gluttony, revenge, fear, and anger. Somehow, the motive could always be found among this very potentially ruinous list of human needs and desires, in some way. James Flanigan was involved with Preston Parker for one or more of these reasons, and I needed to know which ones.

This made me think more about the conversation I had with Michael over the tiramisu. Michael had obviously found his self-esteem in the scientific community, and in particular from his research and the good that it could do society. But what made Preston tick? From my sin list, it seemed to me that it could be all of the above. He had all the appearances of being greedy, especially since he was raised in a privileged environment; he obviously had plenty of lust; perhaps he envied Michael's wholesome desire to make the world better; pride in his own success would be a natural to him; deceit seemed obvious—(cross-reference lust); gluttony was apparent in his lifestyle, living in excess; I'd have to think more about revenge—against whom?; and the same with fear—fear of what? Because Preston was not the biggest and richest in his field, like his daddy was?—maybe; anger at whom? Michael—for not bending the rules a little? Kelly? James?

I didn't have all the answers, but the questions helped me think it through. What about Michael? After all, he wasn't exactly a knight in shining armor. He was being accused of murder and there was a hit man out there who claimed that Michael had hired him to kill. What could Michael's motives be? Maybe for envy of Preston's easy way with the world, his many friends, his confidence, his good looks, his wife? Or was it revenge for hurting Kelly or for mismanaging the company?

And Kelly. What was her game? She seemed motivated most by vanity, greed, betrayal and possibly revenge. It would be easy to understand how she might wish her husband dead for cheating on her and fathering children with another woman. But I couldn't see through her yet. Parts of her seemed so likeable and real; yet, parts of her seemed transparent and fake. She was like a caterpillar stuck in her cocoon—part of her was struggling to emerge into a beautiful butterfly, yet the other part was stuck in the ugly, brown, hairy core.

I couldn't understand how Preston could cheat on Kelly to begin with. She was smart, pretty and interesting. I don't understand infidelity.

The phone rang. It was Kelly.

"I'm in the lobby. Can you meet me in the lounge?" she asked. I agreed.

"Did Michael get you back into your house?" I asked Kelly first thing when I met her in the lounge.

"What?"

"Weren't you just locked out of your house?"

"Oh. Right. Yes. Listen, I wasn't completely up front with you about something," she said. I thought that maybe she was going to give me the real skinny about her dad and Preston. I was wrong. "I suspected that Preston was cheating. I hired a private detective to follow him to Thailand and Indonesia on a trip he took a few months ago. They found him with another woman in Bali and sent me a report."

"Why didn't you tell me earlier?"

"Because I'm embarrassed about it."

"Any other reason?" I wondered whether Michael had said anything to her about Nyomi Janger when he rescued her from her lockout.

"No. I just thought you should know."

"Do you know where the lover is, nowadays?"

"No. I have no idea."

"Did you ever confront Preston about the affair?"

"Yes. I confronted him right before we were supposed to leave on our trip to Jackson Hole."

"What did he do? Did he admit or deny it?"

"At first he denied it. Then I showed him the pictures that the detective had given to me."

"What did he do then?"

"He was furious that I had him followed. He accused me of being paranoid and crazy and things like that. It was the worst fight we'd ever had. I locked myself in the bathroom and cried for hours. It was horrible. I went ahead on the scheduled flight to Jackson because I wanted to get away, but he stayed behind and took a later flight on purpose. He couldn't stand to look me in the eye."

"Did you ever tell anyone else about his affair?"

"No. I wasn't sure what to do about it."

"Were you planning on leaving Preston?"

"I don't know. Initially, yes. I wanted to leave and to never come back. I felt humiliated. I just didn't know what to do, to be honest. The thought of a divorce was so humiliating to me. I needed more time to think it over," Kelly said. She raised her hand toward the waiter. He scurried over to take her order.

I wanted to ask her about the children in the photograph with Nyomi and Preston, but I didn't dare. "How much do you know about Preston's mistress?"

"Enough."

"Do you think that your detective agency could find this woman again, so that we can find out where she was the day of Preston's ski accident?"

"I don't know if they can find her. Preston swore that he would have her fired."

"Did he fire her?"

"He said that he would. I don't know whether he did or not. We never had the chance to talk about it again-"

"Do me a favor, Kelly. Let me contact your detective agency tomorrow and see if they can find the other woman. If I contact them, then any information we gather will be protected by the attorney-client privilege, as if I need to tell you that," I said. Of course, I knew who her detective agency was, but I didn't want her to know what I knew, or how I'd found it out.

"I'd rather not divulge that information-"

"You mean the name of the agency?"

"Yes."

"I don't understand."

Kelly held her vodka martini squarely in her palms as she tilted her head back. "No. I wouldn't imagine that you do." Within seconds, she recovered from sarcasm. "I used a man named Bob Avery. He's with Mason & Associates. I'll call him in the morning and let him know to expect your call."

I left her alone in the lounge to down her martini.

* * * *

Trying desperately to go to sleep, I attempted to ignore the conversation with Kelly. Why had she divulged the information about Preston's lover, information that she had been trying so hard to hide just last week?

Stuck with insomnia, I decided to profile the case. The murderer, if murder it was, likely had motive to kill Preston. Maybe greed or anger was at play—or both. Who could have wanted him dead? Michael—check: corporate greed. Kelly—check: life insurance and infidelity. James: check—defrauded or blackmailed by Preston. Nyomi—check: scorned lover. Duane: check—lust and greed.

The murderer also had to have opportunity. Since Preston was possibly killed on the ski slopes, who of the possible suspects skied? Michael—check. Duane—don't know. Kelly—check. James—check. Nyomi—don't know. But the profile had to fit. Preston suffered blunt force trauma to the head while on the ski slope. Of these suspects, which of them could ski and ski well enough to catch Preston on expert terrain and club him with a blunt object, rendering him unconscious? And why? I just couldn't put it together … yet.

Chapter 13

I applied for a passport my senior year in college with the hope that I could afford to go to Europe after graduation. The bad news was that I couldn't go because I couldn't afford it even on "thirty dollars a day" and my mom refused my idea of the trip being a graduation present. The good news was that I still had a valid passport and so I was prepared to board an airplane to Bali. Michael talked Kelly into giving me part of her file on Nyomi Janger (I had to act very surprised by its contents). The picture of Preston with the children was not included in the package. Michael seemed more than happy to put me on a plane to track this woman down. As a matter of fact, he insisted that I go. I was in the room during the speakerphone conversation when Harry protested my trip.

Harry said, "It's completely unnecessary for Mac to travel halfway around the world to track down Preston's alleged lover. It's sending her on a wild goose chase, and quite frankly, her work is piling up here."

"I understand your concern, but I insist that she go. I believe that tracking down Nyomi Janger is essential to my defense."

"I disagree. I think that deposing the pertinent medical staff at the hospital is critical to your defense."

"That may be. But I hired you to defend me my way. I'm calling the shots. It's my life at stake and I believe that this witness is critical to my defense."

"I'm your lawyer, Michael. You may call the shots at Geyser, but if you want to remain my client, you need to listen and heed my legal advice. If this is so damn important to you for Mac to waste precious time finding this gal, then so be it. But she has three days. After three days, I expect to see her big brown eyes at her desk in Jackson working. Do we understand each other?"

"Three days is fine, so long as you don't mind that your associate doesn't get to sleep, except during long airplane rides. It'll take her a full day to travel back and forth-"

"She has three days."

That was the end of the conversation. Michael grumbled for fifteen minutes after they hung up. Obviously, Harry had ruffled his feathers.

I was busy packing my bags in my suite at the Four Seasons when I took a quick break to check my e-mail. Bob Avery had downloaded an updated file on Nyomi Janger and e-mailed it to me as an attachment.

* * * *

Michael had given me a company credit card, traveler's checks and specific details of what he expected to gain from the trip. I flew direct to San Francisco from Boston and connected to Japan. I changed planes there and flew to Singapor, and then into Bali.

In flight, I read an Indonesian Handbook that explained the topography, history, religion, and language of the Balinese people. This proved to be indispensable over the next several days.

Bali was once connected to its neighboring island to the west, Java, but is now separated by a waterway called the Lombok Straight. Bali is flanked by the Indian Ocean to the south and the Java Sea to the north. It is one of the smallest islands of this fifth largest nation in the world, and the third richest in natural resources.

The Balinese people are small and beautiful. The travel book says that they are a mixture of races—an ethnic blend of Polynesians and Melanesians, with a smattering of Chinese and Indian blood. Indonesians are primarily a Hindu culture, which is a direct correlation to the Indian ancestry.

As we descended on final approach, I could see turquoise blue water in every direction, dotted with islands here and there. Each island was framed with a golden perimeter of sandy beaches, giving way to lush green jungles in the nucleus. Bali is one of about three thousand islands in Indonesia. It is volcanic and near the equator, making it a tropical earthquake zone. After five months of Wyoming cold and snow, the thick, humid air would be a welcome change.

When the jet came to a bumpy rest near the terminal, I walked down the steps of the airplane and onto the tarmac. The warm air smelled of jet fuel and the foliage of the banana trees waved at me in a welcoming gesture. I walked into the airport and was immediately greeted by a small group of Balinese people, eager for the tourist trade. A man with a toothy smile offered to carry my bags to the customs area.

I hired a driver to take me around the island. The driver, Batur, put his hands together and bowed as he introduced himself. He then loaded my bags into his tiny Japanese car. Batur was short, maybe five and a half feet tall. He wore a cream-colored linen shirt with matching pants, a brown leather belt and loafers. I held my breath for a few hours while being wheeled around Denpasar in a wild goose-chase, searching for Ms. Janger's address. Denpasar is the largest city in Bali and is very crowded and noisy. The people drive erratically, as if they are trying to escape from the epicenter of its maze. The streets are lined with open markets and crowded with the types of things a tourist would buy: t-shirts, sarongs, wooden masks, and statues of temples. Batur spoke broken but decent English and offered to explain Bali's history.

"Bali has hundreds of Hindu temples. We worship many times a day," he said, "to keep away the ghosts." I got a glimpse of what he meant while being escorted through the city. There were little baskets with flowers and fruit and incense scattered about in front of homes and businesses. "These are offerings to God to keep the devils away," he explained. I decided to buy a few and place them in Harry's office back home. "We are very good sculptors here," the taxi driver said. "Mostly, we carve wood and other things into masks, to keep the spirits at bay." I was starting to wonder about the place. How many evil spirits were lurking? Did they like young lawyers who were looking for scorned lovers? I wasn't so sure. "Balinese are good artists," he continued. I think he liked having someone to practice his English on. "And we are very good dancers," he continued. "Dance is the center of life here. We perform to please our gods." Of course they do, I thought to myself. I asked him about the address we were trying to find and he nearly sideswiped the oncoming traffic looking at my note. I was disoriented anyway.

I noticed that there were many children wandering around without a parent or caretaker in sight—kids, just playing near the street, riding bicycles, roaming about without someone looking over them and warning them of danger. "I see so many kids wandering the streets," I said to Batur.

"Balinese people idolize their children. When they are very young, we carry them everywhere because they are not permitted to touch the impure earth. We have large ceremonies for their first birthday, which is two hundred ten days after birth. After the priest makes offerings, the child is allowed to touch the ground on the next day. Shortly after a child learns to walk, he or she is set free to roam the streets. We encourage children to find their own way so that they are self-reliant early on in life," Batur said. "That is why you will not see children fighting or crying here. If they do, they will not be aided.

"As a teenager, the child is initiated into adulthood through a ceremony. Young girls are put in strict seclusion and their bodies are cleansed. After three days of seclusion, they are adorned with a crown of flowers and a gold brocade and their upper six teeth are filed to form a straight line in order to weaken the six evil traits of human nature: anger, desire, greed, jealousy, intoxication, and irresoluteness," Batur said. I glimpsed into Batur's rear view mirror to see whether my six front teeth were even. They weren't.

After an hour of driving around in circles, Batur finally realized that the address we were searching for was not in the main city of Denpasar, but in a small town further north called Ubud. We took to the highway, which was really just a two-way street with the cars driving on the wrong side at a high rate of speed. I decided to move over to the driver's side of the back seat in case we were side-swiped, which seemed like a natural progression, at this point.

The winding road took us to a slightly higher elevation into Ubud, which is a Balinese word meaning medicine. The name derives from the healing properties of an herb that grows along a nearby river. I felt naturally connected to this place. And it seemed ironic that I was searching for the mistress of the Geyser fortune in a place known for its medicinal herbs that grow so plentifully near the river. Geyser manufactured a natural remedy found in a hot spring. The parallels were frightening, in a way. I felt like it might be time to make an offering to the gods.

"It's beautiful here," I said.

"Ubud is surrounded by three rivers," Batur said.

"What are the crops on the hillside?"

"Rice fields."

"Batur, everywhere I look, I see the word 'Pura.' What is a Pura?"

"Pura is the word for temple. There are hundreds of temples on Bali. In fact, one of the most famous temples on Bali is here in Ubud. At the end of the Monkey Forest Road is Pura Dalem. It has a natural spring which makes it holy and it is inhabited by gray monkeys. It is distinguishable from other temples by its statues of Rangda devouring children."

Now it was all making sense to me. Nyomi Janger lived in Ubud, near the Pura Dalem, where Bob Avery had taken pictures of her with Preston. I was getting close. I could feel the adrenaline pumping. Just as I saw the sign for Monkey Forest Road, Batur slammed on the brakes.

"What's wrong?"

"Balinese funeral."

"What are they doing?"

"It is a procession. We must pull off the road and let them pass."

As far as the eye could see, there were thousands of people in the most glorious, colorful clothing marching in a procession down the street. The men all wore white cloths for caps and sarongs tied at their waists. They held pyramids of baskets loaded with fruits, flowers and rice balls, some of which cascaded up to thirty feet in the air. Some men carried beach-sized umbrellas of radiant colors and decorated with pom-poms and macramé. But it was the women's parade that captured my attention and my camera. The women were dressed in a rainbow array of lace blouses, all tied at the waist with a different color sash. Many wore sarong skirts in variations of plaid, every color and shade imaginable represented in its most brilliant and dazzling form. On the top of every woman's head was an exalting pyramid of apples, mangos and pears, topped with colorful rice cookie balls stacked into a narrowing triangle, all crowned with a spray of lilies spiked with incense sticks. It was worth the hour-long delay to watch this parade of color.

Batur said that it was not permitted to take pictures of this ceremony, but that if I could sneak my camera up and take a quit shot, he would not oppose it. I took him up on his offer.

"Where are they going?"

"To the Puri Saren, which is the main palace in Ubud. They will offer all of this food to the gods in hopes that the gods will accept the deceased into the next life."

"Do the people eat any of the offerings?"

"No. All of this is left for the gods, to appease them."

"So, all of this food goes to waste?" I asked. "What do the people eat?"

Batur was getting annoyed with me, I think. I decided not to press the issue.

Batur took me through the tranquility of the Monkey Forest and toured the Pura Dalem with me. He dipped his hand into the holy spring and touched his forehead and heart with his wet hand. Then he showed me the entrance to the caves. The pictures that Bob Avery took did not do this temple justice, as the intricate carvings of evil spirits in the stone were zoomed out of the macro lens. The tour was enlightening, and seeing where Preston had made his offering to the gods (or whomever) helped formulate a better picture in my mind. But now it was time to find Nyomi Janger. The clock was ticking.

Batur pulled into a market and asked for directions to Nyomi's place. Within minutes, we pulled into a narrow alleyway and he motioned upward. "This is where Nyomi Janger lives," he said. Just like that. I had given him a picture of

Nyomi from her employment file, along with her address. He took it into the market with him and the man working there recognized her. It dawned on me that I hadn't rehearsed what I was going to say to her when I met her. I was so busy being a tourist that I had forgotten that I was there to do a job. I gathered Bob Avery's manila envelope of pictures and the written report, blotted the moisture from my forehead, applied a light coat of lip gloss, and climbed the two flights of stairs to her very modest apartment on the east side of someone else's house.

I knocked on the eggshell-blue painted door. There was no answer. I peered between the slats of the plastic blinds to see if she was there and just avoiding visitors, but I couldn't detect any movement. I did notice a computer system on a desk, along with an all-in-one fax/copier/scanner. The cop in me needed to see what was on her computer, but the lawyer in me was worried about breaking and entering in a foreign country. I looked down to see if Batur was watching, and of course he was. I gave him a cute little wave. I tried the door, but it was locked. I went around to the other side of the house and tried the window. It was slightly ajar. I slipped my fingers through the opening and lifted with all my might. The window slid up and I slid inside. I signaled to Batur with one finger, hoping he would know that this meant that I would be out in a minute, and I quickly looked around.

Nyomi Janger had more electronic equipment in her tiny apartment than we had in our entire office. I don't know what kind of business she was running, but it obviously was running smoothly. On her nightstand there was a picture of her, Preston and what appeared to be Michael, clad in ski gear atop a mountain. The picture must have been taken by one of those professionals standing at the top of a ski lift because it said, "Snowmass, 2001" on it. Snowmass is a ski area in Aspen, Colorado—I have skied there myself many times. So she could ski, too. Snowmass was known for its family atmosphere, and it doesn't have terribly difficult terrain for skiing, but in order to be at the top of the mountain, Nyomi had to be a good enough skier to make her way down. I couldn't be sure if the guy standing next to Preston in the picture was Michael. He had on a red jacket with the collar zipped to his nose and then a navy hat pulled down over his ears. The reflection on his goggles hid his eyes. Was it possible that Michael knew about Preston and Nyomi?

It got better. Next to the skiing picture was a picture of Nyomi with the two children I'd seen in Bob Avery's package.

On the mantel there was a picture of Nyomi accepting her black belt in some martial art. Black belt. Blunt force trauma while skiing. Hmm.

She had a sophisticated wardrobe of silk suits and blouses, despite Bali's informal dress and high humidity. I was just tampering with the idea of booting up her computer when I heard the sound of tires on gravel. I ran past the second bedroom, furnished with a crib and a small bed and crammed with stuffed toys.

I quickly exited her place and bolted down the stairs. Batur was out of his car trying to defend himself in a language I didn't understand. I hid behind some tall lotus plants and tried to see to whom he was speaking, but my view was obstructed by thick vegetation. As I inched closer, I could hear the voice of a woman, but when I peered around the lotus for a look, she didn't look at all like the pictures I had of Nyomi Janger. She was tiny, maybe five feet tall, with long, dark, straight hair, which fell almost to her waist. She had on no make-up and was wearing a Balinese sarong.

My gut instinct was to flee on foot, but I couldn't abandon Batur, so I inched out from the foliage and I put on my air of confidence as I approached the pair.

I didn't speak immediately. She continued to berate Batur. I asked him what she was saying.

"She wants to know who we are and why we are here."

"What did you tell her?"

"I showed her the picture and told her that we were trying to find Nyomi Janger." So much for lying.

"Do you speak English?" I asked. Yes, I am the naïve, arrogant American, assuming that all other humans on earth should be able to speak and understand English. But, I just didn't know what else to say.

"Yes, I speak English," she said.

"Do you know this woman?" I showed her a picture from the employment file. I thought it was premature to show her a picture of Nyomi on her back worshiping at the Pura Dalem.

"No, I don't know her."

"Do you live here?"

"Yes. This is my house. Now please leave, or I will call authorities."

"Do you know where I can find this woman?"

"No. You must go now. I will move my auto so you can leave. Please leave," she said again, this time with more urgency.

She got in her Jeep Grand Cherokee and backed out, and that is when it dawned on me. She drove an American car. Most cars in Bali were a Asian and European imports—small, economical, and affordable. This woman drove an American car. The pictures I had of Nyomi showed her with shorter, dark hair. This woman had long hair, but it looked too perfect. It didn't move when she did. Also, Nyomi looked tall in photos, but then I remembered her with her four-inch stilettos prancing around Preston's back. This woman was wearing flat shoes. Just as the light went on in my head, the accelerator went down in her Jeep She tore out of there as though wolves were pursuing her. I ran to Batur's car and shouted to him to follow her.

Chapter 14

Batur appeared to be enjoying himself. I, on the other hand, feared for my life. We followed Nyomi through Ubud and headed north on a winding road. Luckily, since it was a two-way road, she couldn't pass any cars and we were able to stay on her tail. She raced through a town called Tampaksiring and continued north until we dead-ended in Bali Aga Village. Suddenly, she jumped out of her car, hailed a small motorboat, and escaped across a lake.

"Batur, we need a boat. We can't let her get away," I yelled. So Batur threw a wad of money at an old man without teeth and he shoved us on to his vessel. He told Batur to drive and the old man sat in the back, using a small plastic bowl to bail out excess water. Something about his missing teeth and his urgency to rid our boat of the flooding water made me anxious. I kept motioning to him that I could help, but he kept shaking his head.

When we got to the other side of the lake, Batur yelled that the small town with the dock was called Trunyan. We could see the boat that Nyomi had tied up there. I looked up to witness on old man dressed in a black cape motioning us to come ashore. I was not convinced that delivering ourselves into his hands was a good idea. The caped man smiled and kept motioning, and the old man kept bailing. I wanted to jump ship and swim back to the village.

"Batur, who is this guy?" I asked.

"He is in charge of the town."

"Why is he motioning to us?"

"It's a holy day here. In Bali, we cremate all of our dead once a year. But in Trunyan, they have a taru menyan, which means 'fragrant tree.' The fragrant tree grows in the cemetery outside the village. There is no cremation here. The dead are left for vultures to feast on—the bodies don't smell because of the fragrant tree," Batur said. I looked overhead and noticed the array of vultures circling what must have been the tree. I was not about to get off my sinking vessel to watch decaying corpses devoured by vultures.

"Let's go back," I begged.

"We can't."

"Why not?"

"It would upset the village," Batur said. He tied our boat to the dock and escorted us off the vessel, which at this point was a quarter full of water.

People were dancing all over the place with masks on their faces and the music was loud. I held Batur's hand and he dragged me though the maze of people and palm fronds and bells and offerings. Suddenly, I spotted Nyomi on the other side of the crowd. I dragged Batur behind me and we caught up to her before she saw us coming. I grabbed her arm tightly and said, "Nyomi, I know who you are. I need to talk with you."

She tried to pull away, but I held my own. Like I said, she is short and I am tall. In moments like these, it pays to be an "Amazon," as Harry sometimes says. I grabbed her hair and gave it a tug. Her wig came off and she stared at me in utter defiance.

"Nyomi, Preston is dead." I waited to see her reaction, but she just stared at me like a soldier. "We need your help in finding out who killed him. Did you know that he's dead?" Silence.

"Please cooperate with me." I put my hand on her arm. She jerked away.

With that, I quickly reached into my bag and handed her a subpoena to testify at the trial. I knew that I wouldn't be making any friends with my "offering," but I had to do it before she got away. She looked at me as if I were the cruelest person on earth.

"Look, Nyomi, I know that this must be confusing and horrible, but if you really loved him, you'll cooperate with us in trying to find out who killed him," I pleaded. She seemed to settle down, and, eventually she agreed to come with us back to Bali Aga Village (on her boat). We finally settled in at a local restaurant, and I bought her and Batur both a Coke. I was starving, since I hadn't eaten since the Japan to Singapore jaunt. I ordered grated coconut meat, rice fried with shrimp and spices, and chicken simmered in coconut milk. Batur joined me in the meal. Nyomi did not. I pulled out my tape recorder.

"Did you know that Preston is dead?"

"Yes," Nyomi said. She looked away. Tears formed in her eyes. She wiped them away with the back of her hand. I noticed that she wore a gold ring on her wedding finger.

"How did you find out?"

"I … read it on the Internet." She shifted in her chair. She tucked her shoulder-length bobbed hair back behind her ears.

"We know that you were his mistress," I said. She looked at me with disdain.

"I loved him. I was *not* his mistress. I was his wife." She straightened her back to the chair.

"Preston was already married."

She shrugged her shoulders, as if what I was suggesting meant nothing to her. "Not in his heart."

"But he was married in his heart to you?"

"Yes. He told me that he loved me."

"Is he the father of your two children?" Nyomi flinched. She leaned in closer to me and squinted her eyes to narrow slits.

"How do you know about the children?"

"Whose are they?" I pressed. Nyomi looked away suddenly.

"I won't discuss the children," she said, hissing her words like a coiled snake.

"Did Preston tell you that he was going to leave his wife for you?" She looked right through me, as if I were a shadow.

"You are very bold, you know? Preston said that it was over between them. He said that I was the woman he loved." Nyomi smoothed her blouse, revealing her bust line. Batur took notice.

"Did he say that he was leaving Kelly for you-"

"I don't remember, exactly. He said that it is complicated in America. He said that we must wait-"

"Did he say he was getting a divorce?"

"He said it would take time-"

"Where were you the day and night of January eighteenth?"

"I was here in Bali." Her answer was quick.

"Do you have any witnesses who can verify that?"

"Maybe yes, maybe no. I keep to myself."

"Don't you have family here?"

Nyomi bit her lower lip before answering. "I refuse to discuss my family."

"Have you left Bali in the last three months?"

"Yes. I leave Bali frequently. I travel to Singapore, Thailand and Japan regularly. I have clients all over."

"I suppose that the Indonesian Customs Department would have an accurate record of your comings and goings."

"I suppose that they would." She crossed her long, thin arms across her chest.

"I've heard that it is a crime in Indonesia to commit adultery," I said. I don't know if this is true, but I thought I could use it for leverage if she wasn't the wiser. "Perhaps we should meet with the authorities and explain this," I said as I handed her the pictures that Bob Avery had snapped. "Perhaps I could talk the local government into letting me escort you back to America to testify at Mr. Parker's murder trial."

"You can't intimidate me. I am Balinese. They will protect me from you."

"I'm not so sure. You may be Balinese, but up until recently, you were employed by Americans, supplied by Americans and paid by Americans. You may not find a sympathetic ear in the Balinese government. You would be wise to voluntarily make a written statement to me now and to agree to enter into my custody until after the trial."

"And what if I don't?" Nyomi stared at me with her magnificent oval eyes. Her red lips trembled as she spoke, yet her fists remained clenched tight.

"Why don't you want to help Preston? If you love him like you say you do, then why not cooperate?"

"You don't understand."

"Try me. If you explain it to me, maybe I will be able to understand. Maybe I can even help you."

"No one can help me."

"What happened to you that's made you feel this way?" I reached over to touch her hand, but she quickly pulled it away.

"I can't tell you. It's too dangerous and awful. You don't know what you're getting yourself involved in." Tears formed in Nyomi's eyes. She batted her eyelids quickly to flush away the wetness.

"Did Preston fire you?"

"Preston? Of course not."

"Are you still employed by Geyser, Inc.?"

"Employed by? Is that what you think? You think that I worked for Geyser?"

"Yes. Michael O'Connor gave me a Geyser employment file on you. Didn't you work for Geyser?"

"Excuse me," she said, "I need to use the toilet." She got up and walked to the bathroom. Batur and I ate and waited a few minutes.

"She has been in there a long time," Batur said. He must have been thinking what I was thinking at the exact same time because as I went in after her, he dropped some money on the table and ran out. She was nowhere in sight. The bathroom window was ajar, and her Jeep was gone. I hung my head out the window as far as I could and I saw her taillights illuminate around the sharp curve of the volcano that hovered over the village.

"Let's go," Batur said. He was already in the car. I ran out the door and jumped in the front seat. He sped away, leaving a dust cloud behind us.

Chapter 15

Nyomi was no stranger to speed. I held my breath as Batur skidded from the soft earth onto pavement. She was also no stranger to this island. She took each turn of the curvy mountain road at a perfectly negotiated high rate of speed. Banana trees lined the highway, making it impossible to see ahead of each turn. Batur, undaunted by the speed at which we were traveling, kept talking like a tour guide.

"Once we go over the top of this hill, we will be in Jatiluwih. You will have a view of the South Bali coast. Jatiluwih means 'truly marvelous.' Once we start down the mountain, we enter the darkest and most mysterious regions of my island. We call it Taman Nasional Barat. This is where the ghosts of Pulaki live. The last tiger on Bali lives in these forests, but no one has seen him for years. We think he is deep in hiding beyond the lotus ponds." Batur motioned with his head to the right side of the road. He kept both hands on the wheel. I looked to the right. The huge lotus plants covered the ground. Beyond the lotus, thick ferns and draping vines covered the earth.

We swerved right and left, following Nyomi's Jeep down a jungle bordered road. I could see a small village ahead. Before I could ask, Batur started up again. "We are entering Mengwi. This village is powerful. It began with the Gelgel Dynasty. See that temple in the middle of the pond over there?" I nodded. "It is called 'taman,' meaning 'garden with pond.' The three shrines represent earth spirits, humans and the gods."

Nyomi's Jeep came to a stop in the village, but then peeled back onto the road. Batur zipped forward, missing a few gears in his little white car. We skidded sideways briefly, and then closed the gap between our car and hers. She took a quick left turn into another tiny village. "This is Kapal. We believe that our oldest temple was built here. It was destroyed by earthquake, but rebuilt. The gods of this temple are very important. If you visit the temple, you will see the statue of the nine gods and seven saints. The lords of the eight directions are surrounded by fifty-four stone seats, representing the wives and concubines of the king."

"You know a lot about your temples," I said, trying to make small talk amidst my nervousness in the car. Batur nodded and grinned.

"It is my livelihood to know. But it is our culture to know. This island is our home. Few natives leave. It is necessary for my generation and our children to understand the history of every temple."

In the thick foliage of the jungle, the air was heavy. I rolled down my window. The humidity was overwhelming, but the breeze was refreshing. "It's cooling off," I said.

"We are getting closer to the sea. It seems that your Miss Nyomi is driving toward Tanah Lot."

"Another temple?"

"Yes, Miss Mac. Tanah Lot is a very unusual temple though."

"How so?"

My question was answered within a minute. We skidded to a stop at a parking lot. I watched as Nyomi raced from her Jeep toward the beach. "Tanah Lot?" He nodded. In the middle of a cove, on an island stood the pyramid stones of another temple. Nyomi charged down the hillside and across a stone bridge to the temple perched on a colossal rock about one hundred feet offshore. The Tanah Lot temple has isolated black towers cascading over cliffs. I grabbed Batur's binoculars to track her movements. I could see one of the shrines. It had two striped sacred serpents on it.

"Why would she come here? She's trapped in an island temple, with nowhere to go." I started walking toward the rocks when Batur grabbed my arm.

"Miss Mac, you cannot go to the temple. It is sacred to the Balinese. Only worshipers are allowed into the temple. See those two men standing there?" I moved the binoculars to the left. I spotted two men standing at the foot of the temple.

"Yes."

"They guard the temple. The will not let you pass. The sign says that tourists may not enter."

"But you can go, can't you?" He paused, and looked at me. Up until this moment, I had thought that Batur had been enjoying the excitement. Now that I had put him on the spot, he seemed less excited to be part of the team.

"Yes, I can go in, but I wouldn't know what to say-"
"Tell her that I am a patient woman and that I will wait for her in this spot until the end of time. Tell her that I will call the authorities and have her taken to jail. Tell her that this is her last chance to surrender." I ran out of things to threaten her with. I was desperate and Batur knew it.

"I will do my best, Miss Mac," he said as bowed in my direction and then turned and walked across the rocks that were slowly being engulfed by the rising tide.

* * * *

Patience was not my strong suit and it seemed like hours had passed waiting for Batur to come back from the island temple. My legs ached from pacing the rocky cliff and my throat was dry. There was a drinking fountain on the outskirts of the parking lot, but women and children were using it to cleanse themselves. The day was coming to an end and the sun was letting gravity take hold. I finally sat and watched the sun rest, thinking about Nyomi's place in Preston's murder trial. Was it necessary that she be present? Maybe it was better that she wasn't. Pictures speak volumes.

Batur emerged solo from the temple about an hour later. "I tried everything, Miss Mac, but she refuses to leave. She said that she would rather die here than be dragged to America. I'm sorry that I couldn't be of more use."

"You did your best, Batur. Thank you."

We drove back to Denpasar that evening in silence. Batur dropped me at a reputable hotel. He promised to pick me up in the early morning so that I could visit "the best temple in Bali" before I departed.

* * * *

Batur was as punctual as the sunrise. He whisked me to one last temple before dropping me at the airport. I said good-bye to him, with a heavy heart. He had been more than a gracious tour guide. I gave him a hefty tip. He bowed, still wearing his white cotton slacks and shirt, and carried my bags to the counter. He waved as he left.

I thought about Nyomi and how she fit into this puzzle. My guess was that she was in love with Preston and apparently really believed that he was going to leave Kelly to be with her. Without notice, just two weeks before his death, Preston had her fired from her job. Or at least that's what the Geyser personnel records showed. Nyomi denied that Preston fired her. Did he break up with her? Did he tell her that he had to fire her for appearance's sake, but that he loved her and would be back for her? Did he tell her that it was over and that he couldn't see her anymore, causing her to lose control of herself? Did she get even? She knew how to ski and she was a seasoned traveler. Maybe she showed up in Jackson, planning on confronting Preston in front of Kelly, and instead, furious at seeing them together, used her black belt skills on him. She was feisty and determined, for sure. Maybe Preston isn't the father of her children. She never answered that question. I seemed to be returning to the States with more questions than answers.

But somehow, I knew that I hadn't seen the last of her.

Chapter 16

I arrived back in Boston around noon. My body clock was ticking midnight, exhausted from jet lag, but I needed to touch base with Harry. I found him at the office. He seemed moderately entertained by my tale of Preston's lover shipwrecked on the deserted temple island, but he told me that I needed to fly back to Wyoming within the next two days. He was overwhelmed by the case and the amount of time that it was consuming.

"It is probably good for us that she isn't available at trial. We can have Kelly testify about hiring Bob Avery, and we'll put Avery on the stand to identify her. Avery can tell the jury about the photographs and the jurists can decide for themselves what it all means. She won't be there to defend herself, and it will be one more element of reasonable doubt. But it is good that you served her with the subpoena. That way, if she does surface in this country at some point, we can either force her to the stand or she will be held in contempt," Harry said. "Witnesses like that need to be controlled carefully."

"What's going on with Bain? Any clue as to plea bargains or strategy on his end?"

"No plea. He's hell-bent on Duane Towns as the hit man hired by Michael and he has set the depositions of the treating doctors and the forensic toxicologist. Also, he says that he got a signed declaration from Steven Taylor, one of Geyser's accountants, stating that Michael withdrew twenty thousand dollars from one of his accounts right before he left for the Jackson convention. That is the same amount of money that Duane Towns once said that Michael jokingly offered to pay him to kill Preston. Bain is pressing ahead. He thinks he can prove it was no joke. Ask Michael about the money. We should warn Michael how bad this looks. This case looks like it's heading for trial and it's going to be expensive. We'll need to up the retainer."

I hate asking clients for money. When I was a young lawyer, Harry never made me beg for retainers. Now that I have client contact, he makes me do the dirty work. He tells me that it's good practice—so that I can run my own firm someday.

"I plan on calling Michael in a few minutes. I need to meet with him before I fly back home. I would also like to meet with his Chief Financial Officer, Dan Silverberg, if he's available. Should I be connecting with Steven Taylor also?"

"Absolutely. But not in the same meeting as Dan Silverberg. Meet with Michael, Dan and Steven separately, if possible. That way, we can compare stories. Before you call Michael, call Jane. She's been worried sick about you."

"I will. Have you been able to track down Kelly's father?"

"Yes and no. I have spoken with him on the phone and he seemed cooperative, but he says that he can't meet with me in person in Jackson, because he has other business commitments at the moment. So I went ahead and had him served with a deposition subpoena. That oughta get him focused. I'm going to call him tomorrow and arrange for our meeting."

"What do you suggest I tell Kelly about my meeting with Nyomi Janger?"

"As little as possible. I think we need to sit on this information as long as we can," Harry said. "I need to run. I have a sentencing hearing in an hour. And after that, I'm taking Jane out for dinner for her sorority chapter annual deal." I pictured Harry at the club having dinner with Jackson society: Oxford navy blazer, gray flannel pants, silk tie, Gucci loafers. He'd bring with him an expensive bottle of wine and then go out of his way educating anyone who'd listen about the wine's origin. He'd order prime rib and green beans, skipping the mashed potatoes.

As he hung up, I thought over his suggestion about Nyomi. I had mixed feelings about it. Part of me would have loved to see her reaction, but Kelly had been cooperative up to this point, and I didn't want to embarrass her. Instead, I e-mailed Michael, filled him in on the trip, and asked that he make time to meet with me soon. I enjoyed a short catnap and a brisk walk, trying to fend off my jet lag. While walking, I saw a woman and a man jogging together in the Public Garden. The woman looked exactly like Kelly. But she had told me when we were at the gym that she doesn't run anymore. In fact, she'd said that she hates running, and only does Pilates or yoga for exercise. As they got closer, I realized that it was Kelly! As the guy she was jogging with looked in my direction, I recognized Michael behind the sunglasses and baseball cap. He might have seen me because he immediately looked in the other direction and said something to Kelly. They swiftly took a path in a different direction.

I took a different route also and headed back for my suite. I logged in to my e-mail. A few messages were awaiting me. One was from Michael.

> "Good to learn that you are back safely. I'm swamped today with staff meetings, etc. Dinner OK? Michael"

I looked at the time the message was sent: 11:00 a.m. EST. Swamped with staff meetings or swamped with jogging dates? I e-mailed back, suggesting an elegant restaurant nearby called Ambrosia that the concierge recommended. But as the day wore on, Michael e-mailed back, begging to pick up Chinese and meet me in the suite. Jet lag was creeping back, so I was happy to stay in my sweats and eat with chopsticks.

*   *   *   *

When Michael arrived, I filled him in about my encounter with Nyomi Janger. He listened more intently than I'd ever seen.

"How was she?" he asked. I was somewhat taken aback by his question. Why would Michael care how she was? A few days ago he hinted that he didn't even know who she was. But what about the Aspen skiing picture? Did he know her?

"Aside from the fact that she was trying to run away from me, she was fine," I snapped, my mood suddenly changing. I took one long look at him and fired my next question. "Why didn't you tell me that you know her?"

Michael nervously started tapping his loafer on the area rug. After a moment, he stood and walked over to the window, running his fingers through his wavy hair. I heard his exhale.

"I didn't want her involved."

"You're protecting her?"

"I'm not protecting her. I'm just trying to stay focused on what's relevant. What's important," he said, rapping his fingers one at a time, from pinky to index, on the window seal.

"But you're the one who *insisted* that I go to Bali."

"Yes. I thought it might be helpful if you understood …"

"Understood what?"

"Nevermind. Let's talk about what's relevant to my defense."

"I'm your lawyer. Why don't you let me worry about what's relevant and what's not? You need to be candid if you want to spend the remainder of your days outside the four walls of prison."

"Listen, my back's against the wall here. I'm doing the best that I can. I'm trying to run a business without my partner, calm Kelly's nerves every other minute, and pacify my employees. They think the company's going belly-up any minute because of this whole mess. Our stock is tanking. I'm not around enough to command the lab. Preston's gone. Our marketing team is bailing. You just don't understand. It's bad enough that I'm standing trial for murder, but I'm also running a huge company. The pressure is intense. So don't lecture me on prison. It would be a blessing at this point in my life!"

"Look, I'm sorry. You're right. I'm looking at this from my perspective only. I need to think about your perspective too. It's just that the heat is on and we're getting down to the nitty-gritty. Harry feels tremendous pressure from Bain's office. Bain's not letting up or giving any indication of a good plea deal. The cards seemed to be stacked against you and at every turn, we keep uncovering more damaging evidence."

"You and Harry need to stop focusing on a plea deal. I'm not dealing. We're going to trial and I'm going to be acquitted," Michael said with undisputable confidence.

I felt like telling him that his arrogance was going to get him convicted, but I decided to bite my tongue. "But you told Harry to see what kind of deal Bain would offer."

"That's what I said when I was arraigned. I was upset and overwhelmed. Since then, they haven't come up with any evidence that seems devastating to me. I've changed the game plan. We're going for the acquittal."

"Then we need to let Harry know right away. Bain will sense that Harry's defense is a weak one if he keeps begging for an offer. If you want a trial, then we need to change gears."

"Then change them."

So I did. I gave Michael a brief update regarding Duane Towns and James Flanigan. I told him how Duane was claiming that Michael had hired him to be a hit man, but that when Harry had questioned Duane about it in jail, Duane had retracted the story. I also told Michael about how Duane's apartment had been covered with Kelly's pictures and about his request to meet with a lawyer. I then asked him about Steven Taylor, Geyser's accountant, and the withdrawal of twenty thousand dollars before the convention.

"I withdrew that money at Preston's request," Michael said, his brows furrowed. "He always took large amounts of money to conventions to *reward* certain suppliers and sales representatives. It wasn't my idea, and I've never liked it, but that's what he did. He had asked me to pick up the money from Steven because he wasn't going to be able to get back to the office in time to pick it up."

"Isn't it too much of a coincidence that Duane Towns had told Bain during his first interrogation that you offered to pay him twenty thousand dollars to kill Preston?"

"It may seem like more than a coincidence, but that's how much money Preston told me to get. I never said anything to Duane Towns about anything."

"How would Duane know about the money?"

"First of all, Duane Towns has been my friend since I was a kid. I don't know what he is saying, but I did not hire him to do anything. Ever. I did try to call him when I was in Jackson, but only to say hello. I've always done that. Every now and then when I've been visiting my mom, I've even taken Duane out for a beer. He's not the brightest light in the world, but he was my neighbor growing up. I've always felt bad for him. His parents weren't very nice to him. Second, I'm glad that you found Nyomi, but I don't think that it matters much whether she is here or there or anywhere. She exists, and that is good enough. Where I think we should be spending our time and my money is on James Flanigan. I have been knee-deep in this business for a long time, and I don't understand why he is involved with us and why I didn't know about it. This is the red-flag, as far as I'm concerned," Michael said while walking back over to the couch. He sat back down, putting his elbows on his knees, then clasping his hands together tightly, forming white blotches around his knuckles while flushing the tips of his fingers with excess blood.

"Harry has served James Flanigan with a deposition subpoena and expects to meet with him soon."

"Good."

"When I mentioned the fact that James was in business with Preston to Kelly, she got visibly defensive. She denied any knowledge of a business relationship between her husband and her father. Does this sound normal to you?"

"Nothing sounds normal to me anymore, but it is possible that Kelly knows nothing about it. She seemed clueless when I asked her about it at the restaurant before we went to Jackson."

"Why did you ask her about it? Would she tell you the truth?"

"Yes. She'd tell me the truth. Why? Did she say something that makes you think that she's not telling me the truth?"

"No."

"Then why did you ask?"

"Why did you?"

"I was trying to figure out what she knew. Remember, Preston was acting very weird and secretive. When I found out about James, I wanted to know if Kelly was involved. If she was, it would have changed everything."

"What do you mean by that?"

"Nevermind."

"No, really. What did you just mean by that statement? It would have changed everything?"

Michael leaned toward me. "I said, nevermind. Why were you asking her the same question?"

"It's my job. I'm trying to make the connection between James Flanigan and Preston. You're convinced that we should be focusing on their relationship. I'm trying to figure out why."

"I'm not sure it matters," Michael said.

I was confused by his suggestion, and decided to press ahead. "Since Harry has a handle on James, let's focus on you and Preston. Before we were interrupted at the Italian restaurant, you were telling me that you suspected that something was wrong so you went snooping in Preston's files. What happened between the two of you after that?"

"When Preston was still in Asia on his last trip, Carol must have told him that I had asked questions about the Rocky Mountain Pharmaceutical client because within twenty-four hours, his password to his computer was changed, even before he got back. When he did get back, he called me into his office immediately.

"When I walked in and closed the door, Preston quickly toggled from his stock market screen to his client summary screen and told me to have a seat. I told him that I preferred to stand. He didn't beat around the bush long before he asked me what I was doing hacking into his computer. I explained that I was trying to figure out who Rocky Mountain Pharmaceutical was. Preston sat back, kicked his loafers up on his desk and folded his hands together, allowing his index fingers to form a steeple. This was his signal to me to continue explaining. Preston was like that. Certain signs had definite meaning. He was indicating to me that he still had patience to listen. So I told him about my conversation with Carol and my concern that there wasn't a master file on RMP. At that point, I stopped talking and waited for an explanation. I didn't get one.

"Preston told me I had it all wrong. Then, he said that I was imagining things and that my depression, coupled with paranoia, had pushed me over the edge. He told me that I was jealous of him because of his business savvy and his wife, suggesting that I had neither, and then he said that I'd better trust him because he was all that I had." I noticed that Michael's right eye had started to twitch.

"Did you push him for more information about RMP?"

"No. I was so flustered by our conversation that I walked out."

"Carol said that you stormed out."

"Stormed out. Walked out. What difference does it make?"

"What did you do after that?"

"I gathered some documents from my lab and I left the office. I needed to make some phone calls, but I didn't trust Preston. I thought he might have tapped the phone or my office or something, so I went to a local coffee shop and used the public phone there."

"Who did you call?"

"First, I called Dan Silverberg, our Chief Financial Officer. He picked up the line, but when I told him that it was me, he told me that he was in a meeting and that he would have to get back to me. I figured that Preston was in his office and he couldn't talk," Michael said. I noticed that Michael's right eye kept twitching. He rubbed it.

"Go on."

"So then, I called our outside CPA firm and asked to speak with the one of the guys who does our independent audit. When he picked up the phone, it dawned on me for the first time that I really didn't know what to ask him. I didn't have any hard facts, and other than knowing about RMP and Powder River Pharmaceutical, I didn't have much to go on. I didn't want to sound dumb or tip him off to a problem, so I suggested that we meet for lunch the following day. He agreed." Michael said. Not only was his eye still twitching, but now his left leg was shaking erratically, as well.

There was a knock on the suite door. Michael jumped up. "I'll get it."

Chapter 17

I had noticed that he didn't show up with the Chinese, and my stomach had started to make growling noises. I was pleased to see a delivery service at the door handing over a paper sack with a juicy stain on the bottom and the aroma of soy sauce and ginger escaping from the top. Michael paid the deliveryman and set out dinner on the coffee table. He opened the steamed rice, cashew chicken, sweet and sour pork and Hunan vegetables. We served ourselves heaping mounds of food and continued the conversation where we'd left off.

"Did you meet with the CPA the next day?"

"Yes. But I went back to the office first and pulled out our quarterly earnings reports over the past three quarters and our annual report. I analyzed our profit and loss statement and our most recent quarterly operating expenses. I pulled up our stock report from the Dow Jones Industrials and recalled that we had earnings per share of twenty-six cents, up forty-seven percent from the previous year's reports. I crunched the numbers from output and inventory until about three a.m. The numbers just didn't add up. In the U.S. market, there was a substantial lack of revenue growth. This didn't make sense against the increase in earnings per share. So when I met with our independent auditor, I had something tangible to discuss."

"What did the auditor say?"

"When I brought the discrepancy to his attention, he acted almost bored. He told me that there wasn't a problem, just a lag time in foreign bookings. I obviously wasn't making shocking headlines with this guy, so I decided to let it rest." Michael took a bite of the sweet and sour pork, and then put down his chopsticks.

"What did you do next?"

"When I got back to the office, I pulled up our accounts receivable and compared it to our operating capital. Cash flow from operations stateside was seriously down and didn't justify our continued growth."

"How do you know so much about accounting?" I was surprised by his business knowledge. Most doctors don't have much, and most scientists have even less.

"Preston indoctrinated me early on in the business of the business. I'm a workaholic by nature, but my drive just isn't about money. I've always been motivated by the interests of the scientific and medical community. Preston commended me for my nobility, but warned me early on that I needed to understand commerce in order to compete. He lectured me constantly on market share and public offerings, cash flow and productivity. I'm a good student. I read money magazines and *The Wall Street Journal*. I'm not a Harvard Business School grad like Preston, but I can analyze a balance sheet."

"Did you figure out what was going on to cause the discrepancy?"

"Not at first. Like I said, I'm not an expert in accounting. But I thought long and hard about what our auditor offered as an explanation. He said that we had a 'lag time in foreign bookings.' I took this to mean that the Asian market had placed orders that had not yet been put on the books. But the more I thought about this, the less it made sense. There was no reason why a foreign commitment should take more time to book than a domestic one. The fact that he suggested such a notion made me dig deeper.

"After going through our price point analysis with our domestic consumers, I realized that there was a discrepancy in what our domestic market was paying for the Geyser drugs versus what the foreign market paid."

"You mean that you charged the Asian market more for the drug?" I asked.

"No. The opposite," Michael said. "Preston knew that we had cash flow problems. He wanted to continue to develop the company, but there was a lag time in the U.S. by sometimes six to nine months to get paid for foreign-based shipments. Our accounts receivable was killing us, and stunting our growth. We needed to motivate the infusion of cash because a company can only grow to the extent that it has viable operating capital. We couldn't hedge our operating capital problems. Our earnings per share were dropping based on a shortfall in revenues. Basically, we needed money fast, and Preston decided to get the money the wrong way."

As he continued to explain the complex market analysis, much of which was over my head, I decided to explore the mini bar to see what was there for the asking. I'd finished my dinner. It was great, but very spicy. I needed something sweet. I had used utmost self-control with the mini bar up to this point, but this confusing conversation made me yearn for a glass of wine and some chocolate. I put my card key into the mini bar and a green light blinked. Access allowed. I then grabbed the mini-bottle of white wine and heard the clacking sound of a calculator—the front desk had just been notified of my selection. I also grabbed a Snickers Bar. Click. I sat back down, opened the bottle, poured us each a glass and cut the candy bar in two. Michael accepted both offerings willingly.

"How did you know that Snickers are my favorite?" he asked.

"You just look like a Snickers guy to me," I lied. He actually looked more like a Hershey's guy to me, but I didn't want to get off the subject.

"Did you figure out what was happening?"

"I wasn't sure at first. I knew that I was begging for trouble if I involved the auditors again. And I hadn't had much help from our CFO, so I decided to talk with Pres about it," Michael said.

"We got into our first discussion about this on a Monday. I met with the auditor on Wednesday. I did more research on Thursday and figured it out. Preston was accepting cash from foreign sales of the products for a discount in price. He had solved his cash-flow problem by breaking the law. I asked Preston to meet with me Friday morning, and we were scheduled to leave early Friday afternoon to go to Jackson Hole for our convention."

"What happened?"

"When I walked into Preston's office Friday morning, Dan Silverberg was there too. I was very surprised to see him. I immediately told Preston that I thought that we should speak in private, but Preston insisted that Silverberg stay. I was guarded at first—afraid to talk openly in front of Silverberg. But it soon became apparent to me that Silverberg knew what was going on. I wanted to know why he was risking the company's reputation and how we could fix it before we got into trouble. When I told them what I knew and started asking questions about what didn't make sense, Preston called the meeting short."

"What do you mean?"

"Well, he must have arranged for some cue from Carol, because just when we were starting to discuss the meat and bones of it all, Carol buzzed in on the intercom and told Preston that he had an urgent call on the line. Dan immediately sprung to his feet and excused himself. I felt obliged to follow suit, although after giving it some thought, it dawned on me that it was rather staged."

"So you think that Preston deliberately had Dan at the meeting and had pre-arranged with Carol to beep him so he could bail if it was getting too hot?"

"Exactly," Michael said.

"How would Carol know when to beep Preston?"

"Who knows? Maybe he pressed his intercom to her. I don't know, but I'm sure that it happened that way."

"Why would Preston play such tricks on you?"

"Because he knew he was in a whirlpool that was sucking him under, and manipulation was his only salvation," Michael said. "He knew that if I could figure out what he had been doing, then the IRS or the SEC could as easily find the paper trail and that both his and Silverberg's careers would be tanked."

"You must have been very upset with him," I suggested. Michael's face flushed a deeper shade of crimson.

"Of course I was upset with him, but I didn't kill him, if that's what you're suggesting," he snarled.

"How was your run today with Kelly?"

Chapter 18

"What are you suggesting?" Michael asked.

"I'm not *suggesting* anything." I don't like to have an antagonistic relationship with my client, but it seemed to me that Michael was playing games with me. I felt like he was telling me half-truths. "I saw you jogging in the Public Garden with Kelly today."

"I need coffee," Michael said, probably to change the subject. He picked up the phone and ordered one decaf cappuccino and one regular latte. He reclined on the cream-colored chenille sofa and propped the pillows comfortably under his head. His loafers had been long discarded. He closed his eyes and rubbed his temples. I felt like I had overworked him and that I should excuse him for the day, but I had a plane to catch the next afternoon and I needed to figure this out before I returned to my obsessive boss. Harry likes to get to the point. Long, elaborate tales confuse him and cause him undue anxiety. He rants and raves around the office about "KISS." When I first started working there, I thought he was referring to the nineteen seventies rock band. One day Harry explained what it meant. "Keep It Simple. Stupid." Harry lives by the acronym: He wants everything to be made simple for him. Nothing is simple to me. And complexities fascinate me, always have and always will.

"What happened next?" I asked Michael. He was about to answer when there was another knock at the door. Room service delivered our coffee. "What happened next is that I couldn't reach Preston for the life of me. Our flight was scheduled to leave at two o'clock p.m. and I tried him at the office and on his cell, but no answer. I felt like we needed to resolve the situation before leaving for a week-long conference in Jackson," Michael said.

"Did you resolve it?" I asked.

"Not exactly. I took a taxi to Logan and checked my skis and luggage curbside and waited at the gate to board our flight to Denver. Kelly and Preston were to meet me at the gate. Kelly arrived on time, setting her stylish carry on luggage at her feet and taking the seat next to me. I glanced around to see if Preston was tailing at a distance, but he was nowhere in sight. I asked Kelly where Preston was, and she told me that he'd had a change of plans and was taking a later flight. I must have given her a curious look because she immediately reassured me that he was coming. I remember feeling suspicious and paranoid and uneasy, all at the same time. I figured that he was pulling a fast one on me.

"The conference in Jackson was an important one. We were meeting with decision-making officers at the conference and Preston was the key contact with most of the players. He needed to be there. And given the circumstances, I wanted to know where he was and what he was doing at all times. I wanted to see who he interacted with and how. I knew that he was up to something and it was up to me to figure it out. I knew that if I hung on Preston that I'd figure it out," Michael said. "I thought that he was either going to try to make fast deals with our American suppliers, or he was going to do some fast talking with our foreign sales representatives to cover his butt. Since the paper trail was so obvious, I knew he had his work cut out for him. The conference was the perfect place for him to play catch-up and to cover his tracks."

"Could it be that Preston deliberately postponed his fight to throw you off? Could he also have had some last-minute arrangements to make?" I asked Michael. I wondered to myself whether the cat was chasing the mouse or whether the mouse was chasing the cat?

"Is it possible? Sure. I don't know what he was up to at that point. I think he was playing games with me. He did that sometimes."

"What happened with Kelly on the flight?" I asked. "Did she seem upset that Preston wasn't with you?"

"She seemed agitated about something, but she told me that she didn't want to discuss it. Kelly's like that. If she doesn't want to talk, she's not going to. If I try to get her to talk to me when she's not in the mood, she gets upset. Anyway, she was busy working on something, and so was I. We didn't talk much at all," Michael said. He took a sip of his coffee and set it down on the table. "She mentioned that she'd had a really bad week, but that's as far as she would elaborate."

"When did Preston arrive in Jackson?"

"He arrived later that evening, I guess. I really don't know about that. All I know is that he was at the opening session of the conference on time the next morning."

"Did you talk with him in the morning, then?"

"Yes and no. Remember I told you about the foreign market problem? Preston was selling the Geyser drugs to the foreign markets for about half of what he was selling them domestically. Basically, he was discounting the product in exchange for a cash infusion. The foreign market paid us immediately for the product in cash, at a discount. This way, Preston was able to make up for our operating capital woes."

"Is it wrong to do that?"

"Yes. It's called breach of contract. We had contracts with our domestic distribution network to sell the Geyser products at a specific price so that we weren't undercutting any competitors. This is normal in our economy. Our contracts also provide that we sell the products to the foreign market at the same price that we sell to the domestic market. That way, foreign economies like Mexico can't get hold of our products at a discount and then re-sell them in America, thereby undercutting the market. If our domestic buyers had discovered that Preston was using an American company to redistribute the Geyser products to the Asian market at discounted prices, our ship would be as good as sunk."

"So, Preston was selling boat-loads of Geyser for fifty cents on the dollar to Asia, and in return, the Asian drug companies were paying Geyser cash immediately?"

"Exactly. This solved our immediate cash-flow crisis, but it made for accounting and domestic relation nightmares."

"Did you ever confront Preston about this?"

"Yes. While skiing, right before his accident."

"Maybe we should back up a bit. Tell me what happened the day the conference started."

"Saturday morning, the conference started with a breakfast meeting. Preston did his best to stay on the move. I noticed a lot of backslapping and whispering, and I noticed that Preston's cell phone rang all day," Michael said. "I stuck as close to Preston as I could, so that I could monitor the kinds of deals he might be trying to set up. I remember Preston saying to me: 'I feel like I've brought my puppy-dog' as I followed him into the bathroom during a break," Michael said. "I was trying to eavesdrop on all of his conversations, to figure out which companies he had cut deals with."

"Why couldn't you just be part of the conversation? You were one of the founding partners of the company."

"Because Preston liked to keep me at an arms-length distance."

"That seems odd to me." Michael rolled his eyes.

"That's just the way he was. Anyway, Preston asked me if we were going to get some skiing in, and I told him that we were set up to ski the following day with my mom. Then, he introduced me to some prospective customers. I remember that Preston continued to talk business and appeared to be more relaxed as the day progressed. He even seemed to want me around, which seemed odd since he had tried to evade me all morning. I could never figure Preston out. The rules Preston played by were always changing. It was like he had accomplished whatever it was that he needed to accomplish, and it was then okay for me to be around."

"What happened the next day?"

"As you well know, Jackson Hole isn't known for its good skiing weather in January. On that particular day, it was crisp and cold, as usual. The four of us, meaning my mom, Kelly, Preston and I, took the aerial tram to the top and took some warm-up runs. After a few of those, Kelly suggested that we ski more advanced terrain. I agreed, but when I told them that I wanted to do Granite Canyon, Kelly and my mom bowed out. I said I would meet them for lunch. Preston insisted on going with me. I told him that I was planning on doing some extreme skiing that I thought might be too advanced for him. But Kelly encouraged Preston to join me, so what could I say? I knew that he could always tree it back to the groomed slopes if he felt he was in over his head. The four of us agreed to meet at the Mangy Moose for lunch and we separated.

"Preston and I made our way over to Granite Canyon and traversed the first few turns. I tried to talk to him about the situation at Geyser, but he seemed reluctant. I think he was still hoping that he could smooth things over for a little while longer, and that we'd be able to catch up, eventually, without getting caught. Then we came to the first chute, which is very steep and technical and surrounded by large granite boulders, hence the name, Granite Canyon. I told Preston to watch where I skied and to follow my tracks. I didn't want him to go first, because it was virgin snow and I was afraid he wouldn't know where to ski. But I was equally afraid of him following too close to me and wiping me out on his way down the mountain. As I explained this to him, I must have freaked him out, because all of a sudden, he bowed out. He said that he was going back through the trees to the groomed runs and would meet us for lunch. That was the last time I ever spoke to him," Michael said.

"Did you deliberately take him into an area that you knew would be too hard for him?"

"Of course not. He knew I was going to ski advanced terrain. I knew that it was too hard for him, but his ego wouldn't allow him to admit that to himself. I wasn't about to argue with Mr. Know-it-All in front of his wife and my mother. I knew that he would figure it out soon enough."

"It seems odd to me, Michael, that Preston had been trying to avoid you all week and then all of a sudden he was your shadow on the ski slopes."

"Whose side are you on, Mac?"

"Yours. But you need to be ready for cross-examination. That's what happens on the witness stand. You tell your story to your lawyer and it all seems so easy. Then the other side's lawyer does everything possible to poke holes in your story. I'm trying to understand to whole picture, that's all." Michael nodded and smiled slightly. I continued. "What about Duane Towns?"

"I haven't seen Duane Towns in years. I've talked with him, but I haven't seen him."

"Didn't you call him when you were in Jackson during the convention?"

"Yes, I called him. I usually do when I'm in town, just to say hello. Unfortunately, I called him from the hospital," Michael said. I looked at him with great alarm.

"You called him from the hospital? Why?"

"Look, I thought Preston broke his collar bone and hit his head, but that he would be better by the next day. I figured that I had some time on my hands, so I decided to make a few phone calls."

"Your business partner is on a gurney with head trauma and you're making social calls?"

"You don't understand. I figured that Preston would be fine! It didn't look like a serious accident."

"Have you ever offered Duane Towns money to do any job of any kind, for you?"

"Never."

"Isn't it possible that you chose this canyon, knowing that Preston's ego would command him to accompany you, and that you had Duane Towns lurking in the trees, waiting for Preston to pick his way back to the slopes, providing Towns with the opportunity to knock Preston off?"

"Is that what you think?" Michael asked in an incredulous tone.

"Michael, I'm on your side. I'm playing the devil's advocate, here, so that we can flush out the possibilities and try to stay one foot in front of the prosecutor-"

"The devil's advocate?"

"You have to think about this from all perspectives. The jury is going to hear this case from Bain's side first, and then from us. First impressions are huge. I need reasonable explanations. Don't be so defensive. I'm asking you what I need to know, not necessarily what I want to know," I said. I hung on my own advice for a moment. I'd never asked him whether or not he'd "planned" for Preston to be in a ski accident, and I never would, because I didn't want to know. What we need to know and what we want to know are often in great conflict.

Chapter 19

It is always good to be back in my own bed, even though I'm still afraid of being alone since being attacked in the office. The trips to Boston and to Bali forced me to deal with my fears head on, but the stalker in Boston set me back a bit. The first thing I did when I entered my apartment was to turn on every light. Then I checked behind doors, under the bed and behind the shower curtain to make sure that no one was laying in wait. Ted, my calico, was still at Harry's. My laundry was out of control, my mail was in a pile on the floor and my houseplants were limp, but my mind was on the murder scene. A few things didn't make sense. I could understand Michael taking an extreme skiing run, since he was essentially an expert skier. But why would Preston tail along, especially that week, when he had been trying to avoid Michael and any questions about Geyser's financial problems? He wasn't a great skier, from all accounts. Why take the chance? I'd skied near Granite Canyon—it's even out of the repertoire of most advanced skiers. Why would Michael agree to have Preston tag along? It would only slow him down and take away from the experience he would normally have been seeking as a skier.

And what about Duane Towns? Why would an upstanding citizen like Michael keep in touch with a sleaze like Duane Towns? And why did he call him this time around? It's not like they were long-lost friends or something. For the first time in this case, I was starting to doubt Michael a little. My mind was spinning. Harry's alarm clock would be ringing much too soon. I needed to be in the office before Harry got there so that I would have time to go through my mail before meeting with him.

✻ ✻ ✻ ✻

Miraculously, I got up before my alarm and went for a jog in the freezing morning air. When something is churning in my mind, I need a cardiovascular flush to help me reboot my system. When I arrived at the office, it was dark. My mind flashed back to that morning before Michael's arraignment. I was afraid to enter. I stood at the door for a few minutes, thinking of excuses for running early morning errands. I'd already had my coffee, but I could grab a cup of decaf at the bakery. I decided that I needed to confront my fears, so I unlocked the door, crossed the threshold and immediately flicked on all of the lights. I checked behind every door to every office and under Harry's, Lela's and my desk. After I felt that the place was secure, I logged in. After an hour of catch-up, I heard the shuffle-hop of my boss entering the office.

"Mac, you're back," he said as he did a little dance into my office, pretending to throw a football on the ground of the end zone like he did in his college glory days. "Meet me in the War Room asap, so we can have a group hug." Only Harry would think of a defense strategy as a group hug. He rarely hugs me, even when I need it. His occasional hugs knock the wind out of my lungs.

I walked into the War Room and gasped. A cyclone of unknown origin had struck, leaving mountains of yellow legal pads, unsharpened pencils, discarded protein bar wrappers, and crumpled up paper everywhere. Poor Lela. What am I saying? Poor me. I'm the one who will have to work in this mess. At least Lela could escape to her "safety zone," as she calls it. I cleared a swath and took note of what Harry was working on. He had obviously met with James Flanigan, Kelly's father. The word "James" was circled on our easel with an arrow pointing in one direction toward "Preston" and in another direction toward countries identified as Indonesia, Thailand, China, Japan, and Germany. Dollar signs united the arrows. The other easel had Michael pointing to Duane Towns. On the side margin it said "Kelly/Nyomi." I didn't know what any of this meant, but I was sure that Harry would tell me more than I wanted to know.

"I met with James Flanigan." Harry tossed another two or three yellow pads onto the pile. "Nice fella. He was on his way to meet a client of his in Boise, Idaho. He was very upfront about his relationship with Preston. He admitted right off the bat that his license to practice medicine had been suspended for improper referrals to an x-ray/MRI center that he partially owned. He claimed that he was ready to retire anyway, and that it was a good excuse to get him out of the medical profession before the HMOs overtook the Wyoming medical community like they had the rest of the country. He didn't seem defensive in the least. He said that he didn't understand the law because it was new but that he never intended to violate it."

"How did he get into business with Preston?"

"He said that Preston called him out of the blue and asked him whether his new medical supply company was a limited liability company. James told him that it was. He said that Preston asked him whether the LLC was authorized to conduct foreign affairs and James again said that it was. Then Preston asked James whether he would be willing to be the sole distributor of Geyser to some of their foreign markets. James's new company hadn't made a profit yet, so James said that he was willing to give it a try. He was candid in telling me that he spent a good portion of his life savings defending the legal action against him to revoke his medical license. He also said his retirement portfolio was too heavy in stocks and when the market took a dive, so did his retirement nest egg. He admitted that the opportunity to make some easy money through Preston's company was alluring."

"Why didn't Kelly know about it? Wouldn't it seem natural for either her husband and/or her father to let her in on it?"

"I asked him that. James said that Preston had asked him not to tell Kelly or Michael or anyone else about it," Harry said.

"Didn't that strike you as odd? Did you ask him why he thought Preston wanted to keep the deal a secret?"

"Of course, but I didn't want to press it, because I wanted to befriend him enough to tell me what kind of distributing he was doing for Geyser. He didn't offer any explanation for why Kelly and Michael were kept in the dark—just business, he guessed. He said that Preston would call him about a shipment invoice and then fax him the invoice on blank paper. James would then transpose the invoice on Rocky Mountain Pharmaceutical invoice letterhead, package the correct amount of product and ship it to the foreign market from his Billings, Montana, headquarters, which was a post office box at a mailbox store in a strip mall. Within a week, Preston would pay on the invoice, plus a commission to James."

"Wasn't James suspicious of this setup?"

"He said that he's been so financially strapped that he didn't really care about the setup. He figured that it was Preston's problem, and that he was only a cog in the wheel."

"But didn't he wonder whether Michael or Kelly knew or approved of it? I mean, if my dad … well, I mean that if someone close to me was doing business with my husband and didn't tell me about it, I would think that something was wrong," I said.

"Like I said, James seemed to only care about James. Maybe that's what got him into trouble in the first place. But, that's not where it ends. James shipped about five hundred thousand dollars worth of inventory to Nyomi Janger in Bali last month. James said Preston never paid him for the shipment. When James confronted Preston for payment, Preston told him that Nyomi claimed to have never received it. James swears that he sent it to her. He said that since Preston had no way of confirming the receipt of shipment, he had refused to pay him. James was out his commission, which amounted to about one hundred fifty thousand dollars. He was furious about it."

"Did he call Preston on it?"

"To say the least. Preston apparently told James he had to prove that the shipment was received, which, of course, is very difficult to do for overseas deliveries. James said that when he couldn't prove it, Preston told him to shove it."

"When did this happen?"

"About a week before the convention," Harry said. His left eyebrow arched. This is when I knew we were getting somewhere. Harry can talk himself blue in the face without ever mentioning anything pertinent or interesting, for that matter, but when the left eyebrow arches, I know it is time to put my pencil on my paper.

"So what did James do?"

"He showed up at the convention uninvited and unannounced." It occurred to me that Michael had never mentioned that James had been at the convention.

"Michael never said that James was at the convention."

"That's because Michael probably didn't see James. Only Preston saw James. James kept a low profile until he found Preston alone. He confronted him in the men's room and told him to pay up or else."

"James told you that?" What fool would admit to that kind of statement in the midst of a murder investigation, I wondered?

"Not in so many words, but that would seem to be one of the purposes of his uninvited and unannounced visit to the convention. Here's the other reason James showed up at the convention. James said that Preston had promised him a percentage ownership of Geyser stock for each million dollars' worth of business shipped. The stock was to be purchased using a street name of some sort, and then James was supposed to be able to convert the stock into a personal portfolio. James said that he tried to convert the stock, but that it hadn't been transferred.

When he confronted Preston about the stock, Preston again told him to take a hike," Harry said, with both eyebrows raised.

"You know that James is a good skier, right?"

"Really?" Now his brows furrowed.

"He taught Kelly and Michael how to ski when they were little kids," I said. "He's in town, livid about being stiffed on his commission. After confrontation, he's irate about the stock. He's a good skier. Motive and opportunity."

"Motive and opportunity," Harry repeated. He nodded his head back and forth.

I walked over to the easel, marker in hand. "Let's chart our suspects and figure out where to go from here," I said.

Chapter 20

Lela buzzed on the intercom to let Harry know that Christopher Bain was holding on line two. I took the opportunity to scoot out of the War Room and down the street to my favorite little log cabin A-frame to grab another cup of coffee. The salesclerk showed me the freshly baked banana bread muffins, and I couldn't resist. So much for the morning jog. I wasn't gone five minutes when I returned to find an irate Harry. Bain had a knack at turning Harry the Benevolent into Harry the Malevolent. Harry was ranting and raving about the police investigation and how it had been slanted against Michael all along. He was grousing about how Tim Marshall, the deputy sheriff, had followed Michael around the emergency room the night of the ski incident and basically focused on Michael to the exclusion of all others as a suspect, even before Preston died. What perturbed Harry the most was that the case wasn't a case at all when Preston was taken to the emergency room—it was simply a ski accident in the trees with the victim at the hospital for medical treatment. It was peculiar that Tim Marshall was there to begin with, let alone there investigating a possible crime.

"Bain has set a deposition for Tim Marshall for tomorrow morning. I'm swamped with client meetings," Harry said. "You'll have to cover it." Harry rattled off the rest of our client commitments for the next several days and we divvied up tasks—or, I should say, Harry assigned the tasks and I accepted them. After Harry shuffled out of the War Room, I set to cleaning up and then arranging our defense into witness and evidence files. I then returned to my office to check e-mails before going to lunch. I scanned a few from friends who wondered if I hadn't met with some horrible demise since I hadn't e-mailed them in weeks.

"Lela," I shouted out my door, "Could you order in a salad for lunch? Order one for yourself too. It's on the house." Lela gave me a wry smile, as if a freebie of a salad on Harry's meager allowance was exciting. She loved any excuse to get out of the office for a bit.

* * * *

I arrived at Bain's office at eight thirty the next morning, and helped myself to a cup of coffee and a donut.

I situated myself directly across the conference table from where Tim Marshall would be seated. The stenographer sat at the head of the conference table, Marshall to her right, me to her left, and then Bain to Marshall's right. This is the way it is at practically all depositions. It makes musical chairs unnecessary. I got out my yellow legal pad and my two pens: blue for taking notes, red for underscoring key concepts or damaging testimony. I was ready to roll. Bain, on the other hand, was late, as usual. Knowing this, I brought my laptop to do work, so as not to allow him to think that I'm wasting my time waiting for him.

Twenty minutes later, the two-inch thick beveled-glass door of the conference room swung open and Bain sauntered in wearing a blue button-down shirt and navy slacks. His tie was a circle in square geometric jumble of primary colors and his belt and shoes were polished black leather. He looked at me with annoyance at first, as if Harry had sent his underling. But Bain quickly gathered himself.

"Good morning Mac. Harry sent his better half, I see," Bain said.

"Good morning to you too, if it still is morning," I said, looking at my watch. Bain smirked at me and took his seat. Enough of the professional courtesies.

Bain turned toward the stenographer. "Please swear in the witness." The stenographer, a middle-aged woman with broad hips and long fingers turned toward Tim Marshall.

"Do you swear to tell the whole truth and nothing but the truth?" she asked.

"I do," Tim Marshall said, holding up his right hand. He was wearing his Deputy Sheriff uniform. His revolver was affixed to his belt and I couldn't help myself staring at the wooden handle of the gun. I've never fired a weapon, which is hard to believe for someone who studied criminal science in undergrad, preparing to be a cop. That's part of the reason I dropped out. I am just not cut out to hold, aim or fire a weapon. The mere sight of Tim Marshall's weapon was making me edgy. When I see a gun, I have these strange impulses to grab it and defend myself. I can't explain why, but the fact that I feel this way made me realize that being a cop was the wrong profession.

Tim Marshall's salt and pepper hair was combed directly back off his forehead, forming a bit of a peak, exposing a large, z-shaped scar on the left side of his forehead. The scar was reddish-purple, making me wonder if he had earned it recently in the line of duty. His gray eyes were deeply set, framed by thick, dark eyebrows that appeared to be a unibrow but for the frequent shavings. He had perfectly white and straight teeth, making me wonder whether they were capped, and he had a slight tuft of hair protruding from the collar of his uniform tie. The index and middle fingers of his right hand had yellowish nicotine stains on them. I could smell cigarettes on him from where I was seated, all the way across the table. He might even be attractive if it weren't for his bubble-butt and his pigeon-toed walk.

After we were introduced on the record, Bain started in. "Deputy Marshall, why were you called to St. John's Hospital the night in question?"

"Our station listens in on the radio frequencies of the local ski areas in case of emergencies," Tim said. "On the afternoon in question, we intercepted a call from the ski patrol requestin' a search for a man in out-of-bounds territory. The Department has been pressing charges over the last two years for people skiing out-of-bounds without proper permission, because it has cost our Search and Rescue team hundreds of thousands of dollars tryin' to find skiers in off-limit places. The State is tired of payin' taxpayer money to rescue thrillseekers, so a law was passed statin' that all people who trespassed out-of-ski-area boundary terrain requirin' search and rescue assistance would be legally responsible for all costs of the rescue operation.

"When we intercept any ski area call requestin' search and rescue for out-of-boundary skiers, we're required to interrogate either at the ski slope, or, if the victim is taken for medical treatment, at the hospital. In this case, Preston Parker was rushed to St. John's Hospital immediately after the ski patrol got him off the slopes, and I was there to meet him when he was brought in."

Bain asked, "Who besides you was there when Preston was delivered by ambulance to the hospital?"

"Kelly Flanigan, I mean, Kelly Parker, Michael O'Connor and Ann O'Connor were there when I arrived. They were busy at the admittin' desk, completin' paperwork. I followed Preston into the ICU. Kelly was the only person allowed into the ICU at first, and she seemed surprised to see me there. We all knew each other. I went to school with Michael, and I'd seen Kelly with him a handful of times while growin' up, so I greeted her by name, which seemed to surprise her. She had only met me once, and that was a long time ago."

"How did you remember her name, if it had been so long since you had seen her?" Bain asked. Tim stopped wringing his hands for the first time.

"Uh, well, I guess you could say that I sorta had a crush on Kelly when I was younger. We all did."

"Who do you mean when you say 'we all did'?"

"Uh, me, Michael, Duane. Some other guys on the block. When Kelly came to town, lots of us went to Michael's house. She was the prettiest girl I ever saw."

"Tim, can you tell us what happened the night Preston was brought into the ICU?" Bain asked, trying to get Tim back on track.

"When Kelly walked into the ICU, she asked me what I was doin' there. I told her that I was investigatin' a possible crime, and that I would need to ask her some questions. I took the spiral notebook and pen out of my front shirt pocket to take notes. She seemed irritated by this and told me that she didn't understand what I was doin' there at all, and that she needed to speak with the doctor in charge. I told her that the doctor would be back shortly. I also said that he had just examined Preston and had stated that he was in serious but stable condition.

"I then asked her when was the last time that she saw Preston, and she just glared at me for what seemed to be quite a few minutes. I remember her askin' me, 'What in the hell are you asking me this for? What business is it of yours? And why now? My husband is laying here unconscious. I haven't even spoken to the doctor about his condition, and you want to know when I saw him last?'

"As she got up to leave, to go look for the doctor, she turned back and said, 'For the record, sheriff, the last time I saw my husband was at the top of the mountain. He wanted to ski with Michael O'Connor—you remember Michael, right?—Well, they decided to ski Granite Canyon. We were going to meet for lunch at the Mangy Moose at one-thirty. He never showed up. What crime are you investigating, anyway? Did Preston do something wrong?' Kelly asked me.

"I apologized to her but told her that I was not at liberty to say at that point in the investigation. This made her mad, I think, because she told me that she was not at liberty to answer any more of my questions, either, and she marched out of the ICU."

"What did you do next?" Bain asked.

"I walked out into the admittin' area of the emergency room and approached Ann O'Connor. I introduced myself and told her that I needed to ask her and Michael a few questions. I asked her where Michael was.

"She told me that he'd stepped outside to make a phone call. She wanted to know what questions I needed to ask him, and I told her that I was investigatin' a possible crime. She, too, asked what crime, and I told her that I couldn't say yet.

Unlike Kelly, Mrs. O'Connor was forthcomin' about what had happened, down to the very last detail."

"What did you ask her?"

"I asked her about the day, the weather conditions, the slopes she had skied and how long they'd waited at the Mangy Moose for Michael and Preston before reportin' them missin' to the ski patrol. Things like that."

"What were her answers to your questions?"

"She told me that it was a beautiful day and she named the slopes they skied. She told me that Michael wanted to take some advanced runs before lunch and that Preston had asked to go along. They agreed to meet a specific time for lunch, she said, and she and Kelly waited for over an hour before they reported them missin'. She said that Michael caught up with them around that time, and that he had appeared surprised to learn that Preston wasn't with them."

"What did she say that Michael said about Preston, exactly, if you recall?" Bain asked.

"Objection," I said. "Calls for hearsay. What Michael told Ann is hearsay. What Ann told Tim about what Michael said is double-hearsay." I can't keep Tim from testifying about the conversation at a deposition because the rules of evidence are much looser in this forum. But I can keep Tim from testifying about this in court. I just wanted to make my objection for the record, in case Bain tried to use deposition testimony in court. Bain rolled his eyes at me and motioned for Tim to answer the question. Bain's glasses were sliding down his nose. He twitched his nose like a rabbit repeatedly until they moved back in place.

"According to Ann, Michael said that they were headin' down the first chute of Granite Canyon when Preston realized that he was in over his head. Preston told Michael that he was goin' back through the trees and would meet him for lunch, as planned. Michael told Ann that this was the last time he'd seen Preston, and he just assumed he would be waitin' with Ann and Kelly for him."

"Did Michael tell Ann why he was so late?"

"Objection. Hearsay," I said again.

"You can answer," Bain said to Tim. Tim looked at me with almost apologetic eyes, as if he didn't want to take sides on whose question to answer or whose objection to obey.

"He told her that he took Granite Canyon to the bottom, but overshot the cut-off point where he needed to be to catch the chairlift, so he had to backtrack to the chairlift to get him back up to the top, so that he could get down the mountain. He had to cross-country it back and it took a long time."

"What happened next?"

"The doctor was enterin' Preston's room, so I followed and listened in. This is how I remember it, but I'm paraphrasin'."

"Let the record reflect that the witness is paraphrasing and not testifying as to specific conversation," I said.

"Go on," Bain said.

"This is how I remember it. 'Mrs. Parker,' he said, 'I am Dr. Conrad. I am afraid that your husband has been in a serious accident. It appears that he was free-falling quite a distance and that he has some blunt force trauma to the head. He remains unconscious, but his vital signs are strong and responsive. We have upgraded him from critical to serious condition. He has a broken collarbone and a broken leg. Those will need attention. However, our main concern is the head trauma. We will need your permission to perform a scan.'

"I was listenin' intently. I understood the broken bones and the head injury. The part I didn't get was the free-fall. I thought that Preston was heading back through the trees to the slopes. It would be hard to free-fall for long in those trees. Maybe the doctor was guessin'. Maybe Preston hit his head really hard on a tree. I wasn't sure at this point what had happened, but the free-fall comment made me suspicious," Tim said.

"Why were you suspicious?" Bain asked.

"Well, the observable injury was on the back of Preston's head. I just couldn't see how that coulda happened in the trees," Tim said.

"What happened next?"

"Kelly asked the doctor what he was lookin' for on the scan, and the doctor said he was lookin' for brain activity. He told her that he was lookin' to see whether Preston was in a coma. This news upset Kelly, so I went over to the nightstand and poured her a glass of water. She signed the forms, and then the nurse unlocked the wheels of the gurney and wheeled Preston out the door."

"What happened next?"

"I remember that Kelly put her head in her hands and began to cry. Ann O'Connor walked in and kneeled beside her. Again, I asked Ann if she could tell me where Michael was, because I still needed to ask him some questions. He was the one who had seen Preston last. I remember Kelly and Ann both glaring at me. Ann said that it wasn't a good time and that the questionin' needed to wait. I told her that it couldn't wait, and I left to go find Michael."

"Did you find Michael?"

"No. I looked everywhere: outside, in the lobby, in the restrooms, everywhere. He was nowhere to be seen."

"What did you do next?" Tim looked at his notes. He flipped forward a few pages and then continued.

"Let the record reflect that the witness is referring to his field notes to refresh his memory," I said.

"I went back to the ICU to see if he was there, but he wasn't. Dr. Conrad walked in right after me, and I overheard his conversation with Kelly. The doctor said somethin' like, 'Mrs. Parker, I have good news. The scan shows fairly normal brain activity. Mr. Parker remains unconscious, but that could be due to the blunt-force trauma to his head, or he could be in a coma. We will continue to monitor his brain activity through an EKG. He is in the casting room now, getting his left leg in a cast and his right arm in traction, so that the collarbone heals. We don't want any more swelling in either of those areas. The rest will be a waiting game'."

Bain looked at his watch and then stood up. "Let's take a lunch break now and resume in about an hour and a half," he said. The stenographer looked relieved. Bain and Tim Marshall walked out of the conference room together and headed left down the hall toward Bain's office. I put my laptop in my briefcase and headed back to my office. When in Boston, I had taped Kelly's version of the emergency room visit. I wanted to listen to the tape during the lunch break to compare her version to Tim's.

Chapter 21

▼

February is either a great month or a terrible month in Jackson. The weather is either starting to improve or freezing cold. Today, the cobalt-blue sky is breathtaking, set off against the sparkling spring snow. Bain's office is only about two blocks away from ours, so I walked through the Town Square and grabbed a sandwich from Shade's Café. The warmth of the sun was melting the frozen landscape and the sidewalks and the streets were finally starting to re-emerge. However the sidewalks, once thawed and wet, often refreeze overnight, making them as "slick as snot" in the morning, as Harry always says.

I closed my office door and opened the wrapper on my turkey and tomato sandwich. I plugged in the tape recorder and hit the play button. I fast forwarded it to the point where Kelly was telling me about her experience at the hospital after Preston was taken there from the ski slopes.

"I got in the ambulance with Preston, and Michael and Ann followed behind in Ann's car," Kelly's voice rang out. "Preston was taken immediately to the ICU, and I had to go to admitting to fill out paperwork. A cell phone was ringing in my fanny pack, and I realized that I still had Michael's phone. I handed it to Michael and he left. As soon as I was done, I went to the ICU. The nurses and the emergency room doctor had intubated him and were checking all of his vitals. While they were doing this and asking me some health questions about Preston, a deputy sheriff came in and started asking me questions about the ski accident. I was surprised at first, because the timing seemed strange. When I asked him if it could wait, he said that it couldn't, because he was investigating a crime. I asked him what crime, and he told me that he couldn't say. This irritated me a lot, so I asked him to leave.

"The doctor then asked to do a scan on Preston's head because he was unconscious and it appeared that he had suffered some blunt-force trauma. I agreed and signed the forms. The doctor came back about an hour later and told me that Preston had more-or-less normal brain activity and that it would just be a waiting game from here. He sent Preston down to x-ray to get his broken bones set. In the meantime, that pesky sheriff came back and was asking both Ann and me questions, and then he wanted to know where Michael was. This was the first time I realized that Michael had not been back to the ICU yet to see Preston, even though he and Ann had received clearance from the staff to come on back.

"The sheriff left. Not more than a minute later, Michael ducked into Preston's room and asked us why Tim Marshall had been talking to us. I remember being surprised by the question. It seemed like Michael should be asking about Preston's condition, but he was more concerned about the sheriff. We told Michael that the sheriff had said he was investigating a crime, but that he wouldn't tell us what crime he was investigating. I asked him where he had been, because the sheriff was looking for him. He said that he had been outside in the parking lot, making some phone calls. Then he asked about Preston's condition, and I filled him in," Kelly said.

"How did Michael react to the news of Preston's injuries?" I asked Kelly.

"I told him that he was unconscious and had some broken bones, but that the doctor had said that Preston's brain was functioning fairly normally. He was unconscious, but probably not in a coma. Michael didn't react much either way. Ann told him that they had taken Pres for bandaging and bone-setting, and that they would be doing further testing for brain activity," Kelly said. "Michael then asked if the doctor knew what had happened to Preston. I told him that the doctor said that he had probably been in a free-fall and then explained what a blunt force trauma to the head was," Kelly said. "I remember saying that I hoped that Preston would be able to tell us what had happened to him very soon. Then an odd thing happened," Kelly said.

"What was that?" I asked.

"Michael abruptly left the room. I watched him walk out. I asked Ann to stay in the ICU in case they brought Preston back and then I followed Michael," Kelly said.

"Why did you follow him?" I asked.

"I followed Michael because he was acting strangely. I followed him out into the parking lot, and watched as he squatted down in between some parked cars. I crouched down a few cars away and heard Michael dialing his cell phone. I hadn't put my coat on and it was freezing. I remember feeling the cold air. I heard him talking on his cell phone, but I couldn't make out his words. There was a short pause and then he said something like, 'I don't give a damn … it must be done.' And then there was silence. My mind was racing. The cloud of my breath billowed out in front of me. I wanted to go back inside, but I had to wait for Michael to leave; otherwise, he would have seen me. Then I heard footsteps. It sounded liked they were getting closer. I bent down to the ground, looking under the cars to see if I could see whoever it was. The footsteps stopped. Then I heard them again. I smelled cigarette smoke and I looked behind me. I saw a pair of shoes, shoes I didn't recognize. I looked up, but the streetlight was directly overhead, so I couldn't make out who it was. I was afraid. At first, I was afraid that Michael had caught me spying on him. Then, I feared for my safety," Kelly said.

She went on. "'Stand up,' a voice said suddenly. I surfaced from the fetal position I'd taken to peer under the car chassis."

"'What are you doing here?' I now recognized the voice. It was Tim Marshall. He was spying on me, or Michael, or on both of us. My fear subsided for a moment, but I didn't know how to respond. Tim was obviously suspicious of me, and now he had good reason. I didn't want to incriminate Michael or myself, but I also couldn't lie to a policeman. I could be disbarred. I remember a long pause," Kelly said.

"'What are you doing here?' Tim finally asked me. I told him that I needed some air. He asked me why I was crouched down on the ground. I told him that I was looking for an earring I'd dropped earlier, and that I had just found it. He asked me where Michael was, and I told him that I wasn't sure. He asked me whether Michael was in the parking lot with me, and I said yes and no. He was out in the parking lot making a phone call, but not with me. It was a half-truth. I felt like a witness in a deposition. Tim told me that it was too cold outside to be out without a coat, and he escorted me back inside.

"Preston's condition stabilized during the night and by morning, he was transferred out of the ICU to a private room on the Moran Ward. His room was called Moran 4. Anyway, he regained consciousness and was making eye contact with us. He wasn't able to speak, really and the nurse on duty instructed us not to ask him any questions. Ann and I took turns sitting with him during the day. Nurses were in and out, checking his vitals constantly. Tim Marshall came back that afternoon, trying to talk to Michael still. I left Preston's room to talk with Tim in the hallway. We went for a cup of coffee.

"As Tim escorted me back to Preston's room, I noticed a lot of activity near Preston's door. The intercom kept repeating, 'Code Blue Moran 4' 'Code Blue

Moran 4.' 'All available personnel respond immediately to Moran 4.' That was Preston's room. Oh God, I thought. The bile in my stomach began to rise. I ran down the corridor to Preston. I pushed past several nurses and doctors. Hospital staff surrounded Preston's bed. 'All clear,' I heard one doctor say. I could hear the thud of the cups sending electrical stimulus to his heart. I could hear his body fall back to the gurney. 'OR 5 is ready,' a nurse yelled out, holding the phone. The staff gathered IVs and machines, and whisked Preston out of Moran 4," Kelly said.

"What was going on?" I asked Kelly.

"Dr. Conrad shouted, 'We must operate. Immediately.' Nobody stopped to explain. I called Preston's parents and they immediately chartered a flight from Boston to Jackson," Kelly said.

The tape picked up the sounds of Kelly standing up as she excused herself to go the bathroom again and get tissues.

"What happened next?" I asked her when she sat back down.

"When Preston's parents Hugh and Phyllis arrived, they were shocked to find him in back in ICU 4, hooked up to every machine imaginable. Phyllis started to cry. She didn't need to be told. When I heard Phyllis, I remember turning to them, sobbing, telling them that they could still say good-bye, even if he was not really there. Phyllis went in. Hugh stood behind her with his hands on her shoulders. Tears were running down his cheeks. The doctor entered the room and introduced himself. 'I'm Dr. Conrad. I am so sorry to inform you that your son has fallen into a coma. The EKG reveals no brain activity.' He didn't need to say anything more. Hugh pulled Phyllis close into his chest," Kelly said.

Kelly continued on. "Hugh demanded to have the best doctors in the country evaluate Preston before anything further was done, so he arranged for two specialists from the Mayo Clinic to evaluate him. That afternoon, a neurosurgeon and a cranial-facial specialist came to the ICU, but after spending several hours evaluating Preston and his test reports, they came to the same conclusion. No brain activity. He was brain dead. A vegetable. It was hopeless," Kelly said.

"What happened next?" I asked Kelly.

"The next morning, Dr. Conrad entered ICU 4 with Hugh's Mayo doctors and they all signed the documents in Preston's chart. I was also asked to sign. Then, after a moment of silence, Dr. Conrad turned off the respirator. Preston's vital signs slowed and stopped. We knelt at his side and said a prayer. 'You'll be with Bri soon, love, she will take good care of you,' I whispered into Preston's ear. I had been told that hearing was the last sense to go when passing away, and I hoped he could hear me. I kissed him on the cheek and said good-bye. Then, Preston was gone," Kelly said.

"After a while, it was time to leave. The coroner and the pathologist needed to take Preston's body for an autopsy as soon as possible. Tim Marshall was questioning Hugh and Phyllis in the hall. Hugh was questioning the doctors and nurses about Preston's treatment and the cause of death. He wanted to know how the ski accident occurred and why a sheriff was investigating it as a crime. He had a lot of questions, but his Mayo doctors told him that they wouldn't have the answers until the autopsy was completed," Kelly said.

"Was that the last time you saw Hugh and Phyllis?" I asked Kelly.

"No, of course not. I saw them at the funeral and have seen them several times since," Kelly said. "They're family. And I now sit on the Geyser board of directors with Hugh, so I saw him last month at the monthly meeting," Kelly said.

The tape ended. I looked at my watch and realized that it was time for the deposition to resume. I would have to run back to Bain's office. Then again, he'd kept me waiting for twenty minutes this morning. He could wait ten minutes for me.

Chapter 22

The rest of Tim Marshall's deposition pretty much mirrored Kelly's rendition of the events at the hospital. After we wrapped it up for the day, Bain told me that he was scheduling the depositions of the treating doctor and the pathologist for the following week. I told him that we were in the process of hiring a forensic toxicologist to review the medical records and to testify as an expert at trial on the matter. We exchanged names and dates and both agreed to confirm all depositions in writing. As I was leaving Bain's conference room, he stopped me at the door.

"I know that we're adversaries at the moment, but after the trial, regardless of who wins, let's meet for a drink … or coffee or lunch."

I looked at Bain for a moment of uncomfortable silence, trying to sense some kind of romantic connection with him. I couldn't. "That might work. We'll see how the trial goes. Maybe you'll have a change of heart by the time this is over."

"I doubt it," Bain said, walking me to the elevator. He pushed the down arrow and watched until the doors closed.

I met Harry back in the office at the end of the day. He was in the War Room, drinking a sports drink and eating a soy bar.

"How'd it go today, Mac?"

"All right, I guess. By all accounts, Tim Marshall suspected that Michael was involved in something illegal from the very beginning. He was dispatched to investigate whether Preston and Michael were illegally skiing out of bounds, in case the locals might need to collect on any search and rescue funds spent to find them. But when he got to the hospital, he thought that Michael and Kelly were both behaving oddly. In his deposition, he stated that Michael avoided talking with him and didn't check in to see how Preston was doing. At the lunch break, I came back to the office to compare Marshall's version to Kelly's and they pretty much match."

"Have you talked to Michael about his behavior at the hospital yet?"

"No. I will do that right away."

"Good, because the pre-trial conference is tomorrow and I want to know as much as I can before appearing. Is Michael flying back out here for the pre-trial?"

"I don't think so. I told him not to unless there was a good chance that Bain was going to offer a plea. It doesn't look likely that he will. Anyway, Michael said that he's not bargaining. He wants an acquittal."

"That's what they all say, until the trial is two days away. Anyway, if this case is bargained, it won't be until after the experts are deposed. Too much at stake and too many unanswered questions," Harry said. "Plus, I think that Bain and the County Attorney's office are enjoying all of the publicity, anyway. Have you seen 'Larry King Live' lately?"

"Yeah. Bain and his cronies have appeared three times via satellite. You would think that there is no other news going on in America right now. Larry King has focused on this case several times, with his talking head lawyers saying the same things over and over—all speculation. Have they asked you to appear?"

"Twice. Larry King has had his station manager call. I told her that I don't make talk show interviews part of my defense. But, I think that I'm going to have to appear tomorrow after the pre-trial conference, just to even the score a little. This case has already been tried by the media. I need to interject some accurate defense strategies into the mix," Harry said.

We formulated our discovery plan and talked strategy late into the evening. I don't get many chances to pick Harry's brain anymore. We used to have these types of pow-wows a lot when I first started working for him. But as time has gone by and Harry has gained confidence in me, he's pretty much let me do my thing and looks over my shoulder only occasionally. He still reviews every pleading I create before it gets filed, but he is hands-off on the day-to-day workload. I love having this time to learn from him—to figure out how he thinks and formulates his strategies. One of the hardest things to do in a case is to be able to see the trees and the forest at the same time. Many lawyers get lost in the trees and fail to see the whole forest. Allocating time for each witness and each piece of evidence is crucial. But what makes Harry masterful is the way he figures out how each piece of evidence fits with all the others, and how each one should come into evidence.

"I'm heading home, Mac. I need to get a good night's sleep before the pre-trial hearing tomorrow morning," Harry said as he gathered his files and an extra yellow legal pad. I stayed later, preparing for the expert witness depositions.

*   *   *   *

"All rise," the bailiff announced. "The Honorable Sheryl Furmer, presiding."

"Please be seated," Judge Furmer stated as she rearranged her black robe and opened the only file on the desk before her. "The People of the State of Wyoming versus Michael Brian O'Connor, case number WC000599. Counsel, please identify yourselves for the record."

"Christopher R. Bain on behalf of the prosecution."

"Andrew J. Harrison on behalf of Mr. O'Connor."

"This is a pre-trial conference. Has a plea bargain been reached in this case?" Judge Furmer looked at Bain.

"No, your Honor."

Judge Furmer looked at Harry. "Any chance that a plea bargain will be reached?"

"Your Honor, it is always possible, but it appears unlikely as this time."

"Well, counsel, as you should be aware, in criminal trials, time is of the essence. Either you can reach an agreement or you can't. What is the percentage of probability of reaching one imminently?" Judge Furmer asked, this time looking into the sea of reporters in the gallery.

Harry turned to me and whispered, "I have never been asked this question in my nearly twenty years of practice. I wonder whether she's performing for the media." Judge Furmer was staring at Harry for a response. I don't think she was happy about his whispering.

"Your Honor, as you know, much can change in the months, weeks and even days preceding a criminal trial. We are in the discovery phase now. We are learning what the prosecution's evidence is and who their witnesses are. I can't possibly give you a hypothesis at this time regarding a plea. I would if I could, but it is unfair to my client to even try, at this point," Harry said. Bain nodded in agreement.

"All right. The trial is set in sixty days, which will be …" Judge Furmer looked at her clerk for the date. "April twentieth at eight thirty a.m. in this courtroom. All pre-trial motions must be filed ten court days prior to trial. The defendant shall remain free on bail under the current bond agreement placed on the record at the indictment hearing, so long as there are no objections." Judge Furmer looked over her glasses at Bain. "Counsel?" she asked.

"No objections, Your Honor," Bain stated.

"No objections," Harry stated.

"Court is hereby adjourned," she said as she pounded the gavel loudly on the bench.

Chapter 23

"Remember, you are to say nothing to the press on the way out," Harry warned me on the way out of the courtroom. "We need to prepare for the Larry King Live segment later this afternoon, but I really need a good sweat beforehand. Are you up for a game of hoops," Harry asked.

"Sure." We went to the YMCA and picked up a fast game of basketball during the lunch hour. When we got back to the office, we didn't recognize the place. There were TV crews pulling cable all over the place and driving Lela crazy. She was patiently telling them where the outlets were, but I could tell that her mask of patience was about to be removed. Lela liked her job because the cases were interesting, it was within walking distance from her apartment, Harry paid her a decent salary (more than mine, I'm afraid), and she had worked for him for so long that her job was second nature. Having a TV crew overtaking her space was not second nature. I thought that she might love the media excitement. She was a thirty-something year-old single woman with a chance to be on national television. But Lela was a private person, despite her short skirts.

The crew turned on their state-of-the-art monitor and it showed Larry sitting in his studio in New York. He was, of course, wearing suspenders and his recently touched-up hair was slicked back off his high forehead. His two-inch square glasses were polished to a shine and he was going through his five by eight inch notecards.

Harry looked quite handsome in his black designer suit. Harry's wife had somehow convinced him to let the camera crew apply a little stage make-up on him (he would have never done it for me) and then the crew put an earpiece in Harry's right ear and tested to see if he could hear Larry and every other participant in tonight's version of round table discussion. I was amazed at the high-tech cameras and equipment, and at how easily they made Harry look like he was in a studio in New York.

"Good evening," Larry said into the microphone sitting on his desk. Larry was wearing a blue dress shirt with a white starched collar and maroon paisley suspenders. "Tonight we have a special guest, one who has been eluding us during the pre-trial phase of Michael O'Connor's murder trial. No, it's not Michael O'Connor. It is his lawyer, Andrew Harrison. Welcome, Mr. Harrison to Larry King Live," Larry said.

"Thank you. You can call me Harry," he said as he repositioned his earpiece.

"What's it like, defending one of the most famous criminal defendants in America?" Larry asked.

"Michael O'Connor is by far one of the most brilliant people I have ever had the privilege of working for," Harry said. "He's honest, forthright and hard-working. This has been a terrible tragedy in his life. He's a highly respected research scientist. Preston Parker, the unfortunate victim, was his best friend and his business partner."

"Do you think O'Connor is innocent of murder?" Larry asked. I held my breath, awaiting Harry's response. Harry has never made a comment to the press regarding his client's guilt or innocence. It is one of his cardinal rules. But America was watching. Potential jurors were watching. Foreigners were watching. What he says right now might materially effect the prosecution and defense of the case.

"As you may know, it is my policy never to comment on the guilt or innocence of my clients. However, due to the public nature of this case, I'm going to tell you outright that the evidence will show that Michael O'Connor is not guilty of murder. The evidence will show that Preston Parker was gravely injured in a skiing accident."

I let out my breath. Lela let out her breath. Larry's crew then panned to Christopher Bain, who was similarly situated in his own office, just down the street. King asked him if he thought he could get a conviction in the case. Bain was a natural in front of the camera. He smiled a relaxed smile and said that he was confident that the jury would find beyond a reasonable doubt that Michael O'Connor is guilty of murder. Larry then consulted with the lawyers employed by CNN to give commentary on high-profile trials. After a long-ish advertising break, Larry came back to Harry at the end of the taped interview and asked him about his defense strategy.

"My strategy is to put on evidence in a chronological fashion that persuades the jurors that Michael O'Connor had nothing to do with Preston Parker's ski accident. There are a number of excellent witnesses who will testify about this case, and their testimony will clearly show Michael O'Connor's innocence. I'm confident that Michael O'Connor will resume his life, but I know that he will miss living it without his best friend and business partner," Harry said. The camera panned out.

"That's a wrap," a crewmember said. It was the cameraman that had followed me to Harry's car on the morning of the arraignment hearing. He caught me staring at him. Before I could avert my eyes, he winked. I couldn't help but smile. Harry nudged me as he pulled out a handkerchief and wiped the sweat from his brow. He looked quizzically at the handkerchief, probably forgetting that he had makeup on his forehead. He stripped off his blazer, removed his tie and unbuttoned the first two buttons on his shirt. Large bluish rings of sweat had formed on his shirt under his armpits.

"How'd you think it went?" Harry asked me.

"Well."

"Bain looked good, don't you think?" I nodded. I turned back to see where the cameraman was, but he was gone. The crew was busy tearing down the equipment. I sought refuge in my office, but I didn't close the door. A few minutes later, there was a light tap on my door.

"Mind if I come in?" he said. I swiveled in my chair to see him. His blond hair was tucked behind his ears. His gray eyes twinkled in the rays of sun beaming through my window. "I'm Greg Fisher. I work for CNN." I started to stand to greet him. "No, don't get up. I just wanted to say hello." He rushed toward my chair with an extended hand.

"I'm Mary MacIntosh," I said, extending my right hand in his direction.

"I know. I saw you at the courthouse. Nice to meet you." His wide hand engulfed mine, sending an electric jolt up my arm and down my spine. He looked a little like a hippie version of Bain. His build was slighter, but his smile was wider, framed by a perfectly chiseled chin. "I'm sure you're busy. I just wanted to say hello." He turned and left before I could find words.

"It was nice to meet you," I yelled out, after he'd rounded the corner of my office. He popped his head back in and winked, and then he was gone. I swiveled my chair back toward the window. A dazzling ray of light shimmered through the glass, warming my heart.

* * * *

I spent the next morning on the aerial tram of the Jackson Hole Mountain Resort. I told Harry that I wanted to see the scene of the incident one more time and I needed to do a little research. This was true. I did want to see the scene again. Something was nagging at me. I had overlooked something, but I just couldn't put my finger on what it was. And I did have some research to do. But let's face it, I had only gone skiing three times during the season because I was trying to save money to buy a new car and Michael was paying for the lift ticket. I was sure he wouldn't mind.

I served the aerial tram operating company with a subpoena a few weeks ago. The documents I had requested in the subpoena were available for pick-up, so that was the first place I went. I reviewed the documents and then purchased a ski ticket. The tram ride was as magnificent, as usual. The view from the top of the tram, at ten thousand feet, is spectacular beyond all reason. If the wind isn't blowing, which it usually is on this unprotected peak, the skiing is fantastic. Usually, the wind is blowing and the visibility is compromised and the snow is a little icy and crusty. Today, I was lucky. No wind. Perfect views. Soft snow. I enjoyed every minute of my investigating.

The site where Preston was found was still roped off with yellow investigation tape. I didn't cross the tape because I didn't want to tamper with evidence, but I was able to get a decent view of where his body was found in relation to the slopes and Granite Canyon. The aspen trees in this area weren't too thick. I skied through the trees adjacent to Granite Canyon, all the way to the bottom. I wanted to see where Michael had said he overshot the ski lift and had to hike his way back up. I also wanted to see if there was access from the snowmobile trails up to the ski slopes. Sure enough, a snowmobile could easily have crossed Fish Creek Road and gone through the backcountry to Granite Canyon.

I skied to the parking lot and got in my car. I drove down Fish Creek Road to where it ended, clocking the number of miles on my odometer. It took me about ten minutes to get from Wilson, where John and Duane Towns said they had been snowmobiling, to get to Granite Creek, traveling fifty-five mph. John had provided an alibi for Duane, but he'd actually said that he'd gotten his snowmobile stuck in Fish Creek near where the creek crosses Fish Creek Road. Duane had told John that he would ride into Wilson, a town only a few miles away, to get a rope to tow him out of the creek. John said that Duane was gone for fifteen to twenty minutes, and returned with the rope. It was possible that Duane had

had a rope all along, and instead of going to town, had driven in the opposite direction, up to Granite Canyon. He could have easily gone to Granite Canyon and back in twenty minutes. John told us that Duane had received several cell phone calls when they were snowmobiling, but that the calls were very short.

    I went back to the ski area and took the ski run again, this time I timed how long it took to get down Granite Canyon. I retraced what Michael told us were his steps that day and kept track of how long it took to get through each segment on his ski run. I'm not as good of a skier as Michael probably is, based on what I've heard, so it probably took me longer to ski Granite Canyon that it did him. Seeing that it only took me about an hour and a half to get down the run, hike back to the chair, take the chairlift back up and then ski down to the Mangy Moose, I decided that Michael must have had a little extra time on his hands on that day. He didn't show up at the Mangy Moose for nearly two hours after he parted ways with Kelly and Ann. I wondered what he did in that extra half an hour?

Chapter 24

Harry and I spent nearly every day until trial preparing witnesses and deposing experts. We prepared jury questionnaires—questions for the prospective jurors which would help determine which jurors Harry would select or reject. Some judges allow the trial lawyers to ask nearly all of the voir dire or juror questions. Other judges prefer to run the show. Judge Furmer is clearly going to run the show in this case. It is her nature to do so anyway, but she is more inclined to do whatever it takes to keep control of the case and the media, not to mention the fact that she wants to remain on center stage as much as possible for her media debut.

A few days before the trial, Michael (and a swarm of journalists) arrived in Jackson. The night before the trial started, Harry and I practiced his opening statement over and over. He had it down pat by midnight.

* * * *

"Ladies and gentlemen of the jury, my name is Christopher Bain and I represent the people of the State of Wyoming. You have been chosen and empowered to decide the fate of this man, Michael O'Connor, the defendant, who has been indicted and charged with the murder of Preston Parker.

"The evidence presented to you during this trial will show that Michael O'Connor met the deceased in college at Harvard University in Boston, Massachusetts. They were college roommates. After college, they became business partners and together they formed a company called Geyser. This company produced and sold pharmaceutical drugs for impotency. Michael O'Connor is the scientist behind the development of the drugs. He is a medical doctor, but he does not practice medicine in the common way. Instead, he channeled his medical mind to the research and development of pharmaceutical drugs. The deceased, Preston Parker, was the businessman for Geyser. He was in charge of marketing the drugs that Michael O'Connor created. He was the dealmaker.

"Michael O'Connor was jealous of Preston Parker for several reasons. First, Michael O'Connor was in love with Preston's wife. He had been in love with her since his teenage years, and when his own wife died of cancer, Michael coveted Preston's wife more than ever. Michael also coveted Preston's business skills. Michael O'Connor is not a very outgoing person. He is uncomfortable in crowds and is painfully shy. Preston often did not ask Michael to join him in business negotiations because Preston was embarrassed by Michael's inability to carry on professional discussions with prospective clients and customers.

"Michael O'Connor was also mistrustful. He was convinced, shortly before the skiing incident, that Preston was involved in some irregular business deals, which is just not true. But, in Michael O'Connor's paranoid mind, the possibility made it so. He spent many nights and weekends in the office hacking into Preston's computer system to find out what Preston was up to. But Preston wasn't *up to* anything. He was expanding market share—as he had done for years, which is the reason that Geyser is such a successful company. Preston was working hard to penetrate the Asian market. He was also negotiating the purchase of several competing pharmaceutical companies, so that Geyser could gain a larger share of the impotency drug market. Preston was a shrewd and successful businessman. Michael was so jealous of him that he became paranoid about the business deals Preston was making.

"The State will call certain witnesses who will testify about the onset of some pretty suspicious behavior on Michael's part. The State will call Preston's secretary, Carol Leahy, who will testify that shortly before Preston's death, Michael was searching through Preston's files and questioning Carol about certain *missing files* of customers. The State will call Preston Parker's father-in-law, who was working with Preston to raise sufficient capital to purchase several competing pharmaceutical companies.

"The State will also call Steven Taylor, Geyser's accountant, as well as Michael O'Connor's personal financial manager. Mr. Taylor will testify that two days prior to the murder, Michael O'Connor withdrew twenty thousand dollars in cash from his management account.

"The State will call Duane Towns, a local thug from Jackson, who has been convicted of many crimes in the county, who will testify that Michael O'Connor contacted him the week of the murder and offered him money to assist him with the murder of his business partner, Preston Parker. Duane Towns will testify that he was to be paid ten thousand dollars to run Preston Parker off the ski slope. Duane Towns will testify that he was to be paid an additional ten thousand dollars when the job was finished, but that Michael O'Connor had refused to pay him, since he hadn't done the job 'right.'

"The State will then present a medical doctor who is a toxicologist, who will testify about the drug found in Preston Parker's body. This drug likely put Mr. Parker into a coma.

"Our local sheriff, Tim Marshall, will testify that he had surveillance on Michael O'Connor from the moment Mr. Parker's body was found on the ski slope. Tim Marshall will testify about how he was able to link Michael O'Connor to Duane Towns, the hired hit man.

"Ladies and Gentlemen, the evidence will show that Michael O'Connor was the mastermind behind the murder of Preston Parker. The evidence in this case is strong and direct. It will tell you that, beyond a reasonable doubt, Michael O'Connor killed Preston Parker. After you have heard the evidence, we are confident that you will find the defendant guilty of murder in the first degree." Bain held his eye contact with the jury for as long as possible before taking a seat at the prosecution's table. He took a drink of water and unbuttoned his suit jacket, taking as much time as possible to let his words resonate with the jurors.

Now, it was the defense's turn for opening statement. Harry wore his dark gray Armani suit with a white custom-made dress shirt and his favorite Robert Talbott blue tie with tiny gray dots. He didn't worry much whether his suit jacket was buttoned or unbuttoned. He did worry about opening statements, though. He knew that a good percentage of jurors made up their minds about the guilt or innocence of a client during the opening, even though jurors promised that they would listen to all of the testimony before they made a decision regarding guilt. He knew that Christopher Bain would, as usual, tell the jurors too much about the case. Harry also knew how to keep it simple and how to use a theme. He'd give them a theme that they could grab hold of like a sword, to use in deliberations to convince other jurors to vote with them, or like a shield, to keep jurors from convincing them to vote a different way. Harry had to think long and hard about his theme for this case. There was ample evidence to convict. Yes, it was circumstantial, but circumstantial evidence is often enough to convict.

Last night, Harry and I had worked late putting the finishing touches on Harry's opening. Harry told me that he had two choices, really. He could argue that Preston died from complications resulting from an unfortunate ski accident or he could argue that Michael had no motive or opportunity to commit the crime. The reality was that Michael did have motive, so we debated late into the evening how best to handle the opening statement. We'd decided to argue that this was an accident with a twist. Harry left my side and shuffled over to the jury box. He rested his hands on the wood paneling that separated the jury from the rest of the courtroom. He looked relaxed and friendly, like a grandfather teaching his grandkids how to build a birdhouse or paint a fence.

"May it please the Court, members of the jury, my name is Andrew J. Harrison. Most people simply call me Harry.

"I represent Michael O'Connor, a local boy who made good. Michael grew up here, was educated here, and then went off to college. He came back here during the summers to work in Yellowstone because he loves it here. He formulated a drug from the geysers here in Yellowstone. This drug has helped millions of people overcome medical problems. Michael is a brilliant scientist and was a loving, devoted husband, a good partner, and a good friend. Michael's geyser research has helped this community benefit. A portion of royalties from his company are funneled back to the National Park Service and, particularly, to Yellowstone National Park, our local treasure.

"Mr. Bain told you a part of the story about this case, and he is a good storyteller. However, as you well know from your own life experiences, there are at least two sides to every story. My job is to help you understand the other half of the story. The truth.

"What really happened on January eighteenth? What really happened is that Michael O'Connor, an excellent skier, was here in Jackson for a business conference with his business partner, Preston Parker. Preston was not as experienced a skier as Michael, but, his ego got the best of him that day. He wanted to keep up with Michael. He didn't want to be left behind with the women while Michael went for some extreme skiing. Preston asked to tag along with Michael. Michael told him that he didn't think that it was such a good idea for him to ski Granite Canyon.

"Michael, who had skied this country most of his life, knew how treacherous Granite Canyon was. But Preston couldn't be dissuaded. When Preston got over to Granite Canyon and took one look at the terrain, however, he decided that he was in over his head. He told Michael that he was going to make his way back through the trees to the groomed runs. Preston told Michael that he would meet him at lunch at the designated time and place that they had agreed to meet Mrs. O'Connor, Michael's mom, and Kelly Parker, Preston's wife.

"What really happened? What really happened is that Preston had a skiing accident. Yes, a skiing accident. They happen every day. He was skiing in an out-of-bounds area. He was skiing in terrain that was too hard for his skill level. He was trying to be macho and it cost him his life.

"The evidence will show that Preston was skiing through the trees, like Michael said. The evidence will show that he must have fallen and hit his head on a tree. He was unconscious when the ski patrol found him, and he never regained consciousness long enough for him to tell us what happened, so we'll never know how he fell. A few short hours after he was brought in an ambulance to the hospital, he regained consciousness. He was transferred out of the ICU and to a separate wing of the hospital. The doctors and nurses wanted to observe him for at least twenty-four hours, since he'd suffered a concussion from the skiing accident. Unfortunately, not long after he was transferred out of the ICU, Preston Parker slipped into a coma and was pronounced brain dead. There is no evidence of foul play involving Michael. Yes, Michael was the last person seen with Preston on the ski slopes. But Michael did not kill him. In fact, Michael tried to persuade Preston not to ski in Granite Canyon.

"Our accident reconstruction expert will tell you exactly how the ski accident happened. And it was simply an accident. Michael had nothing to do with it.

"The prosecution will try to establish that Preston's death was not accidental. Again, we pledge the death was accidental. But if it wasn't, then it was caused by someone other than my client. If someone did cause Preston's death, there are several credible suspects. As I will explain in more detail in a minute, Preston was having an affair. His wife suspected him and hired a private eye. The private eye confirmed her suspicions and gave her pictures of Preston in the act, so to speak, with another woman. Kelly Parker confronted Preston about the affair and he promised to break it off with the other woman and have her fired from the company. So, we have a furious wife and a furious scorned lover as possible suspects, both of whom know how to ski. Also, Preston was secretly in business with his father-in-law, James Flanigan, and had apparently stiffed him on a large commission that he was owed. James Flanigan is a good skier. So, we can add James Flanigan to the list of suspects.

"The evidence will also show that there was no hit man. Duane Towns is a local thug—Mr. Bain was right to describe him as such. And Duane Towns, much as he wanted to get in on the action, is just not a credible witness. He is a convicted felon here in Jackson and was due to serve time on an unrelated arrest. Deputy Sheriff Tim Marshall will tell you that Duane Towns gave his statement to the police on this case in exchange for a reduction in his sentence for a prior felony conviction. Duane Towns has everything to gain from lying, and nothing to lose. He is a liar and a convicted thief. His testimony is not credible. In fact, the evidence will show that he recanted his statement not long after he signed it. In fact, Duane Towns was infatuated with Kelly Parker and would probably say anything just to be a part of this criminal trial because it would involve him in her eye. During our investigation of the case, we searched his apartment and found dozens of pictures of Kelly Parker pasted to his bedroom walls. The evidence will show that if a murder was committed, Duane Towns is likely to have killed Preston Parker on his own in hopes of having Kelly for himself. As a matter of fact, the defense will offer a restraining order into evidence that Kelly had against Duane when they were in high school. The restraining order was issued in Buffalo, Wyoming, where Kelly grew up. During one summer, Duane camped out in Buffalo and stalked Kelly. Her parents filed for a restraining order against him. So you see, ladies and gentlemen, Duane Towns's affidavit isn't worth the paper it's printed on.

"The evidence will further show that Preston Parker had been having an affair with a woman by the name of Nyomi Janger. Nyomi Janger was a sales representative for Geyser, Inc. She worked in Indonesia, distributing Geyser products. Kelly Parker suspected that her husband was having an affair, and had hired a private detective by the name of Bob Avery to follow Preston to an island in Indonesia called Bali. Bob Avery photographed Preston in the act with Nyomi Janger. When his wife Kelly learned of the affair, she demanded that Preston fire Nyomi and stop seeing her immediately. Preston did fire her. Nyomi Janger is a rejected, bitter woman. Further, Nyomi Janger is known to have skied in America in the same mountains where Preston met his demise, perhaps as recently as the month prior to the accident. She has no alibi for the weekend of Preston's death. It is possible that she could have been involved in some way in Preston's untimely death.

"Also, there is the possibility that Kelly Parker's father, James Flanigan, had it out for Preston. Preston had secret business dealings with James Flanigan and had even stiffed his father-in-law on a rather sizeable payment due to him. James Flanigan confronted Preston at the conference the day before the skiing accident and threatened him. So you see, ladies and gentlemen, there were many people that could have wanted Preston Parker dead. But, we believe that none of these scenarios are the truth. The truth is that Preston Parker died of injuries caused by a skiing accident.

"The evidence will also show that a 'drug' supposedly injected into Preston Parker, one that the prosecution claims is responsible for his going into a coma, may not exist. The prosecution has no precise evidence of this. Our toxicologist will testify that no succinylcholine, the drug that the prosecution claims was administered into Preston's IV, was detected in the autopsy. Even if the succinylcholine was in Preston's system at the time of death, it is possible that it was administered to Preston to prepare him for surgery.

"Our expert doctor will testify that Preston Parker suffered from a severe head injury caused by falling into a tree while skiing. The head injury killed him. The same type of accident that happens on the ski slopes every year. Skiing is a dangerous sport. Especially when skiers ski beyond their limits.

"So, yes, ladies and gentlemen, the evidence will tell you the other side of the story, the story of a simple ski accident where the victim sinks into a coma and dies of his injuries in spite of his family's and the doctors' hopes for his full recovery. Accidents happen. Skiing out of bounds in a dangerous area can kill. This is a sad but simple truth. This evidence will prove one thing for sure—that the State will have failed to prove, beyond a reasonable doubt that Michael O'Connor murdered Preston Parker."

Judge Furmer watched Harry walk back to the defendant's desk, looking as confident as ever. He didn't hold the jurors' eyes for a period of time. He didn't stall the proceedings for effect. He didn't have to. After Harry sat down next to Michael, Judge Furmer looked at Christopher Bain. "Your witness," she said.

Chapter 25

Bain stood. Again, he unbuttoned his jacket, as if he were opening the jurors' minds to the truth. "The State calls Kyle Ketchum to the stand." A young, handsome, deeply-tanned man walked to the witness stand. The clerk stood, raising her right hand. "Place your right hand in the air. Do you swear to tell the whole truth and nothing but the truth?" he asked.

"I do," Kyle said. "You may be seated." Kyle sat down in the witness box to the left of Judge Furmer. He tucked his shoulder-length blond hair behind his ears and shifted in his chair.

"Good morning, sir," Bain stated. "Please state and spell your name for the record."

"Kyle Ketchum."

"Could you spell your name for the record, please?" Bain said.

"Oh. Kyle K-Y-L-E Ketchum K-E-T-C-H-U-M."

"Thank you. Where do you live, Mr. Ketchum?"

"In Moose. A few miles from here."

"What is your occupation?"

"I'm on the ski patrol for Jackson Hole during the winter and a river rafting guide on the Snake River in the summer."

"How long have you been on the ski patrol?"

"In Jackson, for eight years. Before that, I was on ski patrol at Big Sky, Montana for two years."

"So, you have had a total of ten years experience on the ski patrol?"

"Yes."

"How long have you been skiing, in general?"

"Most of my life."

"Do you consider yourself an expert skier?"

Kyle smiled a little. "You bet. I've even done a few extreme skiing movies. I've been skiing extreme for at least ten years."

"Could you explain to the jury what an 'extreme skier' is, exactly?"

"Sure. An extreme skier can master radical terrain like virgin powder up to your shoulders. Some extremers are boarders, some skiers. The boarders go for more radical air. The skiers crash the chutes and crags and hang on the vertical."

"When you say 'boarders,' you're referring to snow boards, right?"

"Yeah, snow boarders," Kyle said.

"And what's radical air?"

"You know, when you go off a jump and free fall for a long time. The more air you get, the more radical."

"So, to make sure that the jury understands us, when we're discussing extreme skiing, it can be skiers or snow boarders who ski in steep or very difficult terrain, correct?" Kyle shook his head, agreeing with Bain.

"You need to give an audible answer so that the court reporter can put your answer on the record," Judge Furmer said.

"Yes," Kyle said.

"Extreme skiing can include in-bounds terrain and out-of-bounds terrain, correct," Bain said.

"Yes."

"Can you explain to the jurors what the difference is?"

"Ski areas have boundaries where it's okay to ski. Most of the boundaries are marked or roped off. If a skier or boarder goes outside the boundary, then they're out-of-bounds."

"Have you ever skied Granite Canyon in Jackson Hole?"

"You bet, many times. I'm assigned to it regularly when I am on patrol. I ski down it at the end of the day to make sure that no skier has been left behind there. It's a killer run."

"Move to strike," Harry said.

"So stricken. Mr. Ketchum, please refrain from referring to a ski run as a 'killer run.' Jurors, disregard that statement by the witness." Kyle Ketchum looked confused.

"Would you consider Granite Canyon extreme skiing?" Bain asked.

"Uh … of course. It's out-of-bounds. It's steep and deep and there's a ton of chutes and crags. There's a radical jump after dead man's dip that the boarders crash and burn on. I bet we bag a boarder a day out of there."

"When you say 'bag,' what do you mean?"

"Rescue. Take down on the toboggan."

"What's 'dead man's dip'?"

"It's a steep chute with a gnarly dip at the bottom which propels you over the rock face."

"On January eighteenth, were you asked by your supervising ski patrol officer to look for a missing skier in Granite Canyon?"

"Right. I was told that some dude had been last seen heading back through the trees from Granite Canyon. I followed the ski tracks to the entry point of Granite Canyon off the tram, and then went down the first chute and around the first rock outcropping. There were lots of tracks heading to the next chute, but there were virgin tracks heading back through the trees. I followed the virgin tracks and I spotted this dude laying head down in the snow, yard sale all around him."

"What do you mean by 'yard sale'? Bain asked.

"You know. Yard sale. When a dude falls and loses their gear. Like, their poles and skis are scattered everywhere," Kyle said. People in the courtroom chuckled at his description.

"Madam clerk, please mark this Prosecution's Exhibit No. 1 for identification. Your Honor, may the record reflect that I am now placing Prosecution's Exhibit No. 1 on an easel before the witness and the jury, which is an aerial photograph of Granite Canyon. Your Honor, at this time we move that Prosecution's Exhibit No. 1 for identification be admitted in evidence," Bain stated.

"Any objections, counsel?" Judge Furmer asked Harry.

"No objections, your Honor," Harry said.

"It will be admitted," Judge Furmer said.

"Mr. Ketchum, could you use this pointer and point to the location where you skied and where you found Mr. Parker," Bain asked.

Kyle Ketchum took the pointer and curved it down the first chute and then through the trees. He stopped the pointer at approximately where he found Preston. "This is about where I saw Mr. Parker."

"Let the record reflect that the witness has pointed to trees flanking the left side of Granite Canyon, if you were standing at the top of the Canyon looking down," Bain stated. "Was he bleeding?"

"For sure. His head was bleeding and his right arm was hanging at a weird angle, so I radioed for assistance."

"Did you get assistance?"

"Yes. In about ten or fifteen minutes or so, two other ski patrols arrived with the toboggan. We loaded the dude, I mean, Mr. Parker, into the toboggan and skied him down to the first aid station. We radioed down on the way to have an ambulance meet us there. When we got to the bottom, the ambulance loaded Mr. Parker."

"Approximately how long did it take from the time you found Mr. Parker until he was loaded in the ambulance?"

"Probably about an hour."

"Was Mr. Parker ever conscious during this time?"

"Objection. Calls for an expert opinion," Harry stated.

"Sustained," Judge Furmer stated.

"Did Mr. Parker ever open his eyes or speak to you during the time that you rescued him?" Bain asked.

"No."

"Thank you, Mr. Ketchum. I have no further questions for this witness at this time," Bain stated.

"Your witness," Judge Furmer said, looking over her reading glasses at Harry. Harry stood and picked up the yellow legal pad and pencil that he had been writing on during Kyle Ketchum's testimony.

"Good morning, Mr. Ketchum. May I call you Kyle?" Harry asked. This was a tactical move that Harry often used. If a witness was not an expert and didn't have testimony that hurt his case, Harry wanted to give the impression that he was chummy with them.

"Yes," Kyle said.

"When you spotted Mr. Parker face down in the snow, did you notice any other ski tracks nearby?"

"Objection, calls for speculation," Bain said.

"Overruled," Judge Furmer said.

"You may answer the question, Kyle," Harry said in his parental tone.

"No. I didn't notice any other ski tracks."

"So it appeared to you that Mr. Preston was skiing by himself in the trees?"

"Objection. Your Honor, this calls for speculation," Bain said.

"Overruled."

"Go ahead and answer," Harry said.

"Well, there was fresh snow the night before and there were virgin tracks all over Granite Canyon. But there was pretty deep powder in the trees and I only saw one pair of ski tracks heading into the trees by dead man's dip. That's how I located Mr. Parker."

"So, you didn't see other ski tracks near Mr. Parker?"

"No."

"When you found Mr. Parker, could you describe how his body was positioned?"

"Like I said, he was head first down the mountain, so his feet were uphill. His face was in the snow, and he was mostly on his stomach. His right arm was twisted and his yard sale was scattered around him."

"Describe the yard sale. Where were the skis and the poles?"

"One pole was uphill about ten feet from him and the other was under him. One ski was jammed under a tree root near the uphill pole and the other ski was near his head."

"Where was his head bleeding?"

"Near his left temple and the blood was coming from there."

"Did you notice blood anywhere else?"

"No."

"Did you or any other ski patrol rescuing Mr. Parker take any photographs of Mr. Parker in the position that you found him in Granite Canyon?"

"No. We didn't take any pictures of him," Kyle said.

"Did you move Mr. Parker when you found him?"

"Yes, I turned him over a bit on to his side to check his pulse and breathing, and to make sure he didn't suffocate in the snow."

"Did you check his pulse?"

"Yes. He had a pulse and was breathing."

"Did you do anything else to aid Mr. Parker while you waited for your fellow ski patrols to help you get him down the mountain?"

"Not too much, really. I've been trained not to move a victim much, as they can have head and spine injuries. I just turned his head gently to the side for breathing purposes and felt his right shoulder to see if I could tell what was wrong with it. It was in a weird position."

"Did the ski patrol bring a toboggan on the back of a snowmobile?"

"Yes. The toboggan was brought up by the snowmobile."

"Where was the snowmobile parked in relation to Mr. Parker? You can use the diagram to point, if it is helpful."

Kyle pointed to the tree line that separated the ski slope from the out-of-bounds area. "They parked the snowmobile here."

"Let the record reflect that Mr. Ketchum has placed an 'X' on Prosecution's Exhibit No. 1 indicating where the ski patrol snowmobile was parked. Kyle, after the ski patrol parked the snowmobile, what did you do?" Harry asked.

"They detached the toboggan from the snowmobile and walked it through the trees to where Mr. Parker was. We secured the toboggan in place so that it wouldn't slide down the mountain, and then loaded Mr. Parker into the toboggan. We bundled him with blankets to keep him warm and fastened the safety straps to keep him in place. Then we pulled him through the trees back to the snowmobile and reattached the toboggan," Kyle said.

"Did this appear to be anything more than a ski accident to you, Kyle?" Harry asked. He knew this would draw an objection from Bain.

Objection. Calls for speculation," Bain said.

"Sustained."

"How did you report this incident to your supervisor, Kyle?" Harry said. He knew, once he had asked the objectionable question, how Kyle would answer.

"I reported it as an accident. I told my supervisor that I thought Mr. Parker had crossed his tips or snagged a tip on a branch covered by snow, fell, and either hit his head on a tree or got clobbered by his ski."

"Did you notice any snowmobile tracks near Preston?"

"No."

"But didn't you just testify that the ski patrol brought a snowmobile up with the toboggan?"

"Yes."

"So there were snowmobile tracks, weren't there?"

"I guess so."

"Thank you, Kyle. You have been very helpful," Harry said as his sat down.

Bain stood. "Kyle, you don't know whether this was a ski accident or an attempt to murder Mr. Parker, do you?"

"Objection. Speculation."

"Sustained."

"Do you know how the incident happened?" Bain asked.

"No, I don't know what happened. I can only tell you what I saw."

"So it's possible that this was something other than an accident, right?"

"Objection. Asked and answered," Harry said.

"Sustained. Move on, counsel," Judge Furmer admonished.

"Nothing further," Bain said.

"Counsel, you may re-direct," Judge Furmer said.

Harry stood. "Kyle, when you found Mr. Parker, did you need to take your skis off?" Harry asked.

"Yes. I spotted him, skied to him, and then took off my skis so that I could get close to him and check him out."

"When the other ski patrols came to help, did they take off their skis?" Harry asked. Bain looked confused. Where was Harry going with this?

"You bet. They brought in the toboggan as close as they could on the snowmobile and then walked it over to the scene and supported it horizontally with their ski poles. They took off their skis and then helped me load Mr. Parker into the toboggan. We then secured him, put on our skis and took him down the mountain. I followed on skis."

"So after you left the scene of the accident, there were many ski and snowmobile tracks in the snow?"

"I suppose so."

"And toboggan tracks?"

"Yes."

"But when you first arrived, the only ski tracks you saw were Preston's, right?"

"Right."

"Nothing further," Harry said.

"Mr. Ketchum, you are excused," Judge Furmer stated.

Chapter 26

"The State calls Dr. John Conrad," Bain stated. Dr. Conrad, a short, balding man in his mid-forties was sworn in by the bailiff and sat in the witness chair. His dark brown suit matched the wood stain of the witness box.

"Dr. Conrad, please state your full name."

"John Anthony Conrad." Dr. Conrad explained that he lived in Jackson and was a neurosurgeon.

"Dr. Conrad, you're the doctor who treated Preston Parker after he was involved in a skiing incident, correct?"

"Yes."

"Dr. Conrad, I'm going to ask you some questions about your background as a doctor. Are you licensed to practice medicine in Wyoming?"

"Yes, I am." Dr. Conrad explained that he had been licensed for eight years and gave a brief history of where he was educated. He explained that he was board-certified in neurosurgery and a member of the American Medical Association, the Wyoming State Medical Society and the American College of Neurosurgery.

"Dr. Conrad, are you engaged in the private practice of medicine?"

"Yes, I am. I have a private practice here in Jackson Hole and I'm on call at St. John's Hospital."

"Dr. Conrad, what do you mean by the term neurosurgery?"

"Neurosurgery is the area of medicine which deals with the brain and nervous system. It also involves traumatic—meaning accident-related—and non-traumatic conditions and diseases in these areas of the body."

"How many patients have you treated during the course of your professional experience in which the medical condition related to traumatic head injuries?"

"Oh, I've probably treated three or four hundred traumatic head injury cases."

"Have you ever treated patients who are unconscious as the result of head trauma?"

"Yes, I've handled probably one hundred to one hundred fifty patients who've arrived at the emergency room unconscious."

"Dr. Conrad, let's focus now on the events of January eighteenth. You were the emergency room doctor on call when Preston Parker was brought in, weren't you?"

"Yes."

"Where did you see Mr. Parker?"

"I saw him in the Intensive Care Unit of St. John's Hospital."

"Did you talk to Mr. Parker at that time?"

"No. When he was brought in, he was unconscious."

"Did you examine him at that time?"

"Yes, I did. I checked his pupils for dilation and felt his head for obvious trauma or swelling. I examined his torso and arms and legs for signs of trauma. His right arm was in a splint, due to possible dislocation of his shoulder. I immediately ordered an MRI and a CT scan of his head and spine and an EKG."

"When you say trauma, what exactly do you mean?"

"Trauma means any externally caused damage to or destruction of the body tissue," Dr. Conrad stated.

"Did Preston Parker have trauma?"

"Yes. He had abrasions on his face. He had a gash on the left side of his skull. And he had swelling and bruising on his right shoulder area, on the left side of his ribs and on his left leg."

"When you say that you ordered an MRI, what do you mean?"

"An MRI stands for magnetic resonance imaging. It is a medical test where protons are placed in a magnetic field and electromagnetic energy is then transmitted and received. The test allows a doctor to see different parts of the brain or spinal cord."

"When you say a CT scan, what do you mean?"

"A CT scan is roentgen-ray computed tomography. It's where a beam of light is shot straight through the brain and detects dense living tissue."

"Other than the x-rays or scans, were any other lab tests performed at that time?"

"Yes, we performed the usual preoperative tests; that is, the patient's pulse, blood pressure and respiration were checked and his blood was cross-typed."

"On the basis of the MRI and CT scan, did you reach a diagnosis?"

"Yes. The MRI and CT scan showed no sign of bleeding on the brain or significant swelling of the brain. His brainstem was not swollen, nor did it appear that Mr. Parker had any spinal cord injury. It appeared that he had normal brain activity for a person who had experienced head trauma and was not conscious. Mr. Parker was not in a coma, as he was still responsive to external stimuli, despite his state of unconsciousness. We concluded that he had a concussion. The orthopedic doctor on call determined that he did in fact have a dislocated shoulder and a broken collarbone. He also had bruising to the ribs and a broken left leg."

"On the basis of your diagnosis, Dr. Conrad, did you begin a course of treatment?"

"Yes. Mr. Parker was administered an anti-inflammatory drug to help restrict any swelling, especially to the brain. I prescribed medication to help him cope with pain. His shoulder and leg were reset and bandaged."

"Dr. Conrad, how often did you observe Mr. Parker?"

"He was brought into ICU 4 around five o'clock in the afternoon. I examined him and his scans and test results regularly for several hours. When it was determined that he had normal brain activity, meaning that he was not technically in a coma, and had no visible bleeding on the brain, I looked in on a few other patients."

"When did you see Mr. Parker next?"

"A few hours later. Mr. Parker had regained consciousness, so the nurse called me back to ICU 4. I examined him again."

"How was his condition?"

"Stable and improving. He was conscious. I decided to move him to the Moran wing for a minimum of twenty-four hours of observation prior to release."

"Was Mr. Parker moved to the Moran wing?"

"Yes."

"Did you visit him in the Moran wing?"

"Yes. I checked on him at the end of my ICU shift and he was in stable condition."

"Were you called back to Mr. Parker's room in Moran 4?"

"Yes. The following day. On a Code Blue."

"What is a Code Blue?"

"A Code Blue is when the patient's vital signs are changing rapidly or are non-responsive," Dr. Conrad stated.

"Had Mr. Parker's vital signs changed?"

"Yes. The nurse on duty had noted that Mr. Parker was experiencing an unusually sudden decreased metabolic activity in the brain. She paged me, and I responded immediately by going to Mr. Parker's room. We rushed him to the operating room. Within a minute or so, Mr. Parker went into cardiac arrest. The nurse pushed the Code Blue button and our medical team responded by placing automatic external defibrillators, which are cups, on his chest, and administering electrical stimulation to his heart. We were able to shock his heart back into a normal rhythm and revive Mr. Parker from cardiac arrest. However, Mr. Parker had slipped into a coma. His brain was unresponsive to external stimuli and spontaneous respiration ceased, mandating a mechanical respirator to maintain his vital signs." I watched Dr. Conrad speak. He spoke unemotionally as if he were teaching his children how to inflate a flat bike tire, offering a step-by-step manual of how to get the job done.

"When you say that you put him on mechanical respiration, do you mean artificial respiration?"

"Yes. It was necessary to hook Mr. Parker up to artificial respiration to keep him breathing."

"Did Mr. Parker ever regain consciousness?"

"No. He stayed in a coma. At this point, he was brain dead and unable to breathe without the aid of a respirator." I saw Michael wince slightly at the term brain dead. It was probably hard for him to imagine Preston as brain dead. He had once told me that, of all of the people he had ever known, Preston had had the most active mind he'd ever known.

"Was Mr. Parker taken off the respirator?"

"Yes. The following day, after several physicians had reviewed the lack of brain activity, and after meeting with Mr. Parker's family, his family decided to remove him from the artificial respirator. Mr. Parker died shortly thereafter."

"Do you have an opinion, to a reasonable degree of medical certainty, whether Preston Parker's injuries, as you have described them, were caused by a skiing accident or by some other means?"

"Objection, calls for speculation," Harry interrupted. Harry had been sitting quietly, listening to Dr. Conrad's testimony. It was his practice to allow expert witnesses to testify and not to interrupt unless what they were about to say was in some way detrimental to his side of the case. Some defense lawyers object every now and then just to break the opponent's stride. Not Harry.

"Lawyers, please approach for a sidebar," Judge Furmer stated. I joined Harry and Bain at her podium. She covered her microphone with her hand so that the jury couldn't hear the conversation.

Harry argued, "Your Honor, Mr. Bain is trying to let Dr. Conrad testify about a so-called phantom drug that his toxicologist expert claims killed Preston Parker. It is speculation for him to testify about it, and it is hearsay, too, in that its presence was published in the toxicologist's alleged medical examination and was not a part of the examination performed by Dr. Conrad."

"Your Honor, Dr. Conrad was the treating physician and witnessed the death of the victim here. He has the evidentiary right to tell the jury what his medical opinion is regarding the cause of death," Bain stated.

"Mr. Bain, the toxicologist you are referring to is a post-mortem forensic toxicologist, isn't she?" Judge Furmer asked.

"Yes, Dr. Gilliam is a post-mortem toxicologist, but Dr. Conrad's testimony is simply his opinion of what caused Mr. Parker to slip so rapidly from unconsciousness into cardiac arrest and coma," Bain said.

"How did Dr. Conrad make his medical conclusions regarding death?" Judge Furmer asked Bain.

"Based on his observations of Mr. Parker in the ICU and the OR and based on his review of the lab reports post-mortem," Bain said.

Judge Furmer thought briefly, then said, "I will allow his medical opinion. He was the treating physician. He is allowed to draw his own conclusions based on the medical reports. Please be seated, Mr. Harrison and Ms. MacIntosh. Mr. Bain, you may continue your line of questioning. Stay away from hearsay. He may only testify based on his own conclusions drawn from his observations and his review of lab or toxicology reports."

"Yes, your Honor," Bain stated, great relief flushing across his face.

Harry, on the other hand, was not pleased. We knew that the information would be introduced in evidence—whether Dr. Conrad testified about it or whether Dr. Gilliam did. He would rather have had Dr. Gilliam testify. He knew that she wouldn't be a good witness on cross-examination. She was a very defensive woman and he didn't think that the jury would like her. The jury obviously liked Dr. Conrad. They had all been glued to his testimony for the last hour. Harry knew that he needed to carefully cross-examine Conrad.

Chapter 27

"Dr. Conrad, do you have an opinion, to a reasonable degree of medical certainty, whether Preston Parker's death was caused by a skiing accident or by some other means?" Bain asked.

"In my opinion, Mr. Parker's head injury from the skiing accident rendered him unconscious. My review of the post-mortem forensic toxicology report confirmed my suspicion that Mr. Parker went into cardiac arrest and coma from the reaction to a drug called succinylcholine, which was somehow administered to him while in Moran 4. This drug was not ordered by me or any other medical personnel on staff at St. John's, to my knowledge. In my opinion, the introduction of this drug into his body caused Mr. Parker's death," Dr. Conrad stated.

"You did not order succinylcholine to be given to Mr. Parker?" Bain asked with a note of surprise.

"No, I did not."

"Why would anyone inject Mr. Parker with succinylcholine?"

"Objection," Harry said. "Calls for speculation and the state of mind of another."

"Sustained," Judge Furmer ruled.

"Dr. Conrad, what is succinylcholine?" Bain asked.

"Succinylcholine is a white, odorless powder which is very soluble. It causes profound muscle relaxation and respiratory depression," Dr. Conrad answered.

"Is it used by medical professionals?"

"Yes. It is a depolarizing neuromuscular blocking agent typically used in combination with other drugs for surgical anesthesia."

"So, the drug is used in the medical profession for anesthesia purposes?"

"Yes."

"What happens if too much succinylcholine is used on a patient?"

"If too much succinylcholine is used, it can poison the patient," Dr. Conrad stated.

"Can such a poisoning cause cardiac arrest?"

"Yes."

"And coma?"

"Yes."

"And it is your medical opinion, based on your observation of the patient and your review of toxicology reports, that Mr. Parker was poisoned with succinylcholine, causing him to go into cardiac arrest and coma?"

"Objection, asked and answered," Harry said.

"Sustained. Move on, counsel," Judge Furmer said.

"Did you speak to the medical examiner before the autopsy was performed?"

"No."

"Did you ever speak to the medical examiner about Mr. Parker?"

"Yes. After I received a copy of the toxicology report, I called Dr. Gilliam to go over the results with her."

"Why did you do that?"

"Mr. Parker's case was bizarre. He went from serious condition to stable condition to cardiac arrest and death in a very short period of time. When I got the toxicology report back, I was surprised by what I read."

"Dr. Conrad, I show you the Prosecution's Exhibit No. 2 for identification. Do you recognize it?"

"Yes. It is the post-mortem forensic toxicology report on Preston Parker."

"What part of the report surprised you?" Bain asked.

"The urinalysis detected succinylcholine. Mr. Parker had not been given any anesthesia, so I was surprised to see this on the toxicology report."

"And this prompted you to call Dr. Gilliam?"

"Yes, it did."

"What did you talk with Dr. Gilliam about?"

"Objection, calls for hearsay," Harry interjected.

"Sustained," Judge Furmer ruled.

"Did you tell Dr. Gilliam that Mr. Parker had not been given anesthetic?" Bain continued.

"Yes, I did."

"What else did you tell Dr. Gilliam?"

"I told her that I was shocked to see succinylcholine on the tox report and that I thought that perhaps there had been some mistake. After thinking it over and doing some research, I realized that the succinylcholine could have caused the cardiac arrest and coma."

"What did you do next?"

"I called for an emergency staff meeting at the hospital and questioned every person on staff the night of Mr. Parker's ski incident and the day after when he was in the Moran wing to ask if anyone had administered succinylcholine. No one had. So I called the police."

"Why did you call the police?"

"Because I suspected foul play and the hospital protocol is to call the police if there is every suspicion of a crime," Dr. Conrad stated.

"Whom did you talk to at the police station?" Bain asked.

"I was transferred to Sheriff Tim Marshall."

"And then what happened?"

"Sheriff Marshall questioned me about Mr. Parker's case and asked that I fax him a copy of the toxicology report."

"Did you do that?"

"Yes. And I was interviewed by Tim Marshall. Other members of the hospital staff on-duty at the time of the incident were also interviewed. I told Mr. Marshall my medical opinion as to what happened. Mr. Marshall made a written report of the interview, asked me to read it for accuracy and then sign it. So I did."

"Dr. Conrad, I show you Prosecution's Exhibit No. 3 for identification. Do you recognize it?"

"Yes. It is the police report that I signed."

"What happened next?"

"Not much, actually. I was informed that I could be a witness if there was a trial," Dr. Conrad stated.

"Thank you, doctor. You have been very helpful. I have no further questions at this time." I watched Bain take his seat at the prosecution's table. He looked directly at the jury with confidence. I'm sure that he wanted them to believe every word that Dr. Conrad said. Harry was about to cross-examine Dr. Conrad. Cross-examination was what Harry loved most about being a lawyer.

"Good afternoon, Dr. Conrad. I am Andrew Harrison and I represent Michael O'Connor. It was your initial diagnosis after evaluating Preston Parker in the ICU that he had a concussion and a broken collar bone, correct?"

"Yes."

"After reviewing the results of Mr. Parker's MRI and CT scan, you were confident that Mr. Parker had normal brain activity for a person who had suffered head trauma of this nature, correct?"

"Yes."

"When you evaluated Mr. Parker, all of his vital signs were within a normal range for a person with head trauma, is that correct?"

"Correct."

"In fact, you told Kelly Parker, Preston's wife, that you expected Preston to regain consciousness within twenty-four hours of his skiing accident, right?"

"I believe that I did, yes."

"Mr. Parker's collar bone and rib injuries were not life threatening, were they?"

"No."

"So, as a treating doctor, your biggest concern was Mr. Parker's head injury, correct?"

"Yes. Head trauma is usually more serious than broken bones, Mr. Harrison," Dr. Conrad stated.

"And you testified that you prescribed medication for pain and swelling for Mr. Parker, correct?"

"Correct. I ordered Hydrocodone for Mr. Parker, which is the generic drug for Vicodin, which is a pain medicine. I also ordered Toradol, which is an anti-inflammatory drug to reduce the chance of swelling in Mr. Parker's head and in his upper torso."

"No other medications were ordered by you, correct?"

"Correct."

"And you were the only doctor authorized to order medicine for Mr. Parker, so, no other person at the hospital had authority to give Mr. Parker any medicine other than the pain and anti-inflammatory medicines that you've already testified about, correct?"

"Yes."

"Dr. Conrad, it is medical protocol to watch head trauma patients closely, isn't it?"

"Yes, it is."

"And you watch head trauma patients closely for signs of consciousness, coma, strokes, and conditions of this nature, correct?"

"Yes."

"And it is customary to pay close attention to swelling and bleeding on the brain, correct?"

"Yes."

"And you were concerned that Mr. Parker could have swelling and/or bleeding on the brain when he was evaluated in the ICU, weren't you?"

"Yes."

"And that is why you gave him anti-inflammatory medicine, right?"

"Right."

"You have had other patients die before as a result of head trauma, correct?"

"Yes, I have."

"And some of those patients who have died as a result of head trauma have come into the hospital unconscious and have slipped into a coma, like Mr. Parker, correct?"

"Yes, but …"

"Let's just answer the questions, please," Harry said sternly.

"You testified earlier that you've handled probably one hundred to one hundred fifty patients who've arrived at the emergency room unconscious, correct?" Harry asked.

"That sounds about right," Dr. Conrad said.

"In fact, Dr. Conrad, isn't it true that, in the cases you have handled that have resulted in death from head trauma, in forty-seven percent of those cases the patients arrived at the hospital with some brain activity and died at the hospital in a coma with no brain activity, correct?"

"I am not sure of the exact number, Mr. Harrison, but that sounds about right."

"So it is fair to say that approximately half of the head trauma death cases you have seen had a similar ending to Mr. Parker's, in that the victim arrived unconscious and later died in a coma?"

"Yes."

"And, it is accurate to state that head trauma is one of the leading causes of death in the emergency room, correct?"

"Most likely."

"Dr. Conrad, a coma results from decreased metabolic activity in the brain, correct?"

"Yes."

"And this decreased metabolic activity can be caused by cerebral hemorrhage, inflammation of the brain or abnormal metabolism, correct?"

"Correct."

"So, a coma can result from the inflammation of the brain resulting from head trauma, correct?"

"Correct."

"Isn't it possible that Mr. Parker died of inflammation of the brain due to oxygen deprivation from cardiac arrest?"

"Yes, it is possible."

"In fact, Dr. Conrad, in Mr. Parker's medical chart, didn't you ascribe the cause of death as 'coma resulting from head trauma'?"

"Yes."

"So, you noted the cause of death to be coma." Harry was on a roll. He often joked in the office that when he was on a roll like this one, he was 'Harrisoning' instead of 'harassing' his witness.

"Dr. Conrad, when Mr. Parker went into cardiac arrest in Moran 4, didn't you rush him into the operating room?"

"Yes."

"Why?"

"In case we needed to perform surgery on him."

"What type of surgery were you anticipating would have to be performed?"

"I anticipated performing a craniotomy to relieve brain swelling."

"Was the anesthesiologist who was on duty called into OR 5 to assist you with the surgery?"

"Yes. We were prepared to perform emergency surgery. Dr. Kenehar, the anesthesiologist on call, was present in the OR when we wheeled Mr. Parker in."

"Isn't it true, Dr. Conrad, that you ordered Dr. Kenehar to sedate Mr. Parker for surgery?"

"Yes, I did. But-"

"Please, Dr. Conrad, just answer my questions."

"So you ordered the anesthesiologist to sedate Mr. Parker. After that, you continued to use the defibrillators to shock Mr. Parker's heart back into a normal rhythm, correct?"

"Yes."

"Even though you were able to revive Mr. Parker from cardiac arrest, you noted a lack of brain activity, correct?"

"Correct."

"And once you confirmed that Mr. Parker was in a coma, without brain activity, you then ordered Dr. Kenehar to cease preparations for surgery, correct?"

"Correct."

"Thank you, doctor. I have nothing further," Harry said. He sat down.

Bain had blown it. He looked at Dr. Conrad incredulously. Obviously, Dr. Conrad had never told Bain that he ordered anesthesia on Preston. Dr. Conrad hadn't even told the medical examiner this tidbit of information. I had figured this out when reviewing the medical examiner's report. I compared that report with Conrad's and found the discrepancy. When I told Harry about it, he was elated. Bain's heart must have sunk to his knees as he heard this testimony, for this was a crucial part of his case. He was trying to establish that Michael somehow had sneaked into the OR and administered succinylcholine into Preston's IV—which was apparently what Bain believed had happened. But now, the defense had an easy out. We could argue that the anesthesiologist could have administered the drug that may have led to Preston's death in preparation for surgery.

"Your witness," Judge Furmer said to Bain.

"Your Honor, the prosecution calls for a brief recess," Bain said.

Judge Furmer looked at her watch. "You have five minutes," she said. Bain scribbled a note and handed it to his assistant. She scurried out of the courtroom.

Chapter 28

"All rise," the bailiff announced.

"Your witness," Judge Furmer said.

Bain stepped forward. "Dr. Conrad, you don't know how the succinylcholine got into Mr. Parker's blood stream do you?" Bain asked.

"Objection. Calls for facts not in evidence," Harry said.

"Sidebar," Judge Furmer said.

Harry argued, "Your Honor, Dr. Conrad isn't qualified to testify about toxicology. The question counsel posed assumes that the succinylcholine was administered."

"Your Honor, Dr. Conrad already testified that he read the toxicology report," Bain said.

"But counsel's trying to get evidence in the back door. He's trying to use Dr. Conrad to establish that the drug was administered. Dr. Conrad is not qualified to testify regarding that subject. He can only testify about what he read or saw," Harry said.

Judge Furmer held up her index finger, signaling to Bain to stop the debate. Her right hand remained firm over the microphone. "Counsel is correct, Mr. Bain. You'll have to have your toxicologist testify about her findings. Dr. Conrad can only testify from his personal knowledge."

Bain regrouped. "Dr. Conrad, did you order succinylcholine for Mr. Parker?" Bain asked.

"No."

"Nothing further," Bain said. He sat down.

Harry stood. "Dr. Conrad, you testified that you ordered Dr. Kenehar to sedate Mr. Parker, correct?" Harry asked.

"That's correct."

"Dr. Conrad, it's not your custom and practice to tell anesthesiologists what drugs to administer, is it?"

"No. That's the anesthesiologist's expertise."

"When it's necessary to sedate a patient, you call for the anesthesiologist and he or she makes the determination of what type of drug to use, correct?"

"That's correct."

"Nothing further," Harry said.

"Court is adjourned," Judge Furmer said. "We'll begin again tomorrow morning at nine o'clock."

The first day of trial was over. We now faced a media mob waiting to catch the perfect shot of the tears cascading down Kelly's cheeks or Michael looking desperate or furious or sad.

I glanced up at Judge Furmer as she was leaving the bench. I hate to admit this, but I envied her. It must be tantalizing to be the principal orchestrating the students—being the one to rule on whether someone can or can't testify to something. I would love to be a judge someday—independent from either the prosecution or defense. But most judges come from the prosecution side. Even if I could make it from the defense side of things, I have a long way to go before establishing myself well enough to get to the bench.

Just as I reached over to grab my briefcase and brave the media, Kelly caught my eye. She was looking right at Michael. As far as I could tell from my vantage point, it was the first time they had made eye contact all day. Kelly looked at him with desperate eyes, like she was silently pleading with him. He looked back at her and shrugged his shoulders. When she noticed that I was watching them, she glanced away. I didn't know what to make of this exchange, but it made me feel anxious about Michael's chances for an acquittal.

*   *   *   *

A lawyer never really knows how a trial is going. When I listened to the prosecution's side, I could believe that Michael had killed Preston out of greed and jealousy. If I listened to the defense, I could believe that Preston had had a skiing accident and died from a head injury. It was so easy to be swayed one way and then the other when listening to the testimony. I'm surprised by this notion as a lawyer, myself. I've never been on a jury, but after only one day of testimony, I can see how hard a juror's job is. It must be very difficult to listen impartially to each side and not form a conclusion until the end of the trial. The jurors want to know the truth. The public demands the truth. Hugh and Phyllis Parker need to know the truth. But could they accept the truth? Could Harry and I?

* * * *

On our way out of the courthouse, a young guy with brown hair ran up to me with his hand extended, shoving a note into my hand. At first, I was frightened by his charge, but when I saw him dash back toward Greg, I figured that this kid was a messenger. I opened the note.

> "Mac,
>
> Will you have dinner with me tonight?
> Greg Fisher, the cute CNN Cameraman"

I pulled the pen out of my briefcase and turned the note over.

> "Meet me at the Cadillac Grille on Cache Street (next to the Cowboy Bar) at 7:30. M."

I found the messenger and tucked the note in his shirt pocket. He dashed over to Greg. I smiled and winked at him.

I'm not sure why I accepted so readily. Maybe it's because I haven't had a date in months. I figured that it was an opportunity to think about something other than the trial.

* * * *

Greg was sitting on a saddle barstool positioned in my direction when I arrived. He was wearing faded jeans and a gray sweater. His stark blond hair fell loose to the base of his neck. He had already ordered a microbrewery beer from the selection of ales and he stood when I walked through the door. I'd decided to wear my most comfortable jeans and my favorite, pale-pink, cashmere, v-neck sweater. Certain shades of pink clash with my auburn hair, but pale pink softens my hair color and my mood. I applied a glossy lip color and wore my hair down. My black leather boots have a two-inch heel, making me nearly six feet tall. When Greg reached over to shake my hand in greeting, I was taller than him. He ordered a beer for me.

"Great bar. Looks like it's been here for a while," Greg said, offering me a seat beside him. He whisked his long bangs back with a shake of his head.

"It's famous around here. Until the nineteen fifties, this place was known for its illegal gambling. The bartenders would keep a watchful eye on Teton Pass, where messengers used mirrors to warn of law enforcement coming into town."

"I like the saddles for barstools," he said, adjusting himself in the seat. "Makes me feel like a cowboy again."

"Again?"

"I was raised in Montana."

"Where?"

"A little town called Bozeman. Well, it was small when I was growing up. It's much larger now. It's kind of like Jackson that way. Lots of rich people have ranches outside of Bozeman now, including my boss, Ted Turner. So the town has nice restaurants and lodges these days."

Greg had a charming smile. He told me about his job with CNN and the incredible time commitment it required working for a major network. He asked about my job and a little about my background, being careful not to violate my stipulation that we couldn't talk about the trial or any of the witnesses.

"Do you like your job?" I asked.

"I like the salary. I started out as an assistant freelance photographer for National Geographic. I loved the travel, but I didn't make much money. When this opportunity came up, I couldn't pass. My dad had been hounding me for years about starting to save for retirement. I felt the pressure."

"Do your parents still live in Montana?"

"My father does, I think. I don't know him well. My mother lives in Northern Wyoming with her husband."

"I see." I reached over and touched Greg's hands. He had large, thick palms with deep lines.

"What about your family?" Greg asked. I told him about my father passing away when I was young. I kept it short, not knowing how much is too much when it comes to childhood pain.

After we finished our beers, we journeyed next door to the Million Dollar Cowboy Steakhouse and enjoyed porterhouse steaks, baked potatoes, sautéed mushrooms, and red wine. We both had to get to bed early, so Greg walked me to my car. I begged him not to. He laughed out loud when he saw my old Honda.

"Harry needs to pay you more."

It is funny, so long as you're not the one who has to drive it.

Greg gave me a soft kiss goodnight. Heading home, I could still smell his cologne on my pale pink sweater. I liked the cologne, and I liked the man who wore it.

Chapter 29

"All rise," the bailiff stated with his usual fanfare the next morning. Judge Furmer took her position on the bench and nodded at Christopher Bain.

"The Prosecution calls Dr. Wende Gilliam," he announced with great confidence. Dr. Gilliam rose from her seat in the second row of the gallery. She was wearing a black pantsuit that hugged her large hips. Her shoes were black low heels that looked as if they had seen a few snowstorms over the years. Her sandy-colored hair was short and parted in the middle with no particular attention. She was sworn in and sat down in the witness chair. Bain looked at her and then at the judge.

"The defense has stipulated to Dr. Gilliam's credentials. We have agreed to submit her curriculum vitae into evidence pursuant to this stipulation, as evidence of her education and training," Bain stated for the record. He knew that the jury might get bored if he questioned her about her schooling. They could look at her resume if they wanted to know where she'd studied. He wanted them to pay attention to her findings about the succinylcholine.

"Dr. Gilliam, are you the post-mortem forensic toxicologist who was assigned to perform testing on Preston Parker?"

"Yes, I am."

"What is post-mortem forensic toxicology?"

"It is the analysis of the absence or presence of drugs and their metabolites in human fluids and tissues and the evaluation of their role as a contributing factor or determinant in the cause of death."

"Can you describe for us how you gathered the samples and performed the toxicology analysis on Mr. Parker?"

"Yes. At the time the autopsy was performed, I was called to gather urine and blood samples from the corpse and analyze them for drugs and metabolites."

"What type of testing was performed and what were the results of your testing and analysis?"

"A liquid chromatography-tandem mass spectrometry, called an 'LC-MS-MS' procedure, was used to test the urine, revealing evidence of succinylcholine," Dr. Gilliam stated, while looking at the jury. The youngest juror, a nineteen-year-old waitress, looked back at Dr. Gilliam with a blank stare.

"And succinylcholine is a depolarizing neuromuscular blocking agent used in anesthesia, correct?"

"Objection, he's leading his own witness," Harry stated.

"Sustained. Let the doctor testify, Mr. Bain," Judge Furmer said.

"What is succinylcholine?" Bain asked.

"Like you said, it is an agent used in anesthesia," Dr. Gilliam stated.

"How much succinlycholine was found in Mr. Parker's urine?"

"Approximately five milligrams."

"Is this enough to anesthetize a patient?"

"It could be," Dr. Gilliam answered.

"Is five milligrams of succinylcholine enough to cause a patient to go into cardiac arrest if they are suffering from head trauma?"

"It's possible."

"And did you conclude, to a reasonable degree of medical certainty, that succinylcholine poisoning was the cause of death of Preston Parker?"

Dr. Gilliam put on her reading glasses and referred to the toxicology report. "As stated in the toxicology report, I noted that succinylcholine was detected in Mr. Parker's fluids. The cause of death is noted as blunt force trauma to the head, coupled with cardiac arrest, possibly caused by succinylcholine poisoning, resulting in brain death," Dr. Gilliam said.

"Thank you. No further questions," Bain stated.

Harry stood. He straightened his striped tie and approached the witness. "Dr. Gilliam, isn't it true that succinylcholine has an extremely brief duration of action, meaning that it is extremely difficult to trace in a person's biofluids and tissues?"

"Yes."

"How long after Mr. Parker was pronounced dead did you collect urine and blood samples?"

"Approximately one hour," Dr. Gilliam stated.

"Isn't it true that succinylcholine is metabolized usually in five to ten minutes, due to its rapid hydrolysis in the liver?"

"Yes, it is."

"Then how is it possible that you found trace evidence of this drug an hour after death?"

"It is possible if a large quantity of succinylcholine was administered. Also, neuromuscular blockade by succinylcholine may be prolonged in patients with an abnormal variant of pseudocholinesterase," Dr. Gilliam responded.

"What is pseudocholinesterase, in layperson's terminology?"

"It is basically the speed at which a person metabolizes a certain drug."

"Did Mr. Preston have this abnormal variant?" Harry asked.

"I don't know."

"You don't know?" Harry asked with a theatrical furrow of the brow and a wild gesticulation of his arms, which made him look like a pelican unable to alight.

"No. I was not asked to determine the dibucaine number on Mr. Parker," Dr. Gilliam stated.

"And this dibucaine number would have revealed how quickly Mr. Parker metabolized succinylcholine, correct?"

"That is correct."

"So, you don't know how much, if any, succinylcholine was administered to Mr. Parker, do you?"

"No."

"Or by whom?"

"No."

"Or when it was administered, do you Dr. Gilliam?"

"No, I don't."

"No further questions."

Harry had scored again. The prosecution had to prove its case beyond reasonable doubt. He had extracted reasonable doubt from both doctors, so far. He gave Michael a confident nod as he sat down next to him at the defense table.

"Your witness," Judge Furmer said to Bain.

"No re-direct. The prosecution calls Dr. Richard Kenehar," Bain stated.

I'd spoken to Dr. Kenehar that morning and confirmed that Dr. Kenehar had in fact started the IV anesthetic drip on Preston while in the OR. How could Bain have overlooked this part of the case? I could tell that Bain was worried he was going to lose the case.

I'm sure that he'd thought about not calling Dr. Kenehar to the stand at all, but he must have known that Harry would call him and this would make his case look weaker. So, he was trying to defuse the issue by calling the doctor himself. If he called the doctor and restricted his testimony, then that would, in turn, restrict Harry's cross-examination. It was his only shot.

But, as I expected, Harry tore him apart in cross-examination. Dr. Kenehar had started the drip. He had not administered succinylcholine, but had administered a similar anesthetic, and Dr. Kenehar could not be sure whether the drugs could be differentiated in toxicology. Dr. Conrad had not questioned Dr. Kenehar because Dr. Kenehar was not on staff at St. John's. He was an independent contractor covering for another anesthesiologist on the night of January eighteenth. Since Dr. Conrad had not questioned Dr. Kenehar on hospital protocol, Dr. Conrad forgot to bring up the fact that Preston was being prepped for surgery.

It was time for Christopher Bain to move on.

"The State calls Connie Melnik to the stand." A petite woman in her mid-fifties with short, dark hair approached the stand. After being sworn in, Bain asked, "Ms. Melnik, could you tell the jury what you do for a living?"

"I'm a nurse at St. John's Hospital. I work on the Moran wing."

"How long have you been a nurse?"

"I've been a nurse for thirty-some years now. I've been working at St. John's for probably twenty years. Before that, I worked at St. Joseph's in Denver."

"Were you on duty on January nineteenth, the day that Preston Parker was transferred from the ICU to Moran 4?"

"Yes, sir. I was assigned to Mr. Parker's room."

"What were your duties with regard to Mr. Parker?"

"Normally, I am assigned the west wing of the ward, which includes rooms one through ten. But, the ward was pretty quiet that day, so I only had patients in Moran 4 and 8. I was instructed by Dr. Conrad to keep a vigilant watch over Mr. Parker, so I spent nearly all of my time in his room."

"Was anyone else in the room with you?"

"Yes. Mrs. Parker was there most of the time. And she was relieved every now and then by Ann O'Connor."

"Do you know Ann O'Connor?"

"Yes. We are involved in the same sorority."

"Was anyone else in the room with Mr. Parker?"

"Dr. Conrad stopped by early in my shift to check on him. Otherwise, no one else came in the room, that I'm aware of."

"But you did have to leave from time to time to check on your patient in Moran 8, correct?" Bain asked.

"Yes. That's correct. I was in and out of Mr. Parker's room, but I did spend most of my shift attending to him."

"So is it fair to say that you spend ninety percent of your shift with Mr. Parker?"

"That would be about right."

"How was Mr. Parker's condition during your shift?"

"He was quiet. His vital signs were strong. He moaned and groaned from time to time. He was on pain medication and swelling medication."

"How often did you check his vital signs?"

"I was told to check them every half hour. So I did."

"What, if anything, did you notice about Mr. Parker's vital signs?"

"They were stable all day. No changes to speak of. I noted the recordings in his chart every half hour," Connie said, looking directly toward the jurors. "But around four o'clock, Mr. Parker's pulse shot up and his pulse monitor buzzer went off."

"Were you in his room when this happened?"

"No. I was on my way to his room. I'd been in Moran 8. When I heard the buzzer go off, I ran to his room."

"Who was in his room, other than Mr. Parker?"

"No one. He was alone."

"When was the last time you'd been in his room before four o'clock?"

"I was there around three forty-five."

"Was anyone in the room at that time?"

"Yes. Kelly Parker was there. She'd been there all day."

"She never left the room?"

"Mrs. Parker left a few times, but she was there most of the day."

"Other than Mrs. Parker and Ann O'Connor, was anyone else in Moran 4 with Mr. Parker?"

"No."

"Did you see Deputy Sheriff Tim Marshall in Moran 4?"

"Tim, and I call him Tim because he's a friend of my son-in-law, was there around three forty-five to talk to Mrs. Parker. He never came in the room. He motioned for her to come out and speak with him, and she did."

"When you heard the buzzer going off, did you see anything peculiar?"

"Objection. Leading," Harry said.

"Sustained. Rephrase, Mr. Bain," Judge Furmer said.

"When you heard the buzzer go off in Mr. Parker's room, what did you see?"

"I saw someone coming out of Mr. Parker's room. He ran down the stairwell."

"So someone other than Ann O'Connor and Kelly Parker was in Preston Parker's room?"

"Yes," Connie said.

"What did he look like?"

"He was wearing a white jacket, like a lab coat, and tan slacks. He had on a blue surgery cap and a surgery mask. I couldn't get a good look at him."

"But it wasn't someone on the hospital staff that you recognized?"

"Objection, calls for speculation," Harry said.

"Overruled."

"Did you recognize the person leaving Mr. Parker's room?"

"I'm not sure. He had blond hair, blue eyes and was of medium build. He looked like Michael O'Connor to me." Harry rose to his feet, but it was too late to object. He sat back down.

"Did you report this strange person to anyone?"

"No. In the confusion of the Code Blue, it didn't register to me to mention it."

"Did you call the Code Blue, Nurse Connie?" Bain asked.

"Yes."

"Had you ever had to do that before?"

"No. In my thirty years of nursing, I've never had a Code Blue."

"So is it fair to say that it was a stressful moment in your career?"

"Very."

"So much so that you forgot to tell Tim Marshall about the strange man that looked like Michael O'Connor leaving Mr. Parker's room?"

"Objection. Assumes facts not in evidence and is argumentative."

"Withdrawn," Bain said. "No further questions."

"Your witness," Judge Furmer said to Harry. Harry was already on his feet after making his objection. He quickly approached Nurse Connie.

"May I have some water?" she asked. Harry grabbed a Styrofoam cup from the defense table and filled it with water from the half-full pitcher. He handed her the cup. She drank it in three gulps.

"Nurse Connie, do lab technicians ever come to the Moran wing during your shift?"

"Yes."

"How often do they come?"

"It depends on the shift and the number of patients."

"So on an average day, how many times do lab technicians roam the Moran wing?"

"I guess it would-"

"Don't guess. Give us your best estimate."

"Probably five to ten times during a shift."

"Do you know all of the technicians by name?" Harry asked.

"No."

"Do you know what all of the technicians look like?"

"No."

"Do technicians from the x-ray and radiation departments come to the Moran wing?"

"Yes."

"Again, do you know all of them?"

"No."

"Do technicians wear lab coats at St. John's?"

"Yes. Some of them do."

"And you don't know all of the technicians, do you?"

"No."

"So, it's possible that a technician could have been in Mr. Parker's room, correct?"

"I suppose."

"How long is the Moran west wing?"

"I'm not sure," Connie said.

"I've measured it. It's fifty yards. Half the length of a football field. Does that seem about right to you?"

"Yes, I suppose it does."

"Where were you exactly when you heard the buzzer go off in Mr. Parker's room?" Harry asked.

"I just came out of Moran 8."

"So you were about thirty yards away from Moran 4, right?"

"I suppose."

Harry walked through the gallery to the back of the courtroom. "Your Honor, I would like to engage in a hypothetical for the witness." Judge Furmer looked directly over her reading glasses at Harry. She didn't respond. "Nurse Connie, where I'm standing is about thirty yards away from the witness stand, where you're seated. I'm going to ask this nice gentleman seated to my right to stand up." The man next to Harry stood. "Nurse Connie, what color eyes does this man have?"

Connie squinted. "Brown?" she said.

"Let the record reflect that the gentleman has green eyes," Harry said.

"How tall is this gentleman?" Harry asked.

"Oh, I suppose he's about five foot nine or so," Connie said.

Harry got out his tape measure from his pocket. He measured the man. "Let the record reflect that he's actually six feet three inches tall." Harry walked back to the witness stand.

"Distance distorts perception, doesn't it, Nurse Connie," Harry said.

"Objection, argumentative," Bain said.

"Withdrawn."

"Have you ever seen Michael O'Connor in person before this trial?"

"No."

"So how did you know that he has blue eyes?"

Connie looked to Bain. He grimaced. "The prosecutor told me."

"No further questions," Harry said.

Chapter 30

"The prosecution calls Deputy Sheriff Tim Marshall," Bain said.

Tim, wearing his neatly pressed uniform, walked up to the bailiff. He looked very official and quite serious. His face was flushed, showing off the z-shaped scar on his forehead.

"Please state your name for the record," Bain asked.

"Timothy Brian Marshall."

"What is your official job title?"

"I'm a deputy sheriff here in Jackson Hole, Wyomin'."

"How long have you served on the police force?"

"I was a police officer for nine years and then was appointed deputy sheriff three years ago."

"How are you associated with the investigation of the murder of Preston Parker?"

"Objection," Harry stated. "Assumes facts not in evidence and is argumentative."

"Sustained. Restate your question, counselor," Judge Furmer stated.

"Were you involved in the investigation of Preston Parker's ski incident?" Bain asked, shooting a look at Harry.

"Yes, sir. I was assigned to his case by Sheriff Johnston."

"How long after the ski accident were you assigned to the case?"

"I reckon it was about one hour after we heard about it on the two-way."

"Why were you assigned to investigate a ski accident?"

"Teton County has spent hundreds of thousands of dollars in the past several years rescuin' people from a variety of mountaineering disasters. Our search and rescue units have run out of funding, based on the increase in mountain climbers, extreme skiers and misguided adventurers. We monitor the radio frequency of the search and rescue, and when they're dispatched, and if we have the manpower, we send an officer to investigate. It is a statewide policy now to charge people for the cost of rescuin' them if it's determined that need for the rescue was due to reckless behavior."

"Did Preston Parker's rescue fit into the reckless category?"

"No. He was actually rescued by the ski patrol within the boundary of the ski area."

"So why did you continue to investigate the case, after you had determined that it was a standard rescue?"

"Mr. Parker was a high-profile business man. It's department policy to observe all parties and interview all potential witnesses when there is an accident of this sort," Tim stated.

"Why is that department protocol?"

"For a couple of reasons. There's usually a media issue. We have a lot of movie stars and the like around these parts these days. They get real mad if their privacy is violated. The other reason is that there could be foul play. We make our presence known, so that the media doesn't interfere too much, and we also document anythin' that might seem strange, in case there's a full-scale investigation later."

"And you were the person assigned to monitor and interview the witnesses, correct?"

"Yes, sir."

"Who was the first person you spoke with about this ski incident?" Bain asked.

Tim explained how he got to the hospital and interviewed Kelly and Ann. He went on to explain how he tried to pin down Michael, but that Michael kept avoiding him. Tim told the jury about the parking lot incident where Michael was making a call outside in the parking lot to someone, and about how Kelly was out there eavesdropping, on her hands and knees in between the cars, unseen by Michael.

"Didn't it strike you as odd that the victim's wife was spying on the accused when Preston Parker was in the hospital unconscious?"

"Yes, sir, it did."

"Did you question Kelly Parker about it?"

"Yes. She said that she'd dropped an earring and had come out to look for it."

"Did you believe her?"

"No. I knew that she was spyin' on Michael O'Connor. It was obvious."

"Did you question Michael O'Connor about what he was doing out in the parking lot?"

"I tried to, but he kept avoidin' me the night of the incident. The next day, I stopped by the hospital a few times. He wasn't there when I was. When I went back to the hospital for the third time that day, I saw him. But just as I approached him, there was a big commotion in the hospital. We all went runnin'. That's when Mr. Parker went into a coma. Michael O'Connor refused to speak to me after that time."

"When did the ski incident turn into a murder investigation?"

"A week or so later, I got a call from Dr. Conrad. He was the emergency room doctor in charge the night Mr. Parker was brought in. He said that he got the autopsy and toxicology reports back and that somethin' was wrong."

"So what happened next?"

"Dr. Conrad came down to the station and met with me and the County Attorney. Dr. Conrad showed us the reports. When he told us that Preston Parker died from poisonin', it became a murder investigation. I was already suspicious of Michael O'Connor by the way he was actin' at the hospital. I did some research about his company, Geyser, Inc., and found out that they'd been havin' some partner disputes. Then Duane Towns came forward."

"What happened when Duane Towns came forward?" Bain asked. He walked over to the prosecution's table and took a sip of water.

"He'd been charged with grand theft auto. During his questionin', he said that Michael O'Connor called him from the hospital the night before Mr. Parker died."

"Did you question Mr. O'Connor at the police station some time after the death of Mr. Parker?"

"Yes, with his lawyer present. He said that he had made a business call out in the parking lot."

"Did the police department subpoena Mr. O'Connor's cell phone records to determine who he called from the hospital parking lot?"

"Yes, sir, we did. His cell phone records revealed that he called Duane Towns."

"What happened next? Did the police department interview Duane Towns about his conversation with Michael O'Connor?" Bain asked. Harry started to object, but then refrained. Bain was leading Tim Marshall a little bit, and the question was probably objectionable, but it wasn't worth interruption.

"Yes. I took Duane Towns' statement. He stated under oath that—"

"Objection. Best evidence rule," Harry said.

"Sustained. Do you have an exhibit, counsel?" Judge Furmer said. Bain grimaced. He went to the prosecution's table and rifled through a few documents until he found the right one.

"Sheriff Marshall, I show you Prosecution's Exhibit No. 5 for identification. Do you recognize it?"

"Yes, sir. This is the signed statement from Duane Towns."

"Did you type this statement, Sheriff?"

"Yes. After I interviewed Duane Towns, I typed his statement and gave it back to him to look over. I asked him if it was an accurate summary of his testimony and he said that it was. He then signed the statement in my presence."

"So you watched Duane Towns physically sign this statement, under penalty of perjury, correct?"

"Yes, sir, I did."

"Is that department protocol?"

"Yes, sir."

"In Duane Towns' statement, it says that …"

Harry stood and interrupted. "Objection, calls for hearsay."

"Sustained. Counselor, you can't creep in the back door this way—you know better," Judge Furmer reprimanded. Bain looked up at her sheepishly. He did know better. But this was his best witness. He needed to get in as much information as possible through Tim Marshall. He couldn't call Duane Towns to the stand. Duane wasn't a reliable witness by anyone's account.

"Sheriff Marshall, please read the statement to the jury," Bain said.

Tim put on his reading glasses. He started reading the statement, including the part where Duane Towns claimed that Michael had contacted him about a week before the ski incident. He said that when Michael was in town for the convention, they'd gone out for a beer together. "Over the beer, Michael O'Connor offered to pay me $20,000 to kill Preston Parker." There was an audible response from the jury and the other people in the courtroom upon hearing this testimony. Jurors exchanged glances. People seated in the gallery were whispering.

"Order in the court," Judge Furmer commanded. Once the audience quieted down, Bain continued.

"Continue reading the statement, please," Bain said.

"Michael told me to take my snowmobile up Granite Creek that day. When my phone rang twice, I had ten minutes to get up the canyon and wait. When my cell phone rang once, I was to be hiding in the trees above dead man's dip. When I saw Michael O'Connor and Preston Parker, I was to use my tire iron to whack Preston over the head and kill him. Michael called me the night of the accident and told me that he was only going to pay me half, or ten thousand dollars. The rest would be paid when the job was done." Tim took his reading glasses off and looked at the jury. His face was slightly flushed. His z-shaped scar on his forehead was more pronounced.

"And what would happen if Duane didn't get the job done right the first time. Was there a backup plan?"

"Duane was to finish him off."

"Did Duane Towns indicate how he was to finish Preston off?"

"No. He said that he hadn't ironed out those details yet with Michael," Tim said.

"Thank you, Sheriff." Bain took his seat.

Harry bounded to his feet quicker than I'd ever seen him move. "Sheriff Marshall, Duane Towns agreed to sign a sworn statement in exchange for time off a felony conviction sentence, correct?"

"Yes, that's correct."

"So, Duane Towns had good incentive to give you this testimony, because if he did, he would not have to serve all of the ten-year term for the most recent of the crimes that he had committed, correct?"

"Yes."

"Duane Towns has committed approximately thirty crimes in this area, hasn't he?"

"I'm not sure how many," Tim said.

"Since Preston Parker's death, Duane Towns has been convicted of robbery hasn't he?"

"Yes."

"And Duane Towns is now serving time in jail *for that* robbery, correct?"

"Yes."

"But the robbery that he is now serving time for is a different crime from the one he was on the hook for when he gave you this sworn affidavit, right?"

"Yes."

"What crime was he on the hook for when he signed this statement?"

"Grand theft auto, I believe," Tim said.

"A felony, right?"

"Right."

"So, Duane Towns had incentive to tell you whatever you wanted to hear in exchange for jail time excused, correct?"

"Objection. Argumentative," Bain said.

"Sustained," Judge Furmer stated.

"Sheriff Marshall, isn't it true that Duane Towns recanted his sworn statement within hours of giving it?" Harry asked.

"I wouldn't say he recanted it. He gave several variations of the story," Tim said.

"In fact, didn't he admit that Michael O'Connor never told him to kill Preston Parker?"

"I'm not sure."

"If he gave several variations, how can we know which variation is correct?" Harry said. "Strike that," he said, before Bain could object.

"How many variations did he give before you typed up his statement?" Harry asked.

"A few."

"How was it that you came up with the statement?"

"Objection. Vague and ambiguous," Bain said.

"Sustained. Rephrase," Judge Furmer said.

"If Duane Towns gave several variations of his story, how was it that you were able to narrow down his variations into one accurate statement?"

"I asked him a bunch of questions and verified that he was tellin' me the right story."

"And which *story* was that? The one that he signed as the sworn statement that you typed?"

"Yes," Tim said.

"Did Duane Towns read the statement that he signed?" Harry asked.

"Yes, sir, he did."

"Do you know that Duane Towns failed his high school exit examination in reading comprehension?"

"Objection!" Bain shouted. "Sidebar."

Chapter 31

We approached the bench. "This is highly prejudicial. Its prejudicial value outweighs its relevance," Bain said.

Judge Furmer cupped her right hand firmly over the microphone. "Did you know about Duane Towns' reading ability?" she asked. Bain darted his eyes.

"I don't know it for fact, but I've heard it," Bain said.

"If the guy has difficulty comprehending what he's reading, then it's highly relevant to the authenticity of his sworn statement. I'll allow it," Judge Furmer said. She motioned for Harry to continue.

"I'll ask my question again, Mr. Marshall. Do you know that Duane Towns failed his high school exit exam in reading comprehension?"

"No," Tim said.

Harry walked to our defense table and I handed him Defense's Exhibit No. 3. Harry showed it to Bain and then approached Tim.

"This is Duane Towns' high school exit exam. I'm pointing to the section identified as 'reading.' Can you tell the jury Duane's score?"

"He failed," Tim said.

"So, you testified earlier that you typed a *version* of Duane's statement and then handed it to him to read and sign, correct?"

"Correct."

"Isn't is true that Duane Towns was snowmobiling with a friend on January eighteenth?"

"That's possible," Tim said.

"Sheriff, is Duane Towns an expert skier?"

"I don't know."

"Did you ask Duane Towns how he was able to allegedly run Preston Parker off the ski slope, according to his sworn testimony?"

"No."

"Do you even know if Duane Towns can ski?"

"No."

"Did your investigation reveal a set of ski tracks that could have been traced to Duane Towns?"

"No."

"Did your investigation reveal whether Duane Towns had purchased a ski ticket for January eighteenth?"

"No."

"No, meaning that you didn't research whether Duane Towns had purchased a ski ticket, or no, he didn't purchase a ticket?"

"No, we didn't verify that he purchased a ski ticket the day in question."

This is where my day off on the slopes had paid off. I had subpoenaed the records from the ski area and had discovered there was no evidence that Duane Towns had bought a ticket that day. Sure, he could have paid in cash, but at least we had ruled out the purchase of a ticket with a credit card (although unlikely that he could have qualified for a credit card anyway). Also, I spoke with the aerial tram operator who had been on duty on January eighteenth. She was a local who knew Duane Towns. She didn't see him get on the tram that day.

"So you don't know whether Duane Towns was ever even on the ski slope the day of the accident, do you?"

"We have his word."

"And that means a lot, doesn't it?" Harry saw Bain starting to stand to make an objection. "Strike that," Harry said to the court reporter.

"Did Duane Towns ever get paid anything by my client?"

"I don't know."

"Didn't you ask him whether he had been paid for this alleged crime?"

"Yes, I asked him," Tim said defiantly.

"And what was his response?"

"He said that the defendant stiffed him."

"So, he admitted that Michael O'Connor had never given him any money for any reason, correct?"

"Yes."

"So, you don't know whether Duane Towns can ski, whether he did ski that day, or where, and he admits that he has never received any money from Michael O'Connor, right?"

"Objection, asked and answered," Bain said.

"Sheriff Marshall, were you recently called to investigate Duane Towns' alibi for January eighteenth and discovered that Duane Towns had many photographs of Kelly Parker all over his bedroom wall?"

"Yes."

"Didn't the number of photographs make the police department include Duane Towns as a possible suspect for the alleged murder of Preston Parker?"

"Yes, it did."

Harry walked to the defense table and I handed him Defense Exhibit #4. Harry showed it to Bain and then to Tim Marshall.

"Duane Towns had a restraining order against him for stalking Kelly Parker, didn't he?"

"According to this exhibit, yes."

"As a stalker, Duane might have motive to kill her husband, right?" Harry asked. But before Tim Marshall could answer, Harry said, "No more questions for Sheriff Marshall."

Bain wanted to put Duane Towns on the stand, but he must have known that it would be a mistake. Towns's sworn statement had been admitted into evidence through Tim Marshall. Towns had a long rap sheet. Harry would parade his prior convictions to the jury on cross-examination and this would impeach his credibility. Not to mention that he would be a terrible witness on the stand. According to Harry's son, Duane Towns didn't know a lie from the truth half of the time. The fact that he hadn't been paid also was a problem. Michael O'Connor had gone to high school with Duane, so they had known each other. And Michael told us that he called Duane to have a beer, for old time sake. That was a reasonable explanation. Duane Towns would be easy to impeach. It just wasn't worth the risk of putting him on the stand.

So, Bain moved on. He called Steven Taylor, Geyser's certified public accountant and Michael's personal financial manager. Mr. Taylor testified that Michael had withdrawn twenty thousand dollars from his personal account before the Jackson Hole trip, but that Michael had not told Steven Taylor why he needed the money. Harry made sure that the jury learned from Mr. Taylor that Preston and Michael often withdrew large sums of money before a business trip, usually to pay for business-related costs and for personal expenses.

Bain called Carol Leahy, Preston's loyal personal assistant and the secretary who had been with Geyser since its inception, to the stand. Wearing a light pink suit and silver jewelry, Carol looked stunning on the stand. However, she was visibly shaken, obviously still in shock over her boss's death. She testified about

Michael searching through Preston's files, shortly before the Jackson Hole trip, and asking about a missing file in particular. It sounded a bit suspect, for sure, but Harry played grandpa with her and coaxed her into admitting that Preston often had misplaced files. She had to agree that Michael could simply have been helping Preston locate a missing file. Harry was able to steer Carol in almost any direction he needed her to go with his sweet and understanding tone. It was like watching Fred and Ginger dance. Fred led, and Ginger followed.

I whispered to Harry that Carol was Hugh's mistress and Harry just gave me a nod. "Aren't you going to use this against her in cross-examination?" I asked.

"Mac, there are things you need to learn."

I hate it when Harry says things like this to me. True or not.

"If I bludgeoned her with this information, the jury would hate me," Harry whispered. "Carol is a nice woman. If she were a prominent witness and her testimony was crucial to the case, I might use that kind of information to call her character into question. But since she isn't that important to the overall case, it is best to simply persuade her on the stand in front of the jury that there could be more than one explanation for Michael's behavior."

Harry was right. As usual. That's what I mean about him. He can see the forest and the trees. He doesn't get overly excited about a tidbit of damaging information unless it is pivotal to the case.

I doubt that Bain wanted to end the day of testimony on a high note for Harry, but it seemed like he had no choice. Harry finished the day with his careful and pleasant cross-examination of Carol.

* * * *

On our way out of the courtroom, I asked Harry if he needed any help that night preparing. He said that he didn't and that he was going to take the night off and relax. Harry was not one to overwork a case. He knew that it was equally important to take sufficient breaks to allow the mind to absorb all the information. "Mac, sometimes a modicum of testimony that goes right over your head will be the breakthrough you need, if only you give yourself the time to ponder," he said.

What I was pondering was a little off track. I'd invited Greg to dinner at my apartment.

* * * *

Betty Crocker, I'm not, but I make a delicious pork tenderloin with caramelized apples and wild rice. I ducked into the market on my way home and picked up what I needed. After marinating the meat and placing in the oven, I took a quick shower to freshen up. I slid into comfortable black stretch jeans and a fitted black and jade striped shirt. I fluffed my hair and reapplied my makeup.

Greg showed up right on time. He knocked lightly on my apartment door. I quickly turned on some jazz and lit the candles in the living room before answering the door. He had a bottle of wine in his right hand and a gigantic bouquet of tulips in his left. But instead of handing either to me, he stepped in and gave me a hug. The cold wine rubbed against my lower back, thrusting me forward into him. I started to step back when he pulled me in closer. The first kiss was tender, a careful encounter of soft lips. The second kiss was hungry and passionate.

The oven timer interrupted our kissing, sending us both into the kitchen. He arranged the flowers in a vase and then opened the wine. While I made the final preparations, he wandered about my apartment, studying my photographs.

"Dinner is served," I said, setting the plates on my tiny dining table.

"This is delicious," Greg said, halfway through his first bite. He raised his glass. "Here's to a beautiful woman, smart lawyer and fantastic chef."

"Flattery works wonders on me."

"It should." We talked over a long meal, learning about each other's past, present and future. As we discussed his craft of photography, he said, "I noticed that in every picture here, you are on the perimeter."

"What do you mean?"

He excused himself from the table and took my hand. "Come see." He showed me eight or ten pictures that were scattered about my place. He was right. In every group shot, I was on the outer edge of the group.

"Is this significant?"

"Maybe. Maybe not. But in my experience as a photographer, people place themselves in a particular order during group shots. I love watching it. Normally, people who need to be the center of attention make sure that they're in the middle of a group photo. People who are not quite sure where they fit in often stand toward the edge." I'd never given it much thought before, but Greg was right. "Hey, I didn't mean to hurt your feelings. I was just making an observation."

"No, it's okay. I guess I'm just tired all of a sudden. It's been a crazy month."

"I'm sure that it has. Not to change the subject, and maybe this isn't a good time to ask, but have the police ever found the guy who attacked you earlier in the year?"

"No. They've hit a dead end. As far as they're concerned, he hasn't repeated the crime anywhere around here since then and he didn't leave behind any DNA evidence, so the trail is cold."

"How do you feel about it? I mean, are you worried for your safety or anything? I—I mean, I don't want to frighten you … it's just that-"

"Yes. I do worry. To the point where I think I'm paranoid. But, there's only so much I can do about it. I don't want to dwell on it, but it's always in the back of my mind. Simple chores like going to the market and walking to my car at the end of the day scare me, but I have to live my life. I'm just more careful now. And, thanks for asking. Nobody asks."

"You're welcome. I need to let you get some rest. Thank you for a wonderful evening. I'll see you in the morning," Greg said, as he kissed me goodnight for the next hour.

Chapter 32

"All rise," the bailiff once again announced. Several days into a trial, things begin to work like clockwork. The jurors are seated, the lawyers and clients are situated, the judge walks in, the bailiff makes the announcement and testimony begins. It is very smooth compared to the first few days of jury selection and pre-trial motions, where there are constant interruptions and breaks. It's good to have a rhythm, especially after last night's dream. I dreamed that I was floating in a swimming pool when suddenly, I went cascading over a large waterfall. When I landed in the water after the free fall, I couldn't figure out which way was up. I swam to where I thought the surface would be, but found myself deeper in the water. I flipped myself around and tried to swim to the top, but my left leg got caught on something. As I desperately worked to get myself free, I let out a few bubbles. They rose. I followed my bubbles to the surface, gasping for air when I made it. I awoke with a jerk, realizing that it was only a dream.

By the looks of it, Bain either stayed up late last night preparing for today's testimony or he had nightmares. His eyes were puffy. For Bain, today's line-up of witnesses was critical and pivotal.

Before a trial begins, each side must exchange their respective list of witnesses. That way, both sides are prepared for direct and cross-examination, reducing delays and surprises. However, each side does not have to reveal in detail about what each witness will testify. Depositions can be taken of each witness, but at some point, it can become very expensive. Naturally, then, there are some surprises. Surprises can be either good or bad. But to Harry, any surprise is bad, even if it works in his favor.

"The prosecution calls Dr. James Flanigan," Bain stated, drawing in a big breath of air. Kelly's father walked in the door from the back of the courtroom. He had been waiting outside the courtroom. I could hear the cameras snapping shots of him walking up to the stand. His dark hair had noticeable graying along the sideburns. He walked with a slight hunch to his shoulders. His role as a Geyser product distributor had been splashed across this morning's headlines.

"Please state your name for the record," Bain said.

"Dr. James Michael Flanigan," he responded.

"Where do you reside, Dr. Flanigan?"

"Buffalo, Wyoming."

"What kind of doctor are you?" Bain asked.

"I was a general practitioner for over twenty years. I am now retired."

"Since you retired, have you still been actively involved in the medical community?"

"Yes. Shortly after I retired, I formed a company called Powder River Pharmaceutical. I distributed mainly medical supplies throughout the Rocky Mountain states," James said.

"How did you know the deceased, Preston Parker?"

"He was my son-in-law. He was married to my daughter, Kelly," James said. His eyes glanced in Kelly's direction.

"How did you first come to meet Mr. Parker?"

"He was Michael O'Connor's roommate at Harvard. Kelly, my daughter, also went to Harvard. Michael and Kelly have been friends since childhood. When I visited Kelly during her first year there, Michael introduced me to Preston. Preston later began dating my daughter and a few years after college, they were married," James said. He seemed a little stiff with his answer, as if he had rehearsed it in front of the mirror a few too many times.

"Did you ever have the opportunity to do business with Mr. Parker?"

"Yes. About a year ago, Preston called me and asked if I wanted to create a distribution partnership with him. After many discussions, we agreed to form a company together."

"What was the name of the company you formed with Preston Parker?"

"Rocky Mountain Pharmaceutical."

"Rocky Mountain Pharmaceutical is a different company than Powder River Pharmaceutical, right?"

"Yes. They are two different companies. I am the president and chief executive officer of both companies, but they are completely separate."

"What's the difference between these companies?"

"As I stated, Powder River markets and distributes medical supplies in the region. Rocky Mountain Pharmaceutical distributes Geyser's impotency products throughout Asia and Micronesia."

"Why did you only distribute these impotency drugs to Asia and Micronesia?"

"I'm not sure, exactly. Preston told me that he needed a distributor in that area and told me what he was willing to pay me to do it. The money was too good to pass up."

"Did Michael O'Connor know about this arrangement?"

"Not at first, no."

"Why not?"

"I've known Michael since he was born," James said. "Michael is a smart scientist, but he isn't a great businessman. There is a huge market for these types of drugs, particularly in Asia. Preston said that Michael would not have been happy about the arrangement."

"Did Michael learn about this arrangement at some time later?"

"Objection. Calls for speculation," Harry stated.

"Your Honor, it goes to state of mind of the witness," Bain countered.

"I will allow this line of questioning, Mr. Bain, but don't overstep your bounds," Judge Furmer ruled. "Answer the question, Mr. Flanigan."

"I believe that he did find out about it, shortly before the Jackson Hole convention," James said.

"How do you know this?" Bain asked.

"Preston told me that-"

"Objection. Hearsay," Harry said.

"Sustained," Judge Furmer stated. Her eyes burned holes through Bain. "I warned you, counselor."

Bain had to regroup. This was critical. He had to provide some evidence that Michael knew about the financial arrangements between Preston and James, thus giving him a motive to do Preston in.

"Your Honor, may we have a brief recess?" Bain asked.

"Fifteen minute recess," Judge Furmer stated. When Judge Furmer returned to her podium, she nodded to the bailiff to get the show on the road. The media reorganized in the back of the courtroom. They were ready for something juicy to broadcast to the networks and newspapers that evening. Judge Furmer reminded James that he was still under oath.

"Dr. Flanigan, what type of business arrangement did you have with Geyser?" Bain asked.

"I did not personally have any business arrangement with Geyser," James answered.

"What kind of business arrangement did Rocky Mountain Pharmaceutical have with Geyser?"

"Rocky Mountain Pharmaceutical had a partnership agreement with Geyser," James stated.

"Is this partnership agreement in writing?"

"Yes."

"Do you have a copy of that partnership agreement?"

"Yes, but not on me." James fidgeted in his chair. He accidentally nudged the microphone, making a loud screech in the courtroom. He flinched.

"Could you produce a copy of that partnership agreement by tomorrow, doctor?"

"I sup-suppose I could," James stuttered.

"Your Honor, I move for a recess until this witness can produce a copy of the partnership agreement," Bain said.

"Objection," Harry said. "Michael O'Connor has the constitutional right to a fair and expedient trial. There are no grounds for delay simply for a witness to gather information that the prosecution should have obtained prior to trial."

"Counsel, sidebar," Judge Furmer said. Bain, Harry and I went to the side of her desk for further discussion out of the presence of the jury. "Your Honor," Bain began, "this is critical to the case. This partnership agreement will establish that Dr. Flanigan was in business with Preston Parker behind Michael O'Connor's back. That Rocky Mountain Pharmaceutical and perhaps other companies like it had partnership agreements with Geyser and that Michael O'Connor did not know of these secret partnerships when they were formed. When he found out that he was being deceived, that the drugs he was manufacturing were being shipped to Asia, and that his company had off-the-books partnerships, he was furious. His reputation and maybe more was at stake. What Preston was doing may even have been illegal. The company's viability was being threatened. He confronted Preston about these things, and Preston ignored him. It made Michael even angrier and gave him motive to kill." There. Bain had said it. He wanted Judge Furmer to know where he was going so that she would give him greater latitude with his line of questioning with James Flanigan.

"Your Honor, this whole line of questioning is irrelevant," Harry said. "And any questions that Mr. Bain has for Dr. Flanigan about what Michael did or didn't know about Rocky Mountain Pharmaceutical call for speculation and hearsay. All of this will confuse the jury. You must not let James Flanigan testify as to Michael's state of mind. He is not an expert and he did not have personal conversations with Michael as a foundation for such testimony, Your Honor."

Judge Furmer took off her glasses. She had been staring over the top of her reading glasses, listening to these arguments. She knew that she had to be careful here. It could be misleading testimony if the partnership agreements were simply distribution agreements. She knew that Michael was the scientist, Preston was the businessman—the person most likely to make such agreements. Whether Michael was involved in making these types of agreements would open the door to a whole stream of witnesses. This *could* become confusing and irrelevant.

But if Preston's father-in-law was on the take with Preston, involved in secret partnerships with the company that Michael held a fifty percent interest in, then it *could* give rise to a motive for murder. It was possible that Michael was losing money over the secret deals. She had to allow Bain to at least explore the possibility. "Mr. Bain, I'm going to order the witness to produce it tomorrow in court. After Dr. Flanigan is properly questioned about the agreement and we have learned what relevant information we can, I will rule regarding further testimony along these lines. This trial is not going to become a fiasco. You are not going to be allowed superfluous testimony from secondary witnesses in an effort to get one of your theories to stick. Give me hard evidence in a succinct manner with proper foundation. Understood?"

"Yes, Your Honor," Bain said. Harry looked disgusted and frustrated at the same time as he loped back to the defense table. Judge Furmer put her ruling on the record and recessed for the day.

"This case is going haywire," Harry said, collecting his files from the defense table. "Secret agreements, secret deals, secret lovers. I can't keep up with the secrets."

Michael looked down, averting Harry's obvious stare. "Jim Flanigan is a liar and a thief. I wouldn't get too caught up in his secrets if I were you."

"What's that supposed to mean? A few months ago when you hired us to defend you, Jim Flanigan was like family to you. You told us how he and your father were medical school buddies and that he was like an uncle to you. Now he's a liar and a thief?"

"He tried to screw me over. That makes him a thief in my view. And I know for a fact that he lied to the state medical board so that they wouldn't revoke his license. I don't trust the son-of-a-bitch."

"Trust him or not, he's going to be back on the witness stand tomorrow and he's probably going to try to testify that you found out about his dealings with Preston. Let's get out of here. The walls are starting to close in on me," Harry said. I helped him stuff the files into our trial boxes, which we stacked on top of one another and wheeled out of the side door of the courtroom.

"I'm going to brave the front entrance," I said, hoping to catch Kelly out front. "I'll meet you back at the office."

"Trying to find your photographer friend?" Harry teased.

"No. But that wouldn't break my heart. I want to see if Kelly is with her father. They're relationship intrigues me."

"How so?" Michael asked.

"I don't know. Maybe it's because I never really knew my father. Or maybe it's something else. I can't put my finger on it. I'll catch up with you in a bit."

Michael shrugged me off, like I was wasting my time. Harry was too distracted by the trial to care.

Chapter 33

I don't think I'd seen afternoon sun since before the trial started. We had been marooned on an indoor island for weeks, it seemed. I was nearly blinded walking out of the courthouse into the sunlight.

I followed Kelly and her father down the steps of the courthouse. It was easy to eavesdrop on their conversation. Kelly made no effort to talk quietly. And she made no effort to mask her anger at her father.

"Kelly, I'm sorry. The whole thing was a big mistake. I should never have gotten involved with Preston and I should have told you what was going on," James Flanigan said.

"You must've known that you were going to be called as a witness at this trial," Kelly said, pointing her finger at her father.

"Not really," James said. "I got a notice from the lawyers only a week or two ago."

"Why didn't you call me and tell me about it? Not only am I your daughter, but I'm a lawyer. I could've helped."

"I was ashamed."

"Ashamed of what? Ashamed of doing business with Preston behind my back or ashamed at being caught? You swore to me and to Mom that you'd never get involved in anything like this again."

James must have sensed me coming toward him, for he turned around abruptly and glared at me. I needed to think quickly.

"Kelly," I said, "how are you holding up?"

She looked right through me. "I'm fine," she said, whipping her long dark hair back. She reached in her handbag and pulled out her dark sunglasses and put them on.

"Dr. Flanigan, do you have the partnership agreement with you in Jackson? I mean, did you bring your files, or do you need to have someone get the paperwork and fax it to you?" I asked.

"Why?" James asked.

"Well, if you have the agreement and can produce it, I can go over it tonight and prepare for tomorrow's testimony. I will, of course, produce it for the prosecution at the same time, so that there is no unfair advantage," I said. "It might help speed along tomorrow's testimony."

"I have the file at the hotel," he said.

"Maybe I should look at it first before you turn it over," Kelly snapped.

I followed them to the Wort Hotel, one of Jackson's finest. I waited in the lobby while Kelly went with her dad up to his room. She came back down in fifteen minutes or so and asked the woman at the front desk to copy the agreement for her.

"Here it is," Kelly said. "I'm not sure what any of this has to do with Preston's accident or the trial. It seems like we're getting off focus."

"I agree, but I think Judge Furmer has a good handle on how far she'll allow this line of testimony to go," I said. "Are you okay, Kelly?" I asked. "This has got to be tough on you."

"No, I'm not *okay*," she said and turned around and stomped back up the triple-wide mahogany staircase before I could say good-bye.

I read the partnership agreement through quickly and then asked the front desk clerk at the hotel to make another copy. I walked over to Bain's office and delivered the agreement to him in person.

"How did you get this?" he asked, after I handed him a copy.

"Dr. Flanigan had his file at his hotel, so I asked him to copy it for us," I said.

"If I'd known he'd had the file, I would have asked for a lunch break, not a recess for the day," Bain said. "I'm starting to think that this guy has something to hide. He's not very cooperative."

"He's in a tough position. Kelly's his daughter. Michael is his friend's son. He obviously put himself in a bad situation," I said.

"You're right. But the guy seems a little off to me. He's shifty in the witness chair."

I nodded. "I need to get back to the office. See you tomorrow."

"Hey, before you go, rumor has it that you're seeing one of the CNN guys," Bain said.

"Nothing is sacred in this town."

"How well do you know this guy?"

"Why?"

"Just wondering, that's all."

"I met him when they did that Larry King segment."

"He doesn't look like your type."

"I didn't know that I had a *type*."

"He's a little rough around the edges, don't you think?"

"I wouldn't say that. He's outdoorsy. He used to work for National Geographic."

"Does Harry approve?"

"Approve? It's not like I'm sixteen. I don't think that he even knows about it. But now that you know, he'll probably know first thing in the morning."

"After this trial is over, why don't you have dinner with me?" Bain asked, flashing me a smile.

"Maybe," I said as I fled the scene before it got too personal.

As I walked out of Bain's building and on to Center Street, I noticed a woman crossing Deloney Street. She looked a lot like Nyomi Janger. I tried to catch up with her, but she disappeared into one of the tourist shops, and I couldn't find her again.

*   *   *   *

Harry and Michael were talking in the War Room when I got back to the office. Michael looked angry.

"What's going on?" I asked.

"Dan Silverberg was just personally served with a trial subpoena. He's on his way from Boston as we speak, and he is *not* happy about it. Neither am I," Michael said. "This trial is becoming a bigger nightmare than I ever imagined," he said.

I looked at Harry.

"Geyser's CFO, right?" Harry asked.

"Yes," I said.

"Wasn't he in Preston's office the day that you confronted Preston about short-selling the Asian market?" I asked Michael.

"Yes. Mac, if this trial turns sideways and ends up being a corporate scandal trial, I'm a dead man. The jury will hate me for being associated with a bunch of crooks, or they'll think that I knocked Preston off because I found out that he and the other guys had been acting like a bunch of crooks. Either way, I'm toast," Michael said.

"Michael," Harry said in a calm voice, "if anything, the corporate scandal provides the defense with other possible suspects for murder. The jury isn't going to convict you for the corporate misdeeds of Preston and his cronies, I promise you. Our biggest concern remains alibi and opportunity, in my opinion. You don't have an alibi for the several hours following the ski accident, and you avoided talking to Tim Marshall at the hospital. You even disappeared from time to time. And you called Duane Towns from the parking lot. If we have holes in our case, that's where they are."

"I don't think the judge will let this line of questioning stray too far, Michael. She doesn't have the patience for it," I said.

"Mac's right. Furmer doesn't allow much leeway," Harry said. "You need to explain what was going on with the Asian and Micronesian market to me before tomorrow's testimony." Just as Michael was getting ready to explain, I handed Harry a copy of the partnership agreement.

"Where did you get this?" Harry asked with astonishment.

"I followed Kelly and James Flanigan back to the Wort. He had it in his files in the hotel. He agreed to turn it over to me and I dropped a copy off at Bain's office," I said. Harry looked at the agreement and then showed it to Michael. I left for a minute to grab a bottle of water. When I returned, Michael was talking faster than an auctioneer. He was explaining Geyser's cash flow problems, saying that Geyser's U.S. market had a substantial lack of revenue growth, yet earnings per share remained on the rise. He told Harry about the CPA's explanation that Geyser had lag time in foreign bookings, which didn't make sense. Michael told Harry about the large discrepancy in what the domestic market was paying for the drugs versus what the foreign market paid. Asia paid cash up front for the drugs at a discount, which helped cash flow, but this was in violation of domestic contracts with pharmaceutical distributors. In order to cover up the domestic contract violations, Preston and Dan Silverberg had agreed to cook the books.

"When I confronted Preston about this, he had Dan Silverberg there and refused to talk about it. This was right before the ski trip," Michael said.

I had told Harry all about this a month ago, but sometimes it helps to have it come from the source. Michael was probably better at explaining it anyway.

"I'm sure that Dan Silverberg is not going to be happy about giving testimony on the cash flow problems at Geyser," Harry said.

Chapter 34

The bailiff called the courtroom to order once again. His shiny gun reflected a beam of sunlight shining through the courtroom window. Harry and Michael were whispering furiously and they kept looking back in the gallery, but I couldn't hear what they were saying. "Please come to order," the bailiff said sharply at Harry. Harry stopped whispering. When we were allowed to sit, Michael scribbled on my notepad that Dan Silverberg was in the back of the courtroom.

"I remind you, Dr. Flanigan, that you remain under oath," Judge Furmer said. James nodded. Bain swiftly approached the witness box. He was visibly tense.

"We left off yesterday with a promise from you to produce the partnership agreement between Rocky Mountain Pharmaceutical and Geyser. Do you have that document in your possession, Dr. Flanigan?"

"Yes, Mr. Bain. This is a copy of the partnership agreement that I provided to the prosecution and defense yesterday after court," James responded. James handed the document to Bain. He had it marked. He showed it to Harry. Harry looked it over.

"Dr. Flanigan, please identify this document for the record."

"It's a copy of the partnership agreement between Rocky Mountain Pharmaceutical and Geyser."

"Do you know where the original is?"

"No. I only received a copy once it was signed. I imagine that the original was kept by Preston Parker."

"Is this your signature?"

"Yes, it is."

"What was the purpose of this agreement?"

"It was an agreement for my company to distribute impotency drugs to the Rocky Mountain Region and to certain Asian markets."

"Who approached you to enter into such an agreement?"

"Preston Parker."

"Did you have the agreement drafted or did he?"

"He did. He sent it to me to sign."

"Was Rocky Mountain Pharmaceutical a viable business when Preston Parker approached you to distribute for Geyser?"

"No. Preston suggested that I create a new company for this purpose."

"Why?"

"For liability reasons, mainly."

"Dr. Flanigan, did you distribute impotency drugs to Asian markets in person?"

"No."

"Who performed this task for you?"

"I'm not sure," James answered. He squirmed in his chair a bit.

"What do you mean?"

"Preston shipped me the drugs and I stored them in the warehouse. When he needed a shipment to go to Indonesia or Asia, he would fax me a purchase order and an invoice. I packaged the shipment and sent it to the various representatives in that part of the world working for Geyser," James said.

"So, Mr. Parker would send you the drugs and you would send them back to his representatives in the foreign market? That doesn't make sense. Please explain."

"I'm not sure I can, exactly. I kept track of the paperwork for the foreign markets that I shipped to. And I also distributed Geyser products throughout the Rockies."

"This agreement was purportedly signed by you, Preston Parker and Dan Silverberg, the CFO of Geyser. Did you see Mr. Parker or Mr. Silverberg sign this agreement?"

"No."

"Did you ever discuss the existence of this agreement with Michael O'Connor?"

"No, I did not."

"Do you know whether Michael O'Connor knew about this arrangement?"

"No. I don't know."

"Did you ever discuss this agreement with your daughter Kelly Parker?"

"No." The answer came out of his mouth before he had thought about it. "I d-d-did discuss it with her yesterday."

"Was that the first time you'd discussed the agreement with her?"

"Y-y-yes."

Bain then said, "No further questions."

Harry slowly stood. He sat on the edge of the defense table, with one leg over the front corner of the table. The tassels on his loafer bounced each time he moved his leg. He scratched his head and put on a confused look for the jurors.

"You must have been paid for your services, Dr. Flanigan," Harry said.

"I was."

"How much were you paid?"

"I was paid thirty-three and one third percent commissions on all shipments," James said.

"That's a lot of money! Did Preston Parker ever fail to pay you on a shipment?"

"Yes. The last one to Indonesia."

"How much money did Preston owe you on that shipment?"

"One hundred fifty thousand dollars." The courtroom grew louder. Judge Furmer grabbed her gavel. People hushed before she had to strike it.

"Did you demand that Preston pay you?"

"Yes. I called him several times and left him voicemail messages and even sent a few faxes, but he never responded to them."

"Didn't you confront him in person, at the convention, just before Mr. Parker's ski accident?"

"Yes, I did," James said.

"Dr. Flanigan, would you agree that you are a fairly good skier?"

"I've been skiing for over forty years, so I guess you could say that I'm a good skier," James said.

"Nothing further," Harry said.

I looked over at Bain. His eyes slowly lowered to his legal pad. He had tripped up on one of the first lessons a law student learns in trial advocacy: Never venture down a line of questioning with a witness when you don't know the answers to the questions. You might not like what you hear. Harry had just put another suspect in the jurors' minds. Reasonable doubt.

"Redirect?" Judge Furmer asked Christopher Bain.

"Yes." Bain jumped to his feet. "Dr. Flanigan, were you skiing at Jackson Hotel Mountain Resort on January eighteenth of this year?"

"No," James said.

"Nothing further, Your Honor," Bain said.

One of the first lessons I learned in law school was that "you can't unring the bell," meaning that once the jury has heard something, even if it isn't true, you can't get it out of their heads. The bell rang for the jury when James admitted that Preston had stiffed him on payment and that he could ski well. He was now a suspect, whether that was true or not.

"Judge Furmer, the defense calls for a brief recess," Harry stated.

"Any objections, Mr. Bain?" Judge Furmer asked.

"No objections, Your Honor."

Harry motioned to Dan Silverberg to meet him outside.

"Mr. Silverberg, I'm Harry," he said, reaching out to shake Dan Silverberg's hand. Dan was no taller than five feet five inches with thin brown hair and small brown eyes. He wore a crumpled navy suit with a brown tie. "Let's go into the conference room down the hall to talk," Harry said. "Too many microphones and ears around here." Michael and I followed Silverberg into the conference room and Harry closed the door behind us.

"I was served with this subpoena last night," Silverberg said, "ordering me to testify and to produce copies of all distribution agreements that Geyser has entered into."

"Why?" Michael asked. "I don't get it."

"Michael, there were things going on at Geyser that you didn't know about. I'm not sure I should tell you about them now. Let's just say that certain things were done to boost the market share and, in turn, the stock value of the company."

"Why do you think you have been called to testify?" Harry asked.

"I know about the partnership agreement with Geyser and James Flanigan. There were others like it. I signed the agreements."

"Shouldn't Michael have known about these agreements?" Harry asked.

"Yes, technically, as a majority shareholder and as a member of the board of directors, he should have," Silverberg stated.

"Did you know about them, Michael?" Harry asked.

"Obviously not. I started suspecting that something was up with Preston and James, but I didn't know about the agreement or the distribution deal. I tried to ask you about this before the convention, and it seemed like you and Preston were in cahoots to call the meeting short," Michael said.

"I'm not going to lie to you, Michael. When Preston found out that you were onto the situation, he got very nervous. We decided to try to keep it hushed until after the convention. Preston told me he would explain it to you afterwards, and then try to clean up the mess before it got messier," Silverberg said. "Look, you don't want me to testify about this, Michael. It will hurt Geyser. Our stock is falling as we speak, beginning when the news hit the papers last night about some 'secret agreement.' The stock tanked since Preston died. And you have not been around to give the public hope that any new drugs will be on the market soon. We haven't got much further down to go. Is there any way that you can keep me off the stand?"

"I don't know if I can," Harry said. "You signed the agreement with James Flanigan. Furmer will likely allow Bain to ask you about that. I don't know whether I can limit your testimony to just that act, though."

"What the hell was this all about?" Michael asked.

"Oh, Michael, you don't want to know."

"Yes, I do. I need to know. I am being tried for murder. I don't really give a damn what the company stock does. If I'm convicted, I'll be in prison. My net worth really won't matter, will it?"

"The problem with my testifying, Michael, is that all of these partnerships that I am referring to were 'off the books.' They were shells. We created them so that we could boost production and manipulate overseas market share to upgrade the value of the stock. It worked, too. Geyser has been one of the fastest-growing pharmaceutical companies in America over the past quarter, until Preston's death. Our market share has made you a multi-millionaire. It made Preston and Kelly even richer, because after James and I took our cuts, I diverted the under-the-table money to the Parkers' Swiss bank account and to some other off shore accounts. If I have to testify about it, which I won't—I'll take the Fifth Amendment—the company will collapse. I'll be prosecuted for illegal market manipulations. You might be too."

"Great. Not only will I be convicted of murder, they'll tack on time for white collar crimes," Michael said. He walked over to the window.

"I have our lawyers from Boston here," Silverberg went on. "I'm prepared to take the Fifth. This is a murder trial—not a fraud or conspiracy or a RICO trial. I'm not going to incriminate myself to get you off the hook for murdering Preston."

"I didn't murder Preston!" Michael shouted. "But I might be convicted. I hate this system. I feel like I'm going to throw up."

"Have a seat," Harry said to Michael, pulling out a chair. Michael sat down. "Get a hold of yourself, pal."

"I call an old friend to have a beer, and all of the sudden, I've hired him to kill someone," Michael said. "I do my best to manufacture impotency drugs to help people, and now I'm linked to illicit pharmaceutical sales in another country. I have 'off the books' shell companies with my dad's friend, James Flanigan. I can't tell you how hard my head is pounding right now. What's next?"

The courtroom doors swung open. "Furmer is back on the bench," a reporter shouted into the hallway.

"We need to get back in there," I said.

Silverberg walked back toward the courtroom. Harry held Michael back for a moment, out in the courthouse hall. Michael rested his head back against the white wall. Harry leaned against the wall, shrouding Michael from the cameras. I stood close to Harry, with my back to the courtroom doors. Harry whispered, "It's your call, Michael. I can object like hell and try to keep this testimony out, or we can use it to implicate James and possibly Nyomi Janger—giving the jury a few other suspects to mull over. It's up to you, though. It's your life at stake. And maybe the future of your company. I'm more concerned about the murder charges at the moment," Harry said.

"What would you do if you were me?" Michael asked. Harry hated it when clients asked him that question. He's told me so a hundred times.

"This doesn't look good, Michael. I'll be honest with you. It looks like you figured out that there was monkey business with the company and you took Preston out over it. Or, it looks like you were in on it all along and there was an internal battle over something. Either way, you look bad. You will look like either a crook or a murderer to the jury, once Silverberg testifies. Either way, you're screwed."

*　　*　　*　　*

"The prosecution calls Daniel Silverberg to the stand."

As Harry and Michael rushed back into the courtroom, a petite, dark-haired woman ducked into the ladies room down the hall. I could have sworn it was Nyomi. The woman in the hall had hair that looked just like the wig Nyomi had worn when I first found her in Bali. The woman wore a black scarf and over-sized black sunglasses. She had on black very high heels, an uncommon sight on the icy streets of Jackson Hole in April. After a minute, I followed her into the ladies room. I hid in a stall and peeked under to see where she was. She was right next to me. I heard her flush and open her stall door. And then I heard another familiar voice.

"You're the bitch that ruined my life." It was Kelly. "What the hell are you doing here?"

"I'm here to see Michael hang for the murder of my Preston," Nyomi said.

"Preston was *my* husband!" Kelly shouted. "You're the one responsible for his death!"

"You're a fool," Nyomi said. I heard scuffling and the door of the stall next to me opened. I heard a slapping noise and a screech of pain. I heard another slap and more struggling. "Let go of me, you bitch," Nyomi said as her wig dropped to the ground. I saw her kick Kelly hard in the leg.

"My babies!" Kelly screamed. "Get away from me! You almost kicked my babies!"

"Babies?" Nyomi said.

"Yes, babies. I'm having twins."

With that, I heard the bathroom door slam open. I quietly opened my own stall door and rushed out of the bathroom, but I was too late. Kelly was standing at the top of the courthouse stairs, glaring down as Nyomi fled the building, in tears.

Chapter 35

Furmer looked annoyed that we were late getting settled at the defense table. Michael, Harry, and I quickly took our seats. Michael straightened himself in his chair. Harry followed suit, and then I did the same. We all sensed that something was about to happen. Harry grabbed his yellow legal pad and wrote a large question mark on it and handed it to Michael. He wanted to know what he was up against. Harry had felt confident about the trial up to this point. He'd felt like he was one step ahead of Bain until now. Michael looked back at him blankly. Harry took a deep breath. He loathed surprises.

"Please identify yourself for the record," Bain stated.

"Daniel C. Silverberg." Silverberg repositioned himself in the witness chair and straightened his brown tie. He looked like an accountant. He wore a navy suit, white shirt and black shoes. His round, rimless glasses were perfectly straight across his large nose. His hairline was receding and his lips were thin.

"What is your occupation, Mr. Silverberg?"

"I am the Chief Financial Officer for Geyser, Inc."

"Where is your office?"

"In Boston, Massachusetts."

"What are your responsibilities as the CFO of Geyser, Incorporated?"

"I oversee and manage the financial department of the company."

"Whom did you report to at Geyser?"

"I reported directly to Preston Parker," Silverberg stated.

"Did you report to Michael O'Connor also?"

"Yes, in theory. He's the Vice-President of the company. But he was not involved in the day-to-day operation of the business. I rarely spoke with him about the financial side of the business."

"Other than doing the accounting for the company, were you involved with the creation of any subsidiaries or partnerships of the company?"

"I am going to invoke the Fifth Amendment and decline to answer that question," Silverberg stated. He had rehearsed the line with his lawyer, and it sounded rehearsed.

Judge Furmer looked surprised by this. She interrupted Bain. "Did I hear you correctly, Mr. Silverberg? Are you invoking your Fifth Amendment right to refuse to incriminate yourself?"

"Yes, Your Honor."

"Mr. Silverberg, you have not been charged with a crime here. Do you understand that?" Furmer asked.

"Yes, I do, Your Honor."

"Sidebar," she announced. There was an audible response in the jury box. Bain, Harry and I approached the bench. "What on earth is going on now?" Furmer asked.

"Silverberg cooked the books," Bain uttered before Harry could open his mouth. "He doesn't want to testify about the off-the-books partnerships that he set up for Geyser, so he's taking the Fifth."

"Where are we going with this, counsel? Because I am not going to have a circus in here. You need to prove to me *right now* how this involves Michael O'Connor," Furmer demanded.

"Your Honor," Harry said, "my client knows nothing about this. He was not involved in this part of the business. This is just a trick Bain is trying to play on the jury, to make my client, and all of the higher-ups at Geyser, look like crooks. It is highly prejudicial and the prejudicial value of this testimony highly outweighs its probative value. I strongly object to this line of questioning," Harry stated. "This will create a circus out of this proceeding. The media will be lined up for miles to find out about the book-cooking at Geyser. This won't be a murder trial any more. It'll be a stock market trial." Harry loved pouring on the drama. It usually worked so well.

Bain took his shot. "This is highly relevant information, Your Honor. It goes to prove motive. Michael O'Connor didn't know about these partnerships until just before Preston Parker was murdered. But he did figure out that these partnerships existed, and when he did, he was furious. This is what gave him motive to kill," Bain said.

"Do you have direct evidence that Mr. O'Connor knew about the alleged book-cooking, Mr. Bain?" Furmer asked.

"Yes. I already put Carol Leahy on the stand—Preston's secretary—who testified that Michael was asking her about missing files and, specifically, about Rocky Mountain Pharmaceuticals—which is one of these off-the books partnerships," Bain stated.

"That's tenuous at best," Judge Furmer said. "It's not enough. This is clearly circumstantial evidence, if that. It is not direct evidence. You're going to have to do better than that, Mr. Bain, for me to allow you to go forward with this witness."

But Bain couldn't do better. If Silverberg was going to take the Fifth, there wasn't anything that Bain could do about it. It was a constitutional right, after all. He was frustrated, but he had to move forward with his case.

"Your Honor, I am going to move on with another witness at this time, but the State reserves the right to call Mr. Silverberg back to the stand," Bain said.

"Your reservation of rights is so noted, Mr. Bain," Furmer stated. She looked relieved. Harry took his seat and Bain walked back to the prosecution table.

"I have no further questions for this witness at this time, but reserve the right to recall Mr. Silverberg," Bain stated for the record. Harry declined to cross-examine. Silverberg quickly stepped down from the witness chair.

*   *   *   *

"The Prosecution calls Kelly Flanigan Parker as an adverse witness," Bain stated. When a lawyer calls a witness 'adverse' it means that he or she might be an unwilling or defiant witness, allowing the lawyer to use leading questions to control the testimony. Kelly rose to her feet. She tried to look poised. She'd done her makeup with a soft and natural look. She was wearing a pink silk suit with a cream blouse. I could see a scuffmark on her leg where Nyomi had kicked her in the bathroom. She hobbled to the stand. Every juror had his or her eyes fixed on her. And she hadn't even spoken yet.

"First of all, Mrs. Parker, I am sorry about the loss of your husband," Bain said. He wanted to look like a nice guy to the jury. Kelly nodded as if she accepted his condolence. "How long were you married to Mr. Parker?"

"Six years," Kelly said.

"How long had you known Mr. Parker before you married him?"

"Approximately twelve years."

"How did you meet?"

"We met at Harvard University our freshman year. Preston was Michael O'Connor's roommate and Michael is a childhood friend of mine."

"How long have you known Michael O'Connor?"

"Our parents are close friends. I've known him since he was a little boy."

"So, it would be fair to state that you and Michael O'Connor are very close friends, correct?"

"Yes."

"Have you ever had a romantic relationship with Michael O'Connor?"

"Objection!" Harry shouted. "Irrelevant. Misleading. Prejudice outweighs probativeness."

"Overruled."

"Sidebar," Harry said. I rushed to join Harry and Bain at the bench.

"Your Honor, this is out of line. There's no evidence to suggest that the widow and the accused have ever been romantic. It's highly prejudicial to my client to even suggest such a notion," Harry said.

"It's a fair question, Harry," Judge Furmer said. "She gave grand jury testimony against your client. Her relationship with him is highly relevant."

"But her grand jury testimony can't be used in court. It has nothing to do with the trial. The grand jury testimony was relevant to the indictment. We agreed to waive the basis of the indictment. Bain accepted our waiver. The grand jury testimony was sealed at that point. It shouldn't even be mentioned at this trial, even at sidebar," Harry said. Judge Furmer narrowed her eyes at Harry.

"This isn't about the grand jury testimony, Harry. This is about two people's relationship. If they were romantic, then it would go toward motive. Your objection is overruled."

Bain smiled. He quickly walked back to the podium and resumed his questioning. "Have you ever had romantic relations with Michael O'Connor?"

"No," Kelly said. Her face flushed. Talk about unringing the bell. No matter how she answered, the jury was either going to dislike Bain for being disrespectful to a widow, or they were going to dislike Kelly for cheating on her husband. The 'no' didn't dissuade Bain.

"You haven't ever kissed Mr. O'Connor?"

"Yes, we have kissed. We're friends. Friends kiss-"

"Have you ever kissed Mr. O'Connor outside the presence of your husband?" Bain pressed.

"Yes."

"On the occasion or occasions when you kissed Mr. O'Connor outside the presence of your late husband, where did you kiss him? On the mouth, the cheek, the forehead, or elsewhere?"

"Objection! Argumentative," Harry stated.

"Overruled," Furmer ruled.

Bain was in control right now. A romance between Michael and Kelly? The soap opera was getting juicy. The jurors looked like they had had a good jolt of caffeine. Their eyes were glued to Kelly, awaiting this response.

"I have kissed Michael on the cheek, forehead and lips many times, as a token of friendship. Most of these times, these kisses were in the company of Michael's late wife, Brianna, who was my best friend. She died of cancer. Michael and I have known each other all our lives. If you are suggesting that I kissed-"

"Just answer my question, please," Bain interrupted.

"Did Michael O'Connor ever kiss you outside the presence of your respective spouses?"

Kelly took a deep breath before her answer. "Yes, Michael kissed-"

"A yes or no will do," Bain interrupted again.

"Well, yes." The bell was rung.

"Did Michael O'Connor ever ask you about Rocky Mountain Pharmaceutical?" Bain asked quickly.

"Yes."

"And what did you tell him?"

"I told him that I had never heard of it."

"Did he ask you about your father's pharmaceutical company?"

"Yes, he asked me the name of it."

"And what was your response?"

"Powder River Pharmaceutical," Kelly said.

"Did your husband tell you that he was in business with your father?"

"No."

"Did your father tell you that he was in business with your husband?"

"No."

"You talked with your father frequently, didn't you, Mrs. Parker, about the medical malpractice cases you were working on as a lawyer?"

"I called my father on occasion to ask his medical opinion about a medical malpractice case, when I needed it, yes."

"And *never* during those conversations did your father mention to you that he was in business with your *husband*?"

"Objection, asked and answered," Harry said.

"Sustained."

"When you attended the pharmaceutical conference preceding the death of your husband, you flew here from Boston with Michael O'Connor and not your husband, correct?"

"That's correct. My husband-"

"Just answer the question, please," Bain said.

Kelly bit her lower lip. She tried not to show her frustration. She probably did the same thing when she had witnesses on the stand. Now she probably realized how annoying it was to be cut off when trying to explain something. Bain was obviously trying to make it look like she was having an affair with Michael, and suggest that, possibly, Preston had found out, and that therefore, Michael wanted to get rid of her husband.

Chapter 36

"Do I need to repeat the question, Mrs. Parker?" Bain asked sarcastically.

"Yes, I'm sorry. This has been very painful and stressful," Kelly said, looking toward the jury.

"You flew to the conference with Michael O'Connor, not your husband, correct?"

"That's correct."

"At the hospital, after the ski incident, when your husband was unconscious but not yet in a coma, you were suspicious of Michael, weren't you?"

"I'm not sure what you mean," Kelly answered.

"Isn't it true, Mrs. Parker, that you followed Michael out into the hospital parking lot and crouched down in between two cars to listen to a telephone call Michael was making?"

There was a pause. She couldn't afford to be caught in a lie. "Yes, I did."

"But you told Sheriff Marshall that you were looking for something that you lost, correct?"

"Yes."

"So you lied to the sheriff?"

"I was confused. I didn't know whether Michael was still outside in the parking lot or not when Sheriff Marshall approached me. I didn't want to lie, believe me. I just didn't want to start something based on my own paranoia."

"Why were you paranoid?"

"It was a strange moment. My husband was unconscious in the hospital. I didn't know the severity of his injuries. Michael seemed to be acting strangely. I was upset. I didn't know whether I should contact Preston's parents yet—I didn't want to scare them if he only had a concussion and some broken bones. I was confused."

"You were paranoid because you thought that Michael might have been involved in Preston's ski accident, were you?"

"Objection, asked and answered," Harry said. "The witness has testified."

"Sustained."

"When you say that 'Michael was acting strangely' what do you mean?"

"He seemed nervous to me and he didn't appear to be as concerned about Preston's injuries as I thought he should be. I may have been hypersensitive, though. I was very upset," Kelly said. She was looking at Michael. He was staring at her.

"Isn't it true, Mrs. Parker, that you suspected that Michael was involved in Preston's murder from the time he was admitted to the hospital?"

"Objection. Argumentative," Harry stated.

"Sustained."

"Withdrawn. When Preston was moved to Moran 4, did Michael O'Connor visit you there?"

"No," Kelly said.

"Michael O'Connor never came to visit Preston in the hospital the day after the skiing incident?"

"No."

"Were you at Preston's side the entire day of January nineteenth?"

"Yes, I was. I excused myself a few times to take a break, but I was there the entire day."

"Even when the Code Blue was called?" Bain asked.

"No. I was with Tim Marshall then."

"So you did leave his room from time to time, right?"

"A few times, but not for long."

"And your testimony is that Michael O'Connor never visited you on the Moran wing, correct?"

"That's correct," Kelly said.

"The State offers prosecution's Exhibit No. 16. It's a hospital videotape of the Moran west wing on January nineteenth."

"Objection, your Honor. This video was not included on the exhibit list," Harry said.

"Sidebar," Judge Furmer said.

"Your Honor, we didn't know it existed until yesterday when we were prepping Nurse Connie for her testimony. We just got it this morning. It shows Michael O'Connor on the Moran west wing on January nineteenth," Bain said.

"Even if it does, it is highly prejudicial and it's probative value is outweighed by its prejudice. We have not had an opportunity to see the video and have no way to cross-examine any testimony derived from it. Bain hasn't called a custodian of records from the hospital that can authenticate how the video was taken or how long such recording is stored. There's no chain of evidence verifying that this is in fact *the* hospital video," Harry said.

"I have Jason Smith on call as a witness. He is the surveillance monitor for the hospital. He can verify and authenticate the video," Bain said.

"But it's highly prejudicial to the defense to view it for the first time in front of the jurors. If Your Honor is inclined to allow it into evidence, I strongly suggest that the defense has an opportunity to view it *in camera* in your chambers prior to the jury seeing it. And even so, the defense then requests a recess to hire an expert in the videography field to examine the footage to verify its authenticity," Harry said.

Judge Furmer sat back in her chair. She cupped her right hand under her chin and looked down. She was silent for what seemed like minutes. "I'll need a brief recess to research this issue. Give me the tape. I'll resume our sidebar when I resume the trial. Please step back from the bench." She made her ruling on the record and adjourned the court for an hour.

In an hour, Judge Furmer took the bench. She resumed the sidebar. "I'm inclined to side with Harry on this. The video itself is from too far away to discern anyone's face. It's not constant footage, either. The surveillance cuts in and out of the wing from time to time, on a regular interval. It's too late in the day to allow the introduction of evidence that wasn't disclosed," Furmer said.

"But, Your Honor-" Bain said.

"I've made my ruling. Take it up on appeal if you don't like it. Now continue on with your line of questioning, Mr. Bain."

Bain walked back to the prosecution's table and grabbed his yellow legal pad. He looked back and Kelly and started in again. "Did Michael attend Preston's funeral?"

"No."

"Weren't they good friends?" Bain asked with a staged look of confusion.

"Yes."

"Why didn't he attend your husband's funeral if they were good friends and business partners?"

"I don't know. I assume that-"

"Don't assume. Only answer questions based on what you know. You're a lawyer yourself, right?"

"Yes."

"Didn't it make you even more suspicious when Michael didn't attend Preston's funeral?"

"I was disappointed that he wasn't there," Kelly answered.

"Have you talked with Michael O'Connor since your husband's death?"

"Yes."

"And what did you talk about?"

"We discussed the company. We discussed the future of Geyser."

"Have you discussed what happened to Preston?"

"No."

"Why not?"

"Objection. Calls for hearsay," Harry said.

"Overruled."

"His lawyer instructed him not to talk about it," Kelly said.

"But you did ask him about it, right?"

"Yes."

"Did you ask him whether he was involved in Preston's death?"

"Objection!"

"Overruled."

"Yes, I did."

"And that is when he told you that he couldn't discuss it with you?"

"Yes."

"I have nothing further for Mrs. Parker," Bain said.

Harry stood. He set down his yellow legal pad on the defense table and calmly approached her, as if she was the least important witness to take the stand. He leaned against the witness podium and looked her in the eye.

"Kelly, you and Michael have been friends all of your life, haven't you?"

"Yes."

"You know Michael very well, don't you?"

"I believe so, yes."

"Michael was married to your best friend, wasn't he?"

"Yes."

"You were very supportive of him when his wife passed away from cancer, weren't you?"

"Of course. When Brianna died, Michael was devastated. So was I. I tried to do everything that I could to help Michael through it, but it was a very difficult time."

"You loved your husband, didn't you?"

"Yes."

"But Preston wasn't faithful to you, was he?" Harry asked.

"Well … no."

"In fact, you hired a private detective to follow Preston to Bali, Indonesia, didn't you?"

Kelly looked down for a moment and bit her lower lip. "Yes, I did."

"Why?"

"Because I suspected that he was having an affair and I wanted proof before confronting him."

"Did you get that proof?" Harry asked.

"Yes. Bob Avery, the detective I hired, photographed Preston with another woman." Harry walked over to the defense table and I handed him the packet of photographs and the report that Bob Avery had provided to Kelly. Harry showed them to Bain first. Bain took his time looking through the photographs. Harry then showed them to Judge Furmer. Furmer's expression revealed her surprise. She quickly stacked the pictures and report together and handed them back to Harry. Harry had the clerk mark them for identification and Harry asked for Judge Furmer's permission to approach the witness.

"Kelly, I'm handing you Defense Exhibit Nos. 6-A through H. Do you recognize them?" Harry asked.

"Yes, these are the pictures and the report that Bob Avery gave to me," Kelly said.

"You hired him to spy on your husband and document whether he was having an affair overseas, correct?"

"Yes."

"And your husband was having an affair, wasn't he?"

"Yes."

"Was this other woman's name Nyomi Janger?"

"Yes. These are the pictures of Preston with Nyomi Janger in Bali."

"Nyomi Janger was a sales representative for Geyser, wasn't she?"

"Yes, as far as I know, she was."

"Did you confront your husband with these pictures?"

"Yes."

"When?"

"The night before we were scheduled to go to Jackson for the convention," Kelly said.

"That would have been around January fifteenth?"

"Yes, I believe that's correct."

"How did Preston handle the confrontation?" Harry asked.

"Objection. Vague and ambiguous," Bain said.

"Overruled. You may answer," Judge Furmer said.

"At first he was very angry at me for spying on him. He accused me of being paranoid and things like that," Kelly said, wiping a tear with the back of her hand. "When he settled down, he told me that he had stopped seeing her and that he would agree to having her fired from the company, to cut off all contact with her."

"So, Preston broke it off with Ms. Janger and then fired her?" Harry asked.

"That's what he said he was going to do." Kelly's tears continued to flow down her cheeks. Harry grabbed a tissue from the court reporter's desk and handed it to Kelly. She wiped her eyes.

"Have you ever contacted Nyomi Janger?" Harry asked.

Kelly looked at me, as if I had betrayed her. "I spoke to her for the first time about five minutes ago in the ladies' room."

"Here, *in this courthouse*?" Harry asked. He spun around and glared wide-eyed at the jury for effect.

"Yes."

"Is Nyomi Janger present now in court?" Harry asked.

"No. She left the courthouse a few minutes ago," Kelly said. There was a distinct whisper from the gallery in response.

"What did you say to her?"

Kelly cleared her throat. "I recognized her in the hallway. She went into the restroom, so I followed her. I confronted her about having an affair with my husband. She told me that Preston loved her, not me. I told her that she was wrong. She kicked me in the leg and ran off."

"May we see your leg?"

"Objection," Bain said. "Relevancy."

"Your Honor, if Nyomi Janger is willing to kick someone in a public restroom of a courthouse, imagine what she might be willing to do to a man who just broke off a relationship with her."

"Sidebar," Bain shouted. Judge Furmer motioned for us to meet her at her bench. "Your Honor, Harry's statement just now in front of the jury is highly prejudicial. The prosecution moves for a mistrial."

"On what grounds? Judge Furmer asked. "He was merely responding to an objection. If you didn't want to have an open-court discussion, you should have asked that your objection be discussed at sidebar. There are no grounds for a mistrial. The witness may show the jury her leg." Bain stomped back to the prosecution table.

"Mrs. Parker, could you please show the jury the spot where Nyomi Janger kicked you?"

Kelly stood up and stepped outside the witness box. She lifted her leg and pointed to the large scuffmark on her shin. A bruise had formed and could be seen through Kelly's cream hosiery.

"Nothing further," Harry said. Harry shuffled quickly back to the defense table. He leaned over Michael and whispered to me, "That was a slam dunk, wasn't it?" I nodded, but I couldn't answer yet.

"Redirect?" Judge Furmer asked Bain.

"Just a few questions," Bain said.

"Mrs. Parker, how did you come to hire Bob Avery?" Bain asked.

"I don't understand your question," Kelly said.

"Was Bob Avery referred to you by someone or did you just pick him out of the blue?"

"He was referred to me," Kelly said.

"Who referred him to you?" Bain asked.

Harry stood. "Objection. Relevancy."

Judge Furmer said, "Overruled. Answer the question, Mrs. Parker."

"He was referred to me through Geyser, Inc.," Kelly said.

"Whom at Geyser, Inc. referred him to you?"

Kelly looked down and then away. "Michael O'Connor."

"No further questions," Bain said.

"Re-cross?" Judge Furmer asked Harry.

"No, Your Honor."

"The witness is excused. Mr. Bain, you may call your next witness," Judge Furmer said.

"The prosecution rests, Your Honor," Bain said.

"We will take a short recess before the defense presents its case," Judge Furmer said.

* * * *

Harry turned to me. "How do you know that Nyomi Janger was in the courthouse?" Harry asked.

"That's why I was late getting in here. I was trying to tell you. I started writing you this note, but you had already started your cross-examination. Kelly and

Nyomi got into a scuffle in the bathroom. I was hiding in the stall. Nyomi ran out of the courthouse before I could catch her or get the bailiff to nab her."

"No wonder Kelly seemed so shaken on the stand," Harry said. "She looked too nervous for such an experienced lawyer. That explains it."

"She told Nyomi that she was pregnant with twins!"

"What?" Harry said.

"You heard me. After Nyomi kicked Kelly in the leg, Kelly screamed at her for nearly hurting her babies."

Harry turned to Michael. "Did you know that Kelly was pregnant?"

"What's Nyomi doing here?" Michael asked, almost in a daze. Harry took him by the shoulders and repeated his question, "Did you know that Kelly was pregnant?"

"Oh … well … yes. I did. She is. The stress of the trial … Nyomi here." Michael went off on a tangent of mumbling. Harry looked at me with wide eyes. "Why is Nyomi here?" Michael shouted.

"I don't know," I said. "I swore that I saw someone who looked like her yesterday crossing the street. I followed her into a tourist shop, but I lost her."

"You don't think she's been called as a witness to testify?" Michael asked, looking suddenly pale.

"Not by Bain," Harry said. "He rested."

"I served her with a trial subpoena when I was in Bali," I said. "I doubt Nyomi is here to comply with a trial subpoena. She didn't seem to be the type to worry much about law. Anyway, it wasn't legal service of process. The long-arm statutes don't reach that far."

Michael look confused. "Procedural stuff. Don't worry about it. I served her just to scare her off a bit. I didn't expect her to show up."

"Are you planning on calling her to the stand?" Michael said. He seemed very anxious about it.

"Why?" Harry asked.

"Well, it just seems like this whole trial has become a … big confusing mess. I don't want to make it any crazier than it's been … for Kelly."

"Are you worried about something?" Harry asked.

"No, I'm not worried. Not really."

"It's not like she's going to be able to deny the affair. The pictures tell a pretty vivid story. What are you thinking about?" Harry asked.

"Never mind," Michael said.

"Is it true that you referred Bob Avery to Kelly?" Harry asked Michael.

"Yes. Why? Is that a big deal? She asked for a referral. He's a good investigator. He's done lots of work for me."

"No, it's not a big deal. I just didn't know."

"I've used him a number of times to check out prospective employee's backgrounds and things like that. In the pharmaceutical business, there is a lot of corporate theft of trade secrets. I check out my high-profile people very carefully before hiring them."

Harry turned and looked at me, shrugged his shoulders and said, "We'd better get organized. We're up next."

Chapter 37

Now it was time for Harry to put on the defense's case-in-chief. He put a number of experts on the stand to contradict Bain's experts regarding medical testimony. Harry was able to establish that the ski accident site was initially considered simply an accident, so it was not treated as a crime scene; therefore, it was impossible to determine what had actually happened. He had already cast doubt on whether and how much anesthesia had been given to the unconscious man, during Bain's presentation. Harry was lucky in that the alleged hit man, Duane Towns, was incarcerated and was unavailable to testify as a witness due to the fact that he was in solitary confinement for fighting in prison. His affidavit, however, had been successfully brought into doubt.

"The defense calls Bob Avery," Harry said. A man emerged from the last row of the courtroom and walked to the witness box. I grabbed Harry by the arm as he stood to question him.

"That's Bob Avery?" I asked.

"Yes."

"That's the guy who was following me around Boston! He's the one that was on my flight back," I said.

"What? You're kidding me." Harry said.

"No I'm not. I think Kelly hired him to spy on me while I was in Boston," I said.

"Why would she do that?" Harry asked as he furrowed his brow and then shrugged his shoulders. The bailiff swore Bob Avery in. Harry approached the witness stand, but was still looking back in my direction.

"Mr. Avery, what do you do for a living?" Harry asked.

"I'm a retired security guard. Now I do private investigating."

"Were you hired by Kelly Parker to investigate whether her husband was having an affair?"

"Yes."

"What did Kelly Parker ask you to do?"

"She told me that she suspected that her husband was having an affair in Asia. She thought he was involved with someone either in Hong Kong or Bali. She hired me to follow him and photograph his daily routine during a business trip," Avery said.

"Did you do that?"

"Yes."

"I hand you Defense Exhibit Nos. 6-A through H. Can you identify them for the record?" Harry asked.

"These are the pictures that I took of Preston Parker in Bali."

"Do you know the name of the woman he's with in these pictures?"

"Objection," Bain said, "calls for speculation."

"Overruled. You may answer," Judge Furmer said.

"Nyomi Janger. I followed her around Bali after Preston left Indonesia. When she was preparing to board a flight, I got in line behind her and had a glimpse of her passport. I wrote down her name from the passport while waiting in line behind her. Just as she was putting her passport back in her travel case, I bumped her and the passport fell to the ground. I picked it up for her, but quickly memorized the passport number. Her passport was issued in Indonesia. I wrote down the number and then went to the Consulate's Office and showed him the pictures of her with Preston. I gave the Consulate her name and passport number, and he confirmed her identity. When I returned to the States, I found out that she was a Geyser, Inc. employee through a public records search. I forwarded the information to Kelly Parker."

"Were you asked to follow up on Nyomi Janger since you issued the report to Kelly Parker?"

"Yes, by your office," Avery said.

"Anyone else contact you about Nyomi Janger?"

"The prosecution's office."

"Has Kelly Parker hired you for any other purpose other than to make surveillance on her husband?" Harry asked. Avery shot a look at Kelly, who was seated a few rows behind the defense's table. Harry followed Avery's gaze.

"Answer the question, Mr. Avery," Judge Furmer said.

"Yes."

"What other purpose has Kelly hired you?"

"She hired me to follow the attorney who works for you," Avery said.

"Kelly Parker hired you to follow my associate attorney, Mary MacIntosh?" Harry repeated.

"Yes."

"When was this?"

"When she was in Boston a month or two ago."

"Did Kelly tell you why you were to follow my associate attorney around Boston?" Harry asked, looking confused.

"She said that she wanted to know her whereabouts twenty-four, seven. She didn't tell me much more than that. I was to track where she went, who went into her hotel suite and when those people left."

"Did you do that?"

"I did."

"Did you report back to Kelly Parker regarding the whereabouts of my associate?"

"Yes."

"Were you paid for your services to stalk Mary MacIntosh?"

"Objection," Bain said.

"Strike that," Harry responded, before Judge Furmer ruled on the objection. "No more questions," Harry said.

"Your witness," Judge Furmer said.

"Mr. Avery, do you know Michael O'Connor?" Bain asked.

"Objection. Beyond the scope of direct examination," Harry said.

"Overruled," Judge Furmer said.

"Yes, I know Michael O'Connor."

"Have you ever done detective work for him?" Bain asked.

"Objection. Again, beyond the scope of direct," Harry said.

"I'll allow it. Answer the question," Judge Furmer said.

"I've done work for Geyser, Inc. for years," Avery said. "I've been hired by Michael and Preston from time to time for different types of assignments."

"Have you ever been hired by Michael O'Connor to spy on Preston Parker?"

"Objection, Your Honor. This is far beyond the scope," Harry said.

"Withdrawn," Bain said. "I've no more questions for this witness."

"Redirect," Judge Furmer said.

"No further questions," Harry said. He didn't dare follow up on Bain's question. Harry didn't know whether Michael had ever hired Bob Avery to spy on Preston. It was possible. But Harry didn't want the jury to know about it.

"Brief recess, Your Honor," Harry said.

"We'll adjourn after lunch," Judge Furmer said.

After the crowd cleared, Harry said, "I can't believe that Kelly hired Bob Avery to watch over you! She must have been worried that you'd figure something out. Michael, did you know about this?" Harry asked.

Michael shifted his eyes. "Not really."

"What's that mean?" Harry said.

"It means that I didn't know about it," Michael said.

Chapter 38

Harry's biggest decision was whether to put Michael on the stand. He didn't feel like he really needed to. The defense runs the risk of the appearance of guilt if the defendant doesn't testify on his or her own behalf. On the other hand, if the defendant does testify, he or she can get into hot water very quickly if the prosecution does its job in cross examination.

This was a murder trial. Did Michael need to convince the jury that he didn't do it? After talking with Michael the night before, Harry had decided that he was definitely not putting Michael on the stand. He didn't dare give Bain the opportunity to cross-examine him. Michael's conduct at the hospital was suspect, to say the least. Why had he called Duane Towns from the parking lot of the hospital? He told us that he was calling an old friend to go and have a beer, but had he lied about it? We weren't sure, and it was too risky to find out. If Harry opened the door, Bain would easily get Michael to admit that he'd had a crush on Kelly since they were young. And Harry was convinced that Michael knew more about the corporate irregularities at Geyser, Inc. than he admitted. So, Harry rested his case. Now it was time for closing statements. Harry was to go first. The prosecution gets the last word, since it has the burden of proof.

* * * *

"May it please the court, counsel, ladies and gentlemen of the jury? On behalf of my client, Michael O'Connor, we thank you for your time and the careful attention that you have given this case. We recognize that all of you have busy lives and we appreciate the fact that you have fulfilled one of your civic duties with integrity and honor. When you were being selected as a juror for this case, the judge asked you many questions. One of those questions was whether you could presume that Michael O'Connor was innocent throughout the entire trial unless the prosecution could prove to you, beyond a reasonable doubt, that he was guilty of murder in the first degree. You all gave your word that you *could* presume that Mr. O'Connor was innocent, unless proven otherwise beyond a reasonable doubt. Now, members of the jury, we are calling upon you to fulfill your promise. We are confident that you will fulfill your promise to presume innocence unless proven otherwise.

"Despite the fact that we have been listening to various people testify for nearly two weeks, this is a simple case. Why is it simple, if it took two weeks just to hear the facts? Because the case is simply about a skiing accident. We live in God's country. The Tetons are majestic mountains. We are fortunate to live near them and have the opportunity to explore the most spectacular natural landscapes in America. But, we all know that nature has hazards. The natural hazards on a ski slope are trees. And Preston Parker accidentally crashed into a tree while skiing. He hit his head on the tree, which knocked him unconscious, causing him to suffer traumatic head injuries. In the hospital, only a few hours later, he fell into a coma. As our expert testified, this happens almost fifty percent of the time. It is a tragedy. Mr. Parker was a young, strong, successful businessman, and he was running one of the fastest growing pharmaceutical companies in America. But, accidents can happen to anyone. Every day on earth is a gift. Unfortunately for Preston Parker, that gift of life was taken from him.

"It's time for us to review the facts. Then, you will understand why the prosecution failed to prove beyond a reasonable doubt that Michael O'Connor is guilty of murder. First, Mr. Parker had gone skiing in an out-of-bounds area of the ski slope. The ski patrol assumed from the very beginning that Mr. Parker had accidentally hit a tree while making his way back to the groomed slope. They did not treat the area as a possible crime scene, so no evidence was collected at the scene where Mr. Parker hit the tree. Even so, there was no evidence on the ski slope of this alleged hit man. There is no evidence that Duane Towns was even on the ski slope that day. No one even bothered to ask him whether he had purchased a ski ticket, which would have placed him at the scene of the accident. Duane Towns is just not a reputable witness. He could not testify in court before you because he is serving time for another crime he committed. He did not receive any money from Michael O'Connor. And he later recanted his own affidavit. It is true that Mr. O'Connor knew Duane Towns. They went to high school together. They may have spoken. They may even have gotten together for a drink. But there is no credible evidence that supports this hit man theory. Also, after Duane Towns recanted his statement, we had occasion to visit his apartment and found dozens of pictures of Kelly Parker pasted all over his walls. Obviously, Duane Towns was obsessed with Kelly and was considered a stalker by the police.

"Dr. Conrad, the neurosurgeon, testified that Preston was unconscious when he arrived at the hospital and that he slipped into a coma as a result of the head injury he had suffered from skiing into a tree. Dr. Gilliam, the forensic toxicologist, could not tell us for sure why Preston died. She testified that her toxicology analysis revealed a mystery drug called succinylcholine, but we learned that Dr. Kercher, the anesthesiologist, might have administered such a drug in preparation for an emergency surgery on Mr. Parker.

"Nurse Connie said that she saw someone who resembled Michael O'Connor coming out of Moran 4, where Preston was transferred after he was released from the ICU. But don't forget that Nurse Connie could not accurately determine the distance that she was standing from this unknown person. Also, this man was wearing a lab coat. Nurse Connie admitted that she doesn't know many of the technicians that work in the hospital that wear lab coats. Also, Nurse Connie participated in a hypothetical in the courtroom. I went to the back of the courtroom, which is the same distance from Moran 4 to Moran 8, where Nurse Connie was coming from when Preston Parker's buzzer went off. I asked Nurse Connie to tell us the color of the man's eyes in the back of the courtroom, and she couldn't do it with accuracy.

"Ladies and gentlemen, let's think back about some of the other witnesses we listened to. You probably remember hearing from Dr. Flanigan, Preston's father-in-law. He testified that he was in business with Preston, helping distribute Geyser pharmaceutical products. Michael may not have known about this arrangement, but that is not uncommon. Michael is the research scientist at Geyser. Preston was the businessman. It was Preston's job to run the business. It was Michael's job to do the research and development of the impotency drugs. Dr. Flanigan had words with Preston Parker regarding refusal to pay him for services rendered.

"Preston's wife also testified. She has known Michael all of her life. He is one of her best friends. They are not lovers. There is no love triangle here. Preston and Michael were friends in business together. Kelly Parker introduced them. She also testified that her husband was having an affair with Nyomi Janger, an employee of Geyser. Ms. Janger was fired by Geyser shortly after Kelly uncovered the affair, the week before Preston died. Ms. Janger was served with a trial subpoena, but failed to appear at trial. She is a possible suspect—a scorned lover and a disgruntled employee. As a matter of fact, Kelly testified that Nyomi Janger was at the courthouse and actually confronted her in the restroom and kicked her in the shin. You saw where Kelly Parker had a mark on her pantyhose from this altercation. Nyomi Janger obviously has a bad temper.

"When you leave this courtroom and go back to the jury room, think back on all of the common sense explanations for this ski accident and the coma that resulted from it. Also, think of all of the other possible suspects who had a cross to bear with Preston. Judge Furmer will give you instructions on how to apply the law to the facts you have heard. She will instruct you that the prosecution has the burden of proof in this case, and that this burden of proof does not shift to the defense. The burden stays with the prosecution. The defense is not required to prove anything. We don't have to prove that an anesthesiologist put succinylcholine into Preston's IV, or that succinylcholine poisoning may have exacerbated the head injury and caused him to fall into a coma. We don't have to prove that this was a ski accident. The prosecution is required to disprove the defense theory, and it must do so beyond a reasonable doubt.

"This case will be over for you very soon and you will be able to resume your lives, ladies and gentlemen. Since the prosecution has failed to prove that Michael O'Connor killed Preston Parker beyond a reasonable doubt, we ask that you return the only verdict that is possible here. Allow Michael O'Connor to return to his company, his friends, and his family." Harry pounded on the podium—"Find him not guilty!" He had the rapt attention of every juror. He smiled approvingly at them, then turned and walked to the defense table.

Bain stood. He walked over to the jury and rested his hands on the wooden panel that separated the jury from the rest of the courtroom. He took a deep breath, made eye contact with each juror, and displayed total confidence. Now the jury gave him their total attention.

"Ladies and gentlemen of the jury, on behalf of my client, the People of the State of Wyoming, we thank you for your attention to this case. If you have never been a juror before, I am sure that you now realize how very important your job is and how difficult it can be to sit and listen to a great deal of testimony, much of which contradicts itself. This case is important to the people that it affects directly, but also in the furtherance of the American justice system. This is where you come in. It is your job to dispense justice. We all acknowledge the importance of the jury carefully analyzing the evidence and coming back with the correct verdict. For the careful manner with which I am sure you will soon apply yourselves in the jury room, the people of this beautiful state thank you.

"As I told you in my opening statement at the beginning of this case, we said that you would hear evidence that the defendant, Michael O'Connor, is guilty of the crime of murder. Let's review the evidence that has proven this true.

"We now know that Michael O'Connor withdrew twenty thousand dollars before he got on an airplane to come to Jackson Hole for a pharmaceutical convention. We know that he contacted Duane Towns, a local crook, before he flew west. Duane Towns testified in his affidavit that Michael O'Connor had hired him as a hit man to kill Preston Parker on the ski slope. He said he was to be paid twenty thousand dollars for the job.

"Dr. Conrad testified that Preston Parker was brought into the hospital with a concussion from blunt force trauma to the head and other injuries likely related to falling. He testified that the test results revealed that Preston Parker had normal brain activity and was not in a coma when he was first admitted to the hospital. He testified that he later transferred Preston to the Moran wing for observation purposes. When Preston was transferred, he was conscious and his vital signs were stable. However, the next day, Nurse Connie saw a mysterious man in a lab coat escaping out of Preston Parker's room. She described the man leaving Preston's room as looking very much like Michael O'Connor. Michael O'Connor had the opportunity to slip the succinylcholine in Preston's IV when Preston was in Moran 4. Nurse Connie had gone to Moran 8 to check on another patient. Kelly Parker had left Preston's room with Deputy Sheriff Tim Marshall. Preston was left alone for only a few minutes, and during that time, a man who looked like Michael O'Connor was seen fleeing from his room. Not a second later, Dr. Conrad received a Code Blue call from Nurse Connie, indicating that Preston Parker was in cardiac arrest. He used automatic external defibrillators to shock Preston's heart back into a normal rhythm, which worked, but then, Dr. Conrad testified, Preston went into a coma, and there was no evidence of brain activity after that time.

"Dr. Gilliam, the post-mortem forensic toxicologist, testified that she had detected succinylcholine in Preston Parker's blood during her autopsy. She testified that succinylcholine is a depolarizing neuromuscular blocking agent used during surgical anesthesia. However, succinylcholine poisoning is very difficult to trace and is, in fact, contraindicated in patients with head trauma since it can cause cardiac arrest and brain death. Who administered this drug? There is evidence that suggests that Michael O'Connor either hired Duane Towns to do it, or that he did it himself. He is a doctor, a scientist and a drug maker and certainly knows how to administer drugs, and how to obtain them. Sheriff Tim Marshall testified to Michael O'Connor's strange behavior at the hospital and during questioning. He testified as to how Michael slipped out into the parking lot to make phone calls while his alleged best friend and business partner lay severely injured in the hospital. His phone records revealed that one of the persons he called during this time was Duane Towns, the hit man.

"James Flanigan, who has known Michael O'Connor since he was born, testified that he was involved in secret partnerships with Preston Parker, distributing the impotency drugs to Asian markets. From the testimony of Carol Leahy, Preston's secretary, we know that Michael had discovered these secret partnerships and, in fact, had confronted Preston about them. We know that Preston was making business deals behind Michael's back, and this angered him. We know that Michael also has a, shall we call it *close* relationship to Preston's wife, Kelly. The evidence is circumstantial, but it is overwhelming. We think Michael O'Connor decided to eliminate Preston Parker from his life. The motive? A few of the seven deadly sins. Greed. Love. Hate. Revenge.

"Greed. Michael wanted the business. He was a fifty percent partner with Preston before the company was taken public. Hate. Preston had been cheating on him in business. Love. Michael was possibly in love with Kelly, Preston's wife. Revenge. Michael wanted to get back at Preston after he discovered that he was doing business behind his back.

"This tangled web of a tale is the evidence in our case. The evidence points to this scenario: the greed, revenge, lust, and anger overcame Michael like a tidal wave, crashing upon the shore and shattering a life. This evidence has proved beyond a reasonable doubt that the defendant, Michael O'Connor, intentionally killed, or hired someone to kill the victim, Preston Parker. Now, the People of the State of Wyoming ask that you, the jury, return the only verdict that this evidence supports and fairness demands, a verdict that finds Michael O'Connor guilty of murdering Preston Parker. Thank you."

Bain took a seat, and he let out a large sigh of relief. The most publicized murder trial of his career was over. What the jury did was now beyond his control.

* * * *

Harry always got nervous when a jury deliberated. He knew that no matter how well he had proved or disproved a case, the jury could be persuaded by so many factors over which he had no control that he could only feel he did his best and hope for the outcome to be in his favor. The foreperson could railroad less confident jurors into making a decision. If they had been secluded from their families and friends for too long, they might come to whatever verdict had seemed to be popular in the jury room, just to get the case over with. He knew that some jurors took their jobs seriously, some did not.

But, experience had proved to him that most of the jurors come to the right decision, most of the time. To Harry, this is just the system in which he works. There were times when the jury had acquitted clients when he was certain that they were guilty. There had been other times when a client had been convicted despite what he knew to be their innocence. It's not a perfect system. Harry always cared, though. He wanted to get it right. He wanted justice.

It's also normal for an attorney to care more about some cases than others and Michael O'Connor's case was one of those cases. Harry knew Michael. He had known him for a long time, and he respected him. He knew what a loving, devoted person he was and he believed in his innocence. But the high-profile nature of Michael's case made Harry nervous. There was plenty circumstantial evidence to convict Michael. Yes, he had poked holes in much of the testimony. But, there was enough testimony to convict—not beyond reasonable doubt—but enough to persuade a jury. We could only pray that the jury would follow the law and hold the prosecution to its standard of proof.

I believe that these were Harry's thoughts as he listened to Judge Furmer give the instructions to the jurors about the law.

"Members of the Jury:

"You must base the decisions you make on the facts and the law. You must determine the facts from the evidence received in the trial and not from any other source. A fact is something proved by the evidence or by stipulation. A stipulation is an agreement between attorneys regarding the facts. You must apply the law as I've stated it to you to the facts as you determine them, and in this way arrive at your verdict and any finding you are instructed to include in your verdict. You must accept and follow the law as I've stated it to you, whether or not you agree with the law. If anything concerning the law said by the attorneys during their argument or at any other time during the trial conflicts with the instruction I've just given to you, you must follow my instructions. Statements made by the attorneys during the trial are not evidence. However, when the attorneys did stipulate or agree to a fact, you must regard that fact as proven as to the party or parties making the stipulation. If an objection was sustained to a question, do not guess what the answer might have been. Do not speculate as to the reason for the objection. Do not assume an insinuation suggested by a question asked a witness to be true. A question is not evidence and may be considered only as it helped you to understand the answer. Do not consider for any purpose any offer of evidence that was rejected or any evidence that was stricken by the court; treat it as though you never heard it. Now the duty is upon you to apply the facts to the law. The foreperson is to notify the bailiff when you have concluded deliberations," Judge Furmer stated, keeping eye contact with each and every juror.

The bailiff stood and escorted the jurors out of the courtroom and into the deliberations room. Judge Furmer adjourned the courtroom. Now, the waiting game had begun.

Chapter 39

Normally, we would wait for the courtroom to clear before leaving, but now that the testimony was over and we were waiting for a verdict, along with the rest of the viewing world, we had to get out of there quickly, before the media cornered us. Harry pushed his way through the crowd, pulling Michael and me along with him. Claustrophobia set in as I was engulfed in a mass of moving bodies, pushing and nudging, like wildebeests in migration across the great Rift Valley of Africa. As we finally broke free of the massive herd, Kelly bolted out of the courtroom in front of us and beckoned wildly at us to approach her. Harry saw her closing in on us and pulled Michael and me into the private conference room to the right of the courtroom. He slammed and locked the door.

Kelly banged on the door, but Harry refused to let her in. Harry didn't want Michael associated in any way with her at this point in the trial. I watched through the narrow glass window as Kelly exited the courthouse and tried to escape the press outside. Greg and his CNN entourage mobbed her. She held her handbag up in front of her face and rushed through the town square.

Hours passed like the months of winter. Michael spent his time on his cell phone, taking care of business. Harry paced the room, chatting pre-season baseball scores at me, as if I cared. After two hours of lock-up, I told Harry that I was heading back to the office to get some work done. He promised to call me if the jury came back with a verdict.

As I left the courthouse, I saw Greg interviewing people about the case. He looked a little bored. I approached him. He was wearing a crew shirt with a CNN logo and tan shorts. His sandals looked like they'd seen a few rugged backpacking trips.

"I'm heading back to the office. If you have some down time before the verdict comes in, call me," I said. He shot me a smile full of dimples and white teeth.

When I arrived at the office, Lela was busy cleaning up the War Room. She seemed surprised to see me.

"Is the case over?" she asked. Her long dark hair was pulled back into a clip. Her short, tight denim skirt clung to her thighs.

"No. Jury is still out. I came back to get some work done. Harry's driving me nuts, talking about baseball stats. Michael's talking on his cell phone non-stop. I might as well do something productive."

"I hear that there was a little scuffle in the courthouse bathroom today," Lela said as she bent over to pick up the stack of files on the floor. Her breasts bulged out of her lacy blouse.

"Scuffle?"

"Yeah, between Kelly Parker and that Nyomi woman."

"Oh, that. Right. And who says that trials are boring? You wouldn't have believed it. Too bad that we couldn't get Nyomi on the stand. That would have made for good headlines." I helped Lela put the office back in order as we spoke. The ringing phone interrupted the conversation.

"It's Harry," Lela said, after answering. She listened to him talk and then hung up. "The jury didn't reach a verdict yet, so the judge excused them for the day. He said that he's going home to take a run, then a steam, and then he's going to have a scotch on the rocks. He suggested that you do the same."

"I might," I said, "minus the scotch. Do you want to go and have a drink later?"

"No. I've got some stuff to do," Lela said. She abruptly turned and left the War Room. Lela had been acting strange all week. I didn't know if the demands of the trial were making her crazy or if something else was bothering her. She grabbed her purse and keys from her desk. On her way out the front door, she turned back toward me and said, "By the way, a delivery showed up for you today. It's in your office."

The door closed behind her before I could ask what it was. I walked into my office. A small bowl of forget-me-nots had been placed next to my computer. I grabbed the note. It read:

"Don't forget. You promised me another date after the trial. G."

I set the note back into the prongs that held it and sat down in my chair. After an hour of catch up, fatigue set in. I logged out, locked up and headed for the gym for a good sweat. While driving, my cell phone rang. It was Greg. He agreed to meet me at the gym for a jog.

After the first two miles of running, Greg confessed that he was a rock climber, not a marathon runner, and begged me to slow down before his heart gave out.

"How about a game of basketball?" Greg said. I agreed. We left the running track and took the back staircase to the gymnasium. A basketball game was already in progress.

"Hey, that looks like your boss," Greg said. It was. Harry had the ball and was dribbling down the court. Bain was guarding him. "Isn't that the prosecutor?"

"Harry and Bain play basketball often after work. Let's join them."

"Who's better?" Greg asked.

"Harry's taller, but Bain's younger. Who's side do you want to be on?"

"I'll join Harry. You play on Bain's team." I agreed.

"Hey, mind if we join you?" I asked. Harry and Bain abruptly halted their game. They looked Greg up and down. "This is Greg. He works for CNN." Harry reached out and shook Greg's hand. Bain reluctantly followed suit. "Greg will play with you, Harry." Bain seemed to like the idea and his demeanor perked up.

We played a contested game for over an hour. I guarded Harry, Bain guarded Greg. Bain and I won in overtime. After a shower, Greg and I went out for a light meal.

"Harry's protective of you," Greg said, after the waitress took our order.

"Sometimes."

"So is Bain."

"What do you mean?"

"He gave me the ex-boyfriend look when we first got there. He wasn't shy with his elbows during the game. Have you dated him?"

"No."

The waitress dropped our salads off and scurried away. We enjoyed light conversation over dinner and a lot of good laughs. He was far less serious than Harry, and it was refreshing to let my guard down and enjoy a few jokes. He told me of his travels abroad to faraway places on assignment with National Geographic. I told him about my recent trip to Bali. He'd been there before, and we shared our awe of the simplistic beauty of the people and their lifestyle.

Before we knew it, the waitress was collecting the salt and pepper shakers from the empty tables. He walked me to my car and gave me a lingering kiss goodnight.

✻ ✻ ✻ ✻

Greg was the last face I saw before falling into a deep sleep, and the first face I saw on the courthouse steps the next morning. He looked fresh and handsome in his tan cords and a navy sweatshirt. The wind was brisk and picking up force. He blew me a kiss as I passed his camera lens on my way into the courthouse. Harry was sequestered with Michael in the conference room to the right of the courtroom. I grabbed a cup of luke-warm coffee from the coffeepot and sat down next to Michael. He didn't say a word.

Around noon, the bailiff knocked on the conference room door and bellowed, "The jury has reached its verdict. Judge Furmer will take the bench in twenty minutes." He walked away. Harry didn't even have time to open the door. Twenty minutes. When the jury comes back with a verdict this quickly in a criminal trial, it is usually a unanimous guilty verdict. My heart sank. I could see the fear in Harry's face.

I watched Michael. Harry was talking to him, reviewing all of the possible outcomes, but Michael seemed to be disconnected, staring back at him blankly. Michael walked over to the window and grabbed the blind opener, twisting it back and forth as he watched the media scramble outside.

"Look at this mess. I can't believe how many more press vans, cameras, and reporters have flocked here in the last few hours," Michael said.

"Everyone needs to take his or her seat," the bailiff announced in the hallway with a thundering voice.

Harry escorted Michael into the courtroom. Michael's face was ashen. His future was about to unfold. "Think positive thoughts," is all I could manage to say to him, but I could only think of a jail cell with cellmates like Duane Towns, and worse.

"The defendant shall rise," Judge Furmer stated. Michael, Harry and I stood. I could hear the scuffling of people rummaging to get to their seats. Judge Furmer waited a few seconds to allow the audience to assemble and hush before she continued.

"Ladies and gentlemen of the jury, have you reached a verdict?" Judge Furmer asked.

"We have, Your Honor," announced the forewoman.

Chapter 40

"What say you?" Judge Furmer asked.

The forewoman placed her reading glasses on her nose and stood, looking at the sheet of paper in her hand. She unfolded the verdict sheet and glanced at Michael over the top of her glasses. "In the case of the State of Wyoming versus Michael O'Connor, case number WC000599, we, the jury, find the defendant *not guilty of murder* in the first degree," the forewoman read aloud. Harry turned to Michael and gave him a bear hug. Michael let out a yowl. Had I heard her correctly? Had she said *not* guilty? Michael grabbed me and squeezed me hard.

"Thank you, God," he said out loud. "Thank you." He folded his hands together and then made the sign of the cross over his heart. He looked to the ceiling and whispered again, "Thank you."

Judge Furmer said, "Thank you, ladies and gentlemen of the jury, for performing your civic duty with integrity. You are excused. The defendant is free to go. This court is adjourned." She struck the gavel lightly on her bench. She looked around the courtroom for a second and then at Michael. She picked up a file, took off her glasses and walked slowly into her chambers. The minute the door closed behind her, the noise level in the courtroom exploded.

Bain walked over and shook Harry's hand. No words were exchanged. He went back to the prosecution's table and started packing his briefcase.

* * * *

As we escorted Michael out of the courtroom, Harry stopped in front of lights, cameras, and microphones shoved at us in every direction. "Yes, we are happy with the verdict." "Yes, it was the right verdict." "Yes, Michael will resume the management of Geyser." Every reporter was shouting a question. As we made our way to the staircase, I saw Kelly out of the corner of my eye, standing in the doorway to the private conference room. She motioned for Michael to join her, but I grabbed his arm and steered him closer to Harry. I knew that Harry would not want Michael anywhere near Kelly with this many cameras around. We continued to fight off the press as we made our way to Harry's black Yukon, which was parked out front.

"Anyone up for an acquittal drink?" Harry said as the automatic door latch secured us from the mob.

"I'm buying!" Michael said.

We drove over to the Shady Lady, a cozy tavern at the base of the Snow King Resort. Harry figured that the press wouldn't know about this place and that we could have a drink in peace. Michael, his mother, Ann, Harry and I squeezed into the red vinyl booth in the back of the bar.

"Mabel, a round of drinks," Harry said. Mabel, the owner of the bar, sauntered over to our booth. She was a relic in Jackson.

"Just heard the word," Mabel said, as she adjusted her white bar apron over her broad hips. "Glad that our local hero is free." She patted Michael on the head, as if he was still a little boy. One by one, patrons came over and offered their congratulations to Michael. Just as Mabel was carrying a tray of drinks in our direction, a woman entered the bar dressed in a long, black coat, black high heels, a black scarf and large sunglasses. She looked like Nyomi. She slithered up to the bar and took a seat on a barstool. Michael looked at her and then quickly averted his eyes.

"Excuse me," I said. "I need a little more ice in my drink." I walked up to the bar to get a better look at the woman. The minute I returned to our booth, which was only about twenty feet away from the bar, Michael stood up.

"I'll be right back," Michael said. He slid out of the booth and joined the woman at the bar. We were within earshot of their conversation.

"Nyomi, what are you doing here?" Michael said.

"I've wanted to talk with you for months. I need to set some things straight," Nyomi said. Her voice was muffled, but I couldn't tell whether it was because of the acoustics, or whether she was simply talking quietly. Nyomi waited a bit. Michael said nothing, and did nothing. He stood like a stone, waiting. He was probably on overload. "There's something I have to tell you," she said.

"What?" Michael said.

"I did it," Nyomi said.

"I have no idea what you are talking about."

"Oh, Michael. I'm so sorry. The whole thing, this whole trial, has been like an oncoming train wreck. I couldn't stop it. I should have come forward, but I thought that it would just make it worse."

"What the fuck are you talking about?" Michael demanded. I saw him lean in toward her.

"Succinylcholine is easy to get in Asia," she boasted.

"What does that mean?"

"It's the perfect euthanasia drug. It was so easy, really. I knew that Preston would never allow me to have you, so I needed to get him out of the way," Nyomi said. "Duane Towns was an easy guy to target for the assist. He'd do anything for a buck. But he wasn't supposed to rat you out. He was supposed to have an air-tight alibi. The stupid idiot. Duane was supposed to go for a snowmobile ride with John and then fake some reason to go back to town to get something. He then was to ride his snowmobile up Granite Canyon and park it in the trees. He was supposed to hike up the rest of the way to the first chute and wait for Preston. That way, there wouldn't be any other set of tracks around and it would look like an accident," Nyomi said. I saw Michael's eyes widen, like he was trying to picture what she was telling him.

"How would Duane know that Preston was in Granite Canyon?" Michael asked.

"I followed you skiing that day. You never even noticed. I was only feet away from you in Granite Canyon, back in the trees. I called Duane and told him where you were," Nyomi said. "When the *accident* didn't kill him, I snuck into Moran 4 and put the succinylcholine in Preston's IV," Nyomi said.

"What?" Michael shouted. "You did *what*?" Michael slid off the bar stool and slammed his hand down on the wood. "You did what?" Michael repeated while catching his breath. He walked over to the jukebox and then turned back toward Nyomi. "You murdered Preston and let me take the blame? How dare you? How dare you set me up? I could have gone to prison for life, and you would have let me. I'm damn lucky that I wasn't convicted. I was the last person seen with Preston. God, I can't believe it. You would have let me rot in prison."

"No, Michael. I would not have let you get convicted. I was prepared today, if the jury came back with a guilty verdict, to confess. I would not have let you go to prison, Michael. Please, please believe me. I tried so many times to tell you. I wanted to tell you so, so much, but as time went on, I just kept thinking that you really would be acquitted and we could all move on. And you were, Michael. I was right. I know that you may never forgive me. But please know that it wasn't my intention to put you on trial for Preston's murder. I was trying to make it look like an accident. I was trying to make sure that you weren't connected in any way, but it backfired. Oh God, Michael, I didn't mean for it to be like this. I'm really, really sorry," Nyomi said. "I wanted him dead for what he did to me. He fired me. He left me alone to raise our two children. He's a bastard. I'm glad he's gone. I'm just so sorry that you had to go through this," she said. I watched her try to reach out to him, but he pushed her away.

"Sorry? Sorry? Sorry doesn't cut it. You have ruined my life. My reputation. No one will ever look at me the same way again. They will always think of me first as a murderer, and then they will have to correct themselves in their minds, and remember that I was acquitted. I am marked. Scarred. Forever connected with Preston's death. Because of you! You killed my best friend! No, Nyomi, I can't forgive you. I don't know whether I should call Bain or the press. Do I turn you in? I don't know what to do."

"Michael, don't you understand? That bastard fired me. He promised to marry me. The children are his. He fired me and then told me that he would have nothing to do with the children. He was going to dump us, so I decided to dump him first," Nyomi said.

"So you killed him?"

"What are you going to do, Michael?" Nyomi pleaded.

"For now, I'm going to say nothing, but I might go to the police with what I know at any time. I need to talk with my lawyers first," Michael said.

* * * *

Nyomi ran out the back exit, setting off the emergency door alarm. Michael sat back down on the bar stool and ran his fingers through his hair.

"What's going on?" Harry asked, as we joined Michael at the bar.

"Nothing," Michael said. His right eye was twitching again. He grabbed his beer and swallowed it in two gulps. "Let's get out of here."

Harry downed his drink and threw a wad of money on the table. I didn't even touch my drink. We started toward the front of the bar when Harry noticed that the media had found us. They were assembling their camera equipment near the front door, so Harry steered us to the back exit. We fought off the press and jumped into the Yukon, which was waiting out front. Harry drove to Michael's mother's house. Michael didn't say a word in the car. I kept looking at him, hoping that he would say something. He just starred intently forward, shaking his head from time to time. A saw a lone tear roll down his cheek, which he quickly wiped away with the back of his hand. More reporters were waiting at Ann's doorstep. Ann opened the garage door with her opener, and the reporters raced toward Harry's vehicle. He drove the Yukon onto the sidewalk connecting the front porch to the driveway, blocking their route. Ann and Michael darted out of the back seat of the car through the passenger side and ran into the garage. Harry and I laughed as the garage door closed, protecting them, leaving the reporters with only Harry's black beast to film. Harry threw it in reverse and blasted his horn. To anyone with an ounce of common sense or an inkling of Harry's personality, this meant, "Get out of my way, I have a drink to catch." And he did.

* * * *

"Can you believe it?" Harry said, after Michael and Ann were out of the car. "To think that Nyomi Janger was behind this all along. You were right about her. I didn't think she had anything to do with Preston's death. I guess I should have listened to your woman's instinct."

"Harry, drop me at the office," I said as he sped away from the O'Connor residence. "I've got something I need to do."

"Come on, Mac. It'll wait. What's nagging at you?" Harry asked.

"Why?"

"Because you're biting your fingernails. You bite your fingernails when something's wrong," Harry correctly pointed out.

"You know Mabel fairly well, don't you?" I asked.

"Yeah, I know Mabel fairly well. She's owned the Shady Lady for years. Why?"

"I need her help."

"What? You saw a cute boy in the bar and you want her to set you up?"

"I'm serious," I said, now aware that I was chewing on the remains of my index finger. I tucked my right hand under my lap to avoid further harm.

"What do you need Mabel for?"

"Didn't her bar get broken into a few times last year?" I asked.

"Yes. Some young kids, I heard, broke in the back room and stole some kegs. What's that have to do with anything?

"As I remember it, she had security cameras put in the store room to keep the thieves away, didn't she?"

"I don't remember. She could have. Why?" Harry asked.

"Because I think that we've been tricked."

"Tricked? How so?"

"Let's go back there and I'll show you," I said.

Chapter 41

"Pull over," I said. "I'm driving from here." Harry rolled his eyes, but did as I asked. I could tell that his drink had gone to his head. He hadn't had lunch yet.

"Good. You should test drive a decent car anyway," he shot back, as if it was his idea that I drive all along. "You know, John could set you up in a respectable vehicle."

"I'd need a raise," I said, with a half-grin. "What, you don't like the Accord? I've only had it for twelve years or so. It's got only two hundred thousand miles on it. Well, that's before the odometer broke," I added.

"Seriously, that car's not safe. You could get stranded somewhere," Harry said, as we turned left on Kelly Street on our way to the bar.

"I wish I could, but with my student loans and my rent, I'm barely getting by," I admitted. Nothing like taking advantage of the boss when he's feeling sorry for you.

"Now explain to me why we're going to see Mabel," Harry said.

"I want to see if she has surveillance tapes of the stock room. If she had tape running tonight, I want to see if we can take a look at it," I said. I accelerated quickly, enjoying the power of a car with a commanding engine.

"Why?" Harry asked as he fastened his seat belt.

"Yesterday, I told you that Nyomi and Kelly got into a scuffle in the bathroom before Kelly was called to testify." Harry looked over at me, his left eyebrow raised.

"Yes," Harry said, lowering his eyebrow.

"There's more to it," I protested, fearing that I was losing his attention. "I listened to their conversation. I was hiding in the bathroom stall when it happened," I said.

"Look out!" Harry yelled. I slammed on the brakes, narrowly missing the car in front of us.

"Sorry." I decided it was best to watch the road and disregard Harry's reaction to my every word. "Anyway, Nyomi is petite, maybe only five feet tall and she has a distinctive accent. The woman in the Shady Lady seemed taller and didn't have the same kind of accent."

"So?"

As we pulled into the parking lot of the bar, Harry asked, "Then why do we need the tape?"

"Because I'm not sure that it was Nyomi," I said, lurching the car into park before we'd reached a complete stop. "Sorry. I'm used to a standard transmission."

"I don't get it, Mac," Harry said as he removed his seatbelt.

"What if it was someone else pretending to be Nyomi?" I suggested.

He slapped his forehead with his palm. "Oh my God! Let's go see Mabel," Harry bellowed.

Only the regulars were saddled up at the bar. Mabel was standing behind the bar, going through paperwork and paying invoices. Her broad shoulders and thick bosom drooped over the bar as she peered through her reading glasses. She quickly punched numbers into her old-fashioned adding machine and compared the numbers on the white paper tape to the numbers on the invoices. "Keeping up with the paperwork is half your fun, isn't Mabel?" Harry greeted her.

"Hey Harry. Twice in one day?" she asked.

"Do you still run surveillance on your stock room?" Harry asked.

"Sure do. Haven't had a lick of a problem since them cameras were set up."

"Were they running today?" Harry asked.

"I hope so. They're supposed to run all the time. I have one of them security outfits handling it. They keep the tapes in some storage place. Why? Something happen?" Mabel asked.

"Possibly. How would we get a copy of the tape?" Harry asked. Mabel went over to her Rolodex and spun it around. She pulled out a card and wrote down a name and number on a cocktail napkin.

"His name is Ronnie. He handles the surveillance," she said. "Good luck. Hope you find what you're looking for."

* * * *

"We keep the tapes for thirty days, then we record over them," Ronnie said from across his desk. His office was stark and small, located in a warehouse area outside of town.

"What does the camera record?" I asked.

"Actually, there's two cameras. One of 'em is hidden in the storeroom to watch over the kegs, and one of 'em is hidden in the corner of the bar, to watch over the cash register."

"We need a copy of the tape from the one over the bar," I said.

"I need to call Mabel to make sure I can give you the tape," Ronnie said. He made the call. Once cleared, Ronnie followed us in his truck back to the bar. Mabel greeted Ronnie as he grabbed a footstool and climbed up to the hidden camera. He hit a few buttons, extracted one tape and inserted another. "I'll need to make a quick copy of this before I give this to you," he said. "I'll be back in five." We watched Ronnie scuttle out of the bar waving to a few patrons on the way. He returned in ten minutes. "Here's the copy."

* * * *

In Harry's living room, I hit the fast forward button on the VCR until the coding read four o'clock p.m. Then we watched for a bit until we saw the woman in the black coat sit at the bar. Within a second or two, Michael O'Connor entered the frame.

"Turn it up," Harry commanded from his recliner. I turned up the volume as loud as it would go.

"I don't know what I'm looking for," Harry said.

"That's right. You never met Nyomi, did you?" I said.

"No. Just saw the pictures," Harry said.

"How tall is Michael?" I asked.

"About five feet ten," Harry said.

"Look. The woman is almost the exact same height as Michael seated," I said. "Nyomi isn't more than five feet tall. Even sitting down, she'd only be to his shoulder or so." Harry nodded in agreement, scooting closer to the television.

"Look at her nose," I said. Harry looked closer, without comment. "Okay. Here's the part. The woman is going to turn away from the camera. Look at her hair. See this line?" I asked.

Harry looked closer. "Oh. It looks like a wig. You can see the woman's real hair there," Harry said.

"And the real hair is long," I said. "Okay. She's going to turn back toward the camera again. Watch her lips. They're very full like Kelly's. It looks like they have collagen in them. Nyomi has very thin, heart-shaped lips." Harry nodded. "Here's the ringer. When she goes to leave, she reaches out with her right hand to stand up. See what's on her right wrist?" I asked.

"Kelly Parker's Rolex watch," Harry said.

"Kelly is left handed. She always wears her watch on her right wrist," I said.

"So if this is Kelly on the tape, what's she trying to do? Set Nyomi up for Preston's murder? If she knew this all along, why wouldn't she just turn her in?" Harry asked.

I inched back away from the television and looked Harry in the eye. "If I was trying to get away with murder, I would frame someone else."

"Call Tim Marshall," Harry ordered.

* * * *

"If what you're sayin' is true, then we'd better high tail it to Michael O'Connor's house," Tim said after watching the tape in Harry's living room. He called headquarters and ordered a warrant to search Kelly's room at the Wort Hotel. We jumped in Tim's squad car and raced over to the O'Connor's.

Ann O'Connor opened her front door. "I need to speak to your son," Tim said.

"He left already. He's on his way to the airport," Ann said. We jumped back in the police car and sped to the airport. Just as we pulled in, we saw the white streak take off into the nighttime sky.

"That said 'Geyser' on it, didn't it?" Harry said.

"It's his private jet," I said. "Let's go inside and get a copy of the roster."

Tim showed the general manager of the private plane wing his badge and demanded a copy of the Geyser jet roster. The manager handed him the clipboard.

"It says here that Michael O'Connor and Kelly Parker are on board with two pilots," Tim said. "Guess where they're heading?"

My cell phone rang before I could answer.

"He sold all of his stock in Geyser today in after hours trading," Greg said to me. "I just got word over the wire. So did she."

I put my hand over the receiver and said to Harry, "Michael and Kelly sold all of their stock in Geyser." I have CNN on the line.

"Where are you?" Greg asked. "I'm waiting in front of your office."

"We're at the airport. We just watched Michael and Kelly take off in the Geyser jet. We're on our way back. I'll see you in a minute," I said.

*   *   *   *

"Antigua? Isn't that an island in the Caribbean?" Harry asked.

"Yes. I've heard that they've loosened their restraints on money laundering there. Antigua is the Cayman Islands of the nineties," I said. "What do you bet that Michael and Kelly's Swiss accounts are being re-wired as we speak?"

"So, they really did kill Preston?" Tim asked.

"Looks that way," Harry said.

"That explains why Michael didn't seem petrified when he was indicted for murder in the first place. He wanted to be indicted. He gambled on being acquitted so that double jeopardy would apply. Can't be tried for the same murder twice," Harry said.

"But you can be tried for conspiracy to commit murder," I said.

"I guess I don't get it," Tim said. "Who killed him? Nyomi? Did they hire her to kill him?"

"They killed him," I said. "Kelly figured out that Preston was cheating on her and she wanted him dead. She had been betrayed all of her life by someone, beginning with her father, and she had trusted Preston. She turned to Michael for support. Michael loved Kelly all of his life. He would have done anything for her. They conspired together to get rid of Preston. Michael would sell his share of Geyser. Kelly would sell her share that she owned from Preston's estate. The money would be wired to the Swiss accounts already set up from the illegal proceeds earned from the short sale of Geyser products in Asia.

"Either he or she contacted Duane Towns before the convention and asked him for a favor. They told him to plan a snowmobiling outing with a friend, so that he would have an alibi. He rode his snowmobile up Granite Canyon after she called him from Michael's cell phone, the one she'd borrowed and carefully placed in her fanny pack. Duane hid in the trees near the first chute of Granite Canyon, just as Kelly had told him to do. He used the crowbar from his snowmobile tool kit and smashed Preston over the head.

"In the hospital, Kelly or Michael only needed a few minutes alone with Preston to administer the drug. But there were always nurses around when Preston was in the ICU. So, when Preston was transferred to the Moran wing, they had the perfect opportunity," I said.

"That's why they were so pissed off by my questionin'," Tim said.

"Yes. But when you showed up to talk to them at Moran 4, you provided Kelly with the perfect alibi," Harry said. Tim tilted his head.

"When you went for coffee with Kelly, Michael probably quickly administered the drug. Nurse Connie was probably correct in her testimony. She probably did see Michael leaving Moran 4 dressed in a lab coat. He'd probably just administered the succinylcholine to Preston and then rushed out," Harry added.

"How would he get that kind of drug?" Tim asked.

"Easy. He's in the pharmaceutical business and he's a doctor and a scientist. He can probably get his hands on any kind of drug he wants. He could say that it's for research." *Fertility drugs.* It just dawned on me. I remembered that one of the Geyser employees told Carol that she thought that Michael was giving Kelly fertility injections. She'd seen the vials in his garbage can in his office. "In fact, one of the employees at Geyser even mentioned that they thought he was giving Kelly fertility injections. Maybe he was. Kelly said that she was pregnant," I said.

"Kelly? Pregnant? She sure doesn't look it," Tim said. I agreed. Kelly didn't look pregnant. Maybe she was, maybe she wasn't. She might have just said that to Nyomi to make her crazy.

"I have to hand it to them. They're clever," Tim said.

"They played me like an instrument," I said.

"They played us all," Harry said.

"The thing I don't get is the stage show at the Shady Lady. Why would they do that?" Tim asked.

"That was to throw us off course long enough for them to flee the country," Harry said. "They wanted to be overheard. They wanted us to think that Nyomi was involved so that we'd go after her. That might buy them a little extra time to high tail it out of Jackson."

"So, now what do we do?" Tim asked.

"We turn over the evidence to the County Attorney's office. I don't know what they'll do with it. Maybe Bain will re-try the case," Harry said. He started walking toward the police car.

* * * *

"Drop me at the office, Tim. I need to get my car," I said.

As we rounded Pearl Avenue, Harry turned to me and said, "You staying at our house again tonight?"

I saw Greg leaning against my beat up old Honda, waiting for me as promised. "No. I have plans tonight."

Epilogue

"I needed a vacation," Deputy Sheriff Tim Marshall said to the officer who met him at the airport in Antigua. Tim wore Bermuda shorts, socks to his knees and sandals.

"I'm Jeb Thompson," the officer said, reaching out to shake Tim's hand. "I'm supposed to take you to headquarters. So you're from Wyoming? Is it cold there?" the officer asked.

"Not this time of year. It's summer. Did you get the paperwork?" Tim asked. "I've been worried that I'd get all this way and then you'd tell me that somethin's messed up. My boss will hang me if I don't get them."

"I have a copy of the extradition paperwork right here in my shirt pocket," Jeb said, patting his chest. "My boss told me all about it. We've been staking them out for days."

"You know where they are?" Tim asked.

"They're renting a private home on a cliff above the Caribbean. Are you in a big hurry to meet with my boss?"

"Why?"

"I'll take you for a drive, show you the island. I can point out where they are hiding out. Must be worth some big bucks. What'd they do, rob a bank or something?"

"Somethin' like that. Sure. Let's go for a drive. The minute we get 'em, I'll be back on an airplane for another ten hours." We headed south from the airport.

"If we turn right here, we go to St. John's. That's the capital city and where my office is. We'll turn left instead and head toward Mamora Bay. Antigua is the largest of the British Leeward Islands. About four thousand years ago, it was home to the Siboney people. They disappeared without explanation, so the island was vacant for one thousand years. Columbus found it in 1493. The English, French, Dutch and Caribs fought over it for a long time. The English won."

"You know a lot about your island. Did you have to learn it for school?"

"Yes, but I've been out of school for a long, long time. I'm forty-seven. How old are you?"

"Thirty-nine, and holding. There are so many little islands off the coast. Is the fishin' good?"

"The fishing is very good here. There are over three hundred islands around. Are you a fisherman?"

"Trout. I fly fish. Never fished in the ocean before. I've never seen the ocean before, to tell you the truth."

"You're in luck. See that water over there? That's the Atlantic Ocean. We'll turn right up here in a bit and you'll see the Guadeloupe Passage and then the Caribbean Sea. Most of our beaches are on the Caribbean side. Look up there," Jeb said, pointing to a cliff overlooking a bay. "That's where they're staying."

"The road doesn't go any further?" Tim asked.

"No, sir. The house they've rented is only accessible by boat and helicopter," Jeb said. "If we want to catch them by surprise, we'll have to take the boat. When the timing is right, we'll take you up there."

"The sand is as white as snow and the water is so blue. I'd love to take one of them boats out for a sail," Tim said.

"We won't be taking a sailboat. We'll need a motorized raft to get in that cove. It's pretty rocky. We'll head around the mountainous side of the island and then back towards St. John's."

* * * *

"Here we are at the station. I'll introduce you to the man in charge." Tim followed Jeb into the one-story bright yellow stucco building. Jeb introduced Tim to Clarence Winton, a tall black man with a wide smile and a strong handshake. Clarence escorted Tim into the small conference room.

"We've been running surveillance on them all week. Take a look at the pictures we have," Clarence said, pointing to a conference table laden with photographs.

"What are these?" Tim asked.

"Photographs of Michael O'Connor and Kelly Parker," Clarence said, with conviction. Tim looked at the photographs, one by one. The woman in the pictures was very attractive, but she was older than Kelly. She wore large brimmed hats and oversized sunglasses. The man in the photographs looked even older than the woman.

"There must be some mistake," Tim said.

"What do you mean?"

"This lady doesn't look like Kelly Parker and that ain't the Michael O'Connor I've known since I was a kid."

"That's impossible. We've traced these two people to the plane that landed here a few weeks ago."

"The plane that says 'Geyser, Inc.' on it?"

"Yes. That's the one."

"Do you have a fax machine?" Tim asked.

"Yes," Clarence said. "It's out there, next to the computer. You may use it."

Tim walked out of the conference room and put an enlarged copy of a photograph through the fax. After the fax went through, he borrowed the phone.

"Mac, this is Tim Marshall. I'm in Antigua on the Michael O'Connor assignment. I just sent a fax to you. The police think that it's a picture of Michael and Kelly, but I think there's been some mistake."

"Just a minute. I'll run to the fax machine."

"I'll wait on the line. Somethin's wrong."

"You're right, Tim. That's Carol Leahy, Preston Parker's secretary at Geyser. And from visiting her at her office, I think the guy with her is her husband. Is it possible that they're there with Michael and Kelly?"

"I'll check. I'll call you back." Tim walked back into the conference room and looked at Clarence.

"Any chance that there's another couple stayin' at the house that you've been stakin' out?"

"No, sir. Why do you ask?"

"Because the couple in these pictures is not who we're comin' to arrest."

"Those are the only two people in the house," Clarence said.

"Has the Geyser jet left the island since it landed here?"

"Let me check on that," Clarence said, as he walked over and picked up the phone. He nodded a few times while talking into the receiver and then hung up. "Yes, sir. The plane has taken off and returned several times over the last few weeks. But the airport security officer has not tracked the log, so he has no idea of where it's been. There are thousands of islands in the Caribbean."

"So they could have dropped off the people staying in the house on the cliff and then left to another island?"

"Yes, it's possible. People disappear for years in the Caribbean."

✳   ✳   ✳   ✳

"How long does it take to sail from Curacao to Caracas?" she asked, while taking in the sun on the bow of the thirty-foot sailboat. Her long, dark hair was pulled back behind her ears, revealing her diamond solitaire earrings. Her frameless sunglasses protected her emerald green eyes. A blond-haired man cozily slept at her side.

"Depends on the winds, ma'am."

"That's fine. No hurry," she said, patting her bulging belly. "We've got a few months."

"So, what do we do now, Harry?" I asked, after hanging up the phone with Tim Marshall. Tim had called from Antigua to let us know that Michael and Kelly were no longer on the island. I felt burned. I believed in Michael. He betrayed us all. I wondered whether he and Kelly had planned the whole thing—from the grand jury testimony down to the scuffle in the restroom between Kelly and Nyomi. I wondered whether Nyomi was a hired gun? Did he orchestrate the affair in order to convince Kelly to dump Preston? Or was it her master plan? I decided that the truth wouldn't set me free. What mattered was that I did the best job that I could've done.

"We do nothing," Harry said. "We defended him morally and vigorously and we've turned the matter over to authorities. You figured it out. I'm proud of you, Mac. You've really proven yourself as a lawyer." He reached over to his credenza and grabbed a green file. He handed it to me.

"What's this?"

"It's a new case. We're defending Chance Ballek on a vehicular manslaughter charge. The kid was at a party last month after high school graduation and had too much to drink. He wrecked his car on the way home. Unfortunately, the girl that was with him died in the accident. The arraignment hearing is tomorrow."

"What do you need done?"

"You need to prepare for the hearing. The case is yours, from start to finish. Of course, I'll be looking over your shoulder if it goes to trial, but otherwise, it's up to you." I couldn't believe my ears. After nearly seven years of blood, sweat and tears, I was finally going to take on my own case. I reached out for the file, but before he handed it over he said, "So fill in the blanks for me."

"What blanks?"

"How did Michael do it?"

"Oh. Well, I don't know if I've put every piece of the puzzle together, but I think it started thirty-some years ago when he fell in love with Kelly. He spent his teenage and adult years craving her. When he figured out that Preston was cheating on her, he flipped. He always knew that Preston wasn't worthy of her and when Preston started cheating him in business, he decided to do something about it.

"He's the one who suggested that Kelly hire Bob Avery to spy on Preston, so I think he planted the seed in her mind that Preston was cheating. Then he made his way into her heart by giving her the letter that his wife, Brianna, wrote saying that it was fine with her if Michael and Kelly got together. Who knows if Brianna even wrote the note. Maybe Michael did and signed her name. Anyway, he's the one who hired Duane Towns. He probably convinced Duane that Preston had done her wrong. Michael knew that Duane was obsessed with her. And when that didn't go as planned, he got in Moran 4 and did it himself. He had access to any drug in the world, being a scientist and drug maker."

"But how did you figure out the Nyomi Janger part?"

"Michael insisted that I go to Bali. Remember? You didn't want me to go and he flat out demanded that I did. He needed me to see her in person in order for them to plug her into their plot. But, Michael didn't think that I'd actually get to talk with her or that I'd break into her apartment. When I saw the picture of Michael, Nyomi and Preston on the ski slope, it dawned on me that he knew all about Nyomi. And when she adamantly denied that she and Preston had split up, I knew that something wasn't right. She swore that Preston was having the divorce paperwork drawn up right before the Jackson convention."

"Why did Nyomi come for the trial?" Harry asked.

"I'm sure that she came because she wanted justice. She wanted to see Michael pay for her loss. She truly believed that Preston was leaving Kelly and was going to marry her."

"But that gave Michael and Kelly the perfect ending."

"Exactly. Maybe they were worried about Nurse Connie and the video surveillance at the hospital. I think that Michael was panicky that new evidence might come up against him, meaning Bain could request a new trial."

"Or that somehow Bain would figure out that they conspired to kill him and would charge Kelly with conspiracy to commit murder," Harry said.

"Right. So they staged the act in the bar to throw us off. To pin it on Nyomi so that we'd leave them alone."

"Again, you did a super job. I'm proud of you."

I let those words sink in late into the evening. I don't remember my father ever telling me that he was proud of me. I'm sure that he must have, I was just too young to remember. And my stepfather clearly never uttered such a phrase. When I got home, I picked up Ted and cuddled him over my shoulder. His purring filled me. I looked around my apartment, taking note of Greg's discovery. What he noticed was true. In every group picture, I was standing on the edge, as if I wasn't sure whether I belonged. I picked up the only picture I had of my father, which is my parents' wedding photograph. I found a recent picture and cut it down, so that all I could see was my face and I placed that picture of me in between my parents as they stood that day at the altar. I was in the middle once again.

And I thought about why my mother hastily remarried. Maybe she needed to fill the holes in her heart before she bled out. Maybe that's why Kelly and Michael needed each other—to fill their bleeding hearts. I may never know for sure.

978-0-595-43490-9
0-595-43490-8